T0247869

EBENEZER SCROOGE

SCROOGE

AND THE

GHOST

OF

CHRISTMAS

LOVE

ROBERT MARRO JR.

A POST HILL PRESS BOOK
ISBN: 979-8-88845-394-0
ISBN (eBook): 979-8-88845-395-7

Cover design by Conroy Accord

All English Scripture quotations are from the King James Bible.

Post Hill Press
New York • Nashville
posthillpress.com

Published in the United States of America
1 2 3 4 5 6 7 8 9 10

For my wife and soulmate, Wendy

You inspired this story that November night after we watched the 1951 *A Christmas Carol*. Your sense of justice compelled you to observe that if Scrooge had experienced a life-altering change of heart, why didn't this ardent desire to set right his past wrongs extend to his former fiancée Allyce? This was brought home by Scrooge's poignant reaction when he and the Ghost of Christmas Present beheld Allyce working in a Victorian homeless shelter on Christmas Eve. It took a woman's heart to see the contradiction, and from that heart, a novel was born.

You are forever my Allyce.

CONTENTS

AUTHOR'S NOTE

Our story begins in 1856, several years after the original events depicted in Charles Dickens' novella *A Christmas Carol.* Ebenezer Scrooge is now a fifty-nine-year-old thriving London merchant with a stellar reputation as a fair businessman and *de facto* second father to his clerk Bob Cratchit's family, who call him *"Uncle Ebenezer"* as a term of endearment. This story follows the narrative arc found in the 1951 Renown Pictures Corporation Ltd. UK film *A Christmas Carol,* starring Alastair Sim. In the 1951 film, Scrooge's ex-fiancée Belle was referred to as Alice, here spelled Allyce and depicted as a war widow.

In 2008, A.O. Scott, film critic for *The New York Times*, made a video describing why, out of all the film adaptations of *A Christmas Carol,* the 1951 British film starring Alistair Sim is the best of them all. (Note that the film was originally released as *Scrooge* in the UK and re-titled *A Christmas Carol* for US audiences.) With apologies to Dickens purists, I have endeavored to build this novel off the 1951 film.

1 ❧

A GOOD UNCLE, INDEED

On a frigid, windswept late February night in 1856, Ebenezer Scrooge, his longtime clerk, Bob Cratchit, and Bob's wife, Emily, emerged from London's Royal Opera House into a sudden, fierce snow squall.

"We're ever so grateful for being your guests tonight, Mr. Scrooge," said Emily Cratchit as she tightened her wool scarf against the wind-driven snow. "First, a right fancy dinner at Bella Ragazza and then an evening at the opera. Why, I felt like Queen Victoria herself!"

"I didn't even know there was a restaurant in London town that served proper Italian food, sir," said her husband, Bob, shielding his eyes as a sudden gust blew a stinging cloud of fat snowflakes into his face.

"Why, nonsense, you two," said Scrooge with a smile. "It makes perfect sense to have a nice Italian meal before enjoying Verdi's *Rigoletto*. I should think the two go rather well together—Italian food and the opera. Besides, I do believe Bella Ragazza was the first Italian restaurant to open in London, and you both saw how crowded it was. One of my associates at the Royal Exchange says the owner, Francesco DiStefano, is famous back in Milan and Florence for his restaurants there. Furthermore, Bob, with that enormous family of yours and the crowd of grandchildren forever racing about, I should think you would both enjoy a quiet night away from the hurly-burly of the day." Scrooge raised his hand to hail a hansom cab. He looked over his shoulder at Emily.

"How many grandchildren are you two up to now?"

"That'd be nine, sir, with two more on the way." The Cratchits beamed at the mention of their beloved grandchildren.

Scrooge succeeded in drawing the attention of one of the cabs lined up outside of the Royal Opera House. "Now, let's get a nice warm ride home rather than fight Father Winter on our feet like Napoleon's army!"

Bob Cratchit began to protest, but the words died in his throat as the snow squall suddenly turned into a full-on, heavy, wind-whipped storm. "Me and the missus are much obliged to you, Mr. Scrooge. We *could* walk home tonight, sir; you've already been more than genero—" but Scrooge cut him off mid-sentence.

"Bob, *you* may wish to walk home in this icy winter nonsense, but I think your good missus would appreciate a comfortable and especially *dry* conveyance home, as befits a lady," Scrooge said, playfully winking at Emily Cratchit. "Let's ask the good Mrs. Cratchit. Am I mistaken?"

"Well, no, sir. I don't fancy walking back to Camden Town in this awful nastiness." The snow and the evening darkness hid the blush that spread across her cheeks.

Emily Cratchit was a good, simple woman and not used to what some people would consider the luxury of a hansom cab. Ever since that Christmas when a wonderful change had come over Ebenezer Scrooge, he had become a truly generous friend to the Cratchit family. Scrooge had not only doubled her husband's salary, but also insisted on helping the family with the gift of a down payment for a much better, though unpretentious, house in a nicer part of Camden Town.

Scrooge called up to the driver, "To 87 Pratt Street, Camden Town, my good man! There's no rush in this snowy mess, so take care not to let your horses lose their footing! I trust they are well-shod, sir?"

The driver called down from his perch, "Me 'orses were well and newly shod three days ago, good sir, and I loves them as me own! We'll get you good folks home in decent time, nice 'n' safe!" The brown-and-black carriage trundled away down London's cobblestone streets, its golden lamps just visible in the driving February snow.

Once the little party was nestled inside the roomy carriage, the conversation turned to the Cratchit family. Scrooge looked at Emily and asked, "How did Tiny—oh, I'm *dreadfully* sorry—Tim's latest visit to Dr. Harshaw go? Are his legs still fit?"

Mrs. Cratchit smiled gratefully and said, "Our Tim went for those treatments twice a week for four years, Mr. Scrooge, due to your kindness. As you know, Dr. Harshaw said his condition was a paralysis of the lower extremities caused by rickets. Our Tim's legs are now just like the lad 'imself—as good as gold. No more crutch, no more braces on 'is legs neither. Sir, you wouldn't even know Tim's legs were feeble; he runs with the other lads at school like he was one of the Queen's own deer in Sherwood Preserve, and you yourself have seen the way the boy's grown, shooting up like a weed in me summer garden."

A smile broke out on Scrooge's face before turning to mock sternness.

"Emily, how many times have I told you? *Please* call me Ben or at least Ebenezer. Too many people associate the name Scrooge with someone I'd rather forget. Your Tim played a great part in helping me see that life spent in pursuit of only money *is* the root of evil, as the Gaffer Swanthold would say. But putting money to *good* purpose, now that's a different issue, eh? I'll wager your Tim would agree!"

Mrs. Cratchit still had a difficult time endeavoring to call her husband's boss "Ben." Bob Cratchit broke in.

"You know, sir, Tim's been talking about a calling to the ministry, as they say. He's sixteen and already a senior altar boy at Saint

Hubert's. He sometimes gets a bit peculiar, sir, when he's at Sunday Lord's Supper."

Scrooge cocked his head.

"Peculiar? How so?"

"Well, si…*errr*, Ben, as you please. Perhaps *peculiar* ain't the right word. I'd wager *thoughtful* would put it better. He's ever so attentive to Reverend Braithwaite, and then after the service, he'll ask me questions like, 'Father, if the Lord is so good, then why does He permit men to do such wicked things? Surely, He who raised Lazarus from the dead can put things right in our sad world.' Then, if Tim hears word that the Right Reverend Keble is coming down from Hursley for Sunday services, why, these two horses taking us home couldn't drag him away from Saint Hubert's."

At that point, Emily Cratchit broke in, emphasizing Scrooge's preferred means of address for effect. "Why, *Ben*, like Bob said, our Tim's now sixteen, and I wouldn't at all be surprised by a 'calling' in that one neither. The Lord calls who He will, so if He calls our Tim, God bless him for it."

Scrooge just smiled and changed the topic to the Cratchits' eldest son, Peter, his wife, Charlotte, and their children.

"Now tell me, what's the news of the day about Peter and his family? Is Charlotte still in the hospital?"

Bob and Emily Cratchit took on an inadvertent, somber demeanor at the mention of their eldest son and unfortunate daughter-in-law, who was gravely ill with consumption.

"Well, Charlotte is a more delicate question, Mr. Scrooge, sir."

Bob's never going to stop calling me "Mr. Scrooge," thought Scrooge. And I suppose I'll just go on letting him.

Bob continued, "Begging your pardon, sir, because I don't like to complain, but our Charlotte's consumption doesn't seem to be getting worse, but she ain't getting any better neither. I can't see how being locked up in the Royal Infirmary for Consumption and Ailments of the Chest with all those other poor souls constantly coughing up Lord-knows-what all day has done her health any good these past three months. She just wheezes and coughs. It's absolutely dreadful to see how just the coughing wears down her strength."

An unexpected gloom settled over the previous gaiety as the cab slowly made its way to Camden Town—until Scrooge struck his cane on the cab floor for emphasis as an idea hit him.

"What that daughter-in-law of yours needs is summer in the country, not the soot-filled London air of an infirmary that's little more than a warehouse for the sick! Sitting day after day in a drafty old ward full of consumptives, souls with pneumonia, and Lord-knows-what-other-strange-lung-maladies isn't going to do her a bit of good. Perhaps we can look into sending Peter's family on a nice long summer holiday to the south of Italy, Bob. I'd wager her lungs would clear of consumption in no time at all." Scrooge settled back with a smile, quite pleased with his idea.

Emily momentarily brightened at the suggestion before turning downcast.

"Ben, ordinarily I'd already have the cab going to Charlotte's hospital *right now* with that idea, but I know she'd never leave Peter and her home. And Peter, he's so proud that if the Queen herself offered to help them, he'd turn Her Majesty's generosity down on principle."

At that moment, the cab came to a slow stop, and the driver called out, "Here's 87 Pratt Street, Camden Town!" He yanked the cab door open and helped Emily Cratchit step with attentive care down the hansom cab's steep, snow-covered steps. Once on the street, she turned to look back up at Scrooge as Bob, stepped out.

"Could we trouble you to come in fer a nice cup of hot tea, sir?" asked Emily.

But Scrooge was too wily not to recognize the Cratchits' clumsy attempt to change the subject. *These poor folks are already totaling up the price of treating Charlotte in a nice and dry warmer clime in their heads. When will they learn life's not about money?* Scrooge thought, rolling his eyes. John Heywood's old proverb came to mind: "*You can lead a horse to water, but you can't make it drink.*"

"I'm afraid I'll have to be taking you up on your kind offer of tea when Father Winter doesn't have a say in the matter, Emily. I'm sure Mrs. Dilber has been fretting about my whereabouts and has had a kettle boiling for my evening Twinings for the last hour anyway. I should get home before the water boils away." He called up to the cab driver. "You've got one final stop, my good man: number 38 Belgrave Square down in Belgravia Park!" Leaning closer to the window, Scrooge called out, "A good night to you both!"

Bob and Emily Cratchit's fading voices called back, "Thank you again for a delightful evening, Mr. Ebenezer!" as they hurried out of the snow and into the warmth of their house.

A short time later, the cab pulled up to Scrooge's home at 38 Belgrave Square, a short distance from Buckingham Palace in London's exclusive Belgravia neighborhood. Scrooge lived in an elegant but modestly decorated Georgian townhouse facing the lush Eaton Square Garden, having sold off his former business partner Jacob Marley's drafty old mansion years earlier.

"That'll be one shilling and tuppence, sir," the cabbie said as he opened the carriage door for Scrooge.

Scrooge pulled out his purse and turned away from the blinding snow. He pulled out three shillings and sixpence, handing them to the surprised driver.

The cabbie blinked at the coins in his hand and blurted out, "Thank you, sir!"

"Well, my good fellow, you did make the equivalent of two separate trips in this accursed weather tonight, and your noble beasts acquitted themselves rather well this dreadful night. I think you rather well earned those shillings and sixpence this night. Just be sure to be giving a small share of that extra money in good, fresh hay to your steadfast beasts. I'm sure they had no choice about being out and about in this mess." Scrooge grinned as he patted the brown, snowy flanks of the nearest horse with his gloved hand. As if in agreement, both horses whinnied and shook the snow from their frosty manes.

Scrooge doffed his hat to the driver, bid him a good evening, and hurried to unlock his door. Mrs. Dilber, hearing the key in the lock, rushed to open the door.

"Goodness, Mr. Scrooge! You're the very picture of Jack Frost himself! Come on now. Let's get you out of that wet coat and hat. I've a nice roaring fire for you in the smoking library and a kettle of your favorite tea ready to steep before you retire," she said.

"Thank you, Mrs. Dilber," Scrooge said. "I'll be along to the library presently."

A few minutes later, as Scrooge walked into his library and settled into his favorite chair near the hearth, a dark feline shadow detached itself from the shadows along the wall. The sinewy, dark gray cat rubbed against his leg, jumped up, and curled into his lap. Scrooge began to stroke the top of the cat's head absentmindedly as he stared into the fire. "Were you a good boy for Mrs. Dilber, Julius?" he asked as his housekeeper entered with the tea tray loaded down with a silver service full of steaming Darjeeling tea and a hot buttered cinnamon scone.

"Oh, Mr. Julius and his partner in crime, Mr. Caesar, begging yer pardon, was me polite pals for the whole evenin', sir. I really do think the little moggies know when yer coming home after being out and about. They began wandering about for the last 'alf an hour making their racket the way they always do when yer on yer way home." The big gray cat began a deeper purr as if he agreed with Mrs. Dilber. "Will you be needing anything else tonight, sir?"

"Other than fetching my pipe and a fresh tin of Samuel Gawith tobacco, Mrs. Dilber, I'll be just fine. You can retire for the evening if you'd like. I'll set the tray in the kitchen when I'm off to sleep."

"Very good, sir. You'll be having the cherry tobacco, sir?"

"Yes, Mrs. Dilber. I think Julius and Caesar would approve of the Gawith's Black Cherry. They seem to think it smells like the catnip in the summer garden."

The housekeeper reappeared a few minutes later with a small tin and Scrooge's pipe.

"I trust you enjoyed Verdi tonight," she said. "Have a good evening, Mr. Scrooge. Shall I close the library door?"

"You can leave it open—I wouldn't want to trap Julius in here. Heaven knows that door has seen enough of his claws' wrath. Besides, Caesar will discover where Julius and I are hidden soon enough, and I'll not suffer his jealousy because he thinks Julius is getting special treatment. No, Mrs. Dilber, you go along and sleep peaceably."

Scrooge stared into the flames and embers within the marble hearth as he puffed his old Meerschaum pipe, and tendrils of sweet aromatic tobacco smoke wound their way toward the designs stamped into the tin ceiling. His thoughts kept returning to Bob and Emily Cratchit. They had faced many challenges during their marriage, yet their marriage *endured*. With every tragedy life could employ to discourage the couple, they not only turned aside with a cheerful determination but did it *together*. *Take Tiny Tim, for example*, Scrooge mused, although on consideration he hadn't exactly been "tiny" for years since recovering from rickets. Many families would have taken the shameful but all-too-common road of putting the child away in an orphanage for crippled children instead of dealing with the constant day-to-day strain of raising and caring for a little boy afflicted with such weak legs. *That* was love, Scrooge concluded. Real, enduring love.

The fearsome "Night of the Ghosts," as he looked back on it, ended Scrooge's parsimonious treatment of his long-suffering clerk, who had quietly endured the old Ebenezer Scrooge's abusive treatment for over nine years. Scrooge knew justice demanded it, and so it was. One of Scrooge's first actions after his change of heart and spiritual outlook was to double Bob Cratchit's salary to thirty shillings a week.

But for all his moral change of heart, Ebenezer Scrooge remained a very lonely man whose only real companionship were his playful cats Julius and Caesar. Of course, he saw his own grandnieces and nephews when his nephew, Fred Holywell, and his wife came visiting with their children, but that was becoming less frequent now that Fred had moved the family from London to be near his employer's new factory in Coventry—almost a hundred miles away.

Caesar announced his arrival with a soft meow and curled up on the carpet by the fire. Scrooge smiled when he recalled how he had found the dark gray tabby and his equally diminutive black-and-white brother one drizzly night the previous autumn when the pair of tiny starving kittens followed Scrooge home from his evening after-dinner walk. He remembered it well.

Scrooge heard the mewling noises of the tiny, frightened animals as he was strolling through Eaton Square Garden. Scrooge knew he had pursuers when, after a few minutes, the tiny sounds didn't fade into the distance, but grew louder. Finally, as he prepared to exit the park, he turned to see one of the intrepid kittens peering at him hopefully from underneath a pink rose bush. Scrooge crouched down and began speaking to the frightened orphans in quiet, gentle tones as the kittens inched their way closer. A wide smile crossed his face.

"Come now, my little friends. I don't doubt your bravery, but it's getting much too dark for a couple of intrepid explorers like you to be out and about by yourselves on a wet night like this." When Scrooge saw that the emaciated pair looked as if they hadn't eaten in a day or two, he was sure they had been abandoned—dumped in the park to fend for themselves. His heart immediately went out to the wide-eyed felines staring at him with equal parts fear and hope.

"I'm sure we can convince Mrs. Dilber to part with a nice little piece of leftover chicken or a wee bit of beef, eh? I'll even see that it's washed down with a nice saucer full of cool water." Scrooge remembered wondering what his business associates at the Royal London Exchange would have said if they could have seen him right then, crouched down talking in honeyed tones of reassurance to a couple of stray kittens shivering under a rose bush. Once they had crept close enough, Scrooge deftly scooped up the diminutive, protesting kittens and with great care, deposited each in a deep coat pocket. They were so young their teeth couldn't bite, and their tiny claws felt rather like little brush bristles. Before putting them in his pockets, Scrooge couldn't help smiling and pronouncing them "right soggy moggies."

He remembered Mrs. Dilber's eyes widening in surprise at seeing him pull the shivering kittens from his coat pockets and proclaim with a proud smile that he had "just hired a pair of fearsome mouse-catching beasts." After happily watching his voracious new charges clean off tiny saucers piled with small bits of chopped chicken liver, he had Mrs. Dilber fashion a box lined with an old blanket and place it in the corner of the kitchen near the stove. He crouched at the box and stroked their tiny foreheads until they fell asleep. Naming them Julius and Caesar, they had quickly grown into a pair of lovably mischievous, but immensely loyal sinewy charges who followed Scrooge's every move around the large house with the tenacity of Scotland Yard detectives chasing a suspect.

But for all their affectionate behavior, Julius and Caesar were *cats*, not people, and aside from his business compatriots at the Royal Exchange, Scrooge was very much alone. As his thoughts often did, with some regret, they drifted back to the vision of feminine loveliness to whom Scrooge was once engaged to marry, Allyce Simpson, now Mrs. Allyce Bainbridge. Years earlier, while working his way ever higher in the banking and loan industry, first under the benevolent eyes of old Fezziwig, and then later the rapacious Mr. Jorkin, Scrooge had been engaged for years to the beautiful Allyce.

Scrooge remembered the first time he saw Allyce. It was at a Christmas Eve party thrown by his jolly old boss, Mr. Fezziwig, where he was first apparenticed as a junior clerk of twenty-nine. She was a shy slip of loveliness, almost seventeen years old, and her mother worked as a milliner for Fezziwig's wife. While a gawky Scrooge stood along the wall and pondered how he would work up the courage to approach such a vision of loveliness, old Fezziwig himself, in his Welsh wig and his trademark fashions of a bygone era, came to Scrooge's rescue and clapped his hands, calling for a rest for the dancers and the fiddlers. After a short break, Fezziwig then merrily announced the traditional couples' dance, the "Sir Roger de Coverley," and without thinking, Scrooge had stood and reached for young Allyce's hand with a boldness he did not think he possessed. Upon seeing the usually reserved Scrooge reaching for the beautiful Allyce's hand, his boss smiled and recalled Erasmus's dictum that, "Faint heart never won fair maiden."

Love, bright and white-hot, emerged from that dance and for years afterward with promises of marriage and children. Scrooge kept putting off the marriage until "the time was just right," but in the end, he had pushed the long-suffering Allyce's patience past its breaking point with his growing greed. Scrooge still recalled, as a keen emotional blade of regret and pain twisted in his stomach, the look on Allyce's face as she handed him back his betrothal ring. The plainspoken, anguished truth she told him would come back to haunt him time and again: "Ebenezer, our promise to each other is an old one, made when we were young and in love. Would you seek me out now, a poor girl with no dowry to offer? The look on your face already betrays your answer." The question was rhetorical, for the headstrong, haughty Scrooge knew the answer, and so did Allyce, so she didn't wait for a reply. She hurried off, not wanting the cold, dispassionate businessman Scrooge had turned into to see her tears of grief overflowing and sliding down her face.

Had he been in his right senses, Scrooge mused while stroking the "M" pattern on the purring Julius's forehead, he would have gotten up straight away to pursue Allyce and confess his foolishness. In any case, it would have been to no avail. Scrooge, by then a protégé of the cunning Mr. Jorkin, was priggishly certain Allyce was a silly, ignorant woman who was incapable of seeing the practical importance of accumulating enough wealth for maintaining one's proper station in life. His haughty earlier incarnation had strung Allyce along for far longer than proper courtship and engagement etiquette of the time called for until she realized Scrooge would *never* change back to the dashing but shy man she had fallen for at Fezziwig's Christmas Eve party.

Instead, Scrooge rued that *those* changes required a nightmarish visit from the decomposing ghost of his late business partner, Jacob Marley, and the intervention of three spirits from beyond to scare decency, compassion, and good Christian charity back into him years later.

Besides, he recalled, Allyce *Simpson* didn't exist anymore; she was now Mrs. Tristan Bainbridge, a wife, a mother. He ruminated that as he was now a hale and healthy fifty-nine years old, so Allyce would now be in her early forties. Sipping his tea and tamping a pinch of fresh tobacco into his pipe, he reflected on how much happier his life would have been had he married Allyce. Ebenezer Scrooge was now *very* wealthy—perhaps one of the richest men in all of London (which also meant all of Her Majesty's realm)—but a vault at the Bank of England brimming with gold sovereigns and silver crowns could not purchase *love*. Allyce had truly loved him, and in return, he broke her heart. Was there such a thing as "one true love?" After returning his ring, Allyce met Captain Tristan Bainbridge of Her Majesty's elite Coldstream Guards and was now the mother of two children. Scrooge recalled a line from the new poem by that American poet, John Greenleaf Whittier: "For of all sad words of tongue or pen, The saddest are these, 'It might have been!'"

As he drank his cooling tea and shooed a protesting Julius off his lap to stir the dying embers in the hearth back into some semblance of life, Scrooge ruminated with ineffable sadness that Whittier was right: the most bitter pill a man could swallow in life was *regret*. And it was at times like these, late at night and alone with his thoughts, with only Julius and Caesar and their soft, purring companionship, when he felt the lancing pangs of his unrequited love for Allyce at their fiercest. This was doubly so after having been in the company of contented married folks like the Cratchits. Scrooge thought, aside perhaps from the death of a child, there was no pain in the world more keenly felt than to have lost true love. This is why, at the end of the day, despite his vast wealth, he often fancied Bob Cratchit to be a far richer man than himself. Those times he accompanied Bob home to dinner at the end of the day, whoever of the Cratchit grandchildren happened to be visiting would gleefully greet Bob and them with cries of, "Grandfather! Uncle Ebenezer!" There were no expectations on the part of the Cratchit grandchildren of anything more than a heartfelt hug and kiss, with perhaps the occasional little bag of Heath's toffee sweets thrown in for good measure. Then came the happily noisy commotion of mealtime before they went home or off to bed. Scrooge often thought of his adopted grandchildren as a happy little army whose rallying cry was, "Read us another story, Uncle Ebenezer!"

Watching Julius and Caesar wrestle on the rug in front of the dying fire, Scrooge knew he should be grateful for his new outlook on life these past years, but shadows of much happier times with Allyce lurked at the ragged edge of his thoughts, refusing to be dismissed. The soles of his boots were beginning to feel the warmth from the deep red coals in the hearth, and he wished that the same sort of warmth might enfold his heart again someday.

He roused himself from his melancholy thoughts, announcing bedtime to the ever-watchful cats.

"Come, Julius. Come, Caesar. Time to visit the Land of Morpheus!" The cats immediately sat up at the sound of Scrooge calling their names. "As the morrow is the third Sunday of the month, I promised Tim Cratchit I'd come to Saint Hubert's to hear his famous Right Reverend Keble preach the service." Scrooge padded off to his bedchamber after depositing the tea tray in the kitchen, silently followed by the ever-dutiful Julius and Caesar, padding along behind him like silent sentinels.

2

FAMILY AFFAIR

Several years earlier, in 1852, after numerous attempts, Hawthorne and Cavendish Furniture and Carpentry Works of London was still basking in the glow of receiving its first-ever Royal Warrant of Appointment from Queen Victoria in 1851 as a supplier of fine furnishings and woodwork to the Crown. It was also where Scrooge's nephew, Fred Holywell, worked as a solicitor and Bob Cratchit's eldest son, Peter, was employed as Senior Clerk First-Class. Sir Nigel Fairweather-Hawthorne, a notorious, cutthroat, avaricious businessman, and owner of Hawthorne and Cavendish, was locked in bitter rivalry with London's premier woodworking firm, Holland and Sons Fine Furnishers and Outfitters. The companies competed against each other in every major prestigious International Exhibition of the nineteenth century. Sir Nigel still nursed a bitter grudge against Holland and Sons for their triumph over Hawthorne and Cavendish at the 1851 Great Exhibition of the Works of Industry of All Nations. For this first World's Fair, Holland and Sons had created an enormous, exotic wood bookcase for Prince Albert of Saxe-Coburg and Gotha, Queen Victoria's husband and consort, which won the 1851 Exhibition's "Great Prize" for its beauty, elegance, and unparalleled craftsmanship.

Furious with Holland and Sons for having prevailed over his own company's entries at the 1851 Great Exhibition—and always nursing a perceived slight of some sort or another—Sir Nigel was already scheming with his cousin Grenville Linton-Gower, the 2nd Earl of

Grenville and organizer of the 1862 Great Exhibition, in a bid to become sole Royal Warrant provisioner of milled lumber and furnishings to the Royal Navy fleet reconstruction program. True, there were no royal honors and accolades to be had with this contract, but there was *money* to be made—prodigious sums of money. But as the planning for the 1862 Great Exhibition would not begin in earnest until 1860, for the time being, his cousin Grenville, in recognition and reward for his oversight of the successful 1851 Great Exhibition, was appointed head of the Department of the Permanent Secretary to the Admiralty. Grenville was responsible for the control, direction, and guidance of all administrative functions of the British Admiralty, including contract awards.

Against this backdrop, Sir Nigel received a curious note from his cousin Grenville requesting to meet him and a "special acquaintance" in England's seaside resort of Brighton in late spring 1852 at the Grand Brighton Hotel. The letter from Grenville also stipulated that Sir Nigel was to maintain absolute secrecy and tell no one of his travel plans. Upon arriving at the hotel, Sir Nigel was to announce himself to the front desk clerk as Mr. Remington, a guest of "Mr. William Pembroke in Room 209." Knowing his ambitious cousin always had a touch of grand larceny in his heart, but intrigued nevertheless, Sir Nigel told his senior staff he had been called away on important business for the week and that Fred Holywell was interim company supervisor while he was away.

Sir Nigel arrived at the Grand Brighton Hotel on a bright late May morning in 1852 and, per his cousin's instructions, presented himself at the expansive front desk to the clerk in charge.

"Good morning, my good man," Sir Nigel said, announcing himself to the clerk on duty. "My name is John Remington and I'm here as a guest of Mr. William Pembroke in Room 209."

At the name John Remington, the clerk brightened.

"Very well, sir. We've been expecting you. I've got a note from Mr. Pembroke to send you up to his room straight away on your arrival," the clerk said. "Just take the staircase over there to the right to the second floor and, turning right, proceed down the hall to the ninth room on the left. Please do enjoy your stay, Mr. Remington."

"Thank you," said Sir Nigel, placing a one-shilling tip on the hotel counter as he turned away. Moments later, he was knocking at Room 209 when the door was opened with a sly smile by his cousin Grenville Linton-Gower.

"Come in, Nigel—do come in!" exclaimed Grenville as he closed and locked the door behind his cousin. "I'm so very pleased you could make the journey down from London today, cousin. As it's too early for high tea, I've taken the liberty of having a light early lunch brought up a short while ago. I hope you'll join me."

He beckoned his cousin through a sizeable double-width door to a spacious room patio overlooking the sunny English Channel. A table for two was set with a sumptuous formal lunch, with sandwiches, fruit, and a selection of fine English teas.

After pleasantries were dispensed with, Sir Nigel said, "All right, Grenville, you've got my curiosity going like cats when the fishmonger passes by. What is so bloody important that I had to take valuable time away from the company and sneak off sixty miles from London to meet you under such mysterious circumstances?"

The 2nd Earl of Grenville relished being the bearer of good news.

"I have stumbled upon something, cousin, that will make both of us very rich." He paused to correct himself. "Well, it will make *me* a very tidy little sum," Grenville said, spreading his hands in a trademark gesture of false modesty, "but it has the potential to make your little company famous and *you* very, very wealthy."

"Then out with it, man," Sir Nigel said as he poured himself a cup of fragrant Oolong tea and dropped a sugar cube into the porcelain cup.

Grenville smiled like the Cheshire cat. "I've heard from my friends in the Foreign Office that Czar Nicholas intends to push the Turkish sultan in Istanbul to recognize the Czar as the official 'Protector of Christians in the Lands of the Ottomans.'"

Sir Nigel mulled over this information from his cousin. "And how does this concern *us*, Grenville? Does the czar or the sultan need furnishings or an addition to a palace in Saint Petersburg?"

Grenville paused. "No, *cousin*," he said in a patronizing tone. "I'm talking about *war* and a very profitable war at that if we are patient and don't overreach. There was a meeting between the Admiralty, the Foreign Office, and Prime Minister Smith-Stanley in the last fortnight. If Czar Nicholas invades the Ottoman Turks' empire, then it was agreed at the meeting such an expansion of the Russian Empire would constitute an unacceptable threat to the British Empire and a *casus belli*."

"I don't understand, Grenville," said a perplexed Sir Nigel. "How is Russia such a dire threat to Queen Victoria's realm?"

"It's easy when you step outside your provincial London shoes and think in terms of the 'Great Game,' dear Nigel," Grenville said in a condescending tone. "Picture it as a game of dominoes if you like. We've long been in competition with Russia in Asia. You want to know why the czar would risk a wider war with England and France for the northern wastelands of the Turkish Empire? Because it *would* position Czar Nicholas to gain his long-coveted warm-water ports and naval bases on the Arabian Gulf and the Indian Ocean. From such a position, he could threaten India across the plains of Afghanistan *and* by sea, sever England from Australia, our Chinese colonies of Hong Kong, the Kowloon Peninsula, and our New Territories.

"No, Nigel, those are very real threats to the empire Great Britain *cannot allow*. According to Admiral Finchley, if the Russians march on our Asian colonies, *their* supply lines will be only hundreds of miles long, but *ours* will be measured in *thousands*, sailing around Africa and the Cape of Good Hope. No, cousin, Russian war against the Turks Empire would be a foregone war cry for the British Empire," Grenville concluded.

Grenville saw that the words "a very profitable war" had garnered his cousin Nigel's full attention, if not his exposition of the clear dangers the British Empire faced from Russia.

"I read the minutes of the most recent Admiralty meeting. It is the consensus of the Admiralty and the Minister for War that the Royal Navy is woefully unprepared to support an extended war effort in Asia. As such, they have decided to embark upon the first major rebuilding of Her Majesty's Navy in over *sixty years* since that nastiness with the colonies ended in 1783. I think if we seize the proper moment, Hawthorne and Cavendish will have an opportunity to become the sole supplier of milled hardwood products to the Royal Navy's largest warship program *in the last 150 years*," Grenville emphasized. "It's a chance to put prodigious sums of gold in your accounts *and* a bee in the bonnet of your friends at Holland and Sons Fine Furnishers and Outfitters."

Grenville continued, "The Admiralty has drawn up a proposed list for the complete rebuild and refitting of the Royal Navy's 131-gun *Wellington* class, 121-gun *Royal Albert* class, and the 121-gun *Victoria* class, as well as the first ships to be fitted with those fancy new high-pressure steam engines and iron armor amidships. Think, cousin! You could be the exclusive shipwright for not only twenty-four major Royal Navy warships, but could also become a force to be reckoned with in providing Her Majesty's empire with a navy no other country would dare challenge for decades to come!"

Grenville now had Sir Nigel's full attention.

"Grenville, how much of this is real, and how much is only Foreign Office and Admiralty Board gossip?" Sir Nigel asked.

"Oh, it's not gossip. Too many verified reports have come in of what the Russians are planning for Her Majesty to ignore any longer.

The Admiralty has decided on a budget of just over *£4 million* for this and will be looking to select the winning bidder within the next two to four years at the latest, with the Royal Navy looking for new ships to begin leaving the shipyard slipways in 1860. If your firm can partner with a supplier to help with the heavy lifting, financially and materially, Hawthorne and Cavendish could grow *tenfold* in that time. If you follow this to the logical conclusion, you'll need to purchase your own shipyards, cousin."

Sir Nigel snorted in derision.

"Right, my own bloody shipyards. Have *you* taken leave of your senses, man? Do you know how much it takes to purchase or build a shipyard, Grenville? Not to mention the prodigious quantities of board acreage in every sort of wood it would take for such a venture to succeed. Then, if you're talking about the proposed iron warships driven by those fancy new steam engines, that's another matter of industry altogether."

Grenville smiled. "Perhaps you're not thinking grand enough, Nigel. I know for a fact that the John Scott Russell and Company Millwall Iron Works on Thames has been having difficulty paying its bills and some shipyards are in arrears for money they cannot hope to repay any time soon. Although considerable progress has been made in obtaining machinery for new boilers, steam fittings, pipes, copper, and iron smithing, Russell's Millwall Iron Works is a mere two months from the bankruptcy court."

Sir Nigel poured a bit of milk into his tea.

"I won't presume to ask how you happen to be privy to these rather confidential details. I'm sure old Johnny Russell didn't volunteer them to you."

"No, you're quite right, Nigel, but time-to-time interesting papers come across my desk and I make note of certain...*details*," Grenville said with a smug grin. "That said, if Millwall yards cannot meet their obligations, then the entire enterprise will go up on the auction block for a song. Mr. Russell is most anxious to avoid the humiliation of the Russell family name being sullied. As for sourcing wood like teak, the Admiralty gets most of it from India and certain provinces of Southeast Asia and is keen for the czar not to get his hands on those supplies or cut off our access to it. It already takes four months to sail from Bombay to Portsmouth and a bit longer from Australia. Would Her Majesty agree to surrender our Indian and Australian colonies to Russia?"

Not being schooled in the facts of seamanship nor a knowledgeable grasp of geography and navigation, Sir Nigel pondered the thought for a moment. Finally, he asked, "Then why not just sail southwest from Portsmouth below South America and thence on to Australia or India around Cape Horn at the Tierra del Fuego? You'd avoid the Russian fleet, and we're more than a match for the Spaniards."

Grenville sighed at his cousin's maritime ignorance.

"Nigel, no merchant or naval sea captain in his right mind will sail around South America. At Cape Horn, there are the fearsome, sudden *williwaws* storms. Hundreds of ships and thousands of poor sailors have gone down to Davy Jones's Locker attempting that route. That's not figuring in that safely sailing around Cape Horn adds almost three to four thousand nautical miles to the voyage, entailing expensive port calls and fleet reprovisioning."

"All right, I'm convinced—the Crown has real reason to fear Czar Nicholas's ambitions; the Royal Navy needs an upgrade *and* a new class of iron warships. They'll need a ship-of-the-line shipyard and yards that can handle the new iron ships. But be practical, Grenville—don't we have enough lumber here in England?"

"No, Nigel, most of our shipbuilding lumber comes from Canada, Germany, and the Baltics."

Sir Nigel raised an eyebrow.

"So, the Canadian colonies will source the lumber?"

A peculiar gleam came into Grenville's eye. "No, we'd be looking to the Americans for this venture. We've procured it from Canada because, until now, there's been a lack of viable, and more importantly, consistent alternatives. Canada's railways won't meet the Royal Navy's needs for at least another twenty years, and *that* is far too late. On the other hand, the Americans have two thousand miles of warm Atlantic coastline and any number of major shipping ports located in profitable proximity to their lumber production. Each day their railways expand in every direction of the compass by hundreds of miles. The Admiralty recognizes Her Majesty's Royal Treasury is not bottomless, so there is a keen interest in preserving our gold reserves as far as is practical."

Sir Nigel interjected, "I'm sure the Americans realize their advantages with every sort of raw material. What kind of discounted rates are they *really* willing to offer? I've learned the hard way, cousin, courtesy of that young wizard, Peter, in my employ, that if a business deal seems too good to be true, it is."

Grenville grinned. "How does thirty percent off the prevailing rates strike you, cousin?"

"Are they mad or just stupid?" Sir Nigel found himself wishing he had his prodigy, Peter Cratchit, with him at that moment. *I'm out of my depth discussing naval shipbuilding with Grenville*, Nigel rued, oblivious to the irony.

"Neither cousin. Our American cousins are practical businessmen," Grenville responded. Grenville always relished the opportunity to lecture his cousin about his newfound passion for all things nautical, and this was no exception.

"The Admiralty's naval architects have realized the woodland resources in America are vastly superior to the dwindling forests centuries of harvesting wood from the British Isles themselves have left us with. True, Canada has made up for a good amount of what we no longer have here at home, plus Germany and the Baltics, but even the mighty Royal Navy must pay mind to what the scriveners at the Royal Treasury tell us. But still, the Admiralty gets nervous when they think about the Imperial Russian Navy cutting off our freedom to the open sea."

"What quantities of wood are we speaking about?" Sir Nigel asked. Grenville poured himself another tea.

"You'll recall the HMS *Victory*, Lord Nelson's flagship at Trafalgar? According to Admiralty records, somewhere around six thousand trees were needed to build just HMS *Victory* alone, not to mention the other fleet ships that fought at Trafalgar. Almost a hundred acres of oak trees were cleared using simple hand tools in Kent and Sussex forests. Most of the wood used in *Victory's* construction was oak, a lot of it two feet thick in places on the hull. The largest oak trees available were cut for her because strong one-piece construction is preferred when building a large ship-of-the-line. Gigantic elm trunks are used for the keel and finally, fir and spruce, making up most of the decks, yardarms, masts, and whatnot. Lately we've begun importing teak from India for our ship decks, because teak's oil content gives the ship the highest decay resistance among all natural woods. It's just so blasted expensive, we use what teak we can get for decks."

Sir Nigel sipped his tea and listened patiently, assuming this lesson in shipbuilding *minutiae* was leading somewhere.

"The Americans' New England fir and spruce offer masts and spars of such immense strength and height that our shipwrights don't need to spend months curing and laminating them to make the masts Her Majesty's larger ships-of-the-line need. Their southern live oak offers more advantages for wooden ship construction than many of our existing British shipwrights can even handle. The wood is amazingly strong, and that's where another advantage for *you* comes to the fore."

"Oh?" Sir Nigel stared archly.

"Yes, the American oak is of such strength and durability compared to the Canadian wood that our shipyards and naval carpenters have trouble even working with the blasted stuff because it quickly dulls our tools to the point of extreme frustration. Still, our American cousins have found ways around that too, with a special 'high-carbon' steel, as their metallurgists call it. They've invented a process that keeps the edge on their woodworking planes, adzes, chisels, and what have you, sharp quite a bit longer. Those bits of exclusive expertise in metals smelting and tool hardening will be yours as well, giving you a decided advantage over other shipyards."

Sir Nigel was impressed. Grenville had indeed done his homework on the matter.

"But Grenville, *if* I were interested in participating in your plan, I would still need access to sums of money no bank in England or anywhere else, for that matter, would lend me. I've got no meaningful collateral."

The smug Grenville was endlessly pleased with himself. "Nigel, will you consent to dine with me here in my room tonight, say about seven o'clock? I think the answer to every question you have in mind will be put to rest in a most satisfactory manner."

Sir Nigel got up to leave when Grenville called out.

"Nigel?"

Nigel turned around. "Yes?"

"You've told me many times of your *wunderkind*, that Senior Clerk First-Class you employ. What's his name again?" Grenville asked, feigning ignorance. He had heard of Sir Nigel's young business prodigy, Peter Cratchit, many a time.

"*Cratchit*...Peter Cratchit. Why do you ask?"

"I can say with confidence that if, or rather *when*, he is apprised of this potential arrangement, he will recommend without reserve that you proceed with all possible haste."

When Sir Nigel returned to Room 209 at seven o'clock, he heard boisterous laughter and voices from behind the door, one of whom he recognized as his cousin.

I wonder if this is Grenville's "special acquaintance" he mentioned in his letter? he thought as he rapped on the door, his curiosity aroused. When he opened the door at his cousin's invitation, a most unexpected sight greeted him. Grenville, who stood at a little over five feet, seven inches tall, was standing and smoking cigars next to the largest man Sir Nigel had ever seen—not the tallest, but the *largest*. This bearded Leviathan had to be every inch of seven feet tall and weigh four hundred pounds. As Nigel's stunned gaze took in the behemoth before him, Grenville made the introductions.

"Nigel! Right on time, as usual. May I introduce you to Mr. Cyrus Abernathy, president of the New York and Pennsylvania Coal and Lumber Company? Cyrus, this is my cousin I was telling you about yesterday, Sir Nigel Fairweather-Hawthorne, *and* the key to our success with the Admiralty Board. Sir Nigel is the owner and founder of Hawthorne and Cavendish Furniture and Carpentry Works of London."

Sir Nigel tried not to visibly wince as his right hand was engulfed in the bear-like paw of Cyrus Abernathy's grip.

"A pleasure to make your acquaintance, Mr. Abernathy," Sir Nigel said. "Your reputation as an eminent American man of business precedes you."

"Cyrus is also the current president of the New York Stock Exchange, Nigel," Grenville added in an ingratiating tone, glancing over at Abernathy.

Abernathy gave Nigel's hand a vigorous shake as he exhaled a cloud of smoke from his Cuban cigar. "The pleasure is mine, Nigel. You don't mind if I call you Nigel, do you? I never could get on with all that pompous royalty nonsense. Earls and princes and knights… just a bunch of fairy tale titles for people who never did anything in life except be born to the right parents."

Although he bridled in silence at the implied insult to his knighthood, Sir Nigel held his tongue. *I helped burn down your bloody White House during the War of 1812, you sweaty ox*, he thought. *That's where I got* my *knighthood*.

"Not at all, if I may call you Cyrus," Sir Nigel responded.

"Of course, Nigel," said the immense Abernathy, as he sat back in an oversized dinner chair—one that Sir Nigel observed had to be procured to adequately accommodate a man of Abernathy's tremendous size. The chair's joints creaked in protest as they came under assault from Abernathy's prodigious weight.

"Grenville here tells me your company turns out some of the finest furniture and building construction in England," Abernathy observed.

"No, not *some* of the finest, but *the* finest construction woodwork, cabinetry, and furniture in Europe," Nigel retorted. "We received our Royal Warrant of Appointment from Queen Victoria in 1851 as a fine furnishings and woodwork supplier to the Crown."

The profusely sweating Abernathy pulled a handkerchief from his breast pocket and dabbed at the droplets on his forehead, then said, "Now, why don't you tell this poor American simpleton what a Royal Warrant of Appointment means?"

Sir Nigel gathered his dignity and said, "A Royal Warrant of Appointment is meant to put the public on official notice that the holder has supplied goods or services of such impeccable quality that it has been recognized and endorsed for use in the Royal Household of Her Majesty Queen Victoria. It is meant as an honor and, at the same time, to inspire the general public's confidence. During such times as these when shoddy products are a prominent public issue, a Royal Warrant of Appointment is a *very* sought-after official endorsement from the Crown."

While expostulating on the meaning and value of a Royal Warrant of Appointment, Nigel marveled at the speed with which Cyrus Abernathy consumed dinner and the enormous quantities of food it involved. It consisted of an entire roast suckling pig stuffed with dark turkey meat, a china pot brimming with roasted garlic potatoes swimming in butter-cream sauce, an unfortunate forest of asparagus, and a small mountain of hot buttered rolls; all washed down with two carafes of vintage white wine. Abernathy didn't *eat* food so much as he *inhaled* it, much the way other men breathed the air around them. It was an altogether repulsive, yet fascinating sight.

Abernathy gave an enormous belch as Grenville said, gesturing toward Sir Nigel, "Cyrus, *this* man is the ticket to winning the contract for the Royal Navy's fleet rebuilding program."

Abernathy arched an eyebrow as he fixed a skeptical gaze on Sir Nigel. "You have what it takes to rebuild the British Navy, Nigel? From what Grenville here has told me, what your navy proposes will surely mean rebuilding your largest ships from the keel up, not to mention a new fleet of steam-powered iron warships."

Nigel returned Abernathy's gaze with a steady one of his own. "Yes, provided the proper financing is in place to accomplish the Admiralty's goals. You'd have to secure long-term leasing on capable shipyards, purchase and transport of the necessary lumber, ship chandler's supplies, the services of experienced shipwrights, carpenters, architects, iron workers, pipe-fitters, engineers, and so on. If we could fulfill these requirements, Hawthorne and Cavendish Furniture and Carpentry Works can fulfill the contracts to the Admiralty's satisfaction."

Abernathy bridled at Sir Nigel's long-winded explanation.

Why can't these self-important fops answer a direct question without reciting an encyclopedia? Why can't he just say, "Yes, Cyrus. We can do everything and turn a tidy profit in the process?" Abernathy thought. *Why didn't this blowhard Nigel just bring along his boy genius clerk Grenville's been bragging so much about instead? If he's half the talent Grenville claims, he'd see I'm offering an amazing opportunity.*

Now it was Sir Nigel's turn to satisfy his curiosity. "I'd like to know, Cyrus; what is your interest in this endeavor? Surely Grenville has told you this is only a speculative venture at this point?"

Grenville nervously poured a round of fine port as a plume of cigar smoke erupted from Abernathy's mouth before he replied. Abernathy then removed the cigar from his mouth before jabbing it at Sir Nigel across the table for emphasis. The lies rolled off his tongue, as Abernathy was well-versed in the art of dissembling, and he didn't utter a word about his true reasons for wanting to gain a controlling interest in the massive Royal Navy program. He would buy up the shipyards involved and then sell them off piecemeal and, in the process, hobble the Royal Navy's battle worthiness for years to come.

He still remembered his aged father, Jason, many years earlier telling him how their family had been betrayed by the British Crown at the ignominious end of the revolt in the American colonies. The embittered elder, Jason Abernathy, ruminated to his very deathbed about that black day in November 1783 when the great British fleet sailed out of New York harbor and left hundreds of terrified Tory families still loyal to King George gathered at Manhattan's docks to the not-so-tender mercies of the victorious American rebels. With the failure of his father's mercantile business supplying provisions to the quartermaster of the massive British Manhattan garrison soon after British forces sailed from New York, his father died from bitterness. King George's apparent betrayal of Loyalists consumed his soul like cancer.

The humiliation and the subsequent poverty that afflicted the once-proud Abernathy family made the young Cyrus vow to avenge his father's humiliating death. From shoveling manure in a New York militia stable as a child to clawing his way to an education at Princeton University years later, avenging his father's shameful end was the baleful fire that fueled Cyrus Abernathy's ambition. It was only many years later that he hit upon the realization this could be best accomplished by using his business skills to financially cripple the British shipbuilding industry. By the time the clueless Englishmen realized what had happened to their storied shipyards, they would be presented with the fait accompli that Abernathy had dismantled their legendary shipbuilding industry wholesale right underneath their noses. But for now, noble lies would have to do.

"I only care about *business*, Nigel. I couldn't give a roasted fig about what empires over here go to war over some God-forsaken little parcel of land on the other side of the planet. Grenville here tried explaining it, all about 'Great Games' involving the Russians, the Turks, the Arabs with their camels in the Middle East, and it all made my head hurt worse than a bad cigar," Abernathy said, making a self-deprecating gesture with his hands.

But Cyrus Abernathy was no fool. He knew if the Russian czar coveted the Arab lands for the sea access they offered, the British and perhaps even the French Empire *would* go to war to protect their trade routes and precious Asian colonies. Abernathy knew he would do the same thing to a business competitor back in the United States who threatened his commercial interests. From his reading of history, it stood to reason that empires did the same; however, Abernathy also knew a modern war between empires across oceans and continents consumed immense quantities of weapons, food, and men. He would make the Abernathy name feared if not respected in the United Kingdom and, in the process, would right the injustice done to his father.

"I *do* see a situation here that can provide a very profitable outcome for all concerned, Nigel, if we seize the opportunity," Abernathy said, glancing sideways at Grenville. "War means business, Nigel, and the bigger the war, the more profitable the opportunity. I'm prepared to put up the equivalent of half a million British pounds to start with *and* provide North American lumber to boot at a thirty-percent discount *over and above* the best offer of any other wood supplier in Europe or North America for this project of Queen Victoria's Navy. I'll also sell you high-grade bituminous coal to use in those new steam-powered iron warships you want to build, and I'll give you *that* at an equal discount as well for the first five years."

Abernathy smirked at both Grenville and Sir Nigel's raised eyebrows.

"What? Do you think I don't know about the plans to fashion warships from iron and steel propelled by steam engines? Gentlemen, keep in mind your HMS *Victory* was in active service for fifty-eight years, but time and the science of war do not stand still. Even now, inventors in those deadly arts are readying cannon ammunition that will explode *inside* an enemy ship after striking it, not just punch holes in the hull like iron cannonballs or Congreve rockets do. Whereas the HMS *Victory* was able to withstand bombardment from Napoleon's fleet at Trafalgar, it would only take four or five well-placed shots from these new cannon shells to sink her."

Abernathy pulled another cigar from his vest, clipped the end off, and lit it with a match from the fireplace.

"No, gentlemen," he said, "I'm a plain-spoken man. I want the New York and Pennsylvania Coal and Lumber Company to expand our offerings into Great Britain and beyond into Europe. I also intend to earn a tidy return on my investment to boot; I can't say it any more directly. It's like your Royal Warrants of Appointment. I want the pleasure of knowing my little New York and Pennsylvania Coal and Lumber Company leaves a lasting impression on the Throne of

England," Abernathy said with his greasy false modesty, fixing Sir Nigel with a grin. "Think of it as an American version of your British East India Company."

Abernathy omitted the fact that he was also a majority shareholder in the Pennsylvania Railroad Company, as well as majority owner of any number of the burgeoning freight railways crisscrossing the United States south of the Mason-Dixon line, bringing plantation tobacco, produce, and cotton to market. Cyrus Abernathy held a near-monopoly on getting export goods to market from inland Pennsylvania down to Georgia, meaning he controlled port access between New York City, Philadelphia, and Savannah. His total holdings made him *much* wealthier than the British East India Company.

"Besides, my lawyers—I beg your pardon," Abernathy corrected himself in faux self-deprecation, "my *solicitors* here in England have made quite clear there are certain legal restrictions the Crown has in place regarding reliance on foreign suppliers of items critical to your Admiralty and armaments—especially in a time of war. Even though there's no war on right now, I'm going to assume they'll exercise maximum caution. What I am proposing *is* open and above board; however, I prefer to remain, for the time being, a discreet silent partner for now. Given the terms I've proposed, you have my word of honor that all covenants for the purchase of shipyards and such will be honored ahead of schedule and in full."

Abernathy's explanation was meant to put Sir Nigel at ease. Still, instead of reassuring him, it gave the Englishman a distinct feeling that the enormous American had just stomped across his grave. Abernathy had made it clear that his offer was not contingent on anything other than a handshake over this dinner, with official paperwork to follow at Sir Nigel's solicitors' no later than the following Monday by noon. That timing alone told Sir Nigel his cousin had already been engaged in detailed negotiations with Cyrus Abernathy for quite some time. In all likelihood, that meant there were other members of the Admiralty Board who saw the chance to gain personal profit from this venture. Opportunities to safely profit from the misery of war rarely remained secret very long.

Despite misgivings he could not quite put form to, Sir Nigel recognized the incredible opportunity that Cyrus Abernathy had set before him, and greed won the day. With a prestigious business partner who was also president of the New York Stock Exchange and the bonus of generous financial terms that were almost a gift from Providence, Sir Nigel had no choice but to accept Abernathy's offer. Obtaining and completing a major decades-long Admiralty project would establish Hawthorne and Cavendish Furniture and Carpentry Works of London as a titan to be reckoned with in Britain's shipbuilding industry and beyond. A palpable enthusiasm now infected Sir Nigel and Grenville as the realization of just how wealthy this good fortune might make them dawned on the two Englishmen. Neither of them doubted Cyrus Abernathy was as good as his word.

In contrast, and curiously unnoticed by either of the Englishmen in their avaricious glee, Abernathy sat in his chair like a potentate, contently puffing on his cigar as if he had known all along that Sir Nigel would leap at the opportunity set before him. As one of the wealthiest business tycoons in the United States, along with the dubious honor of being the most ruthless, Cyrus Abernathy was well aware of what his fortune could accomplish once he set his mind to using it. Abernathy was the archetype of what would become known in America as a "robber baron." In several years, due to innocuous clauses that he would have inserted into the contracts, Abernathy would make Hawthorne and Cavendish Furniture and Carpentry Works a wholly owned subsidiary of the New York and Pennsylvania Coal and Lumber Company. *"'Come into my parlor,' said the spider to the fly,"* indeed. Gobbling up Hawthorne and Cavendish was just the appetizer in Abernathy's malign plans for revenge.

"Cyrus, your terms are more than acceptable. In a word, they are quite generous," Sir Nigel said.

Damn right they are, you groveling little toad, thought Abernathy.

As Sir Nigel stood to shake Cyrus Abernathy's hand, he said, "Cyrus, on behalf of Hawthorne and Cavendish Furniture and Carpentry Works of London, I accept your offer. I think we should toast our new business arrangement. Grenville mentioned that you had procured another bottle of fine port for the occasion, so I say let's break it out!"

Grenville clapped his hands with a hearty "Here, here!" and the grinning Abernathy remained enigmatically quiet, puffing his cigar. There was a knock at the door, as if by invisible command, and the head sommelier for the Grand Brighton Hotel entered, pushing an ornate sterling silver rolling cart. In addition to the crystal wine glasses, the cart carried several wine bottles of the most sought-after port wine in the world, the 1735 Tawny Port, along with a large selection of the finest blue, aged gouda, Gruyère, and cheddar cheeses available, and a sealed box of fresh Cuban cigars.

Abernathy's lascivious eyes danced over the cart's contents while Grenville poured the first of many glasses of Tawny Port that night. Once the wine had been poured, and the hotel sommelier had retreated from the suite, Cyrus Abernathy stood and raised himself, along with his glass of port, to his full height.

"Gentlemen, I propose a toast to our new partnership." Ignoring his own unpatriotic sentiment, especially for an American, Abernathy continued. "May our endeavor ensure that Her Majesty Queen Victoria's Royal Navy keeps the world's oceans safe for commerce and trade for many years to come! Rule, Britannia! Britannia, rule the waves, I say!"

Glasses clinked as the three men settled in for several more hours of relaxed, celebratory conversation over their wine, cheeses, and cigars. The Hawthorne and Cavendish solicitors in London and the attorneys for Cyrus Abernathy would draw up the documents marking the official start of the new consortium two days hence. Still, the camaraderie and mutual business interests discussed far into the late spring evening at the luxury hotel overlooking the English Channel were the real beginning of the business partnership. Now all that remained would be for the sclerotic British Admiralty Board bureaucracy to release the proposal requests to refit and rebuild the mighty British ships-of-the-line. But Cyrus Abernathy was a patient man for whom months and years meant little. He had his eyes on larger prizes than a fleet of British warships. His sights were set on humiliating an empire.

3 ₰

A HEART TWICE BROKEN

A weary, but content Allyce Bainbridge marked her fourth month working as a nurse at the Royal Consumption Infirmary on Oxley Street in London with a pleasant detour during the brisk walk to her Georgian-style home just a few blocks off Henderson Square. The poised, beautiful Allyce nodded a cheerful greeting to passers-by and neighbors alike on her way. The confident wife of Captain Tristan Bainbridge of Her Majesty's Coldstream Guards, Allyce was blissfully happy. She reflected that a large part of her happiness was because she had heeded her friend Florence's advice to take the proffered nursing aide's position at the Royal Consumption Infirmary. Working with the sick there had given her another purpose in life—in addition to doting on her children.

Allyce first met Florence Nightingale in early 1850. Both were visiting the Lutheran religious community at Kaiserswerth-am-Rhein in Germany, where they learned innovative medical hygiene procedures from Reverend Fliedner and his deaconess nurses working among the sick and the poor. They realized a specialized education was necessary to prepare a woman to be a proper nurse. As the only English-speaking girls at the Kaiserswerth facility, the wealthy Florence and the decidedly lower-middle-class Allyce formed an unlikely, but tight friendship that wouldn't have ordinarily been possible back in England due to their radically different class backgrounds. But the two young women became fast friends, bound by their common passion for improving English medical care's appalling quality.

Florence Nightingale had left her own comfortable nursing position at the Institute for the Care of Sick Gentlewomen on Upper Harley Street, London, at the urging of then Minister-at-War for Crimea, Sidney Herbert, to travel to the massive British military hospital at Scutari near Constantinople as "Superintendent of the Female Nurses in the Hospitals in the East." Allyce could only marvel at her friend's dogged determination to improve the lot of British troops wounded fighting in the Crimean War, despite the arduous journey and hardships involved. Not many Englishwomen of the day, much less a woman from the very upper crust of British society like Florence, had the stamina to undertake the journey to Asia's very edges, to voluntarily work in vile, unsanitary conditions, motivated purely by compassion and self-sacrifice. Still, Allyce's friend was no ordinary Englishwoman. Religious in the extreme since childhood, Florence Nightingale believed her fiery passion to improve the treatment and conditions of the sick and diseased was a literal call from God. She answered with a determined "yes," much to her wealthy parents' chagrin.

Allyce Bainbridge's practicality, with fraternal twins of her own who were still mere toddlers, meant she couldn't possibly accompany Florence's determined band of nurses to the shores of Constantinople, but following Florence's example, she could still work to improve the lot of the medically less fortunate at home in England. Allyce had begun, here and there, to implement a few of the hygienic and sanitary reforms urged by her best friend. She could do no less.

Due to the indefatigable Florence Nightingale's tireless efforts, the Institute for the Care of Sick Gentlewomen in London had seen a remarkable decline in overall infection and mortality rates among its patients during her time there. Over many conversations, Allyce, a passionate convert to Florence's quest for proper hospital sanitary practices, decided to seek a position at the Royal Consumption Infirmary. When Florence had told Allyce about the results of a discreet visit she had there, Allyce hadn't needed any further prompting to seek a job there.

Florence had visited the Royal Consumption Infirmary in June 1854 and was appalled by the conditions; however, she could not possibly split her time between two very demanding jobs. At the Royal Consumption Infirmary, Florence found the beds packed together, a thousand patients forced to share twelve bathrooms meant for a hundred patients, non-functioning plumbing, and no clean towels, clean water basins, or soap. For a nurse with a passion for cleanliness bordering on obsession, she was horrified. Having heard of the greasy administrator Ainsley Northrup's rumored penchant for dipping his hand into royal funds allocated for hospital expenses, Florence wasn't surprised at the Infirmary's squalor, but remained undeterred. She recruited Allyce Bainbridge and persuaded the pompous Ainsley Northrup—playing off the Nightingale family's prestige and connections with the royal family—to grant Allyce a position as a nurse. In addition to the practical knowledge gained from Reverend Fliedner in Germany, Florence knew Allyce Bainbridge possessed much of her own determination, tenacity, and compassion for the suffering. If Florence herself couldn't accomplish the job, there was no doubt her friend Allyce could. If Northrup thought that the paltry wage of four pounds and three sixpences a week would dissuade Allyce, he was mistaken. Unaware that Allyce's husband was a captain in the Coldstream Guards earning four pounds and four sixpences, Northrup was convinced it would only be a matter of time before the combination of frustration with the miserable working conditions and skimpy wages would force Allyce Bainbridge to quit. He was wrong on both counts.

Allyce remembered the day Florence left for the British Army Hospital at Scutari in October 1854, extracting from her friend the promise that if the Coldstream Guards were in the vicinity, Florence would deliver a letter to Allyce's husband, Tristan, as she hadn't heard from him since he embarked for the Ottoman Empire earlier that year.

She remembered Florence's parting words: "Allyce, I've been told Her Majesty's Army camp at Scutari is absolutely enormous. Please keep in mind, dear, that I'm going to a very messy war zone, so if you don't hear from me right off, it will *not* be due to neglect or forgetfulness on my part. As it is, I must carry a letter from Fox Maule, Her Majesty's Minister of War, just to prove to those arrogant doctors that I'm not a helpless, meddlesome butterfly. I shall do my very best to locate Tristan and surprise him with your letter. I'm sure your tender words will surely lift his spirits higher than heaven itself!"

Allyce blushed at Florence Nightingale's sentiment, but in the secrecy of her heart, was pleased at the thought that her letter might bring her husband even a brief happy respite from his military duties.

This demonstrated the second reason for her happiness that day was the more enduring one. Allyce was married to the man of her dreams, Captain Tristan Bainbridge of Her Majesty's Coldstream Guards, and though for the time being separated by war, in a fortnight they would be marking their eighth wedding anniversary. For years before meeting her husband, Allyce hadn't met any man she cared for, or trusted enough, to allow to court her.

A willowy, raven-haired beauty, Allyce Simpson, when she met Captain Tristan Bainbridge, still carried sad memories of another young man of a higher social station who asked her to dance years earlier at a Christmas party thrown by her mother's employer. He had promised to love her despite her lowly social station and corresponding lack of a dowry to offer. Although he hadn't said so, as he grew more successful in his business career, his interest in Allyce waned as his intense interest in building a successful, competitive business waxed. When she belatedly realized this fact, she had already let almost six years slip by before ending the engagement. Memories of the years wasted engaged to a man who inexorably chose the golden idol of money instead of her love were the only real vestiges of bitterness that lurked in Allyce's heart. Still, the abortive betrothal had wasted too many good years of her young life.

That all changed on that magical Sunday in 1848 when she met Captain Tristan Bainbridge while leaving Sunday services at Saint Mary-on-the-Sea Church in Ilford with her ailing mother. She noticed the dashing officer looking every bit like a storybook hero in his red dress jacket, golden epaulets, and black striped trousers. For his part, without giving any outward indication, Tristan had definitely noticed *her*. His parents had just moved from York to a luxurious estate not far from Ilford, and he had taken to attending church there when visiting them. Now *he* had a definite reason to visit his parents more often. The "silly girls," as Allyce called the wealthy socialites who shamelessly fluttered around the handsome British officer like sparrows, leaving all sense of dignity behind, only reinforced her determination to not pay the captain any attention. For his part, Tristan paid no mind to the small crowd of young women who threw social dignity to the winds in an effort to attract his attention, citing his military duties as an excuse to not engage them on a social basis. But excellent military tactician that he was, Tristan had not only spotted, but was slowly working up the courage to engage the object of his affection.

So, after six weeks of the Army captain ending up seated near her in the cavernous church "by happenstance," he approached her mother after services with a respectful, endearing shyness Allyce hadn't expected and, with dignified politeness, asked that if her daughter was not betrothed to another, might he walk them both home? Allyce's mother, a widow herself after her husband had died some years earlier, was taken by the captain's quiet sincerity and courtly manners. She was equally surprised an officer in Her Majesty's Coldstream Guards would show interest in her daughter, a lower-class commoner. When they reached the Simpson residence, Tristan asked her mother if she would consent for him to formally court her daughter. The neighborhood was soon abuzz with the news of Allyce Simpson's betrothal. Allyce swooned at hearing Tristan's request of her mother, and from that moment on, the ensuing whirlwind romance and wedding bells were a foregone conclusion.

Tristan, a hard-driving military officer, persisted in courting Allyce even though his own parents were decidedly against the marriage. They were mortified at the thought of their son marrying so far beneath his family's social station. His father, Arthur Bainbridge, even threatened to cut his son off from his inheritance if he defied the family's wishes and married a commoner. Why, Tristan was an officer in the Coldstream Guards, and he very well couldn't just up and marry any woman he happened to notice in church! As an officer, Tristan knew certain societal expectations had to be upheld, proprieties observed, and the woman he would take for a wife should be of higher social standing than a commoner from a small English town. Although Allyce's mother did not live to see the wedding, Tristan had assured her throughout the courtship that he would be more than capable of providing a good life for her daughter and that Allyce wouldn't want for anything. After the wedding at Saint Mary-on-the-Sea in Ilford some five miles from London, it wasn't long before Allyce's joy was heightened by bearing her husband fraternal twins, Geoffrey and Amanda, in August 1851.

Although November 1854 was unusually balmy throughout the British Isles, for some reason, on this particular day, Allyce couldn't shake an odd foreboding. Her trepidation deepened when she reached her house. Allyce found a young British Army lieutenant waiting with his horse tethered to a cast-iron hitching post on the street.

"I beg your pardon, but would you happen to be Mrs. Tristan Bainbridge?" he asked.

"Yes, I'm Allyce Bainbridge; my husband is Captain Tristan Bainbridge," she replied. "May I help you, officer?"

Doffing his hat, he said, "I'm Lieutenant Michael Cripps from the War Correspondence Office, ma'am. I have a package addressed to Mrs. Tristan Bainbridge." He held out a parcel a bit thinner than a small sitting-room couch pillow. On the corner of the package was the name *Fl. Nightingale* in the script Allyce knew so well and the words *Scutari Hospital.* Allyce's heart leaptwith joy. Florence had located Tristan and had sent back not just a letter, but what appeared to be a gift from Tristan as well.

The young War Office courier bowed and said, "I bid you good day, Mrs. Bainbridge," swung himself onto the dappled horse's saddle, and trotted off back toward Central London. Allyce went inside her house, where her niece, Penny, served as her children's governess. Her portly young relative came bustling out of the kitchen smiling.

"Hello, Penny. Are the twins still napping?" Allyce asked.

"Yes, they are, Auntie Allyce. Geoffrey and Amanda have been perfect angels all day, and the way they were playing, I shan't be surprised if they sleep for at least another hour." Penny spied the package under Allyce's arm. "What have you got there?"

As she sat down on the parlor couch, Allyce replied in an excited voice, "It's from Florence at the British Hospital in Scutari! Oh, Penny, I can scarcely breathe. I haven't heard a word from Tristan since the Coldstream Guards departed for Crimea this past spring." She began opening the package, and after a moment of puzzlement, she looked up, holding a sealed envelope in bewilderment.

"This is the same letter I wrote that Florence was to give Tristan, and the seal is unbroken." Allyce tried to maintain a happy demeanor but was gripped by a sudden, inchoate fear. "I'll wager she couldn't find the Coldstream Guards encampment, or they had already departed to fight the Russians before Florence arrived at Scutari."

"That's a shame," said Penny Simpson. "Tristan's regiment must have been called away before that Nightingale woman could locate him. I admit I didn't meet Florence more than a few times, Aunt Allyce, but she didn't seem the sort to let rules, regulations, or even stuffy Army officers get in her way. She's not the type to suffer fools lightly. Had Tristan's regiment been in the vicinity, she would have found him."

Then, Allyce spied a second letter, addressed to *"My Dearest Allyce"* in Florence Nightingale's handwriting. Her heart pounding for any word of Tristan or his whereabouts, Allyce slit the second envelope open with trembling fingers, and two sheets of vellum slipped out. Unfolding the letter, she began reading:

Scutari British Military Hospital, Constantinople
November 10, 1854

Dear Allyce,

My hand and heart almost fail me at the sad obligation I must undertake. Our nurses and the French nuns traveling with us arrived in this dreadful excuse for an Army hospital almost one week ago. It makes the Institute for the Care of Sick Gentlewomen where I worked look like the Queen's own dressing rooms in Buckingham Palace. I tried to find Tristan's encampment in the first days after arriving while trying to organize this medical bedlam. It was only in a chance conversation with a wounded Scottish Fusiliers soldier on my fourth day here that I learned to my utter shock and sorrow that enemy guns mortally wounded Tristan at the Battle of the Alma River in September. The official account is that Tristan made so bold as to put his hands on a member of the royal family,

His Royal Highness Prince George, the Duke of Cambridge, during the battle and thereby greatly disgraced himself.

Tristan's men, whom I treated in Scutari, tell a very different story and instead say your husband saved Prince George from his own stupidity and ego. Tristan was leading a valiant charge by the Coldstream Guards against the Russians when he was felled by Russian bullets aimed at Prince George. Although they were vastly outnumbered, I am told Tristan's regiment fought with great courage, ultimately carrying the day. Some of the wounded here say Tristan died defending the Duke of Cambridge. I have met His Royal Highness the Duke, and although he fancies himself a profound military genius and is truly beloved by Her Majesty the Queen, I am not impressed. He carries himself like a dandy. I have no doubt Tristan's actions saved the Duke's life, but the official account of Tristan's actions is nothing short of libel.

You must know, had I been able to offer him succor and comfort, my dear, I would have done everything in my power to return him to you, but alas, Providence had other designs, as Tristan's wounds were very grave. I grieve knowing your Tristan went to his eternal reward before I ever departed England's shores with my nurses. The Fusiliers with whom I spoke told me that your name was on Tristan's lips when he slipped this mortal coil on the field of battle. He was laid to rest here in the Scutari Hospital churchyard, and I have visited his resting place often in your stead.

I sent this package to you via a military express courier on the pretext that it also contained an important update from myself to Minister-at-War Herbert. The letter to Minister Herbert will have already been delivered by the time this reaches you. In truth, dear Allyce, my message to the Minister-at-War was to confirm by direct observations of what we have heard in the penny papers about the dreadful conditions here. It is a fact that more soldiers here die from disease than the guns of the enemy.

I will write you again, dearest, as time permits. We are caring for so many wounded soldiers of Her Majesty that to think of rest is but a fan-

tasy. I think of you often and only wish I was home to console you. Know that I beseech the Lord every day to comfort you.

Your dear friend,
Florence Nightingale

Allyce Bainbridge felt lightheadedness rush upon her as she absorbed the contents of the letter and read it again as if she had somehow mistaken Florence's words or that the words themselves might change. A woman who had always prided herself as having a strong constitution, Allyce fainted dead away back against the parlor couch in a deep swoon. Her head came close to hitting the knurled maple armrest as Penny leapt up in alarm.

"Allyce! Aunt Allyce, what's wrong?" Penny Simpson put aside any lingering thoughts of propriety, picked the letter up off the floor, and read its contents before her own eyes filled with hot tears. *Tristan was dead, killed in Crimea!* Allyce already had her heart broken once before by that nasty merchant, Mr. Scrooge, but this was infinitely worse. Allyce was now a war widow, shorn of her husband, with two children to feed and no more officer's pay to support the family.

After a while, Penny Simpson managed to revive her aunt, at which point Allyce caught sight of the letter and sobbed inconsolably, her breath coming in heaving gulps. She collapsed into Penny's arms in despair and shook with waves of grief. "Tristan! Dear God, those Russians have taken away my beloved Tristan!" In shock herself, Penny could only hold her aunt's frame as she shook and offered awkward comfort and handkerchiefs while Allyce cried for what seemed like hours. Out of the blue, Allyce had joined the growing ranks of England's Crimean War widows. Worse yet, the official accounts had Tristan *assaulting* a member of the royal family on the battlefield!

Later that day, after she somewhat composed herself, Allyce Bainbridge dutifully pulled herself together and began her formal mourning period. With the help of sympathetic ladies in the neighborhood, she purchased a plain mourning outfit for everyday wear and a simple, yet dignified mourning dress for Sunday church services.

Allyce received a small consolation at the beginning of December. Florence's father, William Nightingale, arrived with another letter from Florence; however, citing urgent business in the city, he did not stay to see Allyce read it. Allyce opened the letter with sad resignation. Tristan was dead, so what further grief could the letter bring?

Scutari British Military Hospital, Constantinople
December 6, 1854

My Dear Allyce,

I will not presume to know the depths of your sorrow; just know that I have grieved for you in my heart as one sister to another had I suffered the loss of my own dear father. I plan to return to England when the fighting ends in this wicked devil's playground and will proceed to you straight away. I will not trouble you with a recitation of the details of the wretched conditions I, the nurses under my charge, and the wounded soldiers are forced to endure here daily. Let it suffice to say, my dear Allyce, though many of the cream of Her Majesty's Army have fallen to Russian gunfire, many more have succumbed to typhus, cholera, and dysentery than from Russian bullets. Disease is the real enemy here.

I have also faced another daunting foe here besides disease. It is the British Army "doctors," typified by Sir John Hall, the chief British Army medical officer for Crimea. I am sometimes given to uncharitable thoughts of the man when he dismisses my concerns about the atrocious hospital conditions. When I pointed out the rats running underneath the wounded soldiers' bedsheets, his cavalier response was, "It takes more than a few mice to frighten the British Army." He says I'm "just like a silly English parlor maid who screams at the sight of a church mouse." I told him these rats carry every sort of pestilence from soldier to soldier, but to no avail. We are so scorned by the doctors that we are forced to walk the rows of wounded late at night, with only small oil lamps to guide our steps, lest we incur the doctors' wrath.

Suppose Sir John continues his scorn for the care of our wounded soldiers, in my capacity as Superintendent of the Female Nurses in the Hospitals in the East. In that case, I shall be forced to write Minister-at-War Herbert again for his intervention. I will not hesitate to take this matter to the Crown if necessary, as good Queen Victoria would be most displeased to learn her own army's doctors think so little of the Hippocratic Oath.

Overworked and often drunk to escape the horrors of hacking off diseased limbs, the doctors ignore any offer of assistance. I make certain our efforts are far more attentive than the doctors' if only to justify our presence, despite my official appointment from Minister-at-War Herbert and the letter from Fox Maule. I am fully determined to see that Englishmen back home know what is happening here.

Food supplies are a travesty. We have not seen a drop of milk in over a month, and the bread is stale. The butter is mostly rancid; it is Irish butter in a state of gross decomposition, and the meat is more like moist leather than food. We are still waiting for potatoes until they arrive from France. But now is not the time for you to hear of my travails.

I visited Tristan's resting place again yesterday and, begging your pardon in advance of my words to follow, I grew quite cross that your late husband was so thoughtless as to leave you unprovided for. I have told him so on more than one occasion. I don't care if anyone sees me speaking harshly to his gravestone and thinks me daft. After I told the Catholic nuns that good English Cardinal Manning sent the nuns along with Florence about your Tristan, I've observed them saying their beads each day where Tristan is buried while taking their meal break. Sister Mary Saint Joseph says it is their custom to pray for the repose of a soul that way. Although I do not hold with the Roman religion, I admit seeing those nuns praying at Tristan's resting place gave me comfort. Seeing the conditions here as the work of God's enemies, I shall not refuse assistance from any quarter. Among my nurses, we are not Anglicans, Catholics, or Presbyterians; we are all common enemies of the Grim Reaper.

I know you are a proud woman, Allyce, so I have prevailed upon Father to pay the rent on your house for the next six months by the time you read this. I do hope you locate a position with better pay than the paltry sum Ainsley Northrup is willing to part with. I had Father promise to give you ten sovereigns to help provide for you and your dear children. If I was back in England, you would have me for your governess and quite happy to be so. I count you as one of my most cherished friends and I pray this war ends quickly.

Do give Geoffrey and Amanda a kiss from their Aunt Florence.

Ever yours,
Florence Nightingale

Allyce held up the small leather pouch Florence's father had handed her, and ten gleaming gold sovereigns spilled into her palm. Although her niece was more than happy to remain governess to little Geoffrey and Amanda, without Tristan's Army pay, Allyce's paltry wage of four pounds and three sixpences now put her among the English working poor. Of course, she had always been frugal with Tristan's salary and had never been one to be impressed by finery, but Allyce had one weakness. She loved to dote on her children. Little Geoffrey idolized his father and was always playing a soldier, saying he wanted to be just like his father when he grew up. Still, in little Geoffrey's world, the "enemy" was always invisible, and the brave British Army always carried the day. His little sister, Amanda, wanted to be a nurse, "just like mother and Auntie Florence." In their own childlike way, their aspirations were complimentary. Whenever the "enemy" wounded Geoffrey, Amanda would bring him to her little hospital and wrap his arm in a sling.

Allyce vowed not to let the patients at the Royal Consumption Infirmary see her weep for her husband. For their sake, she was determined to show a face made of sterner stuff. Allyce saved her mourning for late at night, alone in her bedchamber, when she silently soaked her pillow with hot tears of bereaved love for Tristan. As she could not bear to think of Tristan lying on a barren battlefield with his life ebbing away, she redoubled her determination to throw herself into the same demanding pace at the Royal Consumption Infirmary that Florence had taken on at Scutari. Allyce began a grueling work schedule at the hospital six days a week, often for twelve hours or more a day. She was careful to heed Florence's counsel regarding any pestilence that could "be catching." Hence, the bars of soap she brought with her and her diligent hand washing and washing and boiling of the meager bedding and blankets worked their way into her daily work ritual. She also became familiar with some of the patients, the vast majority of whom were poor and elderly, who usually succumbed to their consumption in the night and couldn't be roused in the morning. Although only a nurse, Allyce grew to have more than a passing familiarity with the symptoms of the disease. So many more unfortunates died of consumption than other diseases of the chest combined, including pneumonia.

Allyce continued to cross swords with Ainsley Northrup and his curt hostility on more than one occasion. He thought she was too free to apply "that meddlesome Nightingale's quack theories of sanitary medicine," as he derisively called them. Allyce, for her part, was secure in her position, with the support of Minister-at-War Herbert due to Florence's letters to him about Allyce's situation. Minister-at-War Herbert had even gone so far as to visit Allyce at the Royal Consumption Infirmary just to let Northrup see Mrs. Bainbridge had the ear of a highly influential friend in the government.

For her part, Allyce was too absorbed in caring for the sick and the dying to be bothered by Ainsley Northrup's sarcasm and disdain. He remained flummoxed due to her unassailable connection to Minister-at-War Sidney Herbert, but he also made certain not to go out of his way to be of *any* assistance whatsoever. Allyce's greatest annoyance was the romantic overtures of Northrup's Senior Clerk, Joseph Billingsly. On more than one occasion, Billingsly had intimated that if only Allyce was more receptive to his "overtures of passion," Billingsly could secure Allyce a sizeable increase in her salary. Only the sting from Allyce's palm the first few times the arrogant clerk made his amorous suggestions persuaded him to desist.

4

STORM OF OPPORTUNITY

It was early May 1856, and Peter Cratchit sat at his desk rubbing his temples, willing his headache and eye strain from staring at nine continuous hours' worth of papers and thick ledger books to go away. It was time spent reviewing the status of almost more ongoing work orders than he could keep track of for the Hawthorne and Cavendish Furniture and Carpentry Works. But the indefatigable business prodigy was the youngest Senior Clerk First-Class the company had ever employed, and he was driven to uphold his reputation for excellence. There were castles and mansions of nobility in the House of Lords being renovated, new mansions under construction throughout England, and all of them just *had* to have the latest and best furniture. The papers and ledgers were a mere formality, of course; his preternatural gift for remembering each detail of every project—actual or proposed—made the files superfluous. Peter's modesty wouldn't permit him to brag about his talent; however, these skills made him invaluable to his boss and employer, Sir Nigel Fairweather-Hawthorne.

Fred Holywell, Uncle Ebenezer Scrooge's nephew and only son of Scrooge's late sister, Fan, had secured the position for him with Sir Nigel, Fred himself having worked at Hawthorne and Cavendish in a position of great trust as senior contract review solicitor. And though Fred had secured for Peter the position of Clerk Apprentice at the salary of five shillings and sixpence weekly, or almost a little over fourteen pounds a year, Sir Nigel also had a keen eye for talent.

This salary almost tripled while Peter was in Sir Nigel's employ and rose to forty-seven pounds per annum as Sir Nigel first promoted Peter to Clerk, then Class One Clerk, and finally *Senior* Clerk First-Class—all within the eight years of his employment.

In Sir Nigel's eyes, Peter Cratchit was an extraordinary Senior Clerk First-Class. Peter was brilliant, with a self-deprecating charm. Years earlier, Sir Nigel had realized his solitary Senior Clerk First-Class was the key to his efficiency in running Hawthorne and Cavendish and therefore paid Peter a most handsome salary, quite a bit more than either of the other two First-Class Clerks. Peter also had the added prestige of an office adjacent to Sir Nigel's, with a private door connecting them. Under ordinary circumstances, the other First-Class Clerks would have been jealous of Peter's relationship with the boss, except for Peter's charisma and willingness to help the other clerks solve their projects' stumbling blocks without taking credit.

Having completed his review of assigned contracts for the day, Peter started his end-of-day ritual. He capped his bottles of Witham's India ink, cleaned and dried his steel-nibbed Birmingham pens on fresh blotter paper, and neatly stacked his working papers for the next day on the right-hand side of his large maple desk. Having completed and rechecked his assigned work for the day almost an hour early, Peter hoped for Sir Nigel's permission to leave and visit his wife, Charlotte, still hospitalized with a severe case of consumption at the Royal Consumption Infirmary. Peter grabbed his overcoat and scarf before he headed over to knock at his boss's office threshold. Sir Nigel sat engrossed at his oversized mahogany desk, examining a thick sheaf of papers through spectacles perched midway down his long nose. He looked up at Peter with his ever-crafty grin upon hearing the knock at the door jamb.

He looks like the big bad wolf from "Little Red Riding Hood," Peter thought.

"Peter, my lad, come in, do come in," Sir Nigel said with genuine enthusiasm. Peter knew his boss's enthusiastic and ill-tempered moods began and ended with the bookkeeping department's profit calculations sent to Sir Nigel's richly appointed office each Friday after lunch.

"Sir," Peter said, "I was hoping to visit Charlotte in the hospital tonight before dinner as I haven't seen her going on three days now. I've finished my work for the day and seeing as I have already started on tomorrow's contracts, I've more than—" but was interrupted by his boss.

"Peter, I understand your desire to see Charlotte. She *is* regaining her health, I hope. Consumption is a nasty business." Sir Nigel shuddered.

Peter gave a noncommittal shrug, his deep emotional turmoil kept in careful check. Most people who contracted consumption died of the disease in a matter of months, sometimes a year or two, but surviving it often meant access to financial means he didn't possess. Peter was too proud to ask for charity.

"Well, enough of that. Be at ease, Peter. You will see your dear Charlotte this night. But right now, you can tarry a moment for what I'm going to tell you. I have finally received the news from the Royal Admiralty Board we've been waiting almost four years for, lad!"

Peter's eyebrow arched.

"Those doddering fools at the Admiralty Board have finally made a decision." Sir Nigel brandished the papers in his hand held aloft like a torch, his hand trembling with excitement. "*This is it, Peter!* The official announcement of the first major rebuilding and refitting of Her Majesty's Royal Navy in over fifty years!" Sir Nigel's eyes fairly glittered with excited avarice. "Do you know what this could mean for us? For you and the fortunes of Hawthorne and Cavendish?"

"Not really, sir," Peter answered, quietly anxious to be off to visit his ailing wife but not wanting to seem rude to his boss. "I've been rather busy of late."

Charlotte had been confined in the hospital with consumption for the last four months, and he was anxious to get to the Royal Consumption Infirmary. He frankly didn't see how the matter concerned him, as this was the first time Sir Nigel ever intimated such an effort was under consideration by the Royal Navy.

"Peter, my lad," Sir Nigel could scarcely contain his excitement, "if we can agree on final terms with our American business partner, the New York and Pennsylvania Coal and Lumber Company, we have before us the opportunity to become the exclusive supplier of milled hardwood products and skilled labor to the Royal Navy's most extensive warship rebuild and refit program in *over half a century*. You'll be as wealthy as *any* of those peerage blowhards in the House of Commons, my boy. I daresay you could buy and sell that old miser your father works for a hundred times over. What's his name again?"

"Mr. Scrooge, sir. Ebenezer Scrooge," Peter said. "And he's been quite generous to our family these last few years."

Sir Nigel grabbed the papers on his desk bearing the seal of the Royal Admiralty Board and waved them at Peter. "Yes, well, enough of that. Look here, Peter. This is the request for contract bids by the Royal Admiralty Board, and it includes *all* the major woodworking for the Royal Navy's largest ships-of-the-line. Then there's the addendum for submission of a separate proposal for *iron warships*! Imagine that my boy, iron warships!"

Sir Nigel pointed to the papers in his hand with palpable glee.

"This includes the 131-gun *Wellington* class, 121-gun *Royal Albert* class, the 121-gun *Victoria* class, and the first new Royal Navy ships to be fitted with those new steam engines and iron armor amidships. That's more than *twenty* major Royal Navy warships we can be the exclusive shipbuilders for." A crafty smile stole over Sir Nigel's face. "You've come a long way in the company these past years, haven't you, my boy?"

Peter shifted his stance and glanced down at the floor in a bit of shyness. "Well, sir, I do seem to know when customers are trying to take advantage of us, if that is what you mean, sir."

"Oh, nonsense, Peter. You've got a brilliant mind for numbers! That's why we're going to win this contract!"

"Doesn't that also depend on Mr. Cyrus, sir?" Peter asked, referring to the mercurial Cyrus Abernathy, owner of the New York and Pennsylvania Coal and Lumber Company. Having met the unpredictable Abernathy several times on the man's trips to the United Kingdom and the Continent, Peter knew firsthand Cyrus Abernathy had a well-founded reputation for being a successful businessman—cunning and ruthless in the extreme. There were even whispered rumors Abernathy wasn't above resorting to criminal "intimidation," or worse, if it meant prevailing in a lucrative business deal.

"That's where *you* come in, Peter." Sir Nigel brandished a letter in his hand. "This came in on the SS *Caledonia* that arrived in Portsmouth yesterday. It's a letter from Cyrus requesting that *you* proceed to New York City without delay to meet with his American business agents and solicitors to finalize the details of our joint bid for the Royal Navy rebuilding program. He's got as much confidence in you as I do, my young buck, and for any man to have Cyrus Abernathy's confidence says a great deal, lad."

Peter's mind swam with the grand idea of a trip to America. He had never been outside of England, and the farthest he had ever traveled was with his wife on their honeymoon to Brighton, the English seaside resort. But his momentary excitement was dampened by the thought of being so far away from his beloved Charlotte, especially when she was so very sick. Consumption, which some doctors in Europe had started calling "tuberculosis," was a sickness that did not take pity upon those it afflicted. It was Peter's habit to visit Charlotte in the hospital as often as possible, and Sir Nigel *had* been quite generous in giving Peter time to see his wife as needed.

"If I may be so bold, sir, why didn't Mr. Abernathy ask for Fred Holywell to travel to New York instead of me? Fred is the best contract agent and solicitor we have in the company, and it would seem that's what this situation would call for, not a clerk."

"Yes, yes, I'm sure Fred would do a fine job at making sure the terms and details of the contracts were in proper order, but Mr. Abernathy specifically requested *you*, my boy, and one does not say no to Cyrus Abernathy, Peter. With the unprecedented scope of the Royal Navy program, I would much rather have you as my personal representative. Besides, Cyrus always gets what he wants. He wants *you*, and as *he* is the key to our success, *you* are taking a trip to America."

"How much is the proposed contract for?" Peter asked, as he felt his reluctance beginning to give way to a sense of inevitability.

Again, that crafty look stole over Sir Nigel's face. "Well," he said, lowering his voice to a conspiratorial whisper, "you'll remember my cousin Grenville Linton-Gower?"

"Yes, sir. I recall you once told me he's a distant cousin to Prince Albert?"

"Yes, the very same," Sir Nigel said. "Lord, Peter, how I do envy your memory. Now, this part must be held in the strictest confidence. Grenville is on the Royal Admiralty Board, and he 'accidentally' let slip that the Royal Treasury has final budgeted the value of the overall effort at well over *four million pounds!*"

With his intuition for understanding complex sums and figures, Peter Cratchit felt his vision swimming. Four million pounds sterling was fifty times larger than Hawthorne and Cavendish's pre-tax profit for the last five years *combined*.

As the understanding and implications of the sum involved dawned on Peter's face, Sir Nigel's voice turned from one of undisguised glee to a more serious tone. "Peter, close my office door."

Peter Cratchit walked over, and the heavy oak door swung shut with a solid *cha-clunk* as the robust brass lock engaged. The two men were now in a virtually soundproof privacy chamber.

"Peter, what I am about to tell you cannot leave this office. Do you understand, my boy?"

Peter felt a sudden pit in his stomach. Private meetings with Sir Nigel were very few and far between. It was common knowledge that the only things discussed in Sir Nigel's office were either promotions or tongue lashings, and both of these took place with the door wide open, never locked *shut*. Events were now proceeding at a breakneck pace indeed.

"Of course, sir. Our discussion shan't leave this office."

"Excellent," Sir Nigel continued. "Right now, Peter, as my most trusted clerk, my *only* Senior Clerk First-Class, I pay you forty-seven pounds per annum, correct? I believe that is a full twelve pounds more than either of your fellow clerks, am I right?"

"Yes, sir," Peter replied, "and I'm very grateful for your generosity."

"Well, how would you like your salary to increase by another £120 or so to £165 per annum, along with a guaranteed bonus of £100 per annum for the initial nine-year duration the contracts are in force? Of course, you'll need to use your intellect and charm to see that the proposals are acceptable to Mr. Abernathy *and* thence accepted by Her Majesty's Royal Admiralty Board." The conspiratorial grin returned to Sir Nigel's face. "But I'm hopeful Grenville can put a discreet thumb on the scales in our favor, eh?"

Peter bridled inside at his boss's intimation of his cousin Grenville using nepotism to win the contract, but Sir Nigel read the disapproving look that came over Peter's face.

"Oh, come now, Peter, I can see you disapprove of using my cousin's position on the Royal Admiralty Board as an unfair advantage." Sir Nigel leaned forward on his desk. You're probably thinking I'm not playing by the rules, but I say, *rules be damned*. You know the old saying 'All is fair in love and war,' don't you? Well, that notion also extends to business as well.

"Now, think for a moment; how would a salary increase like that suit you, Peter? Are you up to the challenge of negotiating our company's future fortunes with Cyrus Abernathy?" Sir Nigel grinned, already knowing what Peter's answer would be. He then played a manipulative trump card Peter couldn't resist. Adopting a solicitous, paternal tone, Sir Nigel added, "Just think of the medical treatment we might secure for dear Charlotte! There is not much in this world beyond the ability of money to facilitate. We could have her moved to the best consumption sanitarium possible." Peter quietly noted Sir Nigel's use of the word *we*.

"I…I…" Peter stammered in stunned shock. "That is indeed *quite more* than generous, sir." The normally voluble Peter was at a loss for words. He hearkened back to his first meeting with the American tycoon, Cyrus Abernathy, at the Royal London Exchange a year and a half earlier. Abernathy was a behemoth of a man and Peter had initially thought the man to be suffering from some illness that caused him to be nearly a giant. Still, the intimidating Abernathy had a normal childhood in every way, albeit pampered and with every whim catered to, as Sir Nigel speculated Abernathy came from an exorbitantly wealthy New York family. Peter felt very small in the man's presence, as he had never met a man quite like the Leviathan-esque Abernathy.

The thought of how such a salary windfall would easily permit Peter to provide the very best medical care for Charlotte now became his foremost thought. After all, the Royal Consumption Infirmary was a public institution, and patients crowded into that cramped hospital were mostly left to fend for themselves. Of course, there were rounds made by Infirmary attendants and nurses, like the ever-watchful Allyce Bainbridge, but should the venture with Cyrus Abernathy succeed, Peter would be able to afford to place Charlotte in a cleaner, private sanitarium where she could receive constant medical attention until she recovered.

Peter's mind began racing with the other possibilities the money would enable. His children would grow up with every advantage to make their mark on the world that he didn't have growing up. Not as spoiled brats (Charlotte would never permit *that*), but they would be given every chance in life a first-rate education would provide. He and Charlotte would afford a truly excellent tutor to teach their sons history, literature, Latin, Greek, the great classics, and arithmetic. His boys could attend Eton, Harrow, Oxford, or even Cambridge with a formation like that. Charlotte could hire a governess to teach their daughter the more refined ways of being a proper lady. The more Peter thought of the advantages such an enormous salary increase would bring, the more he warmed up to the idea. His heart beat faster with the possibilities.

Sir Nigel's voice intruded on his thoughts.

"Peter, pay attention, lad; this is no time for wool-gathering! You still haven't told me your answer."

"Oh, begging your pardon, sir. I was just thinking about being able to afford *real* medical care for my wife. Of course, I accept your generous offer with most profound gratitude." He grabbed Sir Nigel's hand and shook it vigorously in thanks. His face then darkened.

"How long will I be away from Charlotte and the children, sir?"

Sir Nigel blithely waved away Peter's concern. "I think you wouldn't be gone for more than a few months at the most. Peter," he stressed, "*these things take time*, and they must be done properly. That's why I'm agreeing to Cyrus's request."

"Well, sir…" Peter hesitated.

"Go on, lad. What is it?"

"You made certain to have me shut your door before you started describing this potential venture, sir."

Sir Nigel sat back in his chair, nodding as Peter continued.

"As I have understood it, this matter is to be held in the highest confidence. How do you suggest explaining to my wife that I may be away in America until just before Christmastide? Charlotte will be most distressed…" Peter left the unspoken implication of the forthcoming difficult marital conversation dangling in the air.

Sir Nigel smirked. "Ah, *now* I understand your dilemma; you're going to be in trouble with your wife. My boy, tell her the truth, but it's not necessary to tell her the *entire* truth. In fact, the very sensitivity of our negotiations with Cyrus forbids it. I know you hold to a very high standard of moral rectitude. Just tell Charlotte that an extraordinary business arrangement has come about in America that I only trust you to handle, and your presence—and yours only—has been requested by Mr. Abernathy, himself. That is true, is it not?"

"Well, yes, as you've described it, sir," Peter replied.

"You *may* tell her this will involve a new salary quite a bit higher than your current pay and that Sir Nigel said to tell her she would be transferred to the consumption sanitarium of your choice on your return to England. *Nothing* in what I said there involves the slightest deception, nor should it trouble your good Christian hearts, but on the contrary, it's only the best of news for your wife and your family. You can both put up with a temporary inconvenience for a guaranteed long-term benefit to your family. Charlotte does not need to know the specifics; indeed, you may not discuss them with anyone except Cyrus Abernathy. I would think that would mollify your dear Charlotte," Sir Nigel concluded solicitously.

Peter appeared satisfied with Sir Nigel's rationale for Peter having to make the long-term business trip to the United States. "When is

Mr. Abernathy expecting me to arrive in New York, sir? I'll be needing to put quite a few things in order."

"The SS *Caledonia* will be departing Portsmouth for New York on June 7, in four days' time. I've secured you a first-class berth aboard the ship, and Cyrus is expecting you to arrive in New York on June 21. The return trip is an open-ended ticket."

The more he thought of Sir Nigel's proposal, the more Peter Cratchit warmed to the idea. "Sir, you've given me quite a bit to digest. May I take my leave for the Infirmary?"

"Of course, you may have the entirety of the weekend to prepare for the trip. I suggest you come in tomorrow for an hour or two so you may familiarize yourself with the specific terms of the Admiralty Board's expectations." Sir Nigel withdrew his purse and slid a letter of credit for the Bank of England across his desk to Peter.

"That letter will allow you to withdraw fifty gold sovereigns this coming Monday to cover your expenses while you're in America. On your arrival, Cyrus will see they are converted into proper American money. He's very generously agreed that you're to lodge at his residence while you're in New York and has a letter of credit waiting for you at the First Commerce Bank of New York City as well. That money should be more than sufficient to provide travel funds for you to inspect his company's woodworking, milling, and mining operations in the eastern United States. Let's suppose you are satisfied that Cyrus's New York and Pennsylvania Coal and Lumber Company has both the capacity and proper resources to partner with us for the entirety of the Royal Navy program. In that case, this letter here grants you the 'power of attorney,' as the Americans call it, to draft with his solicitors a proper consortium contract for our joint work on the project, each company's responsibilities assigned according to our particular talents and abilities.

"The SS *Caledonia* makes a regular run back and forth across the Atlantic every three weeks. That alone is important because we must submit our final bid for the Royal Navy program no later than November 1 of this year. I expect you'll tarry with Cyrus's solicitors and clerks for a few additional weeks and then meet us here in London with his family for the formal award of the contract and the celebratory signing ceremony at *Buckingham Palace*! How would you like to be there to meet Queen Victoria and Prince Albert, my boy?"

Peter was thinking that Sir Nigel was already acting as though the award of the contracts to the joint Anglo-American consortium was a concluded fact. *What deal with the Devil had Sir Nigel's cousin Grenville made to make the usually cautious Sir Nigel so confident? Who knows?* Peter mused. Perhaps with Grenville being an influential voice on the Royal Admiralty Board, Sir Nigel had good reason to be certain of the outcome. Nepotism was common in business, and where unheard-of sums of gold sovereigns were at stake, it would be almost expected.

Sir Nigel continued, "Any communications you wish to apprise me of, write down on vellum in water-fast ink, secured inside an envelope with a wax seal made to your requirements in New York, and insert the vellum inside a separate wax envelope addressed to me here and again sealed with wax. You can even do the same with letters to Charlotte and your family; I'll ensure they get them. Cyrus knows I expect the papers for my final review no later than October 5."

Peter nodded vigorously as Sir Nigel continued.

"I shall follow the same arrangement for all communications to you and Cyrus. The captain of the SS *Caledonia* has been paid a handsome retainer by Mr. Abernathy to directly handle all communications in a confidential manner. Cyrus has insisted that all communications will be handled in this manner to assure us of discretion and privacy while you are away."

Bundled against the still-raw early-April winds slicing down London's cobblestone streets on his twenty-minute walk to the Royal Consumption Infirmary, Peter set off to see his wife. The sudden opportunity Sir Nigel presented him with consumed his concentration to the point of distraction, such that he was compelled to mutter an embarrassed "I do beg your pardon" several times as he bumped into fellow pedestrians along the way. He had met the former Charlotte Lyfield some ten years earlier at a social event for the young ladies and gentlemen of Saint Hubert's parish and, smitten, he had courted her with the ardor and passion only the young in love can muster. Thus far, their marriage had been a happy one until that black day after this past Christmas when Charlotte's constant coughing was first diagnosed as consumption. After that, it seemed every aspect of their lives changed in a blur. Charlotte was taken away by horse-drawn ambulance to the Royal Consumption Infirmary, and Peter began the arduous task of being both father and mother to his three young children, although his own mother, Emily, had busily set about running both households. While his own children were delighted that Grandmother would visit much more often, he did not want to take undue advantage of his mother's generous spirit. She was at the point in life when Peter had hoped things would get *easier* for his parents, not harder.

Peter wasn't naive enough to think Sir Nigel's motives for sending him to conclude the final contract negotiations and factory inspections of the New York and Pennsylvania Coal and Lumber Company were altruistic in the slightest. Sir Nigel knew that the success of this venture would catapult Hawthorne and Cavendish Furniture and Carpentry Works to the vaunted heights of commerce occupied only by the elite of British industry. Sir Nigel, on more than one occasion, was suspicious of a deal that appeared "too good to be real" and sent Peter Cratchit to perform his special brand of highly discreet due diligence. Several times, his loyal Senior Clerk First-Class had ferreted out well-hidden discrepancies and half-truths confirming Sir Nigel's misgivings—and, in the process, had avoided potentially ruinous business entanglements.

Peter walked briskly up to the entrance of a large building where a fading sign proclaimed it the Royal Consumption Infirmary for Consumption and Ailments of the Chest. He clutched the bag of Spanish oranges he had purchased at a provisioner along the way and a special gift for Charlotte lovingly crafted by his mother, Emily. It was a large, sky-blue cotton-backed woolen quilt guaranteed to keep Charlotte warm in the drafty third-floor ward she shared with about two hundred other patients. Peter saw Charlotte in an animated discussion with Allyce Bainbridge, the senior infirmary nurse who had befriended his wife. Allyce quickly moved on to another patient at the sight of Peter's approach. It was a strict hospital rule that outside visitors could visit no longer than ten minutes and then depart. Nurse Bainbridge had also implemented a rule that all visitors had to wear cotton masks while in the building as the staff did and then wash their hands in the main Infirmary exit lobby with strong soap before exiting the building.

The pungent odor of bleach permeated the hospital ward and hallways, another one of Florence Nightingale's innovations Allyce Bainbridge adopted. There was a German nurse with Florence at Scutari who had previously worked at the Vienna General Hospital. She told Florence that the Austrian hospital had begun using bleach to keep "childbed fever," a severe infection that killed countless women after they gave birth, from spreading throughout the maternity ward. Scoffed at by the Infirmary doctors, Florence regardless ordered a large quantity of chlorine bleach for Scutari from her own personal funds. In combination with other measures like diligent hand washing with mild lye-based soap and boiling all hospital clothing, bedding, and towels, it dramatically reduced the mortality rate of wounded British and French soldiers. Allyce then put each of Florence's recommendations into practice at the Royal Consumption Infirmary as soon as possible. Through her efforts, she reduced the Royal Consumption Infirmary's overall death rate by 27 percent.

Peter had long since gotten used to ignoring the nauseating combination of body odor, urine, and bleach wafting throughout the Infirmary, and Charlotte visibly brightened at his appearance.

"Oh, Peter!" she exclaimed. "I was just telling Allyce that Sir Nigel would keep you working late again and that you'd forget all about me." Charlotte gave her husband a playful pout that any other time, Peter would have erased with soft, gentle kisses, but kissing, or any physical contact with Infirmary patients, was strictly forbidden in case their malady was "catching."

"No, my love. I had a last-minute meeting with Sir Nigel involving the contract bidding on a very, *very* large project for the Crown. It's probably the largest order we've ever had, at least in my memory. But enough business drivel. How are you feeling today, my love?" Peter's eyes searched Charlotte's face for a hopeful answer.

"I wish I was up, about, and playing with the children, Peter, but the doctor said yesterday my condition is unchanged."

"It's no wonder, given they have you cooped up in here with these other poor folks. I have some good news on that front, but first…*ta-da!*" Peter produced the oranges with a flourish.

"Oh, Peter, I haven't had fruit in ages!" Charlotte smiled before she was caught in a coughing fit, a dirty towel held up to shield her face. "You really shouldn't have spent—" but her husband cut her off.

"Nonsense, my dear. You need good fresh food if you're to get well and come home to us." He produced the quilt and placed it on the chair beside her bed. "Mother made this just for you. She says it'll keep you warm when the skinflints that run this place neglect the coal furnaces at night."

Peter's face assumed a more serious demeanor. "Sir Nigel also surprised me with some news that, although altogether very good in its own way, means I must travel to America."

Charlotte's eyes widened.

"But then that means I won't see you for ages, Peter! What if something should…" Looking around at their surroundings, Charlotte left the gloomy implication at the end of her thought hanging between them.

Peter grew earnest. "My love, *nothing* will happen to you while I'm away except that you'll continue to fight this blasted infection. Sir Nigel knows this place isn't doing you the smallest bit of good. He's as good as his word, and he told me that not only will he provide me with a substantial increase in my salary, but that if the contracts are accepted, then as a bonus, he'll provide us with enough money to have you transferred to a *real* hospital specializing in ailments of the chest!"

Peter saw the skepticism in Charlotte's eyes. She had heard enough of Sir Nigel's greedy schemes in the past to be suspicious of his promises. "Did he say that? Or did he say what you wanted to hear to entice you into going off to America, like Ainsley Northrup, the rascal running this dreadful place?"

Peter blanched at Charlotte's prescription of the Infirmary administrator, Ainsley Northrup. She had complained many times that he didn't give a farthing for the patients in the Infirmary and instead voiced her opinion that he lined his pockets with Royal Treasury grants and donations to the hospital.

"No, my dear. Sir Nigel most emphatically said that straight away after asking about you." Peter held out the letter of credit so Charlotte could see the Bank of England letterhead across the top.

He lowered his voice. "As you can see, this letter authorizes me quite a sum of money for my expenses while I'm in America. I'm going to leave two sovereigns with my father for your care, so you shan't want for *anything,* my love. Our business partner, Mr. Abernathy, has insisted that I'm to lodge at his residence while I'm in New York. I'm told he has several mansions along the East Coast of the United States. Mr. Abernathy also has a letter of credit waiting for me in New York. I suppose I'll draw on it as needed to personally inspect his company's woodwork and mill operations in the eastern United States. If I'm satisfied that Cyrus Abernathy's New York and Pennsylvania Coal and Lumber Company has both the capacity and proper resources to partner with Sir Nigel for the entirety of the Crown's endeavor, I'll recommend that Sir Nigel proceed with the partnership. In that case, we submit the contract offer papers to the Admiralty as soon as practical. In any event, all the papers must be in the Admiralty offices by the middle of November."

"So, when will you be leaving for America?" Peter saw a look of sad resignation steal over Charlotte's face.

"I'm booked in a cabin on the steamship SS *Caledonia* out of Portsmouth this Tuesday next."

Just then, they heard Allyce Bainbridge's voice.

"I'm sorry, Mr. Cratchit, but you'll be needing to leave now. Infirmary rules and all that," she said.

Despite feeling crestfallen inside, Charlotte looked up at Allyce and managed a smile for Peter's sake. "Peter is being sent to America on important business, Allyce. If he's successful, his boss has promised to have me transferred out of here to a better hospital."

Allyce said, "Then I wish you the very safest of travels, Peter. You're going to need to decide who's going to be on the list of official visitors permitted to see Charlotte in your absence while you're gone off to the colonies. But you can decide that downstairs or have the first visitor in your absence bring a letter by your own hand." But her point was driven home—Allyce made clear it was time for Peter to leave.

Peter looked down at his wife, who was trying to maintain a brave face. Instead, a tear trickled down *his* cheek.

"I shall hold you close in my heart every moment I'm away from you, Charlotte. May the Good Lord and his angels watch over you until my return. I do so love you." Peter whispered it more as a prayer than sentiment as his voice cracked. Allyce felt a momentary pang of sadness. Peter taking leave of Charlotte was all too reminiscent of when her late husband Tristan marched off to war, never to return.

"I love you too, Peter. Write me if they give you any time, and don't tarry in coming back to rescue me from this dreadful place."

Peter smiled, turned quickly on his heel, and strode toward the ward exit, but not before pulling aside Allyce. "You'll take good care of my Charlotte, Nurse Allyce, while I'm in America? She is my *world*." Trying very hard not to let his brimming eyes betray his fears, he searched Allyce's eyes for reassurance.

"Of course, Peter. If I have anything to do with it, Charlotte will be home by the time you return from America."

After Peter left the hospital, Allyce went about her rounds again. Pausing for a moment next to Charlotte's bedside a short while later, she looked down.

"You seem to have quite the dedicated husband, Charlotte," Allyce said. "Let's hope he can come through on his business in America and take you out of this dreadful place. Many are the times he's visited you in this place, and on more than a few occasions, he looks asleep on his feet from working all day. I know from personal experience the pursuit of business and wealth can ruin more than a man's health."

Charlotte sighed and after a moment began to weep softly, giving in to the tears she had desperately held back for Peter's sake. Allyce patted her on the arm for comfort, then began walking away.

"Allyce?" Charlotte called after her.

Allyce walked back over to where Charlotte lay in her bed.

"What is it, Charlotte?"

Charlotte blinked through her tears and held out the bag containing six ripe oranges. "Sometimes I wonder where Peter keeps his brain when it's not in a ledger book. He knows our children are not fond of oranges, and it would be a true waste to throw them out. Please take them for Geoffrey and Amanda."

Allyce saw through Charlotte's generous subterfuge but said nothing. Peter had an important position at the prestigious Cavendish and Hawthorne, so he could provide quite well for his family. In their many bedside conversations, even given Allyce's penchant to keep her home life private, over time, Charlotte had come to realize that Allyce's life outside the Infirmary was a portrait in hardship since Tristan died in Crimea. She would never admit it, but oranges were a luxury that Allyce couldn't afford to buy for her children, and just the fact that the price of a few pieces of fruit was out of Allyce's reach broke Charlotte's heart. She not only considered Allyce her nurse, but had also come to think of her as a friend. Allyce saw the skeptical look on Charlotte's face and relented.

"I'll make a bargain with you, Charlotte. I'll take three of the oranges, one each for Geoffrey, Amanda, and my niece Penny, their governess. Then I will stop by your house and give the rest to your children. Fresh oranges are a treat that shouldn't be wasted!"

Charlotte gave Allyce a wan smile. "Am I as transparent as that?"

"No," Allyce smiled, "you're just too nice to lie."

Charlotte mused that Allyce didn't ever lie either, but sometimes extracting the whole truth out of her was an altogether different matter.

Allyce completed her duties at eight o'clock, well after darkness had fallen outside. The only convenience Ainsley Northrup grudgingly permitted her was to use one of the Royal Consumption Infirmary's ambulance carriages to take her home. Twenty minutes after making her final round of the third-floor ward, Allyce exchanged notes about the more serious patients with the night shift orderlies and prepared to leave for the evening. The first order of the evening after work was to thoroughly wash her hands and face in the washbasin reserved for her in her makeshift nurse's station, converted from a large utility closet. It was unthinkable for Allyce to run the slightest risk of bringing home the dreaded consumption to her young family, so her reddened eyes from the mild sting of the bleach tincture of the water was a small price to pay. She tugged on her heavy woolen coat and climbed into the ambulance waiting for her outside the main entrance of the Royal Consumption Infirmary. Soon the clopping noise of the horses' iron horseshoes on the cobblestone street provided a comfortingly familiar backdrop while Allyce gathered her thoughts.

Charlotte is fortunate to have a husband who loves her as much as Peter does, she thought. He visited her at the Royal Consumption Infirmary several times a week despite the rigors of his job at Hawthorne and Cavendish and his long hours there. And when he didn't, he was working late into the night on some special pet project for Sir Nigel. On those nights when Peter hadn't shown up to visit Allyce, Peter's father, Robert Cratchit, had. Slightly balding, Bob was a friendly, avuncular gentleman who always had a smile and kind words for Allyce. But on those nights when neither man had shown up, Allyce had gotten an earful from Charlotte about Sir Nigel and his love of money. Another man's love of money had destroyed Allyce's first chance at love as a younger woman, and now as a forty-year-old war widow, she was resigned to being alone for the rest of her days.

The ambulance wagon pulled up to her tenement building just outside the seedy Whitechapel section of East London, and the driver, Chauncey, insisted on walking her to her apartment door.

"I'll not be having to tell Mr. Northrup that anything happened to you on yer way home, Mrs. Bainbridge. I suspect the last thing he wants is to explain to Miss Nightingale's friend, Minister-at-War

Herbert, that any harm had befallen you that could've been prevented. Besides, as long as yer my responsibility to get home safe, I'll fight off a hundred East End ruffians to see no harm comes to you," Chauncey said.

Allyce smiled at the thought of the septuagenarian fighting off even a single determined schoolboy, but she thanked him just the same, laying her hand on his arm.

"You're a real dear, Chauncey, and I *do* feel safer not having to worry about highwaymen and brigands on my way home. I truly do appreciate it."

Chauncey tipped his top hat to Allyce as he had done so many times before, and soon Allyce heard his horses' hooves' sonorous clopping sound against the cobblestones as they receded into the distance. Her niece was dozing by the fire when Allyce entered the tiny drawing room, and Allyce gently placed her hand on Penny's arm to awaken her.

"Oh, hello, Aunt Allyce," Penny said as she woke up.

Allyce placed a finger to her lips as she motioned for Penny to remain in her chair. "The children are asleep, Penny?" she whispered.

"Yes, Aunt Allyce, but seeing as you'll be going into work a bit later tomorrow, allowing as it's Saturday, I really do think you should say good night to them. Amanda was as good as an angel, and so was Master Geoffrey."

Allyce smiled and slipped into the twins' cramped bedroom holding a small candlestick. Little Geoffrey and Amanda were asleep in their side-by-side beds as she bent down over them. She kissed Amanda lightly on the forehead, and the little girl opened her eyes.

"Hello, mum," the child said, only half-awake. "I was a good girl for Aunt Penny."

"I'll bet you were, my little love. I wanted to say good night and sweet dreams, my precious little girl."

At the sound of the low voices, Geoffrey stirred in his bed and sat up.

"Mummy! You're home!" the little boy exclaimed. Allyce turned to him and said in mock sternness, "And you're *awake*, Master Geoffrey Bainbridge."

"Oh, Mother," the child sighed. "I'm not a little boy."

"Of course you're not, my love," Allyce whispered and kissed each child again softly on the forehead. "I was working again late tonight and wanted to kiss you good night. As long as I'm your mother, I'm still allowed to tell you I love you."

"We love you too, Mum," the children said in sleepy singsong voices as sleep overtook them again.

Allyce lingered for a moment as she stood in the doorway looking at her precious sleeping children, then entered her own very modest bedchamber. Although a galling choice forced on her by circumstance, moving from the elegant home she had shared with Tristan and her children in London's prestigious Belgravia neighborhood to a three-room apartment in a poor neighborhood's best tenement was the most economical way to stretch her meager Infirmary wages. Allyce lived for only two things now: her children and her consuming passion to improve the condition of London's sick and destitute. She sat on the edge of the bed as she changed into her nightclothes after washing her face. She saw the treasured pen-and-ink drawing of her late Tristan on the diminutive night table next to her bed and felt the familiar burning in her eyes as the tears approached.

It was almost two years since he had died in Crimea, but Allyce still felt a tightness in her chest, and her eyes filled with hot tears whenever she thought of him. *No man will ever replace him*, she thought as soft sobs overwhelmed her again. This was the time of day when she felt most alone. She clutched her pillow in quiet sorrow and desperation at what her life had become in the two years since his death, and it seemed no matter how much time passed, the grief and loneliness only intensified. Tristan's death had numbed an intimate part of her heart in the most profound way possible, and the calumnies against him of assaulting a member of the royal family only made it worse. Although not a choice she consciously made, Allyce had come to the unspoken realization that love would never visit her grieving heart again.

And the hot, salty trails of grief and loneliness flowed.

5 ॐ

COME INTO MY PARLOR

Upon Peter's arrival in New York City two weeks later aboard the SS *Caledonia*, other than the thought of returning to his beloved Charlotte again, he thought that not even Cerberus, the three-headed beast of Greek mythology who guarded the gates of the underworld, could compel him to take a transatlantic steamship voyage again. Sure, he had heard tales of sailors who had bouts of violent nausea from what was called "seasickness," but nothing could have prepared him for what lay ahead on the Atlantic crossing. Ten days into an otherwise uneventful crossing, the captain informed the passengers that the barometer was dropping as the seas increased their tempestuous violence and the North Atlantic winds howled in the ship's rigging, meaning a great storm was in the offing. The crew raced about the ship, struck the sails, sealed off the bulkhead doors, and battened the hatches leading to the decks below.

The first mate went from cabin to cabin and told the passengers that it would soon be unsafe to venture out onto the main deck due to the pitching and rolling of the great ship. When Peter, who hadn't even once crossed the English Channel, inquired why, the first mate responded, "Sir, the captain says it looks like we're heading into a hurricane or the remnants of one, so until it's safe, the captain is confining all passengers to their quarters."

"Hurricane?" Peter asked.

"Yes, Mr. Cratchit, sir. Them's violent storms that are born down in the tropics, given life by the warm winds and waters down there.

The wind and waves in a hurricane could wash a man overboard in less than the time it takes to blink yer eye." The mate thumped a metal bulkhead for emphasis. "We're not in any real danger; the *Caledonia's* been through two or three in the last couple of years just fine. The sextant on the bridge says we're taking a northern route, but all the same, passengers must remain in their cabins for their own safety until the captain says the danger has passed."

Peter Cratchit spent the next thirty-six hours alternating between his berth and retching into the bucket on the floor, a floor that had a habit of pitching back and forth each time the SS *Caledonia* would crest a colossal wave and then race right down the back of the same wave before it repeated the process. In the first seven hours after the great storm struck, Peter had thrown up so much that it wasn't long before he was reduced to dry heaving an empty stomach. The only thing that prevented him from praying for death to end his violent nausea was the thought that his Charlotte had endured far worse trapped inside the Royal Consumption Infirmary.

On the fourteenth day out of Portsmouth, the lookout cried, "Land ho!" as the tip of Long Island at Montauk hove into view, and a grateful Peter thought at that moment there were no fairer words in the English language except *I love you*. Three hours later, the SS *Caledonia* was riding a balmy breeze into the narrows between Staten Island and the city of Brooklyn. Half an hour later, the ship was pulling alongside the dock at Pier 16 on the East River, and the dockworkers were catching the mooring lines to fasten them with complex knots to the great iron bitts on the wharf before the gangway of the ship was lowered.

Peter was fascinated by the hubbub and noise of the famous American port of New York City. Stevedores unloaded the ship's cargo as a parade of carriages waited to take the passengers to their destinations throughout Manhattan Island and beyond. He heard every tongue and language imaginable as the crowds thronging the piers along South Street gawked at the newest arrival from Europe. Sailors, merchants, Black freemen, and Chinamen from the Orient crowded about to see the new arrivals from England. He heard snatches of Cyrus Abernathy's American English along with French, German, Greek, Yiddish, and a veritable babble of other tongues he didn't understand.

The first mate clapped him on the shoulders and restrained him as Peter prepared to disembark.

"Not quite yet, Mr. Cratchit. The captain is under strict orders from Mr. Abernathy that yer not to leave the ship until one of Mr. Abernathy's own carriages comes to collect you. There are cutthroats and thieves in this happy crowd from up around the Five Points and the Bowery who would be more than happy to steal the clothes off yer back, let yer poor body wash up across the river in New Jersey with tomorrow morning's tide and have a good laugh over a pint about the whole thing. No, sir, it wouldn't do to have some of the Bowery Bhoys or the Dead Rabbits get hold of you, seeing, sir, as they don't know yer a guest of Mr. Cyrus."

"The Dead Rabbits? Bowery Bhoys?" asked a perplexed Peter.

"Yessir," said the first mate. "Them's street gangs much like back in the East End of London. Scoundrels and cutthroats all, the Bowery Bhoys are descended from the original Englishmen and Scotsmen who first settled in New York after the Dutch. I guess because they were here a hundred 'n' fifty years before all the Irish Catholics arrived after the Great Famine, they figure they've got claim to New York and most of America, methinks. They see themselves as the defenders of American freedom, always saying the Irish are plotting with the Pope to take the United States away."

Leaning on the ship's railing, the first mate continued, "You know back in London, those East End rookeries around Whitechapel, the places where no self-respecting Englishman like yerself would go? Why, sir, you've got yer poor folk, thieves, cutthroats and prostitutes, and everything else there. Even though we're in the 'New World,' places not 'alf a mile from here are just as dangerous as Whitechapel, and them places in New York are called the 'Five Points.' No respectable folks venture there, leastways not without an escort from the New York City Police."

He gestured with his pipe. "Now, take them fellas what you see over there just layin' about, not a care in the world? Those boys are with the Dead Rabbits; ruffians every bit as nasty as the Bowery Bhoys, but they see themselves as protectors of all things Irish here in the city. I guess you could think of 'em as New York's own 'Wild Boys' from back home in London. They's just as comfortable hiding from the police down in the sewers as they are taking their supper in a fancy restaurant or playin' poker in a bar. One thing they have in common is a healthy respect for Mr. Abernathy's men, so it's best we wait until Mr. Abernathy's men come to collect you."

It wasn't long before a carriage bearing the name *New York and Pennsylvania Lumber and Coal Company* in ornate gilded letters painted on the side pulled up. Two musclebound hulks who looked as if they wouldn't brook interference from the Devil himself jumped off the carriage and, casting sideways glances, made their way to the SS *Caledonia*'s gangway and handed the porter handling the baggage from the steerage compartment a note. The porter took it up to the top of the gangway and gave it to the captain, who then gestured to Peter, motioning for him to approach the gangway.

"Mr. Cratchit, these men will take you to Mr. Abernathy straight away. Remember, if I come by any letters for you from back home, I'll see they get sent right to you at Mr. Abernathy's residence."

Peter bid the captain of the SS *Caledonia* safe travels and walked down the gangway. He thought it peculiar that even though he was now standing on dry land, he could still feel the ship's rocking motion beneath him. One of the men looked over Peter's letter of invitation and, satisfying himself that this was indeed Mr. Abernathy's special guest from London, loaded his luggage on the carriage and helped him inside, but not before Peter caught the eye of one of the ruffians the first mate pointed out moments earlier while still aboard the SS *Caledonia*. Peter gave an involuntary shudder as the lout smirked and touched the brim of his odd little hat with an almost imperceptible smirk as if to say, "We'd be so much better acquainted, Mr. Dandy, if ya wasn't hiding behind Abernathy's bully boys."

The rocking motion of the ship was soon replaced by the trundling vibration of the carriage wheels against cobblestone carrying Peter uptown. Soon the carriage was heading up the Bowery and then along Houston Street before turning up toward Fifth Avenue on the other side of Washington Square. The tenements, factories, and storefronts gave way to more genteel environs the further north the carriage progressed along Madison Avenue. Finally, the carriage turned right onto East 38th Street in Manhattan's tony Murray Hill neighborhood and pulled up before a four-story Neo-Georgian red brick-and-granite mansion with *ABERNATHY* carved in large Gothic letters above the front entrance.

No sooner had Peter alighted from the carriage than he heard the stentorian voice he knew well from Cyrus Abernathy's visits to London.

"*Peter Cratchit!*"

Looking up, Peter saw the ponderous frame of Cyrus Abernathy filling the doorway of the Abernathy mansion. He was accompanied by a severe-looking waif of an older woman with her hair pulled back in a tight bun, and on his other side, stood a stunning young woman in her early twenties in a stylish dress, coquettishly twirling a pink sun umbrella, who, upon seeing Peter, promptly turned and disappeared into the mansion.

As Peter ascended the granite stairs, Abernathy boomed, "Come in, my boy! Come in! We've been looking forward to your arrival!"

Peter was led through an entry foyer and was greeted with the most magnificent house he had ever set foot in. A wide stairway led to the upper floors of the building and flanking the stairs were full-size marble Greek Revival statues set upon solid polished mahogany finial posts. To his left was a long hallway with an arched ceiling and to his right was a large parlor decorated in the most sumptuous manner possible. Peter had never seen such a collection of Gothic Revival furniture outside of a royal manor house he had once been fortunate enough to visit as a guest of Sir Nigel. Everywhere he looked he was overwhelmed with the sight of Gothic Revival furniture in the manner of the castles and homes of the wealthy European nobility such pieces were built for. All of it incorporated beautiful gleaming hardwood—burnished Brazilian rosewood, cherry, walnut, or oak—in various dark stains and colors. There were odd shapes and designs reminiscent of ancient Egyptian glyphs and designs carved as distinctive ornamentation into its design. The luxurious upholstery was equal to the furniture in oozing wealth and power, and it was clear that these exquisite appointments, finished with burnished, aromatic leathers, trefoil brocades, or luxurious, thick velvets, were meant to convey not only authority and influence, but also a carefree, decadent attitude toward money and life in general. As one of the richest men in the United States, Cyrus Abernathy could buy and sell whatever his whims demanded, be it goods, companies, or politicians. Abernathy's latest political puppet and protégé, former New York Congressman William Tweed, known by other New York politicians as "Boss" Tweed for his own corruption and control, was proof of Cyrus Abernathy's reach.

Peter heard and saw a small army of maids, servants, and butlers bustling about in the background.

"Peter," Abernathy said, "let me introduce you to my little family. He gestured toward the prim woman Peter had assumed was Abernathy's spouse. "This is my wife, Gertrude."

Gertrude gave a slight nod of her head. "Welcome to our home, Mr. Cratchit. I do hope your visit with us will be a pleasant one." Her voice was as dry as fallen autumn leaves; nothing about the woman evoked a hint of happiness, joy, or spontaneity; she could have been one of the Greco-Roman statues come to life.

Peter gave a polite bow to Mrs. Abernathy. "I'm honored that Mr. Abernathy has asked me to be a guest in your home. I hope my presence here won't be an imposition."

Peter took note that Mrs. Abernathy had a fair amount of makeup caked on her face that looked like the makeup they used at Charlotte's hospital to cover up disease disfigurement. Then, he took note of the rather stiff way in which Gertrude moved and he got his first insight into the kind of man, or lack of one, that Abernathy was. Try as she might, Gertrude Abernathy couldn't hide the fact that her husband was free with his fists and therefore must have a frightful temper indeed if he was willing to do violence to a woman, much less his wife. No wonder she looked frightened of her own shadow. Peter resolved that Cyrus would bear watching lest he turn his wrath on *him*.

Abernathy turned to the young woman Peter briefly saw on his arrival and spoke again. "And this exquisite gem of a young lady is my daughter, Livinia."

Livinia was sitting in a demure attitude on a richly brocaded couch, and as she got up, she quite deliberately allowed one of her ankles to be exposed to Peter's view, which evoked a chuckle from her father. The act earned her a slight gasp and a stern glare of disapproval from her mother Gertrude, as Livinia walked over to Peter, her gloved hand extended. Livinia, her raven hair in long, curled locks framing an impish face, wore an elaborate peach dress with a deep Bertha collar, exposing Peter to an uncomfortable degree of décolletage. He felt himself redden as she extended her hand.

"How do you do, Mr. Cratchit?" she coyly asked. Peter took her hand and brushed his lips across the back of her glove with studied politeness. "Oh, how very *gallant!*" she giggled.

"Very…well. Thank you, Miss Abernathy," he managed to say in response, taken aback by Livinia's deliberate affront to her mother's sense of decency. A small warning voice told Peter he was treading dangerous ground.

"Mr. Cratchit is a married man, Livinia," her mother remonstrated, but Livinia laughed it off.

"Oh, but he's a very *dashing* married man, Mother," she said in a sultry tone, and Peter couldn't tell whether it was calculated to entice him, scandalize her mother, or both.

Abernathy diplomatically intervened.

"Peter's wife is in a Royal Hospital in London with a severe case of consumption. His children are being cared for by a governess and his mother. He is here to work with me on the final business contracts I have with his employer, Hawthorne and Cavendish in London. For the sake of efficiency, I'm having him reside with us in guest suite number two for the next few months while these business arrangements are all ironed out."

He turned to Peter.

"Jefferson, our senior butler, will escort you to your room. Dinner will be served at six-thirty. Jefferson will come to collect you, as I assume you want to rest for a bit after your voyage."

"Yes, Mr. Abernathy, sir," Peter responded.

"*Cyrus,* my boy…call me Cyrus. I'm not one to stand on ceremony when there's money to be made."

Jefferson cleared his throat and gestured for Peter to follow him. They marched up the wide staircase and turned down a hallway in the labyrinthine home. Everywhere Peter looked, the mansion was decorated in rich dark-stained woods with the same repetitive carvings. They reached his suite of rooms, and Jefferson left him to his thoughts. There was a bedroom with a queen-size bed and a huge open mahogany armoire for a closet, a dressing room, a sitting room with a modest adjacent library containing a formal writing desk, and a washroom with a tub. After washing his face and changing into his business attire for dinner, Peter lay down on the soft bed and soon drifted off.

Almost as soon as he closed his eyes, it seemed there was a knock at the door.

"Mr. Cratchit, dinner will be served in thirty minutes. Are you ready?" he heard Jefferson calling through the heavy door.

Peter got up from the bed, arranged himself in the mirror, and strode to the door, opening it.

"Hello, Jefferson. Why, yes, I *am* rather hungry."

"Mr. Abernathy has had quite the dinner prepared in the main dining room in honor of your arrival. It will be ready shortly."

Peter grabbed his dinner coat and began following Jefferson back down to the first floor, where they stopped at the entrance to a dining room Peter thought was more reminiscent of an opulent medieval manor's dining hall back home in England. The walls looked to be made of ebony, polished to an almost mirror gleam and decorated with inlays and carvings Peter recognized as Egyptian. As dinner was not yet served and the Abernathy family nowhere in sight, Peter began exploring the first floor of the lavish residence. As he walked down one cavernous hallway, he came to an extensive, multi-level library and smoking room where one of the sliding pocket doors was open. Walking in, Peter was taken aback by the collection of literature, some on high shelves accessible only by a rolling ladder fixed to the wall. A large wooden globe stood in the center of the room, easily seven feet in diameter. Among the hundreds of books, every classic book he had ever heard of, and many more he hadn't, was here. He glanced down at a huge rock maple desk to see a list of library titles in delicate script, with a checkmark next to some of them.

The Iliad by Homer
The Epic of Gilgamesh, anonymous
The Republic by Plato
Meditations by Marcus Aurelius
Swanwick's translation of Goethe's *Faust*
The Histories by Herodotus
The Aeneid by Virgil
The Art of War by Sun Tzu
History of the Peloponnesian War by Thucydides
The Egyptian Book of the Dead, anonymous
Ars Notoria: The Key of Solomon by Solomon the King
The Fall of the Roman Republic by Plutarch
The Kama Sutra by Mallanaga Vātsyāyana
The Jewish War by Flavius Josephus
De Nigromancia by Roger Bacon
The Divine Comedy by Dante Alighieri
Le Morte d'Arthur: King Arthur and the Legends of the Round Table by Thomas Malory
The Song of Roland, unknown
The Nibelungenlied, unknown
Arthurian Romances by Chrétien de Troyes
The Prince by Niccolò Machiavelli
Ecclesiastical History of the English People by Bede
The Arabian Nights, anonymous
Confessions by Augustine of Hippo
The History of the Kings of Britain by Geoffrey of Monmouth
The Romance of Tristan and Iseult by Joseph Bédier
The Travels by Marco Polo
Two Lives of Charlemagne by Einhard
Summa Theologica by Thomas Aquinas

"Are you a literary man, Mr. Cratchit?"

Peter turned around quickly; Livinia struck a come-hither pose as she stood in the library's half-open pocket doors. He found himself blushing at being caught by Livinia in her father's library. He was put off balance by Livinia's sudden appearance; he hadn't heard her approach. *Is this room forbidden?* he wondered.

"Well, my education and training have been in the more practical application of business, Miss Livinia." Peter felt a deepening blush of embarrassment spreading across his face, having seen some of the more morally dubious titles on the list, such as *The Kama Sutra* and Goethe's *Faust*.

"I hope this room is not private. I was walking about as there was no one in the dining room when Jefferson summoned me to dinner. I admit to having some knowledge of a few of these titles, but many are unknown to me. I couldn't help but notice some have checkmarks in front of them," Peter said. "Do they signify any particular importance?"

"This is my father's smoking library and study. He says he likes to come here to think and draw inspiration. The books on that list are the titles my father has instructed me to read over the course of this year so as not to fall into cultural ignorance. A checkmark merely means I have finished reading the book."

Livinia continued, "The titles on that list run the gamut from Plato's *Republic* to works by such luminaries as Thomas Aquinas and Augustine of Hippo."

Peter thought, *How odd to think of Aquinas and Augustine as common, profane philosophers!*

As they exited the library, walking back toward the dining room, Peter paused in front of one large carving depicting people kneeling before a large creature with the body of a muscular man but the head of a large dog. He leaned in for a closer look.

"That's Anubis, Mr. Cratchit. Are you familiar with him?"

"I'm only aware he was an ancient pagan god before the Mohammedans conquered Egypt," Peter said.

"He wasn't merely *some sort of god*, as you put it, Mr. Cratchit," Livinia said in a patronizing tone. "Anubis was the proper Latin name given to the ancient Egyptian god of the underworld, *Anoup*, the 'Lord of the Necropolis.' In my history classes at school, I was taught that according to Egyptian mythology, the purpose of Anoup was to bring the spirits of the deceased to the world of the dead, or the Duat, as the ancient Egyptians referred to the next life. Anoup is also said to be the guardian of the tombs of Egyptian royalty."

"So, your father is interested in ancient Egypt, Miss Livinia?"

"My father has many interests, Mr. Cratchit; he cannot abide ignorance. His abhorrence of ignorance caused him to ensure that I received a proper education in arithmetic and history, in addition to Latin and Greek. *Estne conversatus in sermone Latino, Magister Cratchit?*" Livinia asked, the slightest smile playing about her lips. Peter returned her puzzling speech with a bewildered look, so Livinia tried again.

"*Tóte ísos katalávete pós na miláte attiká Elliniká, kýrie Cratchit?*"

His cheeks flushed a deep red; Peter knew Livinia was having fun at his expense. He spoke no language other than English. Livinia gave a haughty laugh as they entered the dining room, an impertinent grin on her face. Livinia plied him with one more taunt, this time in Parisian-inflected French.

"*Peter, Mon père m'a dit que votre chère épouse est très malade dans un hôpital de Londres et souffre de consomption. J'espère qu'elle se remettra rapidement. Tant de gens meurent de cette terrible maladie.*" (*Peter, my father tells me your dear wife is quite ill in a London hospital with consumption. I do hope she recovers soon. So many people die from that dreadful malady.*)

On seeing Peter's look of confusion, Livinia said, "Oh, please, Mr. Cratchit; you can put away your provincial embarrassment, but

I have to admit to being somewhat disappointed. When Father said an important business colleague was coming to New York, I naturally assumed he was speaking of someone of culture and refinement, a man of letters and social station. I *am* somewhat surprised you don't speak classical Latin or Attic Greek. You must be important indeed if Father is willing to give his royal treatment to an uneducated simpleton. You're more like the peasant laborers from Germany and Ireland my father employs unloading shipments from his railroad trains in the West Side rail yards."

At that moment Cyrus Abernathy strode into the room, an angry look on his countenance.

"Is that how your mother raised you, Livinia, to mock and insult our guests?" Abernathy bellowed. "Mr. Cratchit has *extraordinary* skills in business that make him very important to his employer, Sir Nigel, and to me. He is *very* important to the business at hand for Her Majesty Queen Victoria's Royal Navy. You will apologize to Peter, *immediately*."

Livinia stood for a moment, pursed her lips, and blinked at Peter in a doe-eyed manner as if pondering her response before she spoke up, doing her best to sound contrite.

"Mr. Cratchit, I am sorry if I offended your sense of propriety. I just assumed a man of your background, especially from the great city of London, would have certain faculties in Latin and Greek. I do beg your pardon," Livinia said, once again reverting to the coquette, giving a deep curtsy.

Peter couldn't help but feel that Livinia was passive-aggressively mocking him, as he recognized insincerity when he heard it. He summoned the remaining shreds of his dignity and said, "Please don't trouble yourself, Miss Livinia. Although I have certain talents in understanding complex contract negotiations and numbers figuring, you're quite correct. I did not receive an advanced education at university, but as there is no way you could have known that, I can't possibly fault you for it."

Abernathy realized that his headstrong daughter had overplayed her assumed authority over Peter to an inappropriate degree and that returning some measure of dignity to the embarrassed Peter was in order. He turned to his daughter and said, "Livinia, since you were so intent on proving your mastery of classic languages to Peter, perhaps we can have a demonstration of *your* skills in *arithmetic*." She cocked her head in a slight look of confusion as Abernathy asked his daughter, "Livinia, what is 354,939 divided by nineteen?"

Livinia stared at her father. He could see the dismay and embarrassment on her face. Her father knew quite well figuring numbers was not a talent she possessed.

Abernathy turned to Peter.

"Peter, tell me the answer."

"Mr. Abernathy, sir, that would be 18,681," Peter rattled off.

"Thank you, Peter. As I am nothing if not fair, Livinia, I will give you a chance to redeem your pride. What is the square root of 15,422,271?"

Livinia glared at her father. How *dare* he humiliate her like this? She decided to turn the tables on him.

"Father, I don't have the faintest idea, but it occurs to me that perhaps you and Mr. Cratchit have worked out this little game in advance at my expense. If I am to be humiliated in front of a guest, then it is only fair I choose a number for figuring to ask him myself to see if he can calculate the correct answer within ten seconds." Livinia crossed her arms in a fit of pique.

"If he cannot answer, then you shall have him shine my boots for an entire week. If he provides the correct answer, then I shall be his sincere friend, humble companion, and obedient servant for the duration of his stay with us here."

Livinia turned to Peter, smiling sweetly, even as her voice dripped with contempt. "You *do* know how to shine boots, Peter?"

Abernathy had enough faith in Peter to know that Livinia would end up embarrassing herself again; however, in a cunning attempt to appear gallant, he turned to Peter.

"You are a guest in this house. You need not answer to my daughter."

"No, sir. Please let Livinia put her numbers question to me, and I shall answer it," Peter said.

Livinia smiled in triumph. Sitting down at a small side table and taking out a fountain pen, she began writing a calculation on a piece of parchment. When she was finished, she blotted the paper, folded it, and handed it to her father with a look of triumph on her face.

Abernathy opened the paper, momentarily blanched, and casting a glance at Livinia, asked, "Peter, what is the square root of the arithmetic constant *pi*, 3.14, calculated to fifteen decimal places?"

Peter pursed his lips and replied, "*Pi* is an irrational number, and the square roots of irrational numbers are irrational numbers themselves or, in simpler terms, *pi* is a number without end. If, as your daughter has stipulated, the calculation is limited to fifteen decimal places, the answer according to her condition is 1.772004514666935. Should you desire to continue the irrational number for five more decimal places, it would continue as 04019."

The blood drained from her face as Livinia turned a ghostly shade of white while her father clapped his hands and proclaimed, "*Huzzah, Peter!* Well done, *very* well done!"

Peter turned a slight shade of red and responded, "Mr. Abernathy, although your daughter is quite correct in divining that I didn't receive a formal university education, I insist again there is no way she could have known I possess a talent for numbers figuring and I will not take unfair advantage of a lady."

That's what you think, Peter dear. Courtesy of Father, I know a great deal more about you than you could possibly realize, Livinia thought angrily; however, she was not one to surrender without a fight.

She marched off to her father's library and returned with a rather large book, a determined look on her face.

"I assume you have at least read the Bible, Mr. Cratchit. The stakes are the same: I will select a passage, and you will recite it from memory. If you have this gift of 'infinite memory,' as Father says, this should not present a difficulty to you."

"Livinia, this is quite enough…" Abernathy began in a warning tone, but his headstrong daughter was caught up in a fit of pique and would not be denied satisfaction.

"My conditions are the same. I shall tell you the name, chapter, and verse and you will recite them to me as they are in the Scriptures, word for word."

Peter stood silently waiting.

"Recite for me the Gospel of Mark, chapter 9, verses 42 to 44."

Peter thoughtfully glanced at the ceiling for a moment and then began to speak.

"*Et si scandalizaverit te manus tua, abscide illam: bonum est tibi debilem introire in vitam, quam duas manus habentem ire in gehennam, in ignem inextinguibilem.*

"*Ubi vermis eorum non moritur, et ignis non extinguitur.*

"*Et si pes tuus te scandalizat, amputa illum: bonum est tibi claudum introire in vitam æternam, quam duos pedes habentem mitti in gehennam ignis inextinguibilis…*"

Livinia interrupted him. "I win, Peter," she exulted. "I asked you to recite the Bible verses I specified, and instead, you spout Latin at me instead."

What game are you playing at, Livinia? Peter thought. *Not moments ago, you were mocking me for not speaking conversational Latin in your father's library, yet now you pretend not to understand the Holy Scriptures in the same tongue.*

Peter replied, "I beg your pardon, Miss Livinia. I do apologize as I fear I have made a mistake. While we were conversing in your father's library, I saw a volume of the Vulgate of Saint Jerome on a side table written in Latin. I assumed that was the book you brought in here. Although I do not converse in the Latin language, I read the Vulgate many years ago. After I finished it, I went on to read the King James Bible." Peter turned to Abernathy. "Sir, if I may have the chance to correct my mistake, I will answer your daughter's question according to the King James Bible?"

Abernathy nodded magnanimously.

"By all means, Peter. Yours was an innocent-enough mistake. Livinia did not specify the language she desired your answer to be in, so do proceed."

Peter said, "I believe the English translation from the King James Bible would be:

'And whosoever shall offend one of these *little ones that believe in me, it is better for him that a millstone were hanged about his neck, and he were cast into the sea.*

'And if thy hand offend thee, cut it off: it is better for thee to enter into life maimed, than having two hands to go into hell, into the fire that never shall be quenched:

'Where their worm dieth not, and the fire is not quenched.'"

Peter spoke his answer plainly and without a hint of triumph in his voice. He felt embarrassed at having his "talents" displayed as mere parlor tricks. Sensing the tension in the room was only escalating, as his daughter was *always* used to winning a contest, Abernathy said, "I do believe this little intellectual tug-of-war has gone far enough; a dinner of roast beef with mushrooms and asparagus awaits us in the dining room." Livinia placed the Bible down and strode ahead of everyone into the dining room. Peter held her chair out while Livinia seated herself to show that he bore her no ill will.

In a vexed tone, she said, "Thank you, Mr. Cratchit. Despite your lack of formal education, it appears your mother raised you properly."

At that point, Cyrus looked on as the wine was served, and then stood to raise his glass in a toast.

"To Peter Cratchit, whose talents in numbers figuring and 'infinite memory' have indeed demonstrated he will be a most welcome addition to our endeavor on behalf of Her Majesty Queen Victoria. He also gets extra recognition for being the first young gentleman to maintain his composure while Livinia did her utmost to humiliate him. I don't think my daughter was expecting the arrival of a handsome young genius who, although he did not receive the benefits of a classical university education, nevertheless refused to be baited into embarrassment."

Continuing to hold his glass aloft, Abernathy continued.

"So first to toast the president of these United States and my good friend, Franklin Pierce, and then Her Royal Majesty Queen Victoria of Great Britain in honor of our esteemed guest. May they continue to govern and rule to the benefit of civilized people everywhere."

Cyrus Abernathy couldn't help but silently gloat. The first part of his plan to bring down the financially troubled British shipbuilding industry was coming together better than he could've hoped. He knew his overall plan for revenge would take years, but the stealthy acquisition of Hawthorne and Cavendish Furniture and Carpentry Works was proceeding splendidly. Sir Nigel's greed would see to *that*. Livinia was playing her role of the alluring, haughty princess to perfection. It was not yet one full day since the young Englishman's arrival, and Abernathy already sensed tension had begun to build between his gorgeous daughter and the handsome but socially inept Peter Cratchit. He had seen Livinia employ the technique time and again to her advantage, and his strong-willed daughter almost always got her way. Peter Cratchit would be no different, but this time, according to her father's wishes, not as a romantic conquest or plaything. Abernathy relished that corruption of innocence was always more satisfying when cloaked in virtue. If it served his greed, so much the better.

Whatever his daughter might think, Peter Cratchit was invaluable to Cyrus Abernathy's long-range plans for two very special reasons. Abernathy had heard of people with Peter's legendary talent called "infinite memory," rare individuals with prodigious mental recall, enabling them to remember the most arcane detail of any document or book they had ever read or written. He would have sought Peter out for that talent alone. But Peter's uncanny knack for innately divining the value or profitability of a business arrangement after only a cursory examination of the pertinent facts was priceless. For as simple as Peter might seem in fine culture and the arts, he was an unassuming genius at predicting the success of any given business venture.

Abernathy was skeptical when Sir Nigel enthusiastically agreed to engage with him in their proposed business venture after Peter had only briefly reviewed the draft papers in the presence of the two men during an earlier visit to London. Sir Nigel's Senior Clerk First-Class sat at Sir Nigel's desk shuffling and reading papers for only twenty minutes, looked up, and confidently pronounced, "If the New York and Pennsylvania Coal and Lumber Company honors its obligations as stated, then both companies stand to benefit handsomely from the project in the long and short term." It was then that Abernathy suddenly recalled several years earlier Sir Nigel prattling on about his Senior Clerk First-Class's memory abilities. In his naiveté, Sir Nigel didn't realize Peter was the sort of "pearl of great price" that would further Abernathy's fortunes by an order of magnitude, especially with Abernathy's plans to dominate world commerce and drain the Royal Treasury in the process. But first, there was the matter of cementing Peter's loyalty to *him* and not Sir Nigel.

That's where Livinia entered the picture. To the amoral Cyrus Abernathy, it was irrelevant that Peter Cratchit was married. Sir Nigel had remarked to Abernathy in passing that Peter's wife, Charlotte, had contracted a severe case of consumption. Being confined to a run-down hospital like the Royal Consumption Infirmary, her demise was all but guaranteed. But consummate chess player that he was, Abernathy realized his pending moment of opportunity. When the news arrived, real or contrived, that Charlotte had passed on, Livinia would be there to comfort Peter, and as she was known as New York City's most desirable young socialite of marital age, Abernathy had no doubt whatsoever that she would put her charms to work to ease his pain. Besides, Abernathy knew, in her own fashion, his beautiful daughter Livinia's heart was as mercenary as his own. Some months before Peter's arrival, leaving nothing to chance, he had explained in detail the outline of his plan regarding Peter Cratchit to Livinia in a tone that said he would brook no interference or objection from her. When Livinia stomped her foot and announced she would *not* marry some English fop sight unseen, Abernathy sweetened his plan by offering Livinia an estate on the water in Rhode Island and a fully crewed sixty-foot sloop to get her there during the summer. Then, once Livinia had worked her charms beguiling a hapless, heartbroken Peter after Charlotte succumbed to her disease, Abernathy's master plan would be much closer to completion. Abernathy would appoint Peter Cratchit as the New York and Pennsylvania Coal and Lumber's "Vice President for New Contract Fairness and Review." Livinia would be free to do as she wished, but Abernathy was determined to have his game of chess proceed according to his own plan.

The irony was that if Cyrus Abernathy were said to have any sort of devotion approaching formal religion, it would be that he relentlessly built and ran his business empire based on the theories propounded by two of history's greatest strategists, Niccolò di Bernardo dei Machiavelli and Carl von Clausewitz. Machiavelli had always been a controversial Italian official in the Florentine Republic with responsibilities in diplomatic and military affairs. But what set him apart in Abernathy's eyes was that Machiavelli argued in his classic book, *The Prince*, that immoral behavior, even the murder of innocents, was not only desirable, but also perfectly normal and highly effective in politics. Machiavelli also encouraged politicians to commit evil acts in the name of political expediency. It was just this sort of unapologetic argument for embracing "evil" as a foundational principle that Cyrus Abernathy found so appealing. He was also an ardent admirer of von Clausewitz, the great Prussian general and military theorist, whose dictum "War is a continuation of politics by other means" so enamored Abernathy that he refashioned it into the ostentatious personal motto in the Abernathy family crest, *Omnes Commercium Bellum Est*, or "All Commerce is War."

He would not only own Hawthorne and Cavendish outright, but unbeknownst to Sir Nigel, Cyrus Abernathy was already close to owning a majority share of the John Russell and Company's massive Millwall Iron Works on the River Thames, where they were already laying the keel of the massive new ship the *Great Eastern*. Abernathy had also recently finalized the arrangements to become the silent majority owner of the equally huge Thaxter Shipyards on the Lower Thames. The pieces of his complex business strategy slowly came together, and Abernathy loved nothing more than to compare it to a good game of chess. Peter Cratchit would be one of his "knights," so to speak, if Abernathy and Livinia were the king and queen of this wicked game. Peter's ailing wife, Charlotte, on the other hand, was a pawn to be sacrificed and discarded when the time was right.

6

THE PRESIDENT IS
NOT THE QUEEN

Peter Cratchit awoke to the sound of excited voices that buzzed in the Abernathy mansion as his butler, Perkins, knocked at his chamber door.

"Come in!" Peter called out, putting aside the copy of *The Prince* he had been reading.

Perkins, ever the wooden, formal servant, entered.

"Mr. Abernathy asked me to remind you that the family will be departing for the Pennsylvania Railroad terminal this afternoon at 2 p.m. You need not worry about eating lunch here, as the family will be dining on Mr. Abernathy's train."

By now, Peter was no longer impressed by the riches and resources Cyrus Abernathy possessed. If one was rich enough in America, you could not only have your own railway company (he couldn't bring himself to call the endless miles of steel ribbons they had traveled "roads"), but it stood to reason you must then have your personal train. It was certainly a life Peter had quickly grown accustomed to.

"Thank you, Perkins. Please tell Mr. Abernathy I shall be ready to depart whenever you tell me it's time. I'm only reading and doing some last-minute packing."

"Well, on that, sir, Mr. Abernathy asked me to tell you that your black silk jacket and matching trousers for the Presidential Ball tomorrow evening have been delivered, and I will bring them up shortly. I'll also bring up your shoes and the rest of your ensemble.

He asked me to convey that should you forget anything, you will have ample time to purchase them once we arrive in Washington."

Peter nodded absently.

"Bring the clothes up as soon as necessary, and I will try them on for fitting. I daresay there won't be time for alterations."

"Not to worry on that score, Mr. Cratchit, sir. Mr. Abernathy's tailor will accompany the family on the train to Washington." Again, Peter shook his head in wonder; there was truly no limit to what Abernathy's decadent wealth could buy.

Several minutes later, there was a knock at his chamber again.

"Come in, Perkins," Peter said.

To his surprise, it was not Perkins who came in delivering the clothing package, but Abernathy's impudent daughter, Livinia, who strode into the room.

"Father would like you downstairs in half an hour so he might see how you look in these clothes."

She glanced with approval at the book Peter had placed down on the sitting-room table.

"Perhaps you're not as naive as I thought," Livinia sniffed. "Maybe you'll even learn something from Machiavelli," she added as she flounced out of the room.

Peter stood blinking, still getting over his surprise at Livinia entering his chambers unattended. An unattached young woman entering a married man's chambers would *never* be acceptable manners in England. The very idea was so outlandish as to be inconceivable.

Twenty minutes later, Peter looked himself over in his dressing-room mirror.

Good enough to greet Queen Victoria herself, he thought.

Walking downstairs, he encountered the head butler, Jefferson.

"Hello, Jefferson. Where is Mr. Abernathy?"

"He's waiting for you in his main library, along with Mrs. Abernathy and Miss Livinia."

Peter walked quickly down to Abernathy's library, where Abernathy was seated behind his mammoth desk. His wife and an impatient Livinia stood off to the side.

"Peter!" Abernathy boomed. "Let's see if that usurer of a tailor I pay is worth anything."

Peter saw the approving look in Abernathy's eyes as he entered the library, conscious of the scrutiny he was under.

Livinia was the first to speak.

"Well, Father, I don't know how well he can dance, but at least he won't embarrass me in his provincial English work suits."

The implied insult in her left-handed compliment was not lost on Peter as she continued: "I only hope he *can* dance. I would be mortified if the newspapers reported I was seen with a partner who didn't know his right foot from his left."

"I assure you, Miss Livinia, I can hold my own in the waltz or the polka," Peter retorted, more than a hint of testiness in his voice. The constant barrage of sarcasm and belittling in Livinia's voice had diminished somewhat in the weeks since he first arrived in New York; in fact, there had been times when Livinia had been something approaching polite, but she always seemed to be intent on reminding him he was from a lower social class. It almost felt like a constant verbal fencing match.

The Abernathy personal train departed Pennsylvania Station promptly at 8 p.m. that evening. The trip to Washington, DC, was scheduled to last just shy of fourteen hours, with arrival in Union Station at 10 a.m. the following day, eight hours before the grand dinner and dance at the White House. As they walked alongside the private railway cars reserved for Abernathy and his party, Peter got a look at the reinforced iron trusswork underneath as they walked to the stairway at the end of Abernathy's private railway carriage. He had no doubt that the car's supports were especially robust to account for Cyrus Abernathy's massive weight. Peter had his own private compartment on the train and was alone for the entire trip, except for the occasional train porter asking if he needed anything.

After they arrived at the Willard Hotel, the Abernathy party was led to their rooms by a small army of smartly uniformed bell-hops and porters. Although only a couple of blocks from the White House, Abernathy insisted that everyone meet in the main lobby of the Willard by 5 p.m.

When Peter arrived in the hotel lobby, the Abernathys waited for him. Although very conscious that he was a faithfully married man, Peter was nevertheless taken aback by Livinia's stunning appearance. She wore a custom light blue ball gown complemented by small rosettes woven into the trim. Her long tresses were curled to frame her oval face, and she wore her signature diamond earrings, but the tiara in her hair was what really caught Peter's attention. He had no doubt the jewels in the crown were actual diamonds and emeralds; her father could afford to dress her in anything she fancied, and in this case, she wanted to dress like one of the European princesses Peter had seen depicted in newspapers back in Sir Nigel's office.

Abernathy clapped his hands together.

"And Peter makes four!" he boomed. Gesturing toward the hotel doors, he said, "Our carriage awaits, and so does the president of these United States!"

Several minutes later, the carriage pulled up at the black wrought-iron fence surrounding 1600 Pennsylvania Avenue. Gas lights burned bright yellow outside the presidential mansion as the military guards opened the gates to allow the Abernathy party carriage to pass through. Moments later, as the guests of honor, the Abernathy party was escorted by three expressionless butlers and two military honor guards into the expansive White House dining room, where approximately one hundred guests were already waiting. Shortly after they were seated at their table near the presidential seats, the White House senior butler called out in a loud voice, "Ladies and gentlemen, distinguished guests, the president and First Lady of the United States!"

Peter sat as if in a dream as the president of the United States, Franklin Pierce, and his wife, Jane Appleton Pierce, entered the dining room to thunderous applause from a side door. This was a scene he would never have dared dream of back in London. While Peter was enthralled in the presence of the American president, he could not help but notice the contrast between him and his wife, Jane. While President Pierce reveled in being the center of attention, his wife gave off a pronounced aura of sadness. Peter sensed a tragic air about her.

He leaned over and told Livinia, "His wife doesn't look very happy to be here tonight. My mother would say she carries herself with an air of 'perpetual sadness.'"

Momentarily taken off guard by the sensitivity of Peter's observation, Livinia dropped her haughty affectation. She whispered, "Mrs. Pierce never wanted her husband to enter politics. When the Pierces were on their way here several years ago from their home in New England, they were on a train carrying them and their eleven-year-old son, Benjamin. There was a terrible accident, and their little boy died right in front of her when their rail carriage came off the tracks and crashed. They say she never recovered from the shock of that night."

"That's dreadful," Peter replied. "Perhaps that's why she looks so unhappy."

"The Pierces have never been fortunate with children," Livinia continued, more than happy to be able to impart information her father didn't know or didn't care about. "Their son Benjamin was their third child to die. She lost her first baby when he was just three days old, and their second son was lost to typhoid fever when he was only five. Mother says Mrs. Pierce has only her faith to comfort her and attends festivities such as this with the greatest reluctance.

I would say she is the very opposite of her husband's temperament; President Pierce is every bit as ambitious as Father."

At that very moment, President Pierce was engaged in animated conversation with Abernathy when Abernathy beckoned, "Peter! Come here, lad!"

Peter excused himself and proceeded to Abernathy's side of the table.

"Mr. President, I should like to introduce you to a distinguished young businessman from England who is here tonight as my special guest, Mr. Peter Cratchit. He's the gentleman I told you about working to help secure the contracts with Her Majesty's Navy."

President Pierce shook Peter's hand while lavishing extravagant praise upon Cyrus Abernathy.

"A genuine pleasure to meet you, Mr. Cratchit. Cyrus here is effusive in his praise of you, and therefore any protégé of his is fortunate indeed. I am so very sorry to hear your wife is ill with consumption. Mrs. Pierce suffers from the same dreadful malady. When you return to England, you must give her our most sincere regards for an expeditious recovery."

Incredulous that the president of the United States knew of his wife's illness, having been told of it by Abernathy mere moments earlier, Peter could only grasp the president's extended hand and stammer, "Th-thank you, Mr. President." He didn't see Livinia rolling her eyes, a gesture that earned her a visual rebuke from both of her parents. Any mention of a topic that would remind Peter of his sick wife in England annoyed her.

Bit by bit, although she would never admit it, Livinia Abernathy was becoming drawn to Peter—and not in the mercenary way her father first intended. No matter how much she needled and mocked him as being a "provincial," Peter never rose to take the bait. He was always a quiet, unflappable man who carried himself with gentlemanly dignity no matter what verbal slings, arrows, condescension, and insults she threw at him. Livinia Abernathy learned early in life that her extraordinary beauty could be used in getting a man to do almost anything she desired, but not this time. Livinia was always used to men doing her bidding like puppies eager for a treat, but there was an ethical resilience, a moral strength in Peter she had never before encountered. Her inability to penetrate Peter's moral shell only made Livinia that much more determined to prevail.

As President Pierce moved to the podium to give an appreciative speech in honor of Abernathy, starting off with how he was honored that the Abernathy family had traveled to Washington to be guests of the First Couple for long-overdue thanks, Peter glanced over at Mrs. Pierce. It was apparent she would rather be anywhere else than here at a political event. The fine lines etched in the First Lady's face told of tragedies endured with grace and humility. As Abernathy basked in the accolades President Pierce lavished on him for his support, Peter wondered at the contrast between the president and his wife.

So, she is ill with consumption as well, Peter thought. *That would explain why her complexion is as pale as Charlotte's.* His knowledge that the First Lady of the United States shared a common ailment with his wife, Charlotte, cast a sudden pall of melancholy over Peter's enjoyment of the event. He was careful to hide his sentiments as the dinner ended and the United States Marine Corps Band struck up a lively waltz, Frédéric Chopin's celebrated "Minute Waltz." Soon, Peter was whirling about the ballroom floor with Livinia, the receiver of many jealous glances from the eligible men in the White House ballroom.

Livinia played the part of the flirtatious social butterfly to perfection and did her best to make Peter jealous by accepting numerous gentlemen and military officers cutting in on their dances that evening. Peter always yielded with grace and was soon drawn into conversations with Abernathy and an abundance of guests anxious to have the ear of the famous Cyrus Abernathy. He caught Livinia looking his way several times during the course of the evening and couldn't quite make out the emotions that played out across her face. There were times Peter would have sworn that Livinia Abernathy was really jealous he wasn't paying more attention to *her*. Why couldn't she accept the fact that Peter was a married man faithful to his vows? He never tried to hide his wedding ring.

But in that moment, cigar in one hand and single-malt whiskey in the other, Peter was at the center of power and influence in the inner sanctum of an emerging global power and savoring every moment of it. This was a life he could get used to. Abernathy saw the gleam in Peter's eyes and smiled inwardly. Although Peter was outside his proper social element, he adapted quickly to the finer things the world had to offer, provided one had the money.

Later that evening, as they bid farewell to the president and First Lady, Mrs. Pierce extended her hand to Peter.

"My husband tells me your wife suffers from consumption, as do I. I know too well the toll this illness exacts on we who suffer from it, Mr. Cratchit. It does not discriminate according to one's station in society, and therefore you and your wife have my sympathy. Please tell her I shall pray for her swift recovery."

Before he could say a word in reply, Mrs. Pierce was ushered from the room by a White House matron and Peter wondered in silent amazement that genuine humility and sympathy were found in the most unlikely places. Charlotte's jaw would have dropped had she heard what the First Lady of the United States said.

The Abernathy family spent the first hours of the return rail trip to New York City parsing the evening's events with great relish, with only Abernathy's wife, Gertrude, retiring to their compartment to sleep. Peter's brush with the melancholy Mrs. Pierce was soon forgotten in his deep conversations with Abernathy on how President Pierce's support would be able to open a great many doors in England and Europe in expanding business prospects.

"Our first order of business, Peter, when we return to England, will be to introduce you to James Buchanan, the American ambassador to the Court of St. James." In a momentary slip, Abernathy quipped, "I have great aspirations for you, Peter, and they don't involve toiling away in a middling furniture company as a clerk for the rest of your life."

I wonder if Sir Nigel is aware of that, Peter thought.

As they were now alone in the parlor car, Abernathy gave a conspiratorial smile and said, "Peter, I've taken you into my confidence in a great many matters large and small, have I not?"

"Of course, Cyrus, and I have kept your confidences."

"Of course you have, my boy," Abernathy said with an approving nod. "Let me speak frankly with you. I know Sir Nigel has promised that once we win the Admiralty contract, he is going to raise your salary to £165 per annum, along with a £145 per annum guaranteed bonus."

Peter was not surprised to learn that Abernathy knew of Sir Nigel's salary promises to him should the Admiralty Board award the contracts to their consortium. Abernathy seemed to have his ears everywhere.

Abernathy continued, "Peter, how would you like to earn a salary equal to £700 per annum, with a bonus of another two hundred above that for performance? I think Sir Nigel hasn't set his sights nearly high enough for a man of your vision and talents. In time, once everything is signed and sealed, I should like you to formally join my New York and Pennsylvania Coal and Lumber Company as Vice President for New Contract Fairness and Review."

Peter's head swam for a moment at Abernathy's proposed salary offer. Abernathy could see the avaricious gleam growing in Peter's eyes as the young Englishman considered the unfathomable riches being dangled before him.

They all *have their price*, Abernathy thought.

7

OVER THE HILLS
AND FAR AWAY

Charlotte Cratchit was in higher-than-normal spirits that day amidst the gloom of the Royal Consumption Infirmary, for that day had brought another letter from her husband in America.

Tuesday, July 22, 1856

My Dear Charlotte,

I am writing this letter late in the evening in the hope that it will be on its way to you aboard the SS Caledonia *before she sets off for England on tomorrow morning's tide. Though I am here scarcely a month, my time here in America has been nothing short of a dizzying whirlwind. I cannot begin to tell you how many railway facilities I have had to examine, in addition to machine shops, iron smelting works, great lumber mills, and more factories than I care to recall (and it is my peculiar curse to recall them all down to the name of every foreman, engineer, architect, business agent, and solicitor of Mr. Abernathy I have met).*

I must apologize for not writing sooner, but Mr. Abernathy keeps up a frenetic pace I can scarcely believe a man of his ponderous size to be capable of. I speak not just of the business meetings we are being always shuttled to, but he is also quite the social animal (claiming it is all for business, you see). Cyrus—for that is what he insists I call him—says more business deals are consummated over wine and steak in gentle-

men's clubs' dining rooms than company board rooms. We'd no sooner returned from the gala ball in the United States Capitol, where I had the honor of meeting the American president Franklin Pierce, when we were whisked off to what he referred to as another in his calendar of "charity events." These always take the form of dinners and balls, where I should be quite disconsolate were it not for the good fortune of Cyrus compelling his daughter, Livinia, to be my social companion at these affairs. It seems such companionship is a compulsory part of social custom here in the United States and I can't afford to be thought ungrateful.

I am certain I must seem quite the equivalent of a Welsh coal miner to her compared to her wealthy and educated New York society friends. She seems to put up with my presence with a great deal more grace than I would have given any daughter of Mr. Cyrus Abernathy credit for. You would not get on well with her, though, I rather suspect. She spends money like it is her destiny to be wealthy and spoiled. She has a tendency to look down on people of our social station. I rather think she has quite the fine time amusing herself at my expense with all of her sophisticated gentlemen callers when I am off conducting business with her father.

Livinia, although not without her share of wealthy male admirers, has quite a haughty spirit. In fact, her father is quite fond of saying the only qualities Livinia possesses in excess of her beauty are arrogance and pride. I feel compelled to endure her companionship much the way an older brother endures the petty annoyances of a younger sister that insists on following him everywhere. Still, her companionship provides a respite from Cyrus's constant seriousness.

Tomorrow we are off to Albany, New York, to survey another machinery mill owned by Cyrus's New York and Pennsylvania Coal and Lumber Company. Thence, it will be onward to Mr. Abernathy's lumber and wood milling operations in the states of North and South Carolina. My ability to send letters will be constrained during that time; however, I shall seek to do so at the earliest opportunity.

With all my enduring love, I remain,
Peter

Charlotte read and reread Peter's letter several times, and two lines in particular caught her attention: *These always take the form of dinners and balls, where I should be quite disconsolate were it not for the good fortune of Cyrus compelling his daughter, Livinia, to be my social companion at these affairs* and *In fact, her father is quite fond of saying the only qualities Livinia possesses in excess of her beauty are arrogance and pride.*

Charlotte thought, *This is the second letter where Peter has mentioned this girl, Livinia.* Then, she chided herself for her childish suspicions and jealousy. But then the gremlin of jealousy began whispering in Charlotte's ear, *But Charlotte, did you take notice that Peter did not contradict Cyrus's description of his daughter Livinia as possessing "great beauty"? Then, several sentences later, Peter says he should be quite "disconsolate," not because he was away from you, but because he was lacking for companionship—companionship Cyrus Abernathy was only too happy to provide in the person of his "beautiful daughter."* Charlotte went back and forth any number of times, alternating between fear of the corrosive effect this girl was having on Peter, then remonstrating with herself for not having more faith in her husband and his fidelity to her and to their marriage. After all, Peter told her several times that the sole reason he had taken this trip to America was so that he might secure better medical treatment for her once he returned to England.

∾

Wednesday, August 6, 1856

My Dear Charlotte,

I do wish I was there in London visiting you each day after work instead of keeping up this dreadful pace of work. I have noticed that Cyrus continues to take me into his confidence to a great degree and far more than

Sir Nigel ever did. Cyrus has even gone to the point of suggesting that Sir Nigel has taken advantage of my talents and that I have been ill-used.

We have just returned from visiting several great farms in South Carolina and Virginia; they call them "plantations" here in America. While observing the working of one such plantation owned by a business acquaintance of Cyrus, I was dismayed to witness the harsh treatment of the laborers in the lumber harvesting and milling operations we were observing. Although Cyrus insists they are not "his" plantations, this work was performed by African slaves, whom I observed on a number of occasions quite ill-treated by very ill-tempered men Livinia referred to as "overseers." These overseers were large, brutish men who seemed to take great delight in liberal application of the lash when they thought any of the Africans to be laggards in their efforts.

I do not quite know how to express my disgust for what I saw on numerous occasions with the application of the whip. Livinia laughed and said I really needed to lose my provincial attitudes about my "inferiors." It seems to me that the African is every bit the same creature of Providence as we are, but in the American southland, they are held in contempt, on the same level as beasts of burden. Cyrus overheard my conversation with his daughter, and he rushed to assure me that his supplies of wood did not come from such great farms; instead, they would be produced by farms that did not use slaves for labor. He confided to me that he himself thought human bondage was entirely outmoded and would have to be abandoned by America in due course. I hope he is correct.

I find it distressing that a nation founded on the statement "We hold these truths to be self-evident, that all men are created equal, that they are endowed by their Creator with certain unalienable Rights, that among these are Life, Liberty and the Pursuit of Happiness" tolerates the barbarity of indentured servitude. I fear sooner or later, there will be a reckoning with Divine Providence on this matter. I can only say that it is our good fortune that the Crown abolished this vile institution years ago.

I must now conclude this letter, my Charlotte, as we are off in the morning to visit three foundries near Savannah, Georgia, before taking Cyrus's private railway train back to New York City.
I shall write again when I have the opportunity.

Your devoted husband,
Peter

Once again, Charlotte noticed two things. First, it appeared that Peter was becoming altogether too familiar with all members of the Abernathy family in his business travels with Abernathy. If Abernathy's daughter was such the New York City social butterfly, why was she taking such an excessive interest in her father and Peter's travels? It seemed inappropriate for her to be accompanying Peter and her father on these business excursions if—as Peter mentioned in multiple letters—Livinia was nothing more than a social butterfly. The final indignity was that this was now the second such letter in which Peter neglected to say he loved her, and *that* was not the Peter Cratchit she knew and loved. What sort of enchantment were money and business (*and the ubiquitous Livinia*) casting over her husband while he was in America?

Charlotte confided her fears to Allyce, and while Nurse Bainbridge did her best to be reassuring on the surface, she saw a disturbing pattern beginning to emerge—one she was all too familiar with. Although it had been years since Ebenezer Scrooge had succumbed to the siren's song of wealth and riches, no man was truly immune to it. Then, though her Tristan had been faithful to a fault with Allyce, he sometimes alluded to women of loose morality known as "camp followers," who followed soldiers to war zones and preyed on their loneliness so far from home. Allyce's instincts told her that whether going to Edinburgh or three thousand miles to America to pursue business, there would always be women willing to prey on lonely men. Allyce rued that there was more than one type of "camp fol-lower" in this world.

One day, while the consumption ward was quieter than the usual commotion of coughing, wheezing, and cries of pain, Charlotte showed Allyce the letters she had been receiving from Peter in America. Allyce then took Charlotte into her confidence about a man she referred to as Ben many years earlier who had been lured by the call of money and "good business," only to be lost to their spell for-ever. From the way Allyce spoke, and the uncharacteristic bitterness that entered her voice while recalling this, Charlotte knew Allyce was speaking from personal experience. Allyce was, by nature, a kind and gentle spirit; Charlotte could not imagine what sort of man would set Allyce aside for money. But then, given the prosaic tenor Peter's letters back to Charlotte in the Royal Consumption Infirmary had been adopting over time, it seemed there could be troubling changes afoot with Peter as well. Charlotte was confident that Peter would never abjure their wedding vows, but still, his concentration on "concluding great and momentous business arrangements" and his disconcerting familiarity with Livinia was unlike him, and in the confines of her heart, Charlotte Cratchit was troubled.

8

AN UNEXPECTED ENCOUNTER

Bob Cratchit was in quite the fix. He had promised Charlotte that he would visit her as often as possible while Peter was away in America, but not only was late May the busiest time of year for his employer, Ebenezer Scrooge, but of late, Bob developed a toothache of monstrous proportions. These two had conspired to prevent him from visiting Charlotte at the Royal Consumption Infirmary several times in the time that Peter had already been away in America. Bob made sure that Allyce Bainbridge gave Charlotte the notes and letters from him and his wife, Emily, as well as the colored pictures drawn by her own young children, but the Royal Consumption Infirmary was a dismal place. The few times he *had* been able to visit poor Charlotte, Bob had been dismayed at her lack of progress against the dreadful disease, and despite his best efforts, he hadn't been able to hide his discouragement from his wife.

He resolved to ask Mr. Scrooge for a favor. Though Bob was loath to prevail on his boss's kinder nature, he had no choice, as he had promised his wife that he would go to the dentist to have the troublesome tooth extracted after work. Scrooge readily agreed to allow Bob to rest at home for two days before returning to work, but in the meantime, Charlotte could not be ignored in the hospital.

Bob stood up and knocked on the frame of Scrooge's door.

"Begging your pardon, Mr. Scrooge; may I speak with you for a moment?" he asked.

"Of course, Bob. Come in. It's about that tooth of yours, isn't it? I told you my dentist would see you today at 6 p.m." Scrooge looked with pity at Bob's swollen red jaw.

"I know, sir. Me and the missus are right grateful for that."

"Then what is it, my good man? Something more is troubling that scrivener's brain than your swollen jaw."

"No, sir. It's Peter's wife. You see…"

Scrooge interrupted him, the concern on his face apparent.

"Is something wrong with Charlotte besides the consumption? Out with it, man!"

"Well, yes, sir, in a manner of speaking. Charlotte is putting up quite a battle against the consumption, but she's also fighting something I can't help with as much as I'd like. It's loneliness. She misses Peter and the children something awful, sir. Peter's away on business in America for Sir Nigel Fairweather-Hawthorne, and seeing her children is quite impossible while she has the consumption. With this toothache, there's no way I can go to the hospital tonight or the next few days, and I feel obligated to keep Charlotte's spirits from flagging."

Scrooge leaned forward on his desk, supporting himself on his elbows and interlocking his fingers.

"How can I help, Bob?" Scrooge said, his voice softening.

"I know I'm asking an awful lot, sir, but could you see your way to visiting Charlotte in the hospital this night?" Bob regretted voicing his request as soon as the words left his mouth.

Scrooge answered by standing up and grabbing his hat off the coat rack in the corner.

"No time like the present moment, Bob! I'll be glad to visit Charlotte instead of hobnobbing with those pompous buffoons at the Royal London Exchange. Now you get going off to see my dentist before I hear about it from your wife. Charlotte shall not want for cheerful company this night."

"Thank you, sir," Bob said. "Just be sure you abide by her ward nurse's rules for visiting patients with the consumption, in particular washing your hands in those awful basins of chlorinated water she's put everywhere. That Nurse Bainbridge is a regular prison warden. She can be quite fierce in protecting her patients and visitors."

Scrooge hailed a cab on the street a few moments later and told the driver to take him to the Royal Consumption Infirmary forthwith. Fifteen minutes later, the cab pulled up across the street from the hospital, the slightest odor of chlorine bleach wafting on the late afternoon breeze. Scrooge walked up the stairs and into the entry, where an attendant sat behind a receiving desk.

Removing his hat, Scrooged inquired, "My good man, I'm here to visit one of your patients. Her name is Charlotte Cratchit, and I am the employer of her father-in-law. He was supposed to be here tonight, but he has an appointment with the dentist, I'm afraid, so he asked me to come in his stead. Here is my letter of introduction," handing him a note in Bob Cratchit's hand.

After giving the note a brief scan, the attendant on duty consulted a large patient ledger book and pointed to a wide staircase behind Scrooge.

"Go up to the third floor and enter the ward on your immediate right. Mrs. Cratchit will be the seventh bed on your right, going down the middle aisle of beds. She has a bright blue knit blanket beside her bed that will make it difficult to miss her."

Scrooge doffed his hat. "Thank you, my good man."

As Scrooge made his way up the staircase, the smell of bleach became stronger.

Since when did hospitals start using bleach to cover the odors of the patients? he wondered. After some moments, Scrooge reached the third floor and, looking down the hallway, saw a door on his right that could only lead into the medical ward. He already heard the hacking and coughing coming from the multitude of patients crammed inside the cavernous room.

Before reaching the door, he was stopped by a nurse who handed him a cloth mask and the admonition, "Please put that on, sir, if yer visiting someone in the ward. Besides consumption, there are all kinds of other disorders in the air hereabouts. Nurse Bainbridge is awful strict about visitors coming into a place where there's things that are catching, if you get my meaning."

Scrooge looked down at the white cotton mask and figured he could use it to good effect in surprising Charlotte. He fastened it about his face, covering his mouth and nose. *I look like a highwayman*, he thought. *Charlotte will never suspect who I am.* He walked cautiously through the ward door into a sea of hacking and wheezing patients lying or sitting in their beds.

God, preserve me from the ill humors in this wretched place, he thought. Walking over to the central aisle, he began counting the beds on his right-hand side and soon saw a bright blue quilt draped about the shoulders of a pale, emaciated young woman where a nurse in a black uniform sat and spoke with her.

Scrooge's efforts at playful deception were soon banished the moment Charlotte looked up and brightened, exclaiming, "Uncle Ebenezer!" because instead, it was Scrooge who was in for the shock of his life. The nurse sitting by Charlotte's bedside turned to look up at him, and they both gave a mutual start of recognition, Allyce's being more restrained. Scrooge felt his heart leap within his chest, pounding like a carpenter's hammer.

"Oh, Uncle Ebenezer," said Charlotte, "you needn't have come to this dreadful place. I know Dad Cratchit would've been along one of these days." Charlotte then turned to Allyce to make the introduction, unaware it was unnecessary. "Allyce, let me introduce you to the uncle I hadn't been born with, but who's been an absolute treasure to Peter's family for years, Uncle Ebenezer."

For such a wealthy and respected businessman, Scrooge stood there feeling quite silly, his eyes blinking at the sight of his former fiancée, a strong queasy feeling in the pit of his stomach. *Allyce! My God, Allyce...*he thought. Scrooge struggled to keep the sudden emotions roiling his heart under control and to give no outward sign of recognizing his former love. Allyce had matured into a lady of incredible beauty and delicate grace. But there was also something unmistakable in Allyce's gaze that spoke of strength and unyielding determination, forged by life in fires far hotter than any blacksmith's furnace.

Charlotte continued. "Uncle Ebenezer, this is the nurse who will have me home with my family in no time, Allyce Bainbridge. She's been so wonderfully attentive that I think I should already be in Saint Hubert's churchyard if not for her ministrations."

Allyce stood up with the trademark fluidity and graceful dignity Scrooge remembered all too well, nodding at him. Her hair was lightly streaked through with gray, but rather than make her look older, it gave her beauty the distinct appearance of grace and strength formed under pressure, much like a diamond.

"Hello, *Mr.* Scrooge," she said in a peremptory tone that told Charlotte these people had known each other in the past. Looking down at Charlotte, Allyce spoke.

"Be sure to finish all your hot clove and ginger tea before I come round to make my next check, Charlotte. That will belay your coughing so you will be able to eat dinner and sleep peaceably." Turning to face Scrooge, she said a polite, "Good day to you, Mr. Scrooge," before gliding off down the aisle to another patient several beds down, this time a young child whose face lit up at seeing her.

Scrooge was sure he was about to feel his knees buckling beneath him at the shock of seeing Allyce after so many years. Therefore, he was indeed grateful when Charlotte insisted that he take a seat on the chair at the foot of the bed.

"Oh, Uncle Ebenezer, it's so kind of you to visit me among these dark shadows," Charlotte said.

Slowly getting over his shock at encountering Allyce, Scrooge spoke.

"Nonsense, child. You are as dear to me as if I had a daughter in your image. Tell me, Charlotte, is Allyce"—Scrooge hesitated, but belatedly realized he had tipped his hand—"is *Nurse Bainbridge* taking good care of you?" he asked with genuine solicitude.

Charlotte was quick to divine the meaning behind the interaction she had just observed. She recalled Allyce telling her several weeks earlier that a young man named Ebenezer had broken her heart years earlier by pursuing gold coins instead of the golden treasure of love Allyce offered from the innocence of her youthful heart.

After a few more minutes of small talk, Charlotte could no longer abide her curiosity.

"May I ask you a question, Uncle?" Charlotte asked with the slightest quaver in her voice. "I shan't be offended if the subject is unpleasant to you and you do not wish to discuss it."

Scrooge knew the inevitability of the inquiry, given his visible reaction at seeing Allyce after so many years.

"Yes, child. Ask me anything you wish."

Charlotte gathered up her courage and spoke.

"Were you acquainted with Allyce in your youth?"

Scrooge gave a quick affirmative nod, words being superfluous, but an answer was nevertheless in order.

"Yes…"

He continued, his voice carrying an uncharacteristic, thick huskiness.

"The last time I saw Allyce, it was a late summer evening back in 1848, I believe, and she was strolling down Eaton Place near

Buckingham Palace, clutching the arm of a captain in Her Majesty's Coldstream Guards. She was quite smitten with him, and I had heard they were married not long after that."

Charlotte pressed on, undeterred. "Uncle Ebenezer, were *you* the man Allyce was engaged to before she married Captain Bainbridge?" The look in her eyes told Scrooge she already knew the answer.

At that moment, an attendant rang a bell by the doorway, calling out, "The time for all visitors to depart is at hand! Please wash your hands in the basins by the ward doors with a clean towel, dropping them in the marked basins as you leave!"

As he stood up, his composure returned. Ebenezer Scrooge took his top hat off his lap and put it atop his head, the cloth mask concealing his uncharacteristic tears in the gathering darkness as daylight slowly faded from the few windows on the walls.

Charlotte, however, was unflinching. "Uncle, were you..." she began saying.

Ebenezer Scrooge turned to look at the frail young wife and mother lying in the bed.

"Yes, child. I was the covetous villain who broke Allyce Simpson's heart and spurned that gentle creature's love. My only consolation is that she has found happiness with her Coldstream Guards officer," Scrooge said, unable to keep a tinge of bitter regret out of his voice.

With those words, Ebenezer Scrooge turned on his heel and strode directly to a bleach-water basin by the door, desperately wanting to spare Charlotte the embarrassing sight of undignified tears his cloth mask would soon no longer hide. A proper Englishman did *not* shed tears, especially in front of a woman. He was so absorbed in wanting to leave the Royal Consumption Infirmary as soon as possible that he didn't hear Charlotte calling his name as he rinsed his hands and hurried out into the hall and down the stairs.

Charlotte picked up her still-hot tea and took a sip. *He doesn't know Allyce is a widow*, she thought. Some thirty minutes later, Allyce approached with a small meal on a tray and a small fresh pot of clove and ginger tea. Charlotte's curiosity got the better of her timidity.

"I take it Mr. Scrooge was the man you referred to who was more interested in gold than matrimony?"

Charlotte was taken aback by the uncharacteristic bitterness in Allyce's voice. "Yes, Charlotte, if your curiosity must be satisfied, although it really is none of your affair, I will tell you," Allyce said in an officious tone of voice very much out of character with the solicitous nurse who had befriended Charlotte. "Ebenezer Scrooge is the man I spoke of. After five and a half years, I called off our engagement when I had the common sense to see he would *never* amass enough money to be content. And that made me realize Ebenezer would never be content with *me* either." Allyce's gentle voice had adopted a singular tone of bitterness Charlotte found unsettling in the nurse she called her friend. As she moved on to the next patient, Allyce made it clear that the topic was no longer open to discussion.

But Charlotte Cratchit's frail physical condition belied her mental determination. She was made of sterner stuff than Allyce Bainbridge realized and was quite unwilling to drop the matter. After a short coughing spell, she called out after Allyce, "So you don't think someone can have a change of heart, Allyce?"

"Not if the 'someone' you're referencing is Ebenezer Scrooge," Allyce replied as she returned to fluff Charlotte's pillows. "Why do you ask?"

"Because I've known him for just over three years now since marrying Peter and have never seen him utter an uncharitable word to man nor beast. I'm just finding it very hard to reconcile Uncle Ebenezer with the wretched man you described in such harsh terms."

Allyce's peremptory tone returned.

"You have been very fortunate, Charlotte. Your own Peter may not have succumbed to the siren's song of riches. But once a man becomes familiar with the things in life that gold and a fat bank account can buy, he wants more of both, and soon they become a singular obsession, to the exclusion of everything and *everyone* else. I hope your Peter fares better than Ebenezer Scrooge did. Have you heard from Peter again?"

Charlotte pulled out a thin parchment letter dated two weeks earlier.

"Yes!" Charlotte exclaimed. "This was delivered three days ago by a messenger from the SS *Caledonia* after it arrived in Portsmouth. Since his last letter, he's been ever so busy working with Mr. Abernathy's agents and solicitors traveling around the eastern United States examining different factories." Charlotte's face momentarily dropped its enthusiasm.

"What is it, Charlotte?" Allyce asked, genuine solicitude returning to her voice now that the topic was no longer Ebenezer Scrooge.

"It's probably nothing, but this note is not half the length of his last two letters. In those, he stated several times he absolutely couldn't wait to come home and that being apart from me was tearing him up inside. Yes, he says he loves me," Charlotte said, waving the parchment, "but it's subdued. I'm probably just being silly. Peter *is* working for one of the richest *and* most demanding men in the United States."

Allyce kept her opinion to herself. *This is how it starts,* she thought, *always the proclamations of "We'll live on love" until the husband or betrothed realizes love doesn't always bring a dowry or pay the bills.* Then, she spoke.

"Well, if the postal marks on the letters are any indication, your husband has already visited Philadelphia, Washington, and Richmond. Did he ever meet President Pierce while he was in Washington?"

Charlotte brightened at the statement.

"Why yes, I almost forgot to tell you. Peter attended a grand dinner at the White House given in Mr. Abernathy's honor. President Franklin Pierce was in attendance, and Peter met him. Can you imagine? Meeting the president of the United States himself! Why, Peter said that President Pierce's wife herself suffers from consumption and she told Peter to say she would keep me in her prayers. Imagine that!"

Allyce's interest perked up.

"That's quite the honor, Charlotte, meeting the president of the United States."

Charlotte smiled. "Peter said in his last letter that it takes quite a sum of money for a man to be elected president in America, and Cyrus Abernathy donated quite a bit of money to Mr. Pierce for just that reason. Peter says President Pierce is in Mr. Abernathy's debt, as Mr. Abernathy told Peter all political campaign money comes with strings attached."

"*Strings attached?* Whatever does that mean?" Allyce asked.

"Peter says because Mr. Abernathy contributed such a great sum to help Mr. Pierce, it entitles Mr. Abernathy to ask certain...*favors* of the president. I would think *strings attached* is an unflattering reference to making someone in your debt dance like a puppet on a string."

Allyce sighed. "Then thank goodness *we* have the monarchy. Her Majesty the Queen isn't perfect, but I'm certain neither she nor Prince Albert can be bribed."

Charlotte nodded thoughtfully. "I suppose that is true, but I confess to not knowing about American politics. Peter did go on and on about how grand the dinner and dance were, though."

"There was to be a ball as well?"

"Yes," Charlotte replied. "It took place right after the dinner, in the White House ballroom. They traveled down to Washington from New York aboard one of Mr. Abernathy's private railway cars on the Pennsylvania Railroad just for the dinner and dancing."

"Oh, I bet the affair was dreadful for Peter," remarked Allyce. "Your poor husband alone at a prestigious social event, and you are stuck here in this awful place. He must have been quite lonely there."

"Well..." began Charlotte.

"What is it?" Allyce asked.

"Peter wasn't *alone*, not precisely. He explained that proper social etiquette in America demands that a man have a social companion for the evening when invited to the American presidential mansion; as you know, they call the place where he lives the 'White House.' I think it is their American version of Buckingham Palace. Anyway, he told me that Mr. Abernathy didn't want Peter to feel out of place, so Cyrus took the liberty of inviting his daughter, Livinia, to come to Washington aboard the railway car with her mother to be Peter's social companion for the event," Charlotte concluded lamely, her eyes downcast.

"Peter didn't object?" Allyce asked in a tone of incredulousness. "He's a *married man*." The note of disapproval in Allyce's voice was plain.

"Well, I don't think he was in a position to object, Allyce. Peter is in America as a guest of Mr. Abernathy, and I should think it very poor manners to decline such an invitation."

Allyce was troubled but said nothing more to Charlotte than, "You must promise to keep me current with Peter's exciting adventures across the pond."

Later that evening, as Chauncey drove Allyce home to her East End apartment, she was deeply troubled by her conversation with Charlotte. The chance encounter with Ebenezer Scrooge had thrown Allyce into mental disarray, but she had quickly regained her emotional footing. As she reflected on the encounter, she thought seeing Ebenezer Scrooge would have been like seeing any other long-forgotten acquaintance on the street to whom you stop and politely speak before moving on. However, this was not the case.

Then, the more immediate concern of the peculiar way Charlotte spoke of Peter's obligations toward Mr. Abernathy troubled her. A married man did *not* entertain the constant social company of a single woman, especially given the things Charlotte had said about the flirtatious aspects of this Livinia Abernathy's character. Her late husband, Tristan, would have found the idea repugnant. But Charlotte had sounded almost apologetic, as if she, Charlotte, had something to be embarrassed about.

After bidding good night to Chauncey's carriage and heading up into her tenement building to her apartment, her last thoughts were *Poor Charlotte. This will have to bear watching. I will not have her husband, Peter, doing to her what that wretched Ebenezer did to me all those years ago. Peter went off to America in search of a way to get Charlotte out of the Royal Consumption Infirmary—but not out of his life.*

Scrooge removed his cloth mask and discarded it upon reaching the street outside the Royal Consumption Infirmary, and his legs still felt unsteady. Lost in thought, he started walking in the general direction of Buckingham Palace, and, after some time had passed, he paused to get his bearings. It was then he realized just how much time had gone by since he had left the Royal Consumption Infirmary. By his watch, he had been walking for the better part of forty minutes and had overshot his Belgravia neighborhood. Scrooge was perplexed at seeing Allyce working in the hospital, but from what he remembered of her nature, the healing arts and being a nurse *were* well within her character. What really jarred him was seeing how Allyce carried herself with a certain agelessness; the passage of time had not dimmed her beauty, either. To be sure, Allyce's hair was highlighted with slight streaks of gray, but there weren't many people upon whom time did not leave its mark in one fashion or another. During their brief encounter, Scrooge saw no wrinkles on her face or the tell-tale mark of the crow's foot in the corners of her eyes. Instead, when she was looking at Charlotte, all Scrooge could see was a spirit borne of concern, love, and giving in Allyce's eyes. She had been just as surprised at seeing him as he was at seeing her. Perhaps if the circumstances had been more…*congenial*, perhaps she wouldn't have reacted so…coldly.

The unexpected encounter awoke in Ebenezer Scrooge a newfound, but unrequited, longing in his heart. Now married to a dashing military officer in one of the most storied units of the British Army, she was hermetically sealed off from Scrooge's affections just as if he had been walled up in a tomb. Any love that seeing Allyce had stirred anew in his heart must remain unrequited; it was forever consigned to the past. Allyce's marriage to her officer had seen to that. Still, just *seeing* Allyce again, although she had been cool to his greeting, stirred the depths of his heart. Scrooge knew he would be returning to visit Charlotte over the time that Bob was mending from his trip to the dentist. Nothing improper, mind you, but perhaps to glimpse a lovely reminder from his past from time to time would do his heart good.

Sunday, August 10, 1856, dawned to a light morning fog that promised to dispel into those rarest of London days, sunny and fair. Ebenezer Scrooge bid his farewell to young Tim Cratchit and Reverend Braithwaite at the door to Saint Hubert's Church and proceeded with renewed determination back to the Royal Consumption Infirmary to visit Charlotte. It wouldn't be his fault if he happened across Allyce Bainbridge again, not that he intended anything untoward with a married woman, but the sight of her had taken his breath away and set his heart aflame—something that hadn't happened in many years. Scrooge crossed the threshold of the Infirmary and once again donned the cloth mask thick with the odor of bleach before spying Charlotte sitting in her bed, lost in thought. Scrooge strode up to her bed, startling her.

"And why aren't we up and walking about this bright morning, Mrs. Cratchit?" he asked with mock severity.

"Oh, Uncle Ebenezer! You startled me!"

Charlotte gave a wan smile. She just didn't have the emotional strength today to put on a show for her father-in-law's boss, so instead, she brandished a sheaf of letters from Peter in far-off America before setting them down on the small table next to her bed with obvious resignation.

Scrooge sensed something was wrong and, even though he was violating ward sanitary rules, took Charlotte's frail hand.

"What is it, Charlotte dear?" he asked gently. "I'll not reveal a confidence. Tell me, what is troubling you?" At those words, Charlotte felt something inside herself break, and losing all control of her emotions, she broke down, her frame racked with heaving sobs.

"It's Peter, Uncle. He's been away in America for almost three months now, and with each letter that arrives, I feel him slipping further and further away from me."

"Well, perhaps his employer has him rather busy. America *is* a rather large place, and Sir Nigel—"

"It's not Sir Nigel, Uncle!" Charlotte spat out in a fit of unladylike anger. "Peter is at the beck and call of a pair of damnable, conniving American monsters I truly detest. Their names are Cyrus Abernathy and his manipulative minx of a daughter, Livinia." The vehemence in her voice and her use of unladylike language told Scrooge the situation was indeed serious. She gestured to the small stack of letters next to her.

"See for yourself."

"Charlotte, if it is a correspondence of a private sort, perhaps it might be inappro—" But Scrooge was again interrupted by a vehement Charlotte.

"Read them, Uncle! My husband is a puppet at the end of the strings held by one of the richest men in America. The richest and the *nastiest.* On top of that, this Cyrus is forever throwing his daughter, this Livinia...*creature*...at Peter." Scrooge picked up the proffered letters and scanned them, noting a distinct diminishing in the ardor of Peter's professions of love for his wife over time while talking more and more about how wealthy Abernathy would make them when a mysterious project for the Royal Navy came to fruition.

Scrooge did his level best to reassure Charlotte, but as he saw the old familiar signs of how riches had once ensnared him, and that it appeared they were doing the same with Peter, his heart sank. Scrooge knew Cyrus Abernathy, but only by reputation. Abernathy was a new breed of businessman, riding the tails of the great revolution that the new steam engines were making in every corner of industry and commerce. Feeling a twinge of guilt for his previous life as a greedy miser himself, he knew a man of unlimited resources would stop at nothing to get what he wanted. Peter was somehow essential to Abernathy's plans, and it was obvious he was willing to drive Charlotte to an early grave if that's what it took to see them to fruition.

Why the devil does Peter continue speaking of this Livinia girl in his letters? Surely, he must realize all that is going to do is upset his wife, Scrooge wondered. He knew Peter, although brilliant with his numbers and memory, could be a bit naive in the social graces (not to mention common sense) and therefore was unaware of how his infelicitous tales of enjoying lush banquets and glamorous dinners in America with Livinia Abernathy at his side were affecting his wife. Scrooge knew Peter well enough to know he would never betray Charlotte. He also noted some of the titles Peter mentioned in the letters he was reading.

What in the world is Peter doing reading Machiavelli's The Prince? *That is* not *proper reading for a Christian gentleman,* Scrooge thought. He frowned as he saw some of the other questionable titles thrust upon Peter for his "betterment" as a businessman.

Scrooge patted Charlotte's hand.

"Charlotte, I cannot say what has affected this apparent change in Peter, but I promise I'll do my best to assist you," Scrooge said. "Remember, child: I am not without my own resources," he added, even though he realized with an ocean between him and young Peter, there might not *be* anything he could do.

Anxious to turn the subject away from upsetting Charlotte, Scrooge craned his neck, scanning the ward.

Drying her tears, Charlotte noticed Scrooge looking around and said, "She's not here on Sundays, Uncle."

Scrooge feigned ignorance.

"Who do you mean, child?"

Charlotte wasn't fooled.

"You're looking for the widow Bainbridge, Uncle. Today is Sunday and her only day off, so I'll wager she'll be back tomorrow morning as usual."

Scrooge was taken aback.

"*Widow* Bainbridge?"

"Yes, Uncle. Allyce's husband, Captain Tristan Bainbridge, was killed in Crimea. She has been a widow for almost two years."

Scrooge fought to keep his emotions under control. On one hand was his rage that the Russians had robbed the only woman he had ever truly loved of real happiness by killing Captain Bainbridge. But on the other hand, Scrooge felt the tiniest flame of hope flare up and kindle in his heart the idea that perhaps he just might redeem himself in Allyce's eyes.

"I don't suppose..." he began.

"No, Uncle. Allyce has thrown herself into her work and is trying to provide for her children—twins, I believe. After you chanced upon her here, when she brought my dinner by after you had left, she was rather harsh in her comments about your common past," Charlotte said. "I can understand how she might feel, Uncle. One of the other nurses told me that Allyce lives in one of those dreadful tenements over near Whitechapel. If events, people, and fate had been kinder to Allyce, perhaps she would not have to worry about her children being infected by a rat bite while they sleep."

Scrooge paled at her words but remained silent as Charlotte continued. "So, you can see how I fear, after her husband died in Crimea, she has locked her heart away forever."

This time it was Charlotte's turn to be surprised. Ebenezer Scrooge's face betrayed a heartbreaking pain that Charlotte thought no one else in the world was capable of feeling at that moment but herself. There was a sadness in his eyes at once haunting and ineffable. The truth hit Charlotte like a thunderbolt.

Uncle Ebenezer is still in love with Allyce! she realized before the next logical thought arrived. *Of course! He had no way of knowing her husband died in Crimea, so believing Allyce to be married and Uncle being a highly honorable man himself, whatever feelings he carried in his heart he thought would remain locked away, forever unrequited.*

At that moment, Charlotte felt a tremendous surge of pity for her Uncle Ebenezer. Allyce Bainbridge was, by nature, a gentle and generous creature, but when a subject violated her sensibilities—such as injustice toward the gravely ill—she was prone to fast assuming tremendous and stubborn strength. It was obvious that seeing Scrooge had awakened whatever injury of the heart he had committed against her many years before, and it was just this sort of "wound of love" that would only harden Allyce's heart further.

She spoke up, breaking Scrooge's reverie.

"You still love her, don't you, Uncle?"

"Yes," came the husky reply. There was a long pause.

"Charlotte, I had no idea Allyce would be here. Otherwise, I should have waited until this day to visit you and have been none the wiser. But now that I know she is working here, *and a widow with children at that*, my heart compels me to act. I've seen those Whitechapel tenements and the dreadful conditions there. Allyce was always very forthright that she came from a humble background when we were courting, but Whitechapel is an execrable place to live, much less raise children. I must do something about her situation!" he declared.

Unable to control his emotions once again, Scrooge excused himself at the ringing of the visitors' departure bell, but not before telling Charlotte, "Your father-in-law, Bob, will return tomorrow. The atmosphere in this place is unhealthier for a man like me than I realized."

Although Charlotte still felt her own pain, her heart went out to her uncle. *He and Allyce would be wonderful together!* she thought—if only Allyce could trust that Scrooge had changed for the better.

9 ⅔

PAST SINS AND
FUTURE TORMENTS

Leaving the Infirmary, Scrooge began walking back to his Belgravia home, thinking that a good pipe and the playful antics of the ever-enthusiastic Julius and Caesar would do him good. And the doting Mrs. Dilber would be only too happy to prepare something tasty. Almost home, on a whim, Scrooge stopped back at Saint Hubert's Church to sit and ponder the day's events surrounding Charlotte, Allyce, and the revelations about Peter Cratchit during his ongoing trip to America. Oddly enough, Peter's trip and how it affected Charlotte bothered Scrooge the most. Still, seeing Allyce at the hospital left him deeply shaken, and hearing Charlotte Cratchit's tearful suspicions about her husband's fidelity only compounded his own emotional turmoil.

Scrooge had changed for the better since the Christmas Eve night the three spirits visited him, but there were still situations that he found great difficulty coping with. Foremost among these was how to comfort a woman in emotional pain. The singular human skill of consoling a woman seemed to escape him for all his business expertise—not that the occasion arose all that often.

He stared up at the large stained-glass window of Saint Hubert in the apse of the great church behind the main altar. The ancient patron saint of hunters was depicted in the window with a falcon on his arm, a hunting dog, and a great stag with a vision of the crucified

Savior over the stag's head. Scrooge's mind began wandering, but it kept being drawn back to Allyce. He was sure that it was due to her innate goodness of heart that Allyce looked as though time had passed with barely a trace, maturing from the girl he had known into a lady of grace and refinement, *despite* her heartbreak and tragedies endured. During the years Scrooge knew her to be married to Captain Bainbridge, he easily maintained a distance of the heart. Given his moral code, any romantic feelings for Allyce were off-limits and locked away in the recesses of his heart. But now, with the discovery that his beloved Allyce was a Crimean War widow, Scrooge experienced a dagger of heartache he had never known: pining for Allyce, his one true love.

Given her cold, perfunctory reaction at the Royal Consumption Infirmary, Scrooge was sad and depressed about how his miserable former incarnation so destroyed any semblance of any charitable feelings Allyce once had for him. The instantaneous cold that flashed in her eyes that bordered on malice on recognizing him was proof enough. He ardently wished spirits like those who visited him on Christmas Eve years ago would visit Allyce to convince her that he was indeed a changed man…a *good* man, and worthy of such a woman's love and trust. It made Scrooge heartsick to think all Allyce could afford to live in was a Whitechapel tenement apartment. Scrooge was preoccupied with the thought that he would do anything to help her and her young children, without precondition. He looked up at the stained-glass window of Saint Hubert as if imploring the ancient saint for consolation or guidance.

Lost in his sad reverie, Scrooge was startled by a rustling in the pew next to him—and was shocked to see the apparition of his late business partner, Jacob Marley, sitting and quietly staring at him. Marley was tranquil; he no longer dragged moneyboxes connected by ethereal chains. His countenance no longer carried the dark pallor of the grave, but instead radiated an ineffable peace.

"Jacob? *Is it really you, Jacob?*" Scrooge asked, quite stunned. To say Scrooge was taken aback would be an understatement of gross proportion. "When I last saw you, I believe your words were, 'Look to see me no more.'"

"Yes, Ebenezer Scrooge, it is I, the man who was known in your mortal world as your business partner, Jacob Marley."

"Jacob, I almost didn't recognize you. When last I saw you those years ago on Christmas Eve, your countenance bore all the horrid marks of the grave's corruption. Now you radiate light and peace, not torment."

"Ebenezer," Marley said, "I told you, 'It is required of every man that the soul within him should walk abroad among his fellow men, traveling far and wide; and if that soul goes not forth in life, it is condemned to do so after death, doomed to wander through the world witnessing what it cannot share, but might have shared on earth, and turned to happiness.'"

"Jacob," Scrooge made so bold as to reply to the ghost, "I have done my best to keep the spirit and meaning of the message borne by the Holy Child of Christmas every day for years now. Is there more I must accomplish?"

"Ebenezer, it was no certain thing that you would have changed your heart, even with the ghosts who visited you that night. But change you did, and in the realms of the blessed, the good done by a man on earth rebounds to the benefit of the soul who inspired his repentance. Your sincere change of heart brought the great warrior archangel, Michael, to my abode of torment and escorted me to the kingdom of Divine Providence," Marley's spirit said.

"But Jacob," Scrooge said, "what brings you to me this Lord's Day?"

"Your prayers were borne on the wings of sincerity to the realms of the blessed."

Scrooge looked confused. "What are you talking about, Jacob?"

"You visited the Royal Consumption Infirmary today, but the experience left you shaken, did it not?"

"I saw Allyce, Jacob," Scrooge said, nodding.

"I know, Ebenezer, and great turmoil has awakened in your heart at seeing the widow Bainbridge."

"Jacob," Scrooge said to the shining vision next to him, "I had all but forgotten Allyce until seeing her today. I thought she was still married to a Coldstream Guards captain. Thinking of her as happily married made it rather easy to consign my unhappy memories of her and the man I used to be to the past."

Marley spoke.

"Ebenezer, the passage of time allowed you to dim the memories of both the love you once bore and the great pain you inflicted on that gentle creature's heart. But beneath your greed and wickedness, your heart still bore a deep passion for Allyce, and that love was reawakened upon hearing of her husband's death."

"Then surely you also know Allyce holds me in great contempt," Scrooge said. "I have pondered the matter until my head aches with the loneliness, but I cannot think of a way to show Allyce I have returned to being the man she once loved, if not in appearance, then in character. I even thought that if only the spirits that had shown me the error of my ways could visit Allyce, then perhaps…"

"No, Ebenezer," Marley said. "I procured the Ghosts of Christmas Past, Present, and Christmas Yet to Come you encountered that Christmas Eve night because I, myself, was a suffering soul who knew the blackness of your heart best. Divine Providence permitted those spirits to be summoned for *you, and only you*, Ebenezer. They cannot change Allyce's heart or her ill feelings toward you, for they would not have her life's memories to draw upon. Allyce's life has always been lived in Christian charity and love, always seeking to obey the Master's Golden Rule. Even if such spirits would visit her, her life and deeds in your mortal time have been beyond reproach."

Hanging his head, Scrooge quietly said, "So there is no hope? Speak plain words, Jacob. My heart is too heavy this day for riddles."

A slight, mischievous smile played about Marley's face, and he said, "Ebenezer, in the mansions of glory where I now dwell, there are many spirits, and the greatest is the Ghost of Christmas Love. It will take extraordinary sacrifice on your part for that spirit to venture forth to break the chains of pain and bitterness binding Allyce Bainbridge's twice-broken heart. Even though Allyce is an impoverished widow, trusting you again may be nigh impossible. Her heart was broken twice: first, when she returned your betrothal ring, poisoned by your lust for gold—so opening your purse will not avail you. Then, her capacity to love was sundered anew when her husband, Tristan, died without succor in a far-off war. Captain Bainbridge died a heroic death, preventing the Russians from overrunning British and French soldiers near Sevastopol. But despite his heroism, Tristan died without consolation or fellowship on the battlefield. Not even his widow is aware of his valor.

"I am permitted this day to reveal two things, Ebenezer. Consider them to be a boon for assisting me in leaving behind the chains that held me down those many years. If the love you profess to bear in your heart for Allyce is true, you must be prepared to sacrifice greatly. I speak not of gold, but to obtain what your wealth cannot buy, as only love borne of self-sacrifice and without condition is 'true love.' Ebenezer, you have indeed been generous with your riches, but they have been given from your surplus. How far are you willing to go in sacrificing *yourself*, Ebenezer Scrooge?"

Scrooge's reawakened love for Allyce burned like a torch through his torpor at beholding the spirit of his former business partner.

"Jacob," he said resolutely, "I am prepared to do whatever is necessary to obtain a chance for Allyce to know the man I have become since we parted. I know opening her heart to love cannot be compelled, but perchance her heart can be opened enough to listen and see, so that love can be given its moment. And that is all I am looking for: a *chance*."

Marley continued, "You speak with wisdom, Ebenezer. In evoking the Ghost of Christmas Love to Allyce, know this: fate has decreed it is also bound up in the destiny of Peter Cratchit and his wife, Charlotte. Even now, the Reaper beckons to Charlotte from both consumption and a mortal danger arising from her husband's newfound lust for riches that once held your own spirit in thrall. You have read Peter's letters to Charlotte, and his expressions of love grow ever colder as the lure of great wealth beckons, cooling the ardor of his love. Young Peter Cratchit hurtles ignorantly along the same road to perdition you once trod; therefore, you must do for him as I once brought about for you."

Marley's spirit began to shimmer and lose its human shape. He spoke again, "Alas, Ebenezer, my time among the world of mortals again draws to an end. Providence decrees I speak no further. I bid thee hail and good fortune, Ebenezer Scrooge. You shall see me no more."

Scrooge cried out in frustration, "Tarry but a moment, I pray thee, Jacob! You say I must do for Peter what you did for me, yet I am but a mortal man, not a spectral vision from beyond the grave. I possess not the powers to summon spirits from beyond to admonish and teach. Tell me what sacrifice is given and not bought! Do not depart and leave me with a phantasm's riddles!" But Marley's countenance grew dimmer in the church's light. Reflecting upon the remarkable encounter with the shade of his late business partner and, despite receiving no more counsel from Marley's fading apparition, Scrooge resolved to do whatever he must for the chance to win Allyce's love anew.

10

RESOLUTIONS AND PLANS

The following Sunday, Ebenezer Scrooge once again arrived at the Royal Consumption Infirmary with a robust resolution in his heart to win Allyce's forgiveness and trust. Somewhere in the recesses of his heart the words "and her love" echoed as well. It was not impulsive. As the days became weeks, it became Scrooge's passion and *raison d'être*. On the days when Allyce was present, he was careful to be friendly to her and the consummate gentleman as well, without obsequy or overt deference. He had resolved, to start, just to be a Christian gentleman. This specific Sunday, he decided, as Marley's spirit had told him Peter and Charlotte's fate was bound up in his quest to win Allyce's love again, he had to trust Charlotte Cratchit. This meant confiding to her everything that had happened to him, starting with the "Night of the Ghosts" up to the recent apparition of Jacob Marley in Saint Hubert's Church.

After replacing the wilted flowers at Charlotte's bedside with fresh daisies purchased from a street vendor, knowing he had little time due to the Royal Consumption Infirmary's visiting rules, Scrooge decided to get right to the point.

"Charlotte, my child, may I take you into my confidence?" Scrooge asked. "I should be mortified if any of what I'm going to tell you should become common knowledge. They would pack me off straight away to Bedlam if that were to happen," he said.

"Of course, Uncle. You may trust that words between us shall remain ever so," Charlotte replied, her curiosity piqued.

"Well, I'm sure Peter, and if not Peter, then his father, Bob, had told you that there was a time well before you knew me when the name *Ebenezer Scrooge* was a common byword in London Town for a person of a mean, greedy, and altogether uncharitable disposition," Scrooge said. "All that changed about eight years ago one cold Christmas Eve night."

Plunging directly into the topic, Scrooge began to regale Charlotte with the story of what he described as the "Night of the Ghosts." He told an enraptured Charlotte how first the ghost of his late business partner Jacob Marley had appeared to him late one Christmas Eve, followed by three other spirits, the Ghosts of Christmas Past, Present, and Christmas Yet to Come. Each shade had taken him on a journey through his life by turn wistful, melancholy, and finally, terrifying. Scrooge said how, despite his initial disbelief, it was soon made clear that not only was the experience real, but if he *didn't* cooperate with what the spirits warned him of, he would suffer for his negligence, greed, and cruelty for all eternity.

"Now, mind you, Charlotte, when I first beheld the specter of my late business partner, I had the audacity to tell him I thought the vision of him was brought on by a dinner meal that disagreed with my stomach. The memory of the howl Jacob's ghost gave at that intemperate statement still gives me a shiver. But you are free to ask your father-in-law, Bob, the details of the change in my temperament after that Christmas Eve night should you doubt what I'm telling you."

Still entranced at the story, Charlotte nodded for him to continue.

"Well, last Sunday, after leaving here with a heavy heart, I must admit I felt quite sad. I stopped by Saint Hubert's Church to perhaps pray and hope the quiet of the church would give me some clarity of thought. While I was sitting there, I received quite a shock. I had thought I'd heard a noise, and when I turned to look, there was the ghost of Jacob Marley looking quite contented and happy," Scrooge said.

"That must have given you quite the start, Uncle," Charlotte said with wide eyes.

"Oh, indeed it did, and you can imagine my surprise when he told me he knew of my heartache over Allyce. Jacob said, to the best of my recollection, "Ebenezer, there are many spirits in the mansions where I now happily dwell, and among the greatest is the Ghost of Christmas Love. It will take an extraordinary sacrifice on your part for that spirit to venture forth to unlock the chains of despair and bitterness binding Allyce Bainbridge's twice-broken heart. Even though Allyce is an impoverished widow caring for her little family, trusting you again may be nigh impossible. Her heart was broken twice: first, when she returned your betrothal ring, poisoned by your lust for gold—so opening your purse will not avail you—"

Charlotte interrupted him.

"Uncle Ebenezer, it is no less difficult for me to believe a spirit from beyond visited you than to see the ever-so-wonderful changes in you these past few years, if Peter is to be believed. He was rather more descriptive of your former self than you have been, if you'll pardon my boldness. I know Allyce well, and she still has a tight hold over the reins of her dignity. If your former lust for money is what drove Allyce away, then presenting her with a purse full of gold sovereigns would only insult her and drive her further away."

As they pondered what Scrooge might do, the Sunday attendant rang the bell for all visitors to depart. An old man suffering from pneumonia tried sitting up in his bed across the Infirmary ward and screamed in pain as the decrepit, rusting bed frame collapsed under him. Without thinking, Scrooge leaped to help him. The elderly man screamed again as Scrooge bent over without regard for his own health, allowing the patient to grasp him around the neck for support until the orderlies rushing down the ward could help. Charlotte looked on in shock as even the orderlies hesitated to touch some of the sicker consumption patients, yet here in front of her, was the man formerly known as the most grasping personification of greed in the realm letting a grievously sick man cling to him without regard for his own health.

An unbidden thought came into Charlotte's mind from the Sunday scriptures: "Lord, when did we see thee sick...and came to aid thee? And the king answering shall say to them: Amen I say to you, as long as you did it to one of the least of my brethren, you did it to me." From that moment on, Charlotte knew Allyce could have no finer man in her life than her uncle and resolved to help him in any way possible.

"That was quite the brave thing to do, Uncle," Charlotte said as Scrooge came walking back over to gather his coat and hat before leaving. "You've no doubt noticed there aren't that many visitors here. People seem to think consumption is as bad as leprosy, and they treat us accordingly."

"I didn't think about it, my dear. I heard that poor fellow scream and had to do, well...*something*." Before departing, he looked around and asked Charlotte, "Is the rest of the Infirmary in the same state of disrepair?"

Charlotte pointed at the rusting appliances, beds, and peeling wall paint, in addition to wrinkling her nose at the overwhelming stench of urine, and asked Scrooge, "What do you think, Uncle? 'Tis the same on every floor."

Scrooge gave her a perplexed look and asked, "Then why are you here, child? Peter earns a more than decent wage; I *know* he can afford better."

Charlotte turned her face away and wouldn't answer, given the presence of several nearby orderlies who had heard snatches of Scrooge's comments. He persisted, "Charlotte, my dear, this is a *royal* medical establishment under the patronage of Her Majesty; it receives prodigious sums of money from the Crown. Where does all the money go?"

Charlotte relented, turning to her adoptive uncle, and bitterly whispered, "Try looking in Ainsley Northrup's purse, Uncle Ebenezer. He's 'master and commander' of this place."

11 ఎ✦

A NIGHTINGALE SANG
IN BELGRAVE SQUARE

Hailing a cab home, Scrooge pondered the revelation he had just had at the abuse of Her Majesty's good name and reputation by Ainsley Northrup, the Royal Consumption Infirmary's administrator. On a sudden hunch, he told the cab driver, "My good man, take me to the Royal Home of Convalescent Medicine for Her Majesty's Soldiers and Sailors near Bletchley Common." Ten minutes later, the cab pulled up in front of an imposing structure where a sign in slightly better condition than the Royal Consumption Infirmary proclaimed the building to be Scrooge's destination. There were a number of injured soldiers and sailors pushed about the parklike setting in wheelchairs by orderlies in military-style uniforms.

Scrooge, feeling a twinge of guilt at using the late Tristan Bainbridge's name as a pretext, walked into the lobby and up to the attendant at the desk.

"Hello, my good man. I'm here to visit an acquaintance wounded in Crimea; his name is Captain Bainbridge."

Seeing the understated elegance of Scrooge's attire, the attendant asked, "Very well, sir, but was he in the Army or the Royal Navy? They're on different floors and then in different wards on each floor seeing as how they were wounded."

Thinking quickly, Scrooge knew he had to get as thorough a feel for the overall condition of the hospital as fast as possible.

"I don't rightly know. I think he may have been with Her Majesty's Coldstream Guards."

The attendant paused thoughtfully and said, "Well, sir, you'd best start on the second floor and work your way up to the fifth floor on top. If he's here, you're bound to find him."

Scrooge withdrew a shilling and placed it in front of the surprised attendant.

"Thank you, my good man. You've been more helpful than you know."

Scrooge walked up the main staircase and began a cursory inspection of each ward he came across. Although appalled, he was not surprised to find the hospital just as neglected as the Royal Consumption Infirmary, where poor Charlotte was a patient. In addition to the rusting beds, soiled bedding and towels, and scuttling vermin, Scrooge observed there were no bleach-water basins for staff or visitors to wash their hands upon either entering or leaving. There were obviously no sanitary measures in place like those at the Royal Consumption Infirmary.

No one glanced at Scrooge as he passed through the hospital like a phantom, observing all and saying nothing. His anger grew with each indignity of filth and disrepair he saw Her Majesty's wounded fighting men and sailors enduring. By the time he reached the end of the third floor, he had had enough, his temperament morphing from anger to cold fury. The thought that this excuse for a hospital was where Allyce's late husband, Tristan, would have ended up had he survived his wounds only hardened his resolve. His righteous indignation aroused, Allyce notwithstanding, Scrooge resolved to help the voiceless souls languishing in hospitals and asylums across London Town, who had no advocate to speak on their behalf.

Scrooge reflected that he was a very wealthy man and had already donated a large portion of his riches to charitable causes, but now decided to make inquiries for two very specific institutions. First was the rehabilitation of the Royal Consumption Infirmary, where Charlotte Cratchit was confined. The title "royal" notwithstanding, the decrepit conditions and her hint of corruption by the administrator, Ainsley Northrup, were a blight on the good name of Queen Victoria. Second, he resolved to inquire into the rehabilitation of the Royal Home of Convalescent Medicine for Her Majesty's Soldiers and Sailors he had just departed. Scrooge had the presence of mind to know, despite his own fortune, he couldn't accomplish the repairs these hospitals needed solely on his own.

Several nights later, he invited a small group of civic-minded wealthy businessmen to dinner at his Belgravia home for "sensitive discussions of a most urgent nature." He gave Mrs. Dilber a sovereign for the foodstuffs and wines to be served and told her to keep whatever was left over.

That Tuesday night, his eight guests arrived promptly at 7:30. One of them, John Delane, editor in chief of the reigning British newspaper of record, the *Times of London*, was accompanied by a tall, rugged-looking gentleman with long mutton chop sideburns.

"Ebenezer," Delane said, "let me introduce Sir Richard Mayne. He is the head of the London Metropolitan Police at Scotland Yard, and I suspect, based upon our pr.evious conversation, his presence tonight might be most welcome."

Scrooge shook his proffered hand and said, "Welcome, Sir Richard. You honor me by coming to my humble home. Thank you for consenting to join our little group this night."

"It is my pleasure and honor, Mr. Scrooge. I must admit that my curiosity was piqued when John here said part of the evening's discussions would involve Ainsley Northrup." Sir Richard smiled enigmatically.

Scrooge bade all the guests into his dining room, and after a meal of roast goose and mince pudding, followed by Mrs. Dilber's signature apple cake, the small party retired to Scrooge's spacious smoking den. The air would normally swirl with aromatic pipe smoke of every description, except for a special request by one of the evening's guests, Reverend Neville Braithwaite, vicar of Saint Hubert's Church, that the guests refrain from smoking.

"Gentlemen, most of us have known each other for a good many years now," Scrooge said as he stood to speak. "I have been made aware of certain situations that will sooner or later cast a pall of embarrassment over the Crown, and I am convinced that only a like-minded group of businessmen such as us have the resources to spare Her Majesty Queen Victoria humiliation."

John Delane of the *Times* spoke up.

"What could disgrace Her Majesty here, Ebenezer? It *is* Northrup, isn't it? If so, then I shall publish it on the front page of my newspaper and bring the scoundrel to justice!" he thundered.

His statement was followed by the other businessmen joining in a chorus for action if there was a threat to the reputation of the Crown.

Scrooge said, "Gentlemen, would that these matters could be so easily settled as publishing an article in John's *Times*. However, the matter requires a great degree of finesse and delicate handling. I do not doubt that a front-page article in the *Times* may serve a most critical purpose when the time is proper. As some of you know, my clerk Bob's daughter-in-law is confined with consumption to the Royal—"

He was interrupted by Reverend Braithwaite.

"On my word, Ebenezer, Charlotte is confined to *that* rat-ridden pestilence hole? I'd rather spend a week in the hold of a prison barge than be taken sick to *that* place!"

Scrooge was gratified to know that some of the assembled men knew of the execrable conditions at the Royal Consumption Infirmary.

He continued: "But it is not only *there*, gentlemen. I also visited the Royal Home of Convalescent Medicine for Her Majesty's Soldiers and Sailors, where our brave men wounded fighting in Crimea are hospitalized. The conditions at the military hospital are even worse, if you can believe it. I witnessed it with my own eyes and had to leave after only a good thirty minutes, lest I lose my supper."

At that moment, Mrs. Dilber gently knocked at the door and poked her head inside, her excited eyes as wide as the teacup saucers she held in her hands.

"Mr. Scrooge, your 'special guest' has arrived, and she's waiting in the parlor!" she squeaked in a loud stage whisper.

Scrooge turned to Mrs. Dilber with an excited glance. "Please do bring her in, Mrs. Dilber!"

"Who is this surprise that's being sprung upon us, Ebenezer?" asked John Delane.

At that moment, there was a gentle rap at the library door, and Mrs. Dilber entered, accompanied by an attractive and well-dressed lady who nevertheless appeared to be in somewhat ill health, moving rather slowly.

Scrooge leaped to his feet and exclaimed, "Miss Nightingale, how good of you to honor us with your presence!"

Every man in the room was soon on his feet in the presence of England's famed "Angel of the Crimea," astonished at Scrooge's deft move. He guided her to a comfortable chair and told the assembled businessmen, "Miss Nightingale has recently returned from that dreadful war zone where our soldiers called her the 'Lady with the Lamp.'"

Scrooge turned to the famous nurse.

"I was telling my business associates something of the abhorrent conditions at both the Royal Consumption Infirmary and the Royal Home of Convalescent Medicine for Her Majesty's Soldiers and Sailors. I think you would agree with us that in addition to the care of England's brave sons, it is also important that we permit nothing to besmirch Her Majesty Queen Victoria's reputation. This night, I am going to propose that we here and now establish a very discreet group of London businessmen of independent financial means to be known as the 'Honorable Society of Royal Medical Benefactors.' Our only real need for recourse to Her Majesty's Government would be for work permits, building access, working around bureaucratic delays—that sort of thing. Think of it as a charitable endowment of sorts."

"That would be a most satisfactory beginning, Mr. Scrooge. There is much to be changed in the care of our nation's sick and infirm," Florence said.

"Miss Nightingale, would you do us the honor of recounting for us what you discovered upon arriving at Scutari Hospital and the reforms you instituted?" Scrooge asked. "I know your time with us tonight is constrained and I think our group here, in consideration of your recommendations, may be able to have an impact far beyond our modest number."

With an audience thrilled to be in the presence of the famous "Lady with the Lamp," Florence Nightingale proceeded to tell the assembled group of rapt businessmen about her arrival opposite the great city of Constantinople and what she found there.

"First of all, the British Army hospital at Scutari is built on the site of an old Turkish Army barracks and on top of an enormous sewage cesspool," she began. "Wounded and sick patients were compelled to lie in their own excrement on filthy, blood-stained stretchers or scattered about on floors throughout the hallways due to a lack of sufficient beds. Rats, mice, and every manner of vermin scurried over them. As time went on, the basic medical supplies we take for granted here at home—such as clean clothing, bed linens, bandages, and soap—became scarce as the number of ill and wounded grew ever larger. Even *clean water* needed to be rationed. More British and

French soldiers died from dysentery, typhoid, and cholera than injuries received in battle against the Russians. There is a good reason, gentlemen, I called Scutari Hospital the 'Kingdom of Hell.' Some of the good Cardinal Manning's nuns accompanied me, and they did not hesitate to embrace that very description of Scutari in their letters back to His Eminence."

There was not a sound to be heard in Ebenezer Scrooge's study except for his cats, Julius and Caesar, who had taken to Florence's presence right away, sensing her gentle spirit, and Scrooge could not begrudge them. The bold Caesar leaped onto Florence's lap and immediately curled up, purring in contentment. Julius did the same, except curling up around her feet. She smiled, one hand stroking Caesar's gray nose as the cat fell fast asleep.

Reverend Braithwaite spoke up. "Miss Nightingale, first let me say that you do us a great honor consenting to speak with us here on your way home. Aside from physical repairs, what practices would you have us use our modest influence to have implemented in our medical institutions?"

As Florence gazed around the room at the assembled London businessmen, she saw a look of sincere concern on each of their faces. *There's no haughtiness or skepticism here*, she thought. *These men are willing to open their purses to improve the lot of those people in the hospitals, not like that pompous ass, Sir John Hall, senior British Army medical officer for the Crimea back at Scutari.*

"Thank you for inviting me here tonight, gentlemen of the Royal London Exchange. I am in your debt, as there are a great many men in the British medical field, well-intentioned doctors, who think of my practices as medical foolishness, or worse yet, 'silly female quackery,' as some of the doctors at Scutari put it. When we first arrived there, the British Army doctors held the strong opinion that a nurse was the equivalent of a prostitute." The assembled men thereby got a firsthand taste of Florence Nightingale's reputation for direct speech, even if her words might offend more delicate ears.

"These are simple measures to implement, but I am convinced, based on my direct observations, they will save many lives. I will keep my comments short, for you may know I contracted Crimea fever near Sevastopol while there last summer and spent the better part of several weeks in the hospital myself. Some effects of the malady continue their unwanted visitations from time to time, and I still get quite winded if I attempt to speak too much.

"When I saw the atrocious conditions at Scutari, one of the first things I insisted on was a strict policy of hand washing in either soap or water with a mild chlorine bleach solution added to it. The next measure we undertook after scrubbing the entire building from top to bottom was establishing proper ventilation of the hospital wards and setting up a large hospital laundry. Although it angered the doctors, there were times I was compelled to have a group of Cardinal Manning's nuns block a doctor who refused to wash his hands after amputating a limb from moving on to his next patient. Dirty linens, clothing, and robes were constantly collected in tin tubs and washed in vats of boiling water with small amounts of bleach. After several weeks, along with the heroic efforts of Her Majesty's Sanitary Commission to clean out the sewers under the hospital to allow proper drainage and improve overall ventilation, we started to see drastic reductions in mortality among our soldiers."

"Miss Nightingale, is it true that when you arrived at Scutari, a dead horse was floating in the drinking water pond?" Reverend Braithwaite asked.

"Yes, it was decomposing in the drinking pond, and when I asked for it to be removed, as its pestilential effect was polluting the drinking water for the wounded and sick, Sir Dr. Hall at first refused my request. When I told him these diseases were killing our soldiers in the hospital, he rebuffed me to my face and said, 'The poor beast that drowned in the drinking pond has nothing to do with the health of our soldiers. *British soldiers are made of stern stuff!*"

Florence looked around the room at the small gathering. "Would any of you drink from a water basin with a bloated rat carcass floating in it?" she asked. "I thought not," she said acidly after a moment's silence. "It may seem a strange principle to enunciate as the very first requirement in a Hospital that it should do the sick no harm."

Glancing at the clock above Scrooge's mantel, she said, "Gentlemen, my time grows short, and I must take my leave of you directly, but I thank you for indulging me and listening to my advice. For England and humanity's sake, I hope you heed it. I will leave you with these words about the abysmal state of the British medical establishment: "Were there none who were discontented with what they have, the world would never reach anything better."

There was a minor commotion as each member of the assembled group of businessmen rose to express his gratitude for her work among the wounded and sick in Crimea.

As Florence was led through Scrooge's parlor to her waiting carriage, she paused and turned to Scrooge.

"Reverend Braithwaite tells me this *sub rosa* gathering of businessmen to effect change in our medical establishments is your doing, Mr. Scrooge."

Scrooge flushed as his face reddened from embarrassment.

"Yes, Miss Nightingale. It is an endeavor I have an abiding personal interest in." He nodded. "Along with my associates, we have raised the sum of £120,000 for our initial efforts."

Florence's next question rocked him.

"Are you the same Ebenezer Scrooge who broke Allyce Bainbridge's heart all those years ago?" she asked, her piercing gaze making Scrooge feel most uncomfortable. "Allyce and I are quite close friends, and I must tell you, Mr. Scrooge, I do *not* hold a favorable opinion of you, not at all. Quite the contrary. If I were to go by my conversations with Allyce, you would rank among the lowest, most vile of the doctors I had to fight with each day at Scutari just to save a patient from pestilence."

"Yes," Scrooge said. "In my younger days, I was a shallow, craven, and petty tyrant with the hubris to think I knew everything in the world. To my eternal sorrow, I broke Allyce's heart, and it is a shameful pain I shall carry for the rest of my life."

Florence was momentarily taken aback by Scrooge's forthright, abject admission.

"I beg of you, Miss Nightingale, if and when you see Allyce, I pray you do not tell her of my efforts or what transpired here this night."

"Then why are you doing this if not to make a favorable impression on her?" Florence asked. "It has been my experience that a man with the reputation of being a beast and a scoundrel will always have an ulterior motive rebounding to his personal gain."

Scrooge felt the sting in her words but did not refute them.

Paraphrasing what Marley's ghost had told him on that long-ago Christmas Eve, Scrooge said, "Because some years ago, after Allyce and I had our most unhappy parting, it was made known to me in a manner I care not to discuss that "it is required of every man that the soul within him should walk abroad among his fellow men, traveling far and wide to spread Christian charity and comfort; and if that soul goes not forth in life, it is condemned to do so after death, doomed to wander through the world witnessing what it cannot share, but might have shared on earth, and turned to happiness."

Scrooge continued: "Those words were directed at *me*, Miss Nightingale. After that rather harrowing experience, which must remain private, I have always striven to live by those words. I do not seek to convince you of my sincerity in these endeavors; that is not why I asked for you to grace us with your presence here this night. My goal tonight was to have you convince those men in my library of what must be done to assist the souls here in England suffering from the same sort of medical neglect, and you have succeeded beyond my paltry expectations. I just ask that you do not tell Allyce of our encounter; may I ask that of you? I would consider it a great personal favor."

Florence Nightingale searched Scrooge's face for a long minute. After some moments, she spoke.

"Very well, Mr. Scrooge. I will not say anything of this to Allyce, nor that I am even acquainted with your name, on the condition that you give me your word of honor that nothing in your motives involves toying with Allyce Bainbridge's affection or emotions. She is a *sister* to me. Since the death of her husband, Tristan, her life has become difficult enough and is rendered even more so because she is very strong and will not accept assistance from any quarter, not even me. Allyce is a proud woman, and I should gladly give her a house in the country with servants at her beck and call, but she would never accept charity. Should I hear from Allyce that you have further injured her in any manner, I promise you, the consequences to yourself will be most unpleasant."

"Miss Nightingale, you have my solemn word of honor as a gentleman. I...I will not do anything to cause harm or dishonor to Allyce in any way whatsoever." Scrooge faltered. His countenance grew pallid as his mind's eye flew back to that night when he was shown by the Ghost of Christmas Past Allyce sobbing as she returned his engagement ring.

Something about the distant, troubled look in Ebenezer Scrooge's suddenly misting eyes told Florence that she had unexpectedly touched a raw nerve. She had seen that dazed look on the faces of too many of Her Majesty's soldiers in Crimea for her to mistake it for anything else. They were the lucky—or perhaps, unlucky—ones who saw the other side of the Great Beyond and lived to tell of it. Florence instinctively knew the man here in front of her was one such man, and because of it, he was in great spiritual pain. Whatever scoundrel he had been, something had wounded this man's soul. Florence's innate compassion for the wounded and ill pushed aside her initial suspicion about Scrooge's motives and took control of her demeanor as her tone softened into a gentle, probing question. Taking a chance, she asked, "What is it, Ebenezer?"

When he silently stood there struggling to find the words, she asked again, in the same soft tones she used speaking to a traumatized soldier lying on a Turkish cot in Scutari Hospital, "Search your heart, Ebenezer. What would you have me know?"

Knowing he could not tell the woman who was possibly the most famous nurse in the world about the "Night of the Ghosts" years earlier, lest he be consigned to London's Bedlam Insane Asylum, Scrooge managed to say, "Miss Nightingale, whether you believe me or not does not matter a whit. *I would lay down my life for Allyce.*" The anguish on his face told of emotions he couldn't give voice to. Stumbling over his words, he blurted out, "I swear on the destiny of my immortal soul, although she may despise me and curse my name for the remainder of her life, *I will love Allyce forever.*"

For the first time since speaking with badly injured soldiers at Scutari, Florence's intuition told her the man standing before her, as he struggled to get out his halting words, was, at that moment, incapable of lying. Scrooge's mask of the confident, successful London businessman had momentarily slipped. She saw a raw, tortured agony underneath, not unlike the mental damage done to British soldiers subjected to heavy bombardment by Russian cannons in the Crimea.

What happened to you, Ebenezer Scrooge? Florence wondered. *Allyce told me of a rapacious, clutching, wicked miser without a shred of humanity who loved only gold, yet I see before me only a broken man who's spent years trying to repair a grievous moral injury, and more than that, is sorely in need of a woman's touch. You've asked me not to interfere, so I shan't. But you've suffered an injury as grievous as anything I witnessed on the face of a shocked soldier in Scutari Hospital.*

Then the words Scrooge had spoken only minutes earlier came back to her in a rush: *It is required of every man that the soul within him should walk abroad among his fellow men, traveling far and wide to spread Christian charity and comfort; and if that soul goes not forth in life, it is condemned to do so after death, doomed to wander through the world witnessing what it cannot share, but might have shared on earth, and turned to happiness.* She wondered who would have had the wisdom to utter such profound words to Ebenezer Scrooge.

This man was indeed an enigma. Florence would honor his request not to interfere provided he kept his word to her; however, it was Florence, the private citizen, who agreed not to interfere, but Florence Nightingale, *the nurse*, was not so quickly put off. *God has asked me to alleviate suffering, Ebenezer Scrooge, and I shall not ignore the suffering you endure even until this night*, she silently resolved.

"Then we are agreed, Mr. Scrooge. I bid you a good evening and thank you for your hospitality. May this work of yours redound to the benefit of every hospital patient within your little group's reach," she said. With those words, Florence Nightingale stepped out into the cool evening air to her attendant and waiting carriage, soon to disappear into the misty night.

Scrooge collected his thoughts in the cool night air for a few moments before returning to the assembled men in his library, the damp mist from the fog a balm for his tormented thoughts of Allyce. He prayed Florence would honor his request for confidence and discretion.

John Delane was the first to speak up.

"Well done, Ebenezer!" Delane exclaimed. "How in the world did you manage to have Florence Nightingale herself speak to us this night? Again I say, well done, sir! While you were escorting Miss Nightingale out to her carriage, we all agreed she is possessed of a unique moral authority encountered only rarely. Her words alone carry an imperative authority as credible as a sack full of Her Majesty's gold sovereigns; I daresay there is not a man in this group who is not evermore committed to this cause. We must start as soon as possible. In your absence, we have unanimously consented to form the nucleus of the 'Honorable Society of Royal Medical Benefactors.'"

Scrooge nodded as Reverend Braithwaite spoke up, too modest to take credit for having arranged the visit by Florence.

"As you proposed in your discussions with each of us, we have each agreed to contribute the common sum of £15,000. We will be starting with a total of £120,000 for the necessary repair and rehabilitation of the two hospitals we have discussed this evening. We all know of certain merchants and craftsmen who will give of their time, goods, and talent for a cause as worthy as ours."

Scrooge shook off his momentary daze arising from his disquieting conversation with Florence Nightingale.

"This is all well and good, gentlemen," he said. "However, one condition I must insist on is that my name is to be nowhere attributable to our collective endeavor. I am *not* doing this for public acclaim or personal aggrandizement. As we are talking of a hitherto unprecedented private endeavor, I will be contacting certain persons I know well in the Royal Treasury that I am sure will agree to provide proper oversight and auditing by the Crown." He paused to look around the room as the men nodded their concurrence, now puffing contentedly on their pipes after Florence's departure.

"I am sure you are all acquainted with Ainsley Northrup, who oversees the Royal Consumption Infirmary. We shall have to arrange for a Royal Decree to effect the improvements I have in mind, the sort we just heard our 'Angel of the Crimea' endorse as critical, to negate his ability to interfere with us; otherwise, he will frustrate our efforts at best and at worst, confiscate our money for his own purposes," Scrooge said.

Delane spoke up again.

"Ebenezer, it is obvious to the other gentlemen here present, our little 'society,' if you will, you've given considerable thought to these matters. What do you propose we begin with?"

Scrooge did not hesitate to speak up.

"Our priority must be twofold and start simultaneously at each institution. As Miss . Nightingale said, we must see that the quality of food, sanitary linen cleaning, ventilation, elimination of every sort of vermin, and heating are improved forthwith. Another thing, gentlemen; an army of orderlies with scrub brushes and mops will not suffice. The facilities must receive a fresh coat of paint, new beds, sheets and linens, and mattresses." He paused to gather his thoughts; there was much to be done.

"Gentlemen, except for the honorable Sir Richard and Sir Neville, we are all accomplished men of business. From my own experience, I can deduce that the Royal Treasury apportions prodigious sums to the two hospitals I have in mind to start with. Yet, they are as filthy and run down as any slum tenement in London."

Scrooge looked around the room.

"I do not know if the same situation prevails at the Royal Home of Convalescent Medicine for Her Majesty's Soldiers and Sailors, but the situation there was even more execrable. Perhaps Sir Richard can whisper in the right ear at Buckingham Palace about Ainsley Northrup's propensity for enriching himself at Her Majesty's expense? I'm sure I can find a voice at the Royal Consumption Infirmary who can provide substantial corroboration of Ainsley Northrup's, uhhh, *proclivities*. I would think the London Metropolitan Police would be only too happy to lend their assistance from that point onward."

Another member of the Society spoke up, snorting, "Huh! Ebenezer, you are too charitable by half. We all know Northrup is no better than a common East End pickpocket."

Nodding his agreement at the interruption, Scrooge said, "Second, along with sanitary improvements, I know Ainsley Northrup pays the staff at his Infirmary a mere pittance, nothing more than a meager subsistence wage. Now, I grant you we are not in the business of creating wealthy hospital staff; however, I think we can all agree that it is difficult *in extremis* to provide for a family on a wage of only six pounds and four sixpences each week." Members of the Society exchanged looks of consternation as Scrooge continued.

"Therefore, I also propose, once the administration of the Royal Consumption Infirmary has been—uhh—suitably changed in agreement with our goals, that we put in place modest monetary increases to ease the burden on the overworked staff. In the example I cited above, we would see the wage raised from six pounds and four sixpences each week to eight pounds and eight sixpences each week. It is not a grand increase but would ensure those employees can put proper food on their dinner tables and take care of their families. Again, this will have to be done *after* Ainsley Northrup can no longer interfere."

Sir Richard Mayne spoke up. "Gentlemen, whether this is a rare coincidence or perhaps the work of Providence, I cannot say. What I can reveal to you in my capacity as head of the London Metropolitan Police is that I am meeting shortly with a friend inside the Royal Household inquiring about an expedited Royal Decree removing Ainsley Northrup from his position pending resolution of suspected 'financial irregularities.'" Sir Richard did not divulge to the men that his "friend" was his long-time hunting partner, the Royal Consort Prince Albert, himself.

"I can obtain the Royal Decree within the next two weeks if that is acceptable to all of you. It will authorize Ainsley Northrup's removal as discussed. With his connections, he will weasel his way out of time in the Tower of London or Newgate Prison, but I will settle for nothing less than complete forfeiture of the reins of authority at the

Royal Consumption Infirmary to a person of impeccable credentials. Ebenezer, would you be able to reach out to Miss Nightingale to identify a doctor she might recommend? I don't think we'd be able to do much better than a doctor she might vouch for."

Scrooge nodded, still in somewhat of a daze at his final words with the famous nurse. He would send correspondence directly to her at the Nightingale family's Lea Hurst estate.

But along with the others, despite his private words with Florence Nightingale, Scrooge felt an infectious enthusiasm among the men in the room. They were about to accomplish the start of a sincere good. He couldn't possibly know why the head of the Metropolitan Police had such a smile on his face, but then again, it really didn't matter.

12 ❧

A SECRET OR MADNESS REVEALED?

A few days later, after the surreptitious visit of his celebrated new acquaintance, Scrooge sat down at his desk to pen a letter to Florence Nightingale with two thoughts uppermost in his mind.

To the esteemed Miss Florence Nightingale
Lea Hurst Estate, Derbyshire

Dear Miss Nightingale,

I first would like to take the opportunity on behalf of the recently formed Honorable Society of Royal Medical Benefactors to thank you for taking the time out of your very busy schedule to address our little assembly. We have already established a fund at the Bank of England, through a confidential solicitor, as we discussed with you, in the amount of £120,000. I also have reason to believe, for reasons of "police business" of which Sir Richard Mayne could not divulge any substantive information, Ainsley Northrup will soon be removed from his position as High Administrator of the Royal Consumption Infirmary. Once that takes place (and may God grant that it be very soon!), our humble group will begin to effect the repairs and improvements you recommended.

Second, I wondered if I might impose the request for a favor upon you. As you are aware, we are businessmen and do not have any expertise in the field of medicine or the healing arts. From what I've been told, Ainsley Northrup is a singular obstruction to any effort to rehabilitate the hospital. What the Infirmary needs is a competent doctor who may also serve as an administrator. Mr. Northrup is neither. It is the opinion of our Honorable Society of Royal Medical Benefactors that by having served Her Majesty so ably in the Crimea and knowing the challenges of coping with medical facilities in varying degrees of disrepair, you might recommend a suitable personage to us. I assure you that anyone you put forth for consideration will be more than acceptable.

Your obedient servant,
Ebenezer Scrooge

A week later and Scrooge arrived home to find Mrs. Dilber in a highly excited state.

"What is the matter, Mrs. Dilber? Did Julius or Caesar get out again?" Scrooge looked over her shoulder for a sign of his mischievous felines.

"No, sir, but this letter arrived for you earlier today, and I wanted you to see it straight away."

Scrooge took the envelope and looked at the address on the reverse. It read:

F. Nightingale

Lea Hurst, Derbyshire

Taking the letter, Scrooge said, "I'll be in the library, Mrs. Dilber, and will take dinner at the customary time. I would enjoy your company if you have not taken supper yet."

Scrooge retired to his library but, as was his custom, left the door ajar so Julius and Caesar would not feel slighted. Taking a letter opener from his desk, he slit the envelope open and removed a short note written in elegant handwriting on cream-colored vellum.

Dear Mr. Scrooge,

Thank you for your recent note. I was honored to address you and your associates from the Royal London Exchange. I would like to invite you to our family residence at Lea Hurst, Derbyshire, to discuss the matters you raised in your letter on behalf of the Honorable Society of Royal Medical Benefactors. Although highly admirable, there are elements to what your organization is proposing to accomplish that are well beyond the scope of a letter in the post. As time is of the essence, I would like to extend an invitation for you to visit our family home at Lea Hurst no later than mid-August. We have a spacious suite of rooms for guests. Please advise me when you expect to make the trip, and I will have one of the family coaches pick you up at the Derby railway station.

The courtesy of an expeditious RSVP is respectfully requested.

I remain, your humble servant,
Florence Nightingale

Scrooge's hands trembled with excitement. His plans for improving the English hospital system were about to get the benefit of the most famous nurse in the world.

A week later, Ebenezer Scrooge alighted the Great Northern Railway passenger carriage in Derby at one o'clock in the afternoon. The trip on the railway took four hours once the great steam-powered locomotive pulled wheezing and chuffing out of King's Cross Euston Road railway station in London. A dapper attendant dressed like a formal butler holding a sign reading *Mr. Ebenezer Scrooge* stood near the ticket purchasing window. Scrooge walked up to the man with a sense of excitement.

"I'm Ebenezer Scrooge. Are you my conveyance to Lea Hurst?"

"Yes, sir," answered the attendant. "Once we collect your travel bags, I expect it will take us approximately thirty minutes to get to Lea Hurst. The Nightingale family is ready to receive you for afternoon high tea and then a formal dinner at eight o'clock this night."

Scrooge climbed into a waiting carriage where two jet-black thoroughbred horses pawed the ground, anxious to begin the journey to the famous estate of William Edward Nightingale. Scrooge took in the sights of central England on the pleasant carriage ride to the grand estate. He gaped in wonder as the horses approached the grand buildings off Yew Tree Hill. He thought that Florence Nightingale must have been a woman of very strong convictions to leave such a dignified life of opulent luxury as part of the English upper class to relieve suffering in distant Asia Minor.

As the attendant drew the carriage around to the main entrance of Lea Hurst, Ebenezer Scrooge felt very much out of his element. He remembered that Miss Nightingale suffered from the effects of "Crimean fever" and was thus compelled to live at the family's palatial estate, so he considered it to be of little consequence that he had to spend hours journeying here north of London.

He walked up the main entryway into the receiving parlor, where he was bid to wait by the head butler. Several minutes later, he was ushered into a beautifully ornate indoor atrium garden, where the Nightingale family had just sat down for high tea. Florence, spying him walking down the hallway, immediately rose from her seat.

"Mr. Scrooge!" She smiled. "I'm delighted you accepted my invitation to Lea Hurst."

She turned to the three people seated at the table. "May I introduce Mr. Ebenezer Scrooge of London? Mr. Scrooge, this is my mother, Frances." Scrooge bowed deeply, brushing his lips to the back of her outstretched, gloved hand. "This is my father, William. Father, this is Mr. Ebenezer Scrooge." Scrooge shook William Nightingale's outstretched hand with a terse, "Your servant, sir." Finally, Florence turned to a somewhat older but still young woman and said, "Mr. Scrooge, this is my elder sister, Parthenope." Scrooge bowed and said, "I'm honored to meet you, Miss Parthenope."

William Nightingale bid Scrooge take a seat and said, "We were just sitting down to high tea, so your arrival time is most fortuitous. We spend a lot of time fending off the curious and publicity-seekers regarding my famous daughter, so a dignified guest is most welcome indeed."

Scrooge sat to the left of Florence, with her father to his right. In front of him was a massive, gold-appointed sterling silver three-tiered cake stand groaning under the weight of innumerable foods. On the smallest top tier of the cake stand sat a selection of different butter scones dressed in jams and whipped cream. The middle level of the cake stand held an assortment of crustless sandwiches.

Scrooge felt himself reddening with a touch of embarrassment at the opulence surrounding him. "I must confess I'm quite sure her Royal Majesty Queen Victoria is not dining as well as we are this afternoon. I thank you again for your hospitality."

Once tea concluded about an hour later, Scrooge and Florence withdrew to a sitting room appointed with various rare *objet d'art*, including a sixteenth-century French harpsichord and a grand piano.

Florence sat opposite Scrooge in a chair reserved for her while he took his seat at an angle to hers. Scrooge noticed Florence's sister Parthenope hovering just outside the sitting room. When Scrooge remarked upon this, Florence smiled and dryly said, "Parthenope thinks me to be a perpetual fifteen-year-old girl in need of a governess."

Scrooge smiled stiffly and said, "Miss Nightingale, I take no offense. It is an honor to be here. If I may be bold, I would like to go over the lists of improvements to the various medical establishments the Honorable Society of Royal Medical Benefactors has its sight set on."

Florence's next words shocked Scrooge.

"Mr. Scrooge, I have a confession to make, and I hope you will not be cross with me. I have invited you here under somewhat false pretenses."

Scrooge just sat and blinked, wide-eyed.

Florence continued. "That night when Reverend Neville Braithwaite persuaded me to address your little gathering, I did so out of curiosity. As I told you, Allyce Bainbridge is every bit of a sister to me as my flesh-and-blood sister, Parthenope. In fact, I hold no practical difference between my bond with Allyce and Parthenope. I wanted to further acquaint myself with the infamous man who broke Allyce's heart. I genuinely had no idea you were really going to improve English hospitals. I confess I thought it was a ruse to get back into Allyce's good graces."

Scrooge stood up, his face reddening with a wave of anger he felt oddly embarrassed to display, almost as if he had no right to be indignant.

"Please, Mr. Scrooge, rest assured I am *not* your enemy, and the next Great Northern Railway carriage doesn't leave for London until almost noon tomorrow," Florence said gently. "I *do* intend to provide you and your mischievous band of altruistic businessmen with every possible assistance for your endeavors."

She continued. "I first met Allyce in 1850, when I knew her as Allyce Simpson, at the Lutheran religious hospital in Kaiserswerth-am-Rhine in Germany, where we learned medical health and hygiene from Reverend Theodor Fliedner. We were the only English-speaking nursing students there, so naturally we fell into an effortless friendship. As women are wont to do, we were soon sharing intimate details of our lives in lively chatter that would keep us awake half the night before we realized the time. Back then, Allyce was already engaged to Captain Tristan, but she seemed singularly unable to put part of her past behind her."

Scrooge glumly interjected, "Let me guess; the part of her past she couldn't let go of, or forgive, is *me*."

Florence gave an easy laugh that put Scrooge off his guard.

"That's right, Ebenezer—oh, may I call you Ebenezer?" she asked. "I don't wish to take liberties with social convention if it makes you uncomfortable or offends your propriety."

"Only if you accord me the singular privilege of addressing you as Miss Florence."

Florence smiled easily. "*See?* We are friends already."

Scrooge could take no more of Florence's seeming avoidance of the true reason she had invited him to Lea Hurst.

"Florence, I do not wish to seem rude or impertinent, but why did you invite me here? You know everything you need to know about my character deficiencies from Allyce, and you certainly left the Honorable Society of Royal Medical Benefactors with more than enough work for at least the next year."

She looked straight into his eyes and said, "When I spoke at your home and took my leave, I promised not to interfere between you and Allyce, and I fully intend to keep that promise. You must know, however, that it was Florence Nightingale *the private citizen* who gave you her word and agreed not to interfere, but Florence Nightingale *the nurse* is not easily put off. God has called me to alleviate suffering, Ebenezer Scrooge, and when I arrived at your home, I was convinced I would encounter in your personage a beast, a hideous ogre. I found those preconceived notions dashed on the rocks of the pain I saw reflected in your eyes that night. Tell me, Ebenezer, do you believe in God?"

"If I tell you how I came about my belief in God, you shall think me mad. Even to this day, I have not revealed to many people all the details of my 'conversion,' as it were. It was sudden, terrifying, and took place over the course of one night."

Florence gently probed. "So, you had something of a 'Road to Damascus' moment, then?"

Scrooge responded, "I'm afraid I don't understand."

"It refers to the conversion of Saint Paul the Apostle when he was still the learned Pharisee Saul of Tarsus—a Jew, but also a Roman citizen by birth. He was traveling to Damascus to arrest a group of Christians there. While on the road to Damascus, a bright light suddenly shone on Saul and his party that knocked them to the ground. The Lord spoke to Saul from the light, 'Saul, why are you persecuting me?' in a voice heard only by Saul. It does not take much imagination, Ebenezer, to think of the terror that filled Saul's heart. From that moment on, he went by his Roman name of Paul, as it would make him more acceptable to the Roman authorities. Still, his instantaneous transformation from a determined enemy of the Christians to being one of them was irreversible."

Scrooge had a pensive look on his face. Florence stared at him intently as he opened his mouth to respond.

"Yes, some years after Allyce broke off our engagement, I experienced a similar moment, although it was not the Lord that deigned to visit me—would that I were worthy of that." He paused, struggling to find the right words.

"Go on, Ebenezer," Florence softly urged. "I am not here to judge you, and if it sets your mind at ease, you are *not* the wicked man Allyce described to me."

"Well, not anymore," Scrooge allowed. "I look back and think of it as the 'Night of the Ghosts.' It was not the Lord or even an angel who visited me, but a terrible apparition of my former business partner, Jacob Marley. He said he was doomed to wander the world bearing chains of selfishness and greed he forged by his wicked actions in life. Marley told me that the chain I had also forged by the night of his ethereal visit was already far heavier than the one he was condemned to carry. He told me the only chance I had of escaping such a fate was to heed the directions of three ghosts who would thereafter visit me. The first ghost showed me the sins and faults of my past, including, to my everlasting shame, my callous treatment of Allyce. The next spirit, who called himself the Ghost of Christmas Present, showed me how all the people in my life were enjoying the true spirit marking the day of the Babe born in a manger, but it was the third ghost, the Spirit of Christmas Yet to Come who truly terrified me. My hair turned white overnight and I eventually went bald. He had the appearance of the Grim Reaper, only without his scythe. He made quite clear that my fate would be eternal hellfire unless I changed my life. And that brings us to the man you see before you today."

He peered closely at Florence. "So, do you think me mad?"

She laughed. "Ebenezer, my own mother thought I was quite mad when I told her God was calling me to the nursing profession to alleviate the suffering of my fellow man, even though I could have lived out my life in circumstances you see here now." Florence gestured at the opulent surroundings. "Then, she nearly fainted dead away when I told her that I was going to minister to wounded soldiers in the Crimea. So, you tell *me*, Ebenezer, was *I* mad to follow God's call?"

"Of course not! There are thousands of British soldiers who owe their lives to you. But your call was to a noble purpose, to heal and ennoble people's lives."

"Then neither do I think *you* mad, Ebenezer Scrooge. You know the old saying about madness, do you not, Ebenezer?" Florence asked with a gentle smile.

Scrooge shook his head no.

Florence let a small smile play about her lips. "What do people call it when someone is talking to God?" After Scrooge fumbled for an answer, she said, "Why, *praying*, of course! Now, what do people say it is called when *God* talks to *people*?"

Scrooge felt quite the fool, being at a loss again for an answer.

"Madness!" Parthenope called from the hallway, having over-heard the conversation. "When God talks to someone, it is called madness, Mr. Scrooge, and don't think I haven't thought that about my younger sister there on more than one occasion. Had I not seen what she's accomplished, I'd have thought her as daft as Joan of Arc and her 'voices from heaven.'"

Florence waited until Parthenope withdrew before she contin-ued, in her solicitous tone, "Ebenezer, I think you suffer from a 'moral injury,' knowing you had not only the chance, but perhaps the *obligation* to follow a proper and just path with Allyce but proceeded to break her heart in a vainglorious pursuit of riches. But in any case, no, *you are no longer that man*, though you yet suffer the effects of what his actions wrought."

Scrooge set down his tea, a sense of indignation slowly coming to a boil within him.

"So, you think my desire to improve the conditions at the Royal Consumption Infirmary and other medical institutions is only trying to assuage a guilty conscience over what happened many years ago with Allyce? Florence, permit me to be direct with you. I have spent the better part of *years* trying to make amends *every day* for the man I used to be and in every aspect of my life. I am not doing these things to impress *anyone*, as if I were an actor performing for an audience or for public adulation. I am of the firm belief that at the end of my life, I will have to render an accounting of my deeds *and* misdeeds to the God we both profess. I only pray the good I can yet accomplish outweighs whatever damage I have done."

Scrooge almost said he did not care about what Allyce thought, but he also knew that would be a lie. He cared a great deal about what she thought, but of *him*, not his charitable deeds.

"But I sense there is more to this than the unhappy end of a romance years ago, isn't there?" Florence said. "That night when you saw me off from your home in London, you professed to still love

Allyce very much. I know that to be true because a man in that agitated state was incapable of uttering a lie. I happen to be an expert in lies and deception, Ebenezer, for I contended with the British Army's officer corps at Scutari Hospital, and they are some of the best liars in the world."

Scrooge felt himself growing red in the face.

"There *is* more, Florence," he said. "The very Sunday before you spoke to the Honorable Society of Royal Medical Benefactors, I visited my clerk Bob Cratchit's daughter-in-law, Charlotte Cratchit. She is confined to the Royal Consumption Infirmary with severe consumption. I had taken to visiting her on Sundays, as it is the one day of the week Allyce is permitted with her children. After leaving the Infirmary, I stopped at Saint Hubert's Church a few blocks off Radley Circus. I didn't really think I was praying, but rather collecting my thoughts in the quiet amidst the smell of beeswax and incense." At this point, Scrooge could not hold Florence's gaze. His eyes shifted to a pattern on the floor as he continued.

"I hadn't been there for more than a few minutes when I beheld the spirit of my former partner Jacob Marley again, and *he told me he knew of my unrequited love for Allyce.*"

Florence said, "My word, Ebenezer!"

"See? I *knew* you would think me mad."

"No, I am not judging you; I'm merely taken aback. Please, go on," she said.

"Before I do, I must ask you to renew your pledge that you will never speak to Allyce of *anything* that passes between us on this subject. I must follow my own path—to ruin or happiness I cannot say—but mine is to be a solitary journey regarding Allyce. I know Allyce is family as far as you are concerned, but *you* were the one who invited *me* here, so I am being as forthright as possible."

Florence Nightingale was impressed. Knowing the tight bond uniting the two women, Scrooge could have easily asked for her intervention in this affair of the heart with Allyce, given the closeness of their friendship, and she would have consented.

"Ebenezer, I shall not speak to Allyce of this. What is spoken today here at Lea Hurst will remain unsaid outside of the two of us. Please, do go on," Florence urged.

"Well, Marley's soul, spirit—what have you—told me several things that had transpired or may yet come to pass. He looked to be at peace, Florence, not the rotting apparition from the grave I first beheld years ago, the sort of horrifying vision one reads of in children's ghost stories. When I inquired about how his release from his suffering came about, Jacob told me *my* change of heart *here* had lifted the burden of the chains his greed in life had forged. He said he was happy now. In a moment of selfishness, I asked him straight away if the spirits that haunted me that Christmas Eve night might visit Allyce to tell her of my 'redemption,' if you will."

Florence Nightingale sat in rapt attention as Scrooge continued.

"Jacob told me that those spirits who visited me that night were borne of my own life's miserable work and unhappy memories. They could not change Allyce's heart or her ill feelings toward me, for they would not have her life's memories to draw upon. Jacob said, and I do believe as much, that Allyce's life has been one that has been lived in Christian charity. Even if such spirits would visit her, Allyce's life and deeds in our mortal time have been so beyond reproach, my spirits would serve no purpose."

"So then why did Jacob manifest himself if not to offer you solace?"

By her question, Scrooge knew Florence was solicitous toward his situation.

"Well, he went on to say that there was a particular spirit he called the Ghost, or Spirit, if you will, of 'Christmas Love,' that might be able to prevail upon Allyce's heart to at least consider that I was not beyond redemption and might yet prove to be a positive influence in her life."

"Well, Ebenezer, you professed to me that you still love Allyce."

"And I most assuredly *do*, Miss Nightingale," Scrooge responded, slipping for a moment back into formal address. "Then, Jacob told me that if the love in my heart for Allyce was true, then I must be prepared to sacrifice greatly to obtain that which my gold cannot buy, as only love arising without selfish attachments is 'true love.' He said I have been generous with my riches, but they have been given from my surplus, not my want. Then, he asked how far I was willing to go in sacrificing *myself*."

Listening to Scrooge's tale, Florence was impressed. This was no tale borne of madness, but a most special intervention brought about by Divine Agency.

"So, you now know of my situation, Florence. I have racked my poor mind trying to figure out the meaning of his cryptic words, but shortly thereafter, he just faded away, and I was left alone in Saint Hubert's Church with burning candles and these thoughts I tell you now as my only company. The Jacob Marley who exists in the hereafter, Charlotte Cratchit, and you are the only persons to know of my feelings toward Allyce."

Florence looked at Scrooge, who at least seemed somewhat relieved at having told his rather outlandish tale to someone who wasn't predisposed to judge him a madman.

"So how may I help you, Ebenezer? I was prepared to offer words of solace, but yours is a most extraordinary situation. I admit to a deep belief in God and that He has chosen a path for me, but I am at a loss as to how I might assist you."

"If there is some way for the chains of mistrust and bitterness Marley told me that still surround Allyce's heart might be removed, I think it must be entirely of my own doing. Of a more pressing nature, that detestable lout Ainsley Northrup is in a position to block any further improvements at the Royal Consumption Infirmary. Considering the conditions at other institutions, Allyce has per-

formed remarkable work, but Northrup is still in a position to frustrate any meaningful sanitary improvements. Among my associates,
we have heard rumors of Northrup's malfeasances, but nothing of
substance. I admit it is a vexing situation, but that leaves us with
a void to fill. We were hoping we might use your influence to help
effect the removal of Northrup and recommend a suitable doctor
to take his place. It needs to be a compassionate doctor, willing to
embrace your ideas for improvement of sanitary medical care, and
capable of administering a large facility like the Royal Consumption
Infirmary."

Florence didn't hesitate. "I cannot violate a confidence, Ebenezer,
but this much I can tell you. Ainsley Northrup's conduct as administrator of the Royal Consumption Infirmary has been suspect for
quite some time. I have collected information on him that directly
shows he has embezzled funds for his own gain."

Florence stood up and made her way over to an ornate writing
desk, where she pulled out a sheaf of papers. She unfolded a fair-sized
chart that displayed two odd-looking circles side by side. Although
different in size, each circle was segmented into wedges that resem-
bled an odd pie of sorts.

She pointed to the larger circle on the left.

"This diagram represents the number of confirmed patients,
deaths, and recoveries at the Royal Consumption Infirmary over the
last two years. As you can see, the wedge representing deaths takes up
the majority of the chart."

She then called his attention to the smaller pie-shaped chart on
the right.

"Although speculative, this chart shows what the number of
confirmed patients, deaths, and recoveries *should* be, given what the
Royal Treasury appropriates for the Royal Consumption Infirmary.
You can see the number of people I projected to have recovered from

consumption is far greater than the people who have actually been healed. Ebenezer, far too many people die than recover."

Florence pulled out another chart with similar illustrations, one larger than the other.

"These pictures depict the causes of death that prevailed at Scutari Hospital for the first year I was there and the same causes of death when I left. You can see that death by disease had greatly diminished."

Scrooge wrinkled his brow.

"I'm not following you, Florence."

"If we compare both charts, although they are not directly related, but using the same method to examine them, we can see that if the funds allocated to the Royal Consumption Infirmary for health and sanitary purposes were used precisely for those purposes, the number of deaths should logically be far fewer. I suspect that some of the monies from the Royal Treasury are being misdirected, and if I had to guess, I would agree it is Ainsley Northrup."

Florence wrinkled her nose in distaste.

"I met him when I accompanied Allyce to her interview. That was before I went to the Crimea. He gave off an air of shiftiness, and my opinion has been confirmed in the years since. I'm not at liberty to say anything further, but you can rest assured that Ainsley Northrup will not be in a position to interfere with your group's efforts.

"I've also got the perfect doctor in mind for you. Grant Entwistle, *Dr.* Grant Entwistle," Florence said. "Dr. Entwistle was one of very few doctors who recognized what we might accomplish with better sanitation at Scutari, and I ended up having a most productive partnership with him. Together we reduced the mortality rate at Scutari by almost *sixty percent*. He has now returned to London, having completed his term of service with Her Majesty's armed forces. This evening I shall write a letter of introduction for you to my friend Sidney Herbert, former Minister-at-War for Crimea. Sidney will ensure the

Crown appoints Dr. Entwistle to the Royal Consumption Infirmary forthwith."

Scrooge stood up and kissed the back of Florence's hand.

"Florence, your reputation for solicitude and intelligence precedes you and is well deserved. Since you are in a generous mood, might I prevail upon you to write a letter of introduction for me to the administrator of the Royal Home of Convalescent Medicine for Her Majesty's Soldiers and Sailors as well? We have resolved that will be the next institution on our list."

"Why there, Ebenezer?"

"Well, thinking to see where Allyce's late husband would have recovered had he lived to return to England, I also visited there. I must confess, although the administration at that hospital does not appear to have the deliberately cruel neglect of Ainsley Northrup, the conditions there can be best described as the fruits of *benign neglect.*"

As a final test of Scrooge's intentions, Florence decided to try one more provocative question. "Are you hoping to impress your sincerity upon Allyce by rehabilitating *that* institution simultaneously with the Royal Consumption Infirmary to win romantic favor with her?"

"That *was* foremost in my thoughts after seeing Allyce at the Royal Consumption Infirmary with Charlotte, but then I visited the place. Once I crossed the threshold, every thought of Allyce vanished. There was one noticeable difference with the Royal Consumption Infirmary, where Charlotte is confined. Of course, there are the same sort of old rusting beds, antique equipment, and peeling paint, but I noticed in the military hospital that there were no bleach-water basins for staff or visitors to wash their hands upon either entering or leaving. Allyce has taken your advice to heart in improving the sanitary lot of the consumption patients at the Royal Consumption Infirmary, but she can do only so much being a nurse. I wish I could say the same for where Her Majesty's injured fighting soldiers and sailors must recover.

"From what you have told me of the conditions at Scutari, it would seem as if the British military wanted to set a standard for medical neglect. The robes and clothing of the patients were filthy and covered in dried blood. I saw more poor souls there with suppurating wounds and unchanged, reeking bandages than there are crows in Bletchley Park. These men charged straight into the guns and cannons of the Czar with the greatest of bravery, yet when they once again returned to England's glorious shores, their welcome committee consisted of rats, lice, and assorted vermin. Tell me, Florence. Do those veterans of service to Her Majesty the Queen deserve their thanks to lie helpless and in pain while maggots and flies crawl on the stumps where noble hands once embraced a wife or cradled a child?" By this point, Scrooge veritably trembled in outrage.

"Well, Ebenezer, now you know what greeted my nurses at Scutari Hospital. Sidney Herbert still carries quite a bit of influence in Parliament and enjoys the favor of the Crown as well. I should think that as sending me with my nurses to the Crimean Theater of War was *his* idea, he would be most enthusiastic regarding your Honorable Society's plans to rehabilitate the military convalescent hospital as well."

Although Scrooge couldn't help but feel that he had passed yet another test with the "Angel of the Crimea," he was nevertheless grateful.

"I cannot thank you enough, Florence. You may be assured that a suitable member of our Honorable Society of Royal Medical Benefactors will be at Dr. Entwistle's disposal to ensure he does not want for anything he requires for any improvements. We are prepared to make up for whatever may be lacking in funds from the Royal Treasury." Scrooge observed a tired look stealing across Florence's face and took the opportunity to excuse himself.

"I have enjoyed our conversation most sincerely, Florence. With your permission, I'll retire to my chamber until dinner. I have already had a long day."

The smile on his face was sincere, and Florence was impressed.

He could have asked me to intervene with Allyce on his behalf, yet he didn't. I shall pray for him and Allyce nonetheless, she thought. Then, another thought crossed her mind. *I did promise Sidney Herbert to soon visit him in London. In addition to seeing Allyce, I think my itinerary will now include a discreet visit to the Royal Home of Convalescent Medicine for Her Majesty's Soldiers and Sailors.*

The following day, Scrooge departed for London via the same Great Northern Railway train that had brought him to Lea Hurst. He carried two wax envelopes sealed with Florence's ring addressed to her close friend and advocate Sidney Herbert, 1st Baron Herbert of Lea and former Minister-at-War for the Crimea. Florence had permitted Scrooge to read the letters before she sealed them. Upon handing the envelopes to him, she said she was confident Sidney would approve of the Honorable Society's plans to repair and refurbish the Royal Home of Convalescent Medicine.

13

SETTLING OF ACCOUNTS

It was a stroke of luck for the new Honorable Society of Royal Medical Benefactors that on the evening when Sir Richard met the famous Florence Nightingale, the very next day, on his way home after work, Ainsley Northrup's clerk would be arrested by the Metropolitan Police just before arrival at his home.

Sir Richard knew that on the testimony of both Florence Nightingale and Allyce Bainbridge, Joseph Billingsly was the sort of craven coward who wielded the bully's authority of being Ainsley Northrup's clerk like a whip, where no such authority existed. He had even attempted romantic advances toward Allyce Bainbridge but was rebuffed at every turn. With these thoughts in mind, Sir Richard planned on working very late into the night. He derived great satisfaction in seeing an arrogant criminal, certain he was beyond the reach of the law, watch his world of manipulation and deceit collapse. He was well acquainted with Billingsly's type of corrupt bureaucrat, and watching his bravado vanish would be worth looking forward to, especially given the dramatic turn of events at Ebenezer Scrooge's home.

The clock in Sir Richard Mayne's office chimed nine o'clock in the evening. His energy was fueled by a roast chicken dinner and several cups of strong Turkish coffee as much as his anticipation of the night's events about to unfold. Finally, two officers entered with a resolute Allyce Bainbridge accompanying them, a package of documents tightly clutched in her hands. She was quickly ushered into another side office accompanied by the two officers. Right thereafter, the sounds of a commotion were heard down the hallway and grew louder. Soon, two hand-picked detectives from Sir Richard's "Flying Squad" entered, an angry but frightened Joseph Billingsly held between them, and roughly pushed the protesting man down into a large wingback chair—a chair designed to make an accused man feel small and powerless. Ainsley Northrup and his weaselly clerk didn't know it right then, but their exorbitant lifestyle would end this night.

Sir Richard Mayne drew himself up to his full six feet three inches.

"You are Ainsley Northrup's Senior Clerk, Joseph Billingsly?" Although phrased as a question, it came out as more of a statement.

"What if I am?" Billingsly sneered. "I ain't done nothing wrong." Billingsly's churlish attitude returned with a vengeance as he regained his composure, and a measure of arrogance reasserted itself. It was not to last.

"Do you know who I am?" Sir Richard asked.

"You could be the Lord Mayor himself, and I wouldn't care a farthing," Billingsly replied.

"Then let me introduce myself, Mr. Billingsly. I am *Sir* Richard Mayne, chief of the London Metropolitan Police Department, and as far as your 'not caring a farthing,' well, that's where you're very, *very* wrong. If I were in your situation, I should care very much, Mr. Billingsly. Let me ask you, do you know that embezzlement of funds from the Royal Treasury over a thousandfold pounds is a capital offense punishable by hanging?"

"So what?" Billingsly sneered. "I couldn't care less. Like I said, Your *Highness*," Billingsly turned on his trademark sarcasm, "*I* ain't stolen a ha-penny."

"Oh, permit me to say again, I should care a great deal if I were you, Mr. Billingsly. You see, the public street in front of Newgate Prison is where they erect the gallows for public hanging."

Billingsly grew ever so slightly less confrontational.

"How does this concern me?"

Sir Richard took his chance and, leaning in toward Billingsly's face, thundered in his most authoritative voice, "The Metropolitan Police Department knows your boss, Ainsley Northrup, has been stealing funds from the Royal Treasury, bribing provisioners of services and supplies for the Royal Consumption Infirmary, and avoiding all required fees and excise taxes in the process for at least five years, perhaps longer."

Billingsly managed to maintain his blustering front.

"So what? What Mr. Northrup does in his private time outside the hospital is none of my concern. I only maintain the official ledgers for hospital expenses and Treasury funds for him—nothing more."

Sir Richard violently slammed his hands down on the thick oak desk for effect.

"*No sir!*" he exploded as Billingsly shrank back in his chair. "I will not tolerate lies in this august office!" Sir Richard roared, his righteousness blazing like a Guy Fawkes Night bonfire. "We *know* you've been Ainsley Northrup's water boy, making illegal payments to corrupt merchants and provisioners. You've kept the records for every farthing embezzled from the Royal Consumption Infirmary's patient medicine supplies and general hospital operation accounts."

Regaining a modicum of bravado, Billingsly said with a smirk, "You ain't got no proof of any of this, Sir Richard."

"That's where you're *wrong*, Mr. Billingsly. Three nights ago, you met with a Mr. Tremaine," Sir Richard turned to glance at the door to the next office before continuing, "at the Ancient Copper Pint Inn in Liverpool. You handed him a small sack containing three hundred gold sovereigns. The merchants and drovers then returned a sizeable part of the monies paid to you through a network of corrupt officials Ainsley Northrup has cultivated over the years. What he didn't count on was that a number of these officials would grow remorseful at their silence having been bought and thereby informed us of Mr. Northrup's operation. You also slipped up because you didn't read the confidential note from Mr. Tremaine to Ainsley Northrup acknowledging the payment, did you?"

"There is *no* note, and I…I *demand* my rights as an Englishman," Billingsly sputtered.

Sir Richard nodded to one of the detectives in the room, and he exited into the adjoining office, where he returned with Allyce Bainbridge, a resolute look on her face.

Despite his sallow complexion turning a further pale, Billingsly declared, "I don't know what trick you're playing, Sir Richard, but this woman is nothing but a common nurse at the Royal Consumption Infirmary, and I am the Senior Clerk to the Administrator."

Sir Richard nodded, and one of the detectives pulled out a parchment note that Billingsly recognized as a secret bill of lading for a padded linen shipment.

"I take it this is your signature, Mr. Billingsly? Let me take the liberty of reading the note aloud, '*Acknowledgment of shipment number 149, consisting of nine hundred sets of bed linens and cotton towels. Proceeds are to be forwarded forthwith to the account of Ainsley Northrup at the Bank of England. Signed Joseph Billingsly.*'"

Sir Richard laid the parchment down on his desk before continuing. "Do you have anything to say *now*, Mr. Billingsly?"

Defiant to the very end, Billingsly thrust forward his chin and declared, "This is all a plot to discredit my good and noble employer, Ainsley Northrup."

"That is too bad, Mr. Billingsly," Sir Richard said. "I had hoped you would realize the foolishness of defending an employer who would toss you to the hangman's noose to save his hide. You see, one night when Ainsley Northrup, you, and several of his corrupt business merchants to the hospital were making rather merry with John Walker's finest whiskey, you all imbibed a bit more than prudent.

In your so very inebriated state, you mentioned in the presence of a…let's say a respectable hospital personage," Sir Richard glanced at Allyce, "whom I know to be of impeccable integrity that you had forgotten to bring the 'special ledger books' with you that evening. There would be hell to pay with Mr. Ainsley in the morning if you didn't go home straight away and retrieve them from the bottom of your wife's dowry chest. But since you were falling-down drunk, you had no way to retrieve the books from your home, did you?"

Right then, there was a knock at Sir Richard's door.

"Come in and be quick, man! It's almost eleven o'clock!" Sir Richard boomed.

His trusted senior detective entered with another detective holding not one, but two ledger account books.

"Here they are, Sir Richard, right where you said they'd be," the detective said, casting a sideways glance at Billingsly. "His wife put up quite the argument until we showed her the arrest papers you signed, and we threatened to clap her in irons if she interfered further."

Sir Richard looked at Billingsly with a combination of disgust and pity.

"One of these books shows all the official monies received from Her Majesty's Royal Treasury and thence disbursed to corrupt merchants to deliver non-existent hospital supplies and services. The other book shows the actual smaller sums paid to all corrupt parties involved. The interesting fact, Mr. Billingsly, is that all of these notations and entries are in your hand. You see, we cross-checked them against correspondence from the Royal Consumption Infirmary you have signed on behalf of Mr. Northrup. Every word, every sentence down to the smallest jot and tittle we know with unassailable certainty to be in your hand. Now, need I remind you *again* embezzling funds from the Crown is a *capital offense*, Mr. Billingsly?"

Before he realized what he was saying, Billingsly looked over at Allyce and screamed in a shrill voice, "*Bainbridge, you bitch! You turned rat on me and Mr. Northrup while we were making merry! You'll pay for snitching about those ledgers. They were none of your business!"* Allyce blanched in fear but maintained her composure. Sir Richard imperceptibly nodded at the nearest detective, a hulking beast of a man, who slapped Joseph Billingsly backhanded so hard it overturned his chair.

Sir Richard calmly said as Billingsly's seat was righted, "Mr. Billingsly, Mrs. Bainbridge is my guest here this night and you will address her as a lady, even though you're no gentleman. Prior to her entering this room, I never mentioned anyone's name from the Royal Consumption Infirmary during our little chat tonight. But you've just now implicated yourself and your boss in front of six witnesses because Nurse Bainbridge *did* mention that little detail to a Royal Consumption Infirmary patient whose husband is a detective in my employ. We have a notarized statement from Nurse Bainbridge as to your drunken ramblings, and these ledgers were precisely where she said they would be found in your residence."

Sir Richard leaned in close to a now utterly defeated Billingsly's face.

"Now, how did Detective Pierce know the precise location to look among your wife's, *ahem,* 'delicate garments' for these *fascinating* ledgers?"

He then pressed his advantage home.

"Unless you wish to be swinging from the gallows in front of Newgate Prison within a fortnight, I'd be right quick in telling us what you know about Northrup's side businesses."

A deflated Billingsly looked up and asked, "If I provide you with a sworn statement of what I know, will it spare me the gallows?"

Sir Richard looked down at Northrup's disgraced clerk.

"As the chief of the London Metropolitan Police Department, I have the discretion to exercise a certain amount of leeway in criminal matters. We'll decide after we see how forthcoming you are this night."

And so began the worst night of Ainsley Northrup's life as a corrupt little bully. It was a night of Joseph Billingsly going through each book, page by page, every line entry a damning indictment of himself as a minor partner in a scheme hatched by Northrup in early 1850 to enrich himself at the expense of the Royal Treasury. It was all premised on the well-founded assumption that no one from the Royal Treasury would dare set foot inside the Royal Consumption Infirmary for Consumption lest they become infected with the dreaded disease. It was almost foolproof, but the elaborate plan unraveled due to the old maxim *In Vino Veritas.*

When a light purple hue in the east announced the approach of Tuesday morning, Sir Richard brought an end to the proceedings. He told Billingsly, "You'll go to your job today and act like nothing is amiss. You will be watched *very* closely. If you tell Mr. Northrup *anything* of what transpired this night, we shall know of it, and there will no further talk of leniency for your offenses, Mr. Billingsly. You will not know where we are, but rest assured, if you or Mr. Northrup so much as go for a walk around the Infirmary, we will pounce on you like starving cats on mice. If you so much as whisper an imprecation or threat against Nurse Bainbridge here, we will know of that too. *Do not doubt me, sir.*" The palpable menace in Sir Richard's voice left Joseph Billingsly convinced the very walls of the Royal Consumption Infirmary had eyes.

Three days later, at eleven o'clock in the morning, Sir Richard Mayne, clutching a Royal Warrant of Arrest and Dismissal and accompanied by a flying squad of six handpicked Scotland Yard detectives, showed up unannounced at the Royal Consumption Infirmary. They were led by a terrified orderly to the office chambers of Ainsley Northrup, who happened to be meeting with a linen supplier.

Sir Richard and his officers burst into the inner office of a thoroughly outraged Northrup.

Leaping to his feet, Northrup demanded, "What is the meaning of this violence? You've intruded upon one of the Crown's most beloved infirmaries! Who are you?"

Ignoring Northrup's outrage, Sir Richard Mayne, observing the formalities, pulled out the Royal Warrant of Arrest and Dismissal and began reading:

To the attention of Ainsley Northrup. I, Sir Richard Mayne, chief of the London City Metropolitan Police Department, read in the presence of the accused, Ainsley Michael Northrup, this Royal Warrant of Arrest and Dismissal from all authority and control over any and all activities having to do with the Royal Consumption Infirmary for Consumption and Ailments of the Chest. Signed this Day, Third of September in the Year of Our Lord Eighteen Fifty-Six, by Albert Prince Franz August Karl Emanuel and Royal Consort to Her Majesty, Victoria, Queen of the United Kingdom of Great Britain and Ireland.

Like his weasel of a clerk, Ainsley Northrup was defiant to the end.

"I shall not go quietly in the face of this travesty of justice."

As the shackles were placed on Northrup's hands and feet by the detective whose wife had died in the Infirmary the day before of severe pneumonia, Sir Richard went nose-to-nose with the nobleman accused of embezzlement. "You have no choice, you worm. The only way you'll *ever* return to this building will be as a patient. You'd best pray they treat you better than you've treated these poor wretched souls abused by your callousness and greed."

As hospital staff looked on in utter amazement, a humiliated Ainsley Northrup was led out of the Infirmary by the Metropolitan Police. The capstone on his mortifying exit was the sudden burst of a well-aimed rotting egg from an upper window of the Infirmary thrown by a gleeful cook. It exploded against the back of the accused as he was led to the jail carriage. Northrup was so dazed from the swiftness of his downfall, he didn't notice.

14

A MEASURE OF JUSTICE

The repairs to the Royal Consumption Infirmary began toward the end of the week after the very public removal of Ainsley Northrup, to the amazement of patients, staff, and doctors alike. No one knew where the sudden largess for the repairs had come from, other than the hitherto unknown "Honorable Society of Royal Medical Benefactors." Charlotte sat up wide-eyed in her bed at the bustling activity of workmen in every part of the Royal Consumption Infirmary's ward where she was confined. Allyce Bainbridge came by on her regular rounds with a wide smile.

"I have good news, Charlotte, although by now the rumor mill has no doubt spread the news. Ainsley Northrup is no longer in charge. I received a letter from Florence Nightingale that the Crown asked her to recommend a doctor who would put into practice each of Florence's recommendations that so drove down the death rate at Scutari Hospital. She recommended a Dr. Grant Entwistle as the new administrator. She had met him at Scutari when he was near the end of his service in Her Majesty's British Army and was one of the only doctors to heed her advice instead of looking after his ego."

Charlotte didn't look as pleased as Allyce might have hoped.

"Aren't you pleased with this turn of events, Charlotte? It will not be paradise, but the Royal Consumption Infirmary *will* be a proper hospital," Allyce said. "*Charlotte?*"

In response, Charlotte handed Allyce her latest letter from Peter in America.

"I don't recognize the man in that letter, except the signature, Allyce. All Peter does is rave about the value of this deal or that contract, with hardly a caring word for me. He's having a fine time with that Cyrus Abernathy's daughter, Livinia, too, and why shouldn't he? She's six years younger than me, well-educated, and in good health."

Allyce grimaced as she scanned the letter. Charlotte was not exaggerating; Allyce noticed every sign she saw years ago in young Ebenezer Scrooge emerging fourfold in Peter Cratchit: the constant talking about money, contracts, fortunes to be made, grand houses to be lived in upon his return to England. The seed of fierce resentment Allyce still bore Ebenezer Scrooge broke out of its little shell deep within her heart, and she permitted herself a rare display of emotion.

"This is terrible, Charlotte, just terrible." Allyce saw the tears welling up in Charlotte's eyes and tried to offer some comfort. "I'm sorry, dear. I know this seems very discouraging, Charlotte, but you must keep fighting the consumption. Your children are counting on seeing their mum soon!"

A despondent Charlotte replied, "Does it matter, Allyce? This vile Abernathy creature who enticed my husband away can afford a hundred governesses and a hundred houses to keep them in. But that is not what hurts the most. How could Peter fall under the charms of such a worldly woman like this Livinia?" Tears of despair began sliding down Charlotte's face. "I knew it was all too good to be true when Peter told me he was going to America," she sobbed.

Allyce felt helpless at that moment, and there was little she could do aside from offering words of comfort. Momentarily laying a hand on Charlotte's shoulder, Allyce walked away and down to the offices of the new hospital administrator, Dr. Entwistle.

Allyce knocked at his door, and his affable voice resounded in the office.

"Come in." He smiled at seeing Allyce.

"Nurse Bainbridge, what do you think of the improvements we're making to the Infirmary? I know you had to fight that scoundrel, Northrup, just to have bowls of sanitary hand-washing water set about. I trust our friend Florence would approve."

"Yes, doctor, it will be a very different hospital in no time at all. Everything Florence told me she put in place at Scutari Hospital is being followed here."

"Oh, I can assure you of that, Nurse Bainbridge. My wife became quite good friends with Flo, and she wouldn't tolerate anything less than me following all of what we called the 'Nightingale Procedures' with precision."

Allyce's curiosity got the better of her.

"But how did this all come about? Not two weeks after Mr. Northrup was taken away, you arrive with an army of repairmen, craftsmen, and literally every building trade imaginable. Where did the money come from? I know the accountants at the Royal Treasury cannot possibly work that quickly, nor are they that generous."

Dr. Entwistle didn't entirely reveal as much as he was privy to but said, "To the best of my knowledge, a group going by the name the 'Honorable Society of Royal Medical Benefactors' has pledged the necessary funds, and I was meeting with their solicitor just earlier today."

Entwistle changed the subject and smiled. "I also have some good news for you, Nurse Bainbridge. I shall be direct; this is a rather large hospital, and I need experienced staff to help me run it. Forthwith, you are hereby appointed the new Superintendent of Nurse Staff here at the Royal Consumption Infirmary, and it comes with this."

Entwistle slid an envelope across his desk toward Allyce.

"Go ahead," he said with a grin. "Open it. It's your new weekly wages."

Allyce opened the envelope and read the letter from Dr. Entwistle, who at the recommendation of Florence Nightingale had appointed her

Superintendent of Nurse Staff at a weekly wage of one pound and eight sixpences. Several gold sovereigns tumbled out of the envelope and onto Dr. Entwistle's desk. Allyce counted them, and they came to *eight pounds and nine sixpences*! Dr. Entwistle looked on, wearing a huge smile.

"The extra funds account for your pay increase being made retroactive for two full months. I heard from a number of quite trustworthy patients here that there have been many days and nights where you worked twelve, sometimes fourteen hours a day. Flo"— he quickly caught himself—"*we* didn't think it proper for our new superintendent of nurse staff to be earning a mere pittance and not have a proper staff of nurses to supervise."

Overcome by the happy turn of events, Allyce Bainbridge impulsively broke protocol and gratefully hugged Florence's old friend so recently back from the Crimea. "Thank you, doctor. This…this will mean the world for my children."

"Oh, before you go, there's one thing. You can't be the Superintendent of Nurse Staff without a proper staff to supervise. There will be seven experienced nurses here tomorrow who served with Florence at Scutari. I don't think anything here at the Royal Consumption Infirmary can scandalize them worse than the conditions they found at Scutari when they first arrived there."

For the first time in months, Allyce Bainbridge went home a happy woman, and she would be writing a letter of thanks to Florence Nightingale that very night. Still, Allyce had no way of knowing the letter wouldn't be going to the person *really* responsible for all the wonderful changes happening at the Royal Consumption Infirmary.

15

WHEREIN SCROOGE
LEARNS OF TRUE BRAVERY

Two days later, Scrooge left his house on Belgrave Square in the early morning in high spirits and, on a whim, decided to visit the Royal Home of Convalescent Medicine for Her Majesty's Soldiers and Sailors again, as his appointment with former Minister-at-War Sidney Herbert was not until 1 p.m. He thought he might seek out some of the Coldstream Guards at the Royal Home of Convalescent Medicine who fought at the Battle of the Alma River, where Allyce's husband, Tristan, was mortally wounded. He walked up to the greeting desk again. It was a stroke of luck the desk attendant was an older fellow who would have no way to know Scrooge had already been there on a pretext.

"I beg your pardon, but are there any members of her Majesty's Coldstream Guards from the fighting in Crimea recuperating here?" he asked the attendant in the lobby.

"Why, yes, sir. I believe there's a fair number of the Coldstream boys in the second-floor ward." He handed Scrooge a damp cloth. "I'd hold this over your nose when you go up there, sir. It's soaked in an extract of lilac and alcohol and will serve to dull the...*ahem*...odors you will encounter on entering the ward. Some of those wounded men are in pretty rough condition."

Remembering the stench of the hospital wards from his first visit, Scrooge looked down at the patch of cloth in his hand and handed it back.

"I'm not here for pleasant purposes, my good man. I'll be fine," he said as he turned to ascend the staircase. Upon entering the ward on the second floor, he momentary gagged from the smells that assaulted his senses and made his eyes water, but proceeded forward with a resolute gait.

Walking up to an orderly, he asked, "Are there any wounded Coldstream veterans here who might be in proper condition to have a short conversation?"

The orderly pointed to the far corner of the ward, where a number of men lay on their cots or were propped up to speak with each other and avoid bed sores. Scrooge thanked him and strode over to the area indicated by the orderly.

"I beg your pardon, gentlemen, but the orderly said you were Coldstream veterans."

He was answered by a series of simultaneous grunts and eye rolls.

"You wouldn't know it by this place, sir," one amputee offered.

"Were any of you acquainted with a Captain Tristan Bainbridge?" Scrooge asked. That got their attention. At the mention of the name "Bainbridge," a number of the wounded veterans piped up quite vocally.

"Hello, sir! We served under Captain Bainbridge at the Battle of the Alma. He was quite the hero, that one was."

Scrooge ignored the stench and walked over to where the men lay in their beds.

"Hero? Please, I would like to know something about the manner of his passing, as the official record says he was rudely insubordinate to Prince George, the Duke of Cambridge, before receiving his mortal wounds. I am acquainted with his widow; she works as a nurse at the Royal Consumption Infirmary. I believe it would provide her with a measure of consolation to know of his bravery."

A sarcastic joker with a heavily scarred face several rows away piped up.

"What, his widow's a regular *Florence Nightingale?*" Bitter laughter ensued.

"Why, yes," Scrooge retorted. "She trained with Florence Nightingale in Germany to be a right proper nurse and now devotes her life to caring for people with consumption. With all due respect, young man, bravery comes in more ways than carrying a gun."

A lieutenant with a blood-stained bandage covering the right side of his scarred face spoke up.

"I knew Captain Tristan, sir. He was leading us in the fighting at the Alma River. The Russians were making their stand on the high ground south of the river. They must've had almost a hundred cannon up there."

Another wounded veteran spoke up.

"*A hundred?* More like one hundred and fifty, I recollect."

The lieutenant spoke up again. "It was a large, well-fortified enemy cannon redoubt guarded by at least a company of Russian snipers atop a small mountain, sir, giving us bloody murder despite the bombardment they were getting from the Royal Navy offshore. There was great confusion, seeing as our own Light Division charged up the hill before we did. The Light Division caught bloody murder from the Russian cannons, and they were counterattacked by a screaming battalion of bloody Russians with wicked sharp bayonets, if you'll pardon my speech."

Scrooge motioned for him to continue.

"Well, sir, it was at that moment the order was given for the Scots Fusilier Guards to charge uphill, but it was a mess of confusion because the Scottish Fusiliers ran straight away into our retreating boys of the Light Division. Soon, it was a helluva tough go telling the

Russians from the Englishmen. The Scots faltered but pressed on in a rather confused state.

"Meaning no disrespect, sir, but it was then that Prince George, the Duke of Cambridge himself, decided to observe the Russian cannon emplacements up close on horseback. It was a damn fool thing to do because decked out in his finery on that grand horse of his, he made a fine target for the Russian snipers guarding the cannons. Captain Bainbridge, seeing that the Russians could not fail to notice the prince, began arguing with him that he was in great danger. But Prince George insisted that the entire Allied attack was in danger of failing, and he ordered our troops, the 1st Battalion, Coldstream Guards, to charge the Russian cannon position from the left flank. His Highness was mighty frustrated and said he wasn't going to merely observe, but would lead the charge personally. Captain Bainbridge saw the foolishness of a member of the Royal Family putting themselves in harm's way for a dubious effort, so he grabbed the reins of the prince's horse, screaming and yelling like a madman that the prince was going to get himself killed. I swear, again, begging your pardon, sir, it was like Captain Bainbridge was bloody-well possessed by banshees, because a man in his right mind *would never* put his hands on a member of the royal family. The Duke was fit to be tied and struck at Captain Bainbridge with the flat of his cavalry saber. At that moment, the Russian guns opened up. Captain Bainbridge was yanking the prince off his mount when the Russian bullets meant for Prince George hit him instead. If not for Captain Bainbridge, Queen Victoria would be mourning the loss of her nephew. Despite being shot, Captain Bainbridge was still trying to rally Her Majesty's troops, but he took another bullet—this time in his thigh—and went down. Some of us endeavored to bandage him, but his bleeding was most fierce, sir. He died whispering the name *Allyce* over and over before his eyes went glassy."

"Damned right!" muttered an old sergeant in another bed. "If it weren't fer Captain Bainbridge, that idiot the Duke of Cambridge would be dead, and that bastard Prince Menshikov and the rest of his bloody Russians would be pissing down on us from atop that accursed hill! I say we lost the better man that day."

Scrooge bridled.

"What did His Highness do?"

The amputee sergeant snorted. "He galloped out of there as fast as his poor 'orse would carry him. He made sure the whole mess was hushed up because it wouldn't do for it to become public knowledge a lieutenant-general and nephew of Her Majesty had no more battlefield sense than a Yorkshire village idiot. It wasn't until the Coldstream boys carried the day that we found out, to save his own skin, the Duke of Cambridge was spreading the rubbish that Captain Bainbridge was guilty of assaulting a superior officer on the battlefield."

An hour later, a disheartened but determined Ebenezer Scrooge left the Royal Home of Convalescent Medicine with the names and ranks of the Coldstream Guards wounded who had dictated their testimony to hospital clerks about Captain Bainbridge's extraordinary bravery in the face of murderous Russian infantry fire. Allyce had indeed lost a *hero* and, in that moment, Ebenezer Scrooge felt like a very small man indeed.

Scrooge hired a carriage to the Parliament buildings for his appointment with Sidney Herbert that afternoon. After presenting his card to Herbert's secretary, Scrooge was ushered into his office.

Former Minister-at-War Sidney Herbert stood up from behind his desk and came around to greet Scrooge, extending his hand in greeting.

"I received a telegraphic message from Florence Nightingale that you would be seeking to meet with me today at my earliest possible opportunity, Mr. Scrooge. I have been in meetings all morning, so I apologize if I have kept you waiting." He held Florence's dispatch up in his hand, reading from it. "She says, '*Ebenezer is a man of sincere and noble intent. I have provided him with a personal letter of recommendation. If you should find yourself in agreement with my observations after meeting with him, I would greatly appreciate it, Sidney, if you would render all appropriate assistance he might request.*'"

Scrooge sat in silence as Herbert continued.

"She says you have organized a charitable effort on the part of a discreet group of London businessmen from the Royal London Exchange who go by the name the 'Honorable Society of Royal Medical Benefactors' and that you wish to improve the conditions of our wounded veterans from the Crimean campaign." He set the letter down on his desk. "Nasty business, that, but if we hadn't allied with the French Empire and the Turks, Czar Nicholas would have marched his armies to the tip of the Arabian Peninsula. The current round of the 'Great Game' would have left Her Majesty's empire in a most precarious position."

"I have just come from the Royal Home of Convalescent Medicine for Her Majesty's Soldiers and Sailors on Bletchley Common, Minister Herbert," Scrooge said. "I was speaking with some of the veterans there who fought in the Battle of the Alma. I must tell you, the conditions in that hospital make me ashamed to be an Englishman. The poor souls I was speaking with had a fine time watching this proper English gentleman do his best not to vomit at the conditions there. My God, man, I would lay money that there are regions of Hell itself that smell better than the pestilential air those men must breathe."

Herbert took on an embarrassed air before speaking again; it was obvious conditions at military hospitals were a sore point for him.

"I am not immune to nor ignorant of the suffering those men languishing there must endure, Mr. Scrooge. Miss Nightingale spent seven days a week down at Scutari during the war trying to improve their lot."

Scrooge realized that he had likely overstepped the bounds of propriety in his passion.

"I didn't mean to imply the situation there was your responsibility, Minister Herbert; please accept my apology."

Herbert looked up from the note again.

"Your words did not wound, nor did they insult me, Mr. Scrooge. I haven't heard of this 'Honorable Society of Royal Medical Benefactors.' Tell me, Mr. Scrooge, is your society seeking money to improve medical facilities? I must be direct with you, sir. If that is your intent, Miss Nightingale and I have been trying to correct the deplorable conditions in our military hospitals for several years now. We have met with precious little success, and the small-minded men in charge of the Royal Treasury are not a beneficent lot."

"No, Minister Herbert, we are not seeking money. We have already raised £120,000 from our personal resources and have the ability amongst ourselves to raise quite a bit more. No, Mini—"

Herbert interrupted him as he gestured for Scrooge to take a seat.

"Please call me Sidney, if I may call you Ebenezer," he said with a smile. "It is a singular privilege for *anyone* to receive an endorsement from Florence, so I treat it with the gravest urgency when she would deign to send me such a message. Florence said your number includes some of the most forthright individuals in our fair city; however, before I determine if there is any assistance I might render, I must know some of the personages among you. We cannot succeed cloaked in anonymity."

Scrooge folded his fingers under his chin in thought. He looked up and asked, "Do I have your word of honor that the identity of my associates will not leave this discussion?"

"Of course."

Scrooge appeared satisfied. "Our number, besides myself, includes John Delane, editor-in-chief of the *Times of London*. Another distinguished member is Sir Richard Mayne, head of the Metropolitan Police Department, and Neville Braithwaite, vicar of Saint Hubert's Church."

Herbert held his hand up.

"That is sufficient." His smile grew wider. "I am impressed, Ebenezer. Any man who can gain Florence's confidence *and* recruit John Delane and Sir Richard Mayne to his cause by moral suasion must be formidable indeed. Are you here to ask me to join your 'Honorable Society'? If so, I would certainly be honored."

Scrooge was momentarily flustered, thrown off balance by Sidney Herbert's offer. He hadn't considered that such a prestigious government minister would want to participate in the "Honorable Society," much less volunteer.

"I…I mean we…would be most honored if you would consent to participate in our endeavor, Sidney. It is not clandestine, but I must stress we do not seek to bring attention to ourselves. Florence told me that if our effort is to succeed, we must follow something she quoted from the Good Book: '*Therefore when thou doest thine alms, do not sound a trumpet before thee, as the hypocrites do in the synagogues and in the streets, that they may have glory of men. Verily I say unto you, They have their reward. But when thou doest alms, let not thy left hand know what thy right hand doeth: that thine alms may be in secret: and thy Father which seeth in secret himself shall reward thee openly.*'

"Sidney, we are not seeking praise or a cheering crowd; we only seek to relieve suffering," Scrooge continued. "It is not money we require. Florence and I agreed the best way you might assist us would be to use the authority of your office to cut through bureaucratic entanglements and the egos of the senior officials presiding over the hospitals most in need of repair and better sanitary conditions."

"Scutari..." Herbert said.

"I beg your pardon?"

"She is asking me to do here in London what she asked of me by letter while she was at Scutari Barracks Hospital. Every letter I received from her told of how Florence was constantly battling the egos of obtuse British Army doctors. Can you imagine men of high station would be so vain that they would feel threatened by a small band of women seeking to comfort the sick and dying? Why, the chief doctor down there assumed when she arrived that they were..."

"Prostitutes," Scrooge said, not mincing words.

Sidney Herbert nodded ruefully.

"Ebenezer, your little band of charitable conspirators has grown by one this day, with your permission of course. I should hear of it from Florence if I did not offer to join your efforts. Is there anything else I might assist you with?"

Scrooge pulled out notes he had written at his office before coming to Herbert's office, along with the sworn Coldstream veterans' testimonies, detailing the heroic exploits of Allyce's late husband, providing the names and ranks of the men who tried to outdo each other at the hospital in their praise of Bainbridge's exploits. Herbert held a hand up when he heard of the altercation between Captain Bainbridge and the Duke of Cambridge.

"That's not how the Duke speaks of the battle. He told some of us that an impertinent young officer tried to prevent him from leading a heroic charge against the Russians and that he would have had him brought up on charges in a court martial—but that the officer later died in the same battle."

Scrooge reddened as he fought to control his anger. He withdrew a fistful of letters from the Coldstream veterans fresh from his recent visit to their hospital that morning.

"Even allowing for some enthusiastic exaggeration on the part of the considerable number of surviving wounded from the Coldstream

1st Battalion," Scrooge pointedly said, "Captain Bainbridge's self-less heroism should not be wasted, nor his memory lost to posterity. Those men I spoke with this morning didn't have the time to concoct the story they all told me about what happened between the Duke of Cambridge and the late Captain Bainbridge. It's obvious Prince George concocted his calumny against the captain to salvage his own reputation. We are seeking to clear his name and see what sort of posthumous honor might be accorded to Captain Tristan Bainbridge. Clearly, he saved the life of a member of the royal family and played a singular, pivotal role in the victory at the Battle of the Alma."

"That will require considerable thought, Ebenezer. I cannot confer honors and privileges upon a military officer, as I no longer hold the position of Minister-at-War. By tradition, those honors are bestowed by Her Majesty, Queen Victoria. I cannot promise anything, but I shall see what I can do. I know *I* do not possess the fortitude to lead a charge against a Russian cannon emplacement defended by the Czar's riflemen." Herbert smiled conspiratorially. "For that matter, I've met Prince George and cannot picture him charging headlong into anything other than the general officers' mess hall for dinner. I can easily see him speaking ill of a dead officer if it would spare him humiliation in front of Her Majesty his aunt."

Scrooge stood up to shake Herbert's hand.

"Captain Bainbridge's widow, Allyce, works at the Royal Consumption Infirmary on a pittance to provide for her children."

"Not that pestilence hole where Ainsley Northrup is the administrator?"

Scrooge gave a grim, if satisfied, smile. "*Was*…Northrup *was* the administrator until he was arrested by Scotland Yard a few days ago on charges of embezzling from the Crown. I am told Sir Richard Mayne led the arresting officers himself."

"Was that arrest orchestrated by the 'Honorable Society,' Ebenezer?"

"No, our little group doesn't have that kind of authority, but consider that Sir Richard is a member of our organization. His men had been keeping a close eye on discrepancies between the funds sent by the Royal Treasury for the general upkeep of the hospital and the actual conditions at the Royal Consumption Infirmary. It was only a matter of patient detective work, combined with Northrup's arrogance and love of spirits, before the entire plot was revealed."

"Hold up just a moment, Ebenezer." Herbert walked over to a large, locked secretary desk in the corner of his office and, taking a key from his vest pocket, unlocked the central drawer. He counted out ten sovereigns from an inner, separate locked drawer and, sitting back down at his desk, took his fountain pen and scribbled a short note.

To Allyce Bainbridge, from a mutual friend aware of your late husband's sacrifice and heroism. I do hope your situation and the grieving in your heart are daily improved. —S. H.

Placing the note and coins in a small purse, he reached to hand them to Scrooge, who read the note and politely demurred.

"I cannot deliver that to the widow Bainbridge, Sidney. It is quite impossible."

"Whatever do you mean, Ebenezer?" asked a perplexed Herbert.

"Years ago, I was a suitor of Allyce, and we were engaged to be married. In my ignorance and blind greed, I broke her heart. To this day, it pains me to admit it, but that is the truth of the matter, and it was only then I learned the most bitter medicine a man may swallow in life is regret. If I give her your gift, it would be seen as a blatant attempt at ingratiating myself, and I have no intention of doing that," Scrooge explained.

"I see your predicament," Herbert said. "Very well. If she would not accept this from you, she would without question accept it from her 'sister' in Derbyshire. The widow Bainbridge could not possibly discern an ulterior motive in *that*." He tore up the first note he had written. "I must make a better showing than that if I am to prove myself a worthy member of the 'Honorable Society,' eh?" he said with a conspiratorial wink.

Herbert reached for his pen again.

Allyce, I ask you to accept this small token of appreciation from a mutual friend of ours, B. S. H., who is mindful of your late husband's sacrifice and heroism. He prays your situation and the grieving in your heart are daily improved. I think of you daily and hope to visit London within the month. I should like to see you when I do.

With deepest affection, your friend,
Florence

Handing it to Scrooge, Herbert smiled in triumph.

"What do you think of *that*?"

Scrooge stood there with a puzzled look on his face.

Herbert said, "I'm sending this note and the money to Florence at Lea Hurst. She in turn will have it delivered to Allyce by special courier at the Royal Consumption Infirmary. I shall send Florence a telegraphic dispatch today with a proper explanation. There is no way Allyce will connect these funds to you and, having some knowledge of the paltry sum people in her station are paid, I am certain it will be appreciated. Keep in mind, Ebenezer, Florence and I had recourse to subterfuge *many times* while she was battling the insufferable Army doctors at Scutari and the British military bureaucracy back here. She will immediately divine my purpose behind this."

"That is most generous of you, Sidney."

Sidney Herbert clapped him on the back. "Our friend Florence is not the only person who can put scripture to good use. I believe there's also a passage saying, '*Be ye therefore wise as serpents, and harmless as doves.*'"

As Scrooge began to leave, before reaching the door, he turned around.

"Sidney, it was my sincere honor to make your acquaintance. I am in your debt, sir—your debt and Florence's as well."

Sidney Herbert gave the slightest bow.

"The pleasure is mine, Ebenezer. I will instruct my secretary that all communications from you on behalf of the 'Honorable Society' are to be brought to my immediate attention. You have my word that they will be treated with the utmost discretion."

16

A SACRIFICE MONEY CANNOT BUY

Scrooge left the Parliament buildings in high spirits after meeting with Government Minister Herbert and began walking back to his house on Belgrave Square. He had entered the Parliament's grand buildings expecting to have a somewhat formal meeting with the former Minister-at-War but did not expect to encounter a sympathetic soul and new friend. Allyce aside, Scrooge's newfound passion for Her Majesty's wounded veterans had put a determined stride in his step and lent him a vitality of purpose he hadn't felt in years.

The realization dawned on him it was not enough to abide by the meaning of Christmas each day of the year with a cheerful disposition, but if one were given the means and opportunity, it was important to *make the difference for the good happen* in the lives of the less fortunate. As winning back Allyce's affections were never far from his thoughts, Scrooge pondered the enigmatic words of Marley's ghost, *"You must be prepared to sacrifice greatly to obtain that which your gold cannot buy."* How was this possibly bound up in the fate of Peter and Charlotte Cratchit? On a sudden whim, while walking past the Whistling Kettle Pub, Scrooge decided to let Mrs. Dilber rest for the evening and not have to fret about preparing him a proper dinner. Upon entering the pub, he scribbled a quick note to Mrs. Dilber and, handing a messenger boy half a crown, sent him on his way.

As he made his way toward an empty table in the bustling eatery, he heard a familiar voice call out, "Hello, *Ebenezer!*"

Scrooge looked around and saw a fellow member of the Honorable Society of Royal Medical Benefactors, Reverend Neville Braithwaite, waving him over to his table. A man Scrooge didn't recognize sat with Reverend Braithwaite.

"Good evening, Neville." Scrooge smiled. "I trust you are well. Please, do not let me interrupt your dinner, gentlemen."

"No, Ebenezer, please join us. I insist."

Despite Scrooge's protestations, turning to his dinner guest, Reverend Braithwaite said, "Michel, I would like to introduce you to a good friend of mine, Mr. Ebenezer Scrooge. He's part of the efforts I told you of earlier to improve the lot of Her Majesty's military veterans wounded in the Crimean War."

Reverend Braithwaite's dinner companion stood up and reached across the table to shake Scrooge's hand.

"It is a pleasure to meet y'all, Mr. Scrooge. The name's Michel St. Tutelairé, and I represent Bennington, Vermont's Sturdy Eagle Fine Wood Products Company. We're a lumber and millwork cooperative in New England, and I'm their European sales and supply representative."

"Your servant, sir." Scrooge clasped St. Tutelairé's surprisingly firm grip, as Michel St. Tutelairé looked as though he didn't weigh more than 140 pounds. "I beg your pardon, Mr. St. Tutelairé, but I couldn't help noticing your accent. Are you from the United States yourself?"

"Yes, I am, Mr. Scrooge. I hail from Savannah, Georgia, by way of Bennington, Vermont. It throws people off when they hear my American southern accent and then I tell them I'm from Vermont." There was a mischievous twinkle in St. Tutelairé's eyes. Michel St. Tutelairé was a tall, thin, impeccably-dressed man in his mid-thirties, with long, slicked-back blond hair and penetrating icy blue eyes who spoke with the easy, relaxed southern accent of his native Georgia. He exuded an aura of calm confidence.

After the men ordered their meals, Reverend Braithwaite asked Scrooge, "Are you quite all right? You look troubled, my friend." Braithwaite saw Scrooge cast a quick glance over at Michel St. Tutelairé. "Ebenezer, you needn't worry about Michel here; he's the soul of discretion. He's a good friend who shows up from time to time when he's in London running about doing whatever he does for his carpentry firm." Something in St. Tutelairé's reassuring grin put Scrooge at ease.

Scrooge cocked his head. "Neville, how did a right proper Anglican vicar come to be friends with an American lumber representative?" Scrooge was puzzled.

St. Tutelairé gave an easy chuckle.

"I'm a longtime student of Gothic church architecture, Mr. Scrooge," he said. "Neville here caught me skulking around his church a few years ago, as Saint Hubert's is one of the few churches in London proper that survived King Henry VIII's wrath intact. It was known for the Legend of the Sword of Saint Michael back then."

"The Sword of Saint Michael?" Scrooge asked.

St. Tutelairé nodded. "Most people have forgotten it. In October 1479, a great plague ravaged all of Britain for an entire year and tens of thousands of people died in London alone. Then, a small child said he beheld a great angel in armor holding a great shining sword over the main altar while pastor was leading the congregation in the Litany of the Angels. In his innocence, the child asked the angel who he was. The angel announced himself as Saint Michael, and he told the young boy that God had heard the prayers of the English people and that the plague would end in one month. It so happens that the plague ended one month later in October 1480."

"I never heard of that legend, Michel," said Reverend Braithwaite, "but then again, there have been many plagues to strike our fair isle, and many of the parish histories were destroyed when the Church of England was established, and the Dominican friars were sent packing back to their Roman hideouts."

Scrooge saw the briefest shadow cross Michel St. Tutelairé's face at the reference to "Roman hideouts." He sensed perhaps it was a rare topic of discord between these two friends, so Scrooge adroitly changed the conversation. Perhaps St. Tutelairé was Catholic and took offense?

"Well, I might as well tell you both, if you don't mind listening to a knotty situation I find myself in," Scrooge said. "I would appreciate your insights." He paused. "But I must warn you that you may think me a candidate for the madhouse by the end of my tale."

Scrooge waited until the waiter pouring the wine left the table before continuing. He began telling his dinner companions much of what he had related to Florence Nightingale about his visions during the "Night of the Ghosts" long ago.

St. Tutelairé spoke.

"But I take it the visits of this vision from beyond turned y'all away from the wicked path you were on and in a more helpful direction, Mr. Scrooge? If everything worked out for the best, why do you look so worried?"

Scrooge glanced from man to man as if unsure of whether he should continue. Braithwaite saw the mental anguish flitting across Ebenezer's face and said, "You're among friends. I daresay, given what you've said up to this point, you couldn't scandalize us if you wanted to."

He urged Scrooge, "You said the visions from beyond succeeded in persuading you to reform your life, but I sense there is something of it still troubling you."

Sensing that dissembling would not help his cause, Scrooge said, "Neville, the other day when I stopped in Saint Hubert's to mull things over in a quiet place for a bit, I beheld Jacob Marley again in your church."

"Indeed!"

Scrooge looked from face to face, but neither man betrayed any sign of disbelief; instead, they were caught up in rapt attention, so he kept going.

"Jacob said in bringing forth the Ghost of Christmas Love to Allyce that fate has decreed it is also bound up in the destiny of Peter Cratchit and his wife, Charlotte. To what end I do not know. He said, and I repeat this as well as I may recollect his words, '*Even now the Reaper beckons to her from both consumption and a mortal danger arising from the lust for riches that once held me in thrall.*' He said young Peter Cratchit was hurtling along the same road to perdition I once trod in ignorance; therefore, according to Marley's words, I must do for him as Jacob once did for me.

"At any rate, Peter has been away on business for several months now, and Jacob Marley's spirit was quite correct. When I visited Charlotte in hospital, she bade me read his letters to her. I hesitated, thinking they would be too intimate for my eyes, but she begged me to read them. At first, Peter's letters home were filled with his longing to be with his wife and family again, but over time, the letters came to be dominated more and more by talk of money and the great wealth Peter stands to gain if this 'grand contract' he spoke of is won. His first few letters spoke of his emptiness of heart and strong home-sickness, but as Peter grew accustomed to the luxuries showered on him, the letters have spoken of the riches he stands to gain and what it shall do for their station in life. To make matters worse, from the tone of some of the more recent letters, it would seem young Peter has been tempted to infidelity as well."

Reverend Braithwaite spoke. "I'm confused, Ebenezer. Why does Charlotte's husband write her letters? If you can visit her in hospital, then surely he can as well, no matter where in England he may be visiting for business. Surely his boss would permit him to take a day or two off once in a while given Charlotte's illness, no?"

Nodding toward Michel St. Tutelairé, Scrooge continued: "I forgot to tell you Peter is in America on an extended business trip for his employer, Sir Nigel Fairweather-Hawthorne, owner of Hawthorne and Cavendish Fine Furniture and Carpentry Works. It seems there is a huge business contract brewing with the Royal Admiralty Board that Sir Nigel has taken a very keen interest in and has sent Peter Cratchit to the United States to oversee whether the American end of the prospective business arrangement has merit. Peter is now the guest of Sir Nigel's American business partner, the president and owner of the New York and Pennsylvania Coal and Lumber Company, a Mr. Cyrus Abernathy. From Charlotte's observation, this Cyrus Abernathy is not only powerful in American business circles, but is also an immensely disagreeable sort of person. For Charlotte to even hint at that means he is quite likely a tyrannical character."

At the mention of Cyrus Abernathy, Scrooge could have sworn he saw an unnerving light momentarily gleam in St. Tutelairé's eyes, but chalked it up to the heady wine. St. Tutelairé then sighed, his countenance darkening. He shook his head and remarked, "I know Cyrus Abernathy quite well, Ebenezer. Abernathy is a vile man, one of the few I have ever encountered without redeeming qualities or honor."

Reverend Braithwaite looked up, stunned at the sharp condemnation of Abernathy by his friend.

"Michel! You can't mean that. As Ebenezer has shown us, even the hardest of hearts can reform their ways."

St. Tutelairé uncharacteristically shook his head in rare disagreement.

"No, Neville. I have crossed swords, so to speak, with Cyrus Abernathy on several occasions and I fear he bears no benevolence toward any man, only his own bank accounts and business fortunes. I say again that he is a man without redeeming qualities. In fact, if a business arrangement worth a great deal of money is at stake here, then I have no doubt the 'temptation to infidelity' Peter's wife frets over is his daughter, Livinia. She's a regular Salome to Cyrus Abernathy's Herod.

"She is a most beautiful, headstrong woman, with a mercenary personality molded by the upbringing of her greedy, rapacious father and timid mother. Cyrus has catered to Livinia's every whim her entire life, so her sense of entitlement is boundless. She sees how her father uses people until they are of no further utility and then he discards them and, observing the material benefits of such a manipulative attitude, she has grown up imitating him. Livinia is much sought after for marriage by New York City's most eligible bachelors; however, despite her physical beauty, her heart is as icy as her father's. It too would take a great sacrifice to melt it. In fact, Ebenezer, much as the spirit you beheld in Neville's church told you about trying to change Allyce's heart with a sacrifice that cannot be purchased, I'm afraid only a similar selfless sacrifice might free Livinia from the grasp her father holds over her heart."

Scrooge said, "So you can begin to see the depths of my predicament; my conundrum about Allyce remains. I have already put my wealth and profits to good use to better the condition of my fellow man when and where I can. But if not my fortune, what in the world *can* I sacrifice to obtain what my gold cannot buy?"

The three men ate their meal in silence while they pondered Scrooge's question.

Reverend Braithwaite looked up with a start.

"Ebenezer, I think I may have the answer to your conundrum! My friend, perhaps you've been looking at this from the wrong end of the telescope, so to speak. If young Peter Cratchit has been trapped by greed and infidelity, the only way you might free him from these snares could be if you *appear* to revert to your miserly former self. I'll also wager there is not a prospective contract with the Admiralty that our friend in the 'Honorable Society' John Delane hasn't heard of with his newspaper connections.

"Once we determine exactly what this Admiralty Board business actually is, *you* could compete for the contract against Peter's employer, Sir Nigel, and that American tyrant, Cyrus Abernathy. Mind you, you will need to beat Abernathy at his own game and *appear* to callously treat Peter Cratchit as your pawn. I have no doubt that soon enough, tongues in London will wag that your change of heart was a mere expedient. Don't you see? Those things could be what you must be willing to sacrifice: your good name, your honor, and the reputation you've worked so hard to rebuild. Money cannot buy respect, only fear, just as it cannot buy love. Look at Nigel Fairweather-Hawthorne or Cyrus Abernathy."

Scrooge looked to Michel St. Tutelairé.

"You say you met this Abernathy fellow, Mr. St. Tutelairé. What do you think of Neville's plan?"

Tutelairé said, "Please, call me Michel, if I may call you Ebenezer."

Scrooge nodded as St. Tutelairé continued: "Sir Nigel and Cyrus Abernathy could each afford to buy half of London, yet as Neville says, neither is respected, only feared. I have known Abernathy for many years, and he will stop at nothing to get what he wants— including dangling his daughter like bait on a fishhook before Peter.

"Neville's plan has considerable merit, but do not doubt me, Ebenezer; it will be a *very* hard thing you must do. You must be prepared to be made an object of contempt and derision in London again. I have no doubt that Allyce will hear of your apparent reversion to greed and wickedness in pursuit of riches, and it will only harden her further against you. But once you beat Sir Nigel and Abernathy at their own game and have Peter Cratchit take the blame for the failure of whatever scheme they are hatching, I have no doubt Sir Nigel Fairweather-Hawthorne will kick Peter to the gutter before you can say 'lickety-split.'"

Reverend Braithwaite glanced at Scrooge and smirked as if to say "*these Americans*" but concurred with St. Tutelairé. "Yes, my friend, I think you must be willing to risk humiliating Peter Cratchit before the London business community, and you will again be the heartless, conniving miser of days gone by; you will sacrifice your good name and a significant portion of your business. Contracts *will* be canceled, notes *will* be called due, and you *must* be ready to embrace Lady Poverty. Therein may lie *your* sacrifice money cannot buy."

Before Scrooge could object, Reverend Braithwaite continued: "If this Ghost of Christmas Love perchance manifests only by a great sacrifice on your part, I have no doubt this may indeed do the trick. Short of losing your life, there is not much else you could give up."

At the mention of the Ghost of Christmas Love, the tiniest hint of a smile played about Michel St. Tutelairé's face, unnoticed by either of his dinner companions.

"Look, Ebenezer, once Peter faces destitution and has learned his lesson, our 'Honorable Society of Royal Medical Benefactors' will find him gainful employment and a position that will keep him close to his wife," Reverend Braithwaite said. Gesturing skyward with a bony finger, he continued: "If what you beheld in my church was of Divine Providence, despite any necessary subterfuge the effort may entail, only good will come from your effort. I've known Allyce since she was a child while I was a sexton at Saint Mary's Church in Ilford, and healing her broken heart *will* take a miracle, and though a kind, selfless woman of deep faith, she is very headstrong. But remember, *my* business *is* believing in miracles."

"You know, Ebenezer," said a thoughtful St. Tutelairé, "it occurs to me there is another way you could make a great sacrifice that your riches cannot purchase without going to such elaborate lengths to sully your name."

Scrooge leaned forward across the oak table.

"Well, out with it, man!"

"Very well," said St. Tutelairé. "I would ask you to consider the idea that all of your efforts to bring Allyce back into your life may come to naught, even if perchance you unlock the secret to having the Ghost of Christmas Love brought to Allyce and he releases her heart from the pain she carries. You should consider a possibility you may not have thought of even if your endeavor is successful. *What if you succeed in bringing the capacity for happiness and true love back into Allyce's life, but her heart chooses another?* Knowing human nature as I do, your own heart would be crushed, and no amount of money would ease *that* pain. That is truly the sacrifice all of your gold cannot purchase. You could always recover your good name in time, but knowing you could well lose Allyce's heart to another suitor forever, would you *still* try to unburden Allyce of her sadness? Especially if it meant losing her *twice*? After all, no matter your actions, her free will is still her own."

The contrast of altruism versus selfishness of the heart hung heavily over the rest of the dinner conversation and lingered in Scrooge's mind far into the night. Would he still try to set Allyce's heart free even if, like a bird whose broken wing was healed, she flew into the arms of another man once her own heart could love again?

His love for Allyce decided the issue. Scrooge would try whatever it took to heal her heart, even if she ultimately chose the arms of another man. Otherwise, Allyce would merely be a prize, not a precious woman to love and cherish.

17 ❧

WHEN GOD AND
DESIRE COLLIDE

Sunday, October 12, 1856, dawned a glorious, unusually warm autumn day in New York City. As a day of rest, the innumerable horses and carriages on Manhattan's bustling streets were far fewer in both number and clamor; a pall of sleepiness lay over the city like a fine silk sheet. Peter awoke at his customary 7 a.m. and quickly dressed to slip out to attend church services. He had stumbled upon a small High-Church Anglican parish on 29th Street back in July, the Episcopal Church of the Transfiguration, while on a getting-acquainted-with-Manhattan tour with Livinia. On a whim, to her annoyance, he had stopped the carriage and bid Livinia and the driver to wait a few moments while he went inside. Livinia, in a fit of pique, ordered the carriage driver to drive off and left Peter to find his way back to the Abernathy residence three hours later, sweaty and tired, having gotten thoroughly lost in Manhattan.

Finding the front door unlocked, Peter entered the dim church to find a clergyman who introduced himself as the Reverend Dr. George Hendric Houghton. Dr. Houghton was a kind, white-bearded spirit as welcoming as the quaint little church he presided over. Transfiguration was a small, unpretentious church designed in the Neo-Gothic style of a modest English country parish, complete with a spacious, airy rose garden that immediately enchanted Peter. It would also prove to be an England-in-miniature for the occasionally homesick Peter.

However, this day would prove to be more than merely a test of wills between Peter and Livinia. While it didn't altogether reverse Peter's growing greed, it set in motion the reversal of his views of Abernathy as a benevolent, quasi-father figure and Livinia as a cunning, beautiful minx.

When he reached the first floor at 7:30 a.m., while Abernathy and Gertrude were still fast asleep, he was startled to find Livinia waiting by the front door to the mansion in one of her more form-flattering dresses, her hair worn straight, twirling a lady's parasol.

"Livinia," Peter asked, "what are you doing awake so early? It's *Sunday.* Not even the house staff is awake yet."

"I've decided to accompany you to services this morning. Father and Mother go to church only at Christmas and Easter, and I'm *bored* to tears. I thought perhaps I might learn why you go week after week, and if it could perhaps profit *me?*" she asked disingenuously. "You know very well Father does not hold with what he calls 'all that angels and incense rubbish,' so I thought I might go with you if you don't mind the company," Livinia said, twirling her sun umbrella.

Of course, Livinia was again lying and playing on Peter's loneliness to find yet another excuse to be with him, as the riches promised to her by her father were never far from her mind. For his part, Peter was too enthused that a member of the aloof Abernathy family had deigned to accompany him to Sunday services to give any thought to Livinia's motives.

Once they arrived at the Church of the Transfiguration, Peter escorted Livinia inside. Throughout the service, Peter paid careful attention to the Reverend Houghton expounding on the wedding feast at Cana. At the same time, Livinia sat and did her best to look simultaneously bored *and* alluring—a feat not easily pulled off. She caught the roving eye of more than one man among the worshipers, as the stunning daughter of Cyrus Abernathy was a beautiful jewel for the male gaze.

Since it was still an early hour when the service ended, Peter and Livinia took a roundabout way back to the Abernathy mansion in the carriage. After some minutes of small talk, Livinia could no longer hold her tongue or curiosity.

"Peter," she asked, "do you think I'm pretty?"

Peter, caught off guard, turned a deep red at being put on the spot and pondered her question. Livinia interpreted his hesitation as evasion.

"Peter," Livinia said as she turned to face him with a sly smile, "if you should like to kiss me here in the carriage, no one but us would know of it. Not Father, not Mother, and not...*Charlotte*."

Peter was stunned at her brazen invitation to infidelity, but he was also homesick and ached for someone to confide in. Since he had arrived in New York, his conversations had revolved around business. He had no friends in America to speak of, no one to unburden himself to, for that matter.

"Livinia, I think you're quite lovely, and you certainly make for a quite, ah, *interesting* social partner, but you must remember I *am* a married man and have to think of..." Peter was in the process of coming up with a suitably polite rebuke when a loud noise spooked the horses and the carriage hit a bump in the road. Livinia was tossed close against him. Peter felt the warmth of her breath and the delicate scent of her rosewater perfume. But instead of pulling away when the opportunity presented itself, Livinia instead made her move, passionately kissed Peter on the mouth, and lasciviously swept her tongue across Peter's lips as she pulled away.

When she pulled back with a triumphant look glittering in her eyes, her face was as flushed as Peter's, but for a different reason. Livinia was confident that she had broken through Peter's moral defenses. Poor Peter was immediately gripped by deep remorse at having been trapped into a compromising situation by Livinia, who used a ruse of accompanying him to church, of all places, to get him to lower his guard. Not that *he* had initiated the kiss—far from it—but such a minor difference wouldn't matter to the conniving Livinia. From that point on, Peter feared Livinia would redouble her efforts to add him to her list of romantic "conquests," given the challenge he posed, not to mention the opportunity for blackmail the situation presented.

As she was considered New York City's most eligible, beautiful socialite, Livinia had her share of dalliances with wealthy married men in New York. Still, there was a particular satisfaction she took in setting her sights on a married man with a moral shell around his heart who seemed immune to her wiles. The material inducements from her father aside, Peter Cratchit *was* a very appealing challenge. Livinia always won out in the end; it was only her devious stratagems that differed.

"Livinia," Peter haltingly said. "Please accept my apology. I did not mean to be so...*forward* with you." His gallant admission of being at fault was his first mistake.

Her response took him off guard, especially her high-pitched girlish giggle.

"Oh, Peter, you and your high-minded morality. It was just an accidental kiss." Livinia decided to slip her verbal dagger into Peter's conscience a little further to satisfy her cruelty. "Don't be such a prude; I rather enjoyed it. I may even permit you to kiss me again," she said with an inviting smile.

Peter felt a momentary flush of panic at Livinia's response to his apology. He was so flustered with confusion that he didn't even try to point out that Livinia had kissed *him*, not the other way around, but he was still mortified. He had been unintentionally unfaithful to his wife, but nevertheless, Peter was very ashamed. He was convinced Livinia would in time tell her father or Charlotte. She also wasn't above dangling the *threat* of telling them over his head like the Sword of Damocles, much the way a fox will toy with a rabbit before moving in for the kill.

Arriving back at the mansion, Peter and Cyrus eventually retired to Abernathy's palatial library for their Sunday review of the new week's planned activities. Peter waited until Jefferson had secured the library doors and Livinia had left on an afternoon outing with some of her wealthy friends.

"Sir," Peter began haltingly. He felt his face reddening in a combination of humiliation and embarrassment.

Abernathy knew straight away something was amiss, as much by Peter addressing him as "sir" as by Livinia's gleeful attitude at breakfast, where she had patted Peter's forearm and announced to the family that she would from now on "take great spiritual consolation in accompanying Peter to Sunday services." This statement alone drew a guffaw from Abernathy.

"Livinia," he said, "I'm just surprised the holy water didn't burn your fingers when you entered the church."

Back in his library, as they pored over the contract figures, after several obvious mistakes by Peter, Abernathy finally reached the limits of his patience.

"*Out with it, Peter.* You have a look about you like a prisoner at the Tombs facing the hangman's noose," he said, referring to New York City's infamous jail in the notorious Five Points neighborhood.

Peter began, his words halting and hesitant: "After we took our leave of the good Reverend Houghton after services, on the way back here, the horses were spooked by another animal or perhaps a gunshot, and the carriage was thrown violently to one side, as were I and Miss Livinia. We were thrown together in the tumult, and I kissed her. I must admit that although it was quite a pleasant kiss, Mr. Abernathy, I mean *sir*, er, *Cyrus*, I want to assure you that I would *never* take advantage of Livinia's virtue in such a manner. After all, I *am* a married man and a Christian gentleman." Peter was shaking in trepidation and tripping over his words, as lying did not come easily to him. Still, his code of honor would not permit him to betray a woman—not even the conniving Livinia—no matter how provocative and inappropriate her actions were.

Abernathy couldn't contain the mirth building within him and he loosed an uproarious gale of laughter, which only confounded Peter even further. When Abernathy did stop shaking with laughter, he wiped the tears of incredulity from his eyes and asked, "Peter, are you sure it was *you* who kissed Livinia and not the other way around?"

Hesitating, Peter stared disconsolately at his shoes. "Yes, sir..."

"Come now, Peter. The situation cannot be as bad as you make it out to be," Abernathy said.

He stared at Peter in bemusement as his guest continued:

"As you know, sir, I am *deeply* devoted to my wife, and again, I *did not* mean to act in such an untoward manner toward your daughter," Peter declared, his feigned indignation building.

Abernathy thought, *There is no way that Peter would kiss Livinia, at least in the way he described it happening; it's not in his character. He's also a terrible liar.* He resolved to let the matter go. However, upon seeing that a distracted, distraught Peter was unable to concentrate on the critical contract negotiation details Abernathy was depending on him to have memorized for the coming week's meetings, he soon realized that whatever happened on the carriage ride back from church that morning had been more than just an accidental kiss. Abernathy would have a full accounting of it from his daughter post-haste.

Finally, after Peter made yet another glaring error tabulating net acreage of southern live oak required for a full re-hulling of a 121-gun *Royal Albert* class ship-of-the-line, Abernathy realized whatever fun and games Livinia was up to on her own had now gone beyond his *modus vivendi* with his daughter and jeopardized Peter's reason for being in New York in the first place. He saw Peter's hand trembling and realized something had to be done.

"Peter, I know you're an honorable lad and a gentleman to boot," he said. He poured the normally abstinent Peter a stiff shot of single-malt scotch and, as he handed it to Peter, boomed, "Drink!"

Peter did as Abernathy commanded and sputtered his way through tossing back the whiskey in a single swallow.

"Now, in this matter of kissing Livinia, I will take care of it. I can't have a momentary fixation with my daughter's games interfering with our work. You have my word, Peter; *nothing* will come of this incident."

And you're a terrible liar, Mr. Cratchit, even if you think you're defending Livinia's honor. She knows her place in my little plan, and I won't have her messing it up by taking things too far before I am fully prepared, Abernathy silently concluded.

Somewhat reassured, Peter did his best to focus on the matters at hand.

Cyrus Abernathy was not a man to let things linger, especially anything that touched on critical business affairs. First, he summoned his Sunday carriage driver, who confirmed that there had been a gunshot near 31st Street and Madison Square Park, which startled the horses, causing the carriage to jerk with some violence to one side.

"Mr. Williams, after you drove Livinia and Mr. Cratchit to church, what did you do while they were inside at the services?" Abernathy asked.

"Well, sir, seeing as it was Sunday and there was no traffic on the street, I lock-tied the carriage team to one of the iron hitch posts in front of the church. Then I went and stood in the back of the church to hear the good reverend preach."

"What did he talk about today, Mr. Williams?" Abernathy asked.

"Well, sir, he spoke at length about the Lord's first public miracle when He changed the water to wine at the wedding feast."

Satisfied his chauffeur was telling the truth, Abernathy dismissed him.

At dinner that evening, a subdued Peter kept his eyes lowered to his plate, speaking and eating little, while Livinia was the very picture of animated excitement and triumphant confidence. She was unprepared for the verbal and physical ambush to follow. Abernathy didn't often have the chance to put his headstrong daughter in her place, no matter her importance to his plans.

"Livinia, Peter tells me you had an exciting ride home from church this morning," Abernathy said. "Why don't you tell your mother and me about it?" The question had more of a commanding air to it than an inquiry.

Taken off guard, Livinia blushed and blurted out, "Well, Father, if you must know, we were riding home as pretty as you please and enjoying a discussion on the Sunday sermon when out of the blue, Peter kissed me!"

Her mother's eyebrow arched at her daughter's statement. She was only too aware of her daughter's reputation as a flirtatious tease.

"He just leaned over while we were riding home in the carriage, put his hands on me in quite the rough fashion, and kissed me in an impure manner, right on the mouth," Livinia sputtered in mock outrage. "I tried to push him away, but he was most insistent on taking liberties with me while we were alone! Only when I threatened to scream for the carriage driver did he finally desist."

Peter's jaw dropped at the boldness of Livinia's lie, but Abernathy acted before he could even draw a breath.

Two things told Abernathy his intuition about Peter being the innocent party was right. First, even as she embellished her lie in detail, Livinia's complexion turned an ever-deeper shade of red.

Second, Peter did not speak up or even attempt to defend himself. From his time spent with Peter, Abernathy knew Peter's outmoded English chivalry would not permit him to accuse a woman of lying, even in his own defense.

"So that's it, then? You discussed the sermon, and Peter grabbed you and rudely kissed you, eh? He took advantage of your virtue in a moment of weakness?"

"That's *just* what happened, Father. I was quite outraged." She sniffed.

For a young woman who had suffered such an indignity, Livinia was in high spirits, even as Abernathy went in for the rhetorical kill.

His voice lowering an octave in menace, he asked, "Livinia, what was the Sunday sermon you were talking to Peter in the carriage about?"

"Well, Father," she faltered, realizing she had fallen into a trap of her own making. "We were talking about the Sermon on the Mount in the gospel of Mark and the importance of humility—"

Abernathy interrupted her.

"Come here, Livinia," he said in a low tone.

Obeying immediately, Livinia turned on her sense of aggrieved charm as she bounced to his side.

"Yes, Father?" she asked.

His open palm moved with a speed Peter's eyes didn't even have time to register. Abernathy slapped Livinia's delicate face so hard it left a red welt.

"*Liar!*" her father roared. "Today's scriptures were from the book of John the Evangelist, and the subject was the wedding feast at Cana. When Peter and I discussed our plans for the forthcoming week's meetings, I asked him if he had heard anything at church I might profit from. He told me the subject of the reverend's sermon, and if you had been paying attention, young lady, you'd have known that as well. Shall I summon Reverend Houghton as well to see who is telling the truth?"

While tears of pain and humiliation cascaded down her cheeks, Livinia attempted a feeble defense.

"P-p-perhaps Peter is conspiring to make me out to be a liar," she stammered while imperceptibly trying to move out of range of her father's meaty hand. For the first time in the months since his arrival in the Abernathy household, Peter saw real fear in Livinia's eyes. She was no longer the brash, arrogant woman desired by men; at that moment, Peter saw nothing more than a terrified little girl.

Abernathy was now convinced that whatever had happened in the carriage, it was *not* Peter's doing, despite Peter's earlier gallant attempt to take the blame. The chauffeur did not know Abernathy had asked Peter the topic of the sermon as well, so there was zero likelihood of collusion between the two of them. Enraged that his daughter had dared lie to *him* of all people, Cyrus Abernathy pushed back from the table, rising to his full seven-foot height. What happened next was a blur.

As he sputtered in inchoate rage, Abernathy pulled back his arm to strike his daughter again, and Livinia's terror rooted her feet to the floor, unable to move. Peter instinctively sensed the next blow from her father would *seriously* hurt Livinia. He leaped out of his seat to intervene between Abernathy and his daughter, and this time Abernathy's hand was balled into a fist the size of a small melon as he yelled at his daughter, "You lying little trollop!" The blow meant for Livinia caught Peter full in the face, breaking his nose and knocking him unconscious. Before he even hit the floor, a bright crimson spray erupted from his face, arcing across the dinner table linens and Livinia's ivory dress as she screamed and fled the room.

Stunned by the unexpected turn of events, Abernathy could only stare down at an unconscious Peter Cratchit lying prone at his feet as his face bled profusely onto the polished hardwood floor, while his wife called for the servants to bring ice and clean towels. Abernathy was momentarily flummoxed; he hadn't foreseen that Peter's chivalry would compel him to defend Livinia at his own personal risk. Unable or unwilling to justify his violence, he angrily stalked from the dining room, roaring Livinia's name. Moments later, the heavy slam of his library pocket doors echoed throughout the mansion.

For all her cunning, a dazed Livinia Abernathy knew when she was beaten. Under normal circumstances, she would have fainted dead away at the sight of so much blood pouring from Peter's damaged face, had her own instinct for self-preservation not kicked in. Her heart pounded in mortal terror as she listened from her temporary refuge in the kitchen while her father angrily stormed by on the way to his library, roaring her name. Her mother, Gertrude, promptly took charge and directed several servants to carry Peter up to his chambers and bed.

"I'm sorry, Peter," Livinia whispered in a barely audible voice from her hiding place in the scullery. "I am *so very* sorry."

It dawned on Livinia that until that moment, no man had *ever* come to her defense or had shown anything like Peter's decisive bravery on her behalf. Since his arrival, she had continuously treated Peter in a manner calculated to increase his discomfort. He had responded to her constant teasing and condescension with an act of spontaneous, noble courage, taking the potentially lethal punch her father meant for her. "I *am* truly sorry, Peter," she said in a somewhat louder tone as uncharacteristic tears of remorse formed in her eyes.

She could still hear the awful, sharp *thud* as the back of his head bounced off the dining room's burnished oak floorboards while she fled the room. Throughout her twenty-three years, Livinia had heard of her father's murderous rages, but they were only spoken of in whispers, and she had never been a target of one of them. And for her capricious actions, an innocent man had paid a potentially lethal price.

After some minutes of gathering her composure and hearing her father storm out of the house to a waiting carriage, Livinia could have sworn she heard a familiar sentence whispered in her ear in a mellifluous southern accent:

"Livinia, 'greater love hath no man than this, that a man lay down his life for his friends.'"

Whirling around, fearing she had been discovered, Livinia saw no one in the kitchen but herself. Where had the voice come from? Gathering her courage, Livinia proceeded upstairs to Peter's chambers. Her mother was just emerging and shot a warning look at her daughter.

"Livinia, I think you're the last person Mr. Cratchit would want to see right now, even if he were awake."

She looked her mother in the eye and said in a surprisingly resolute voice, "Mother, *I* am the cause of Mr. Cratchit's grievous injuries, and I will tend to him. The house staff may assist me, and you can watch if you like." The uncharacteristic adult tone in her voice brooked no interference. It caught her mother off guard and, stepping to the side, Gertrude silently acquiesced as Livinia entered Peter's suite of rooms.

In his bedroom, two maids were diligently applying ice packs to his swollen face.

At least most of the bleeding has stopped, she thought.

As she quickly forgot the unbidden voice in the downstairs kitchen, going to his side, Livinia took a damp cloth and wrung it in a basin of water already tinted pink with his blood, and tenderly dabbed at his disfigured face. Her mother stood in the doorway, amazed as much by Livinia deigning to put her delicate hands into a basin of bloody water as by the words Livinia spoke aloud to the still unconscious Peter, unconcerned with who might overhear her.

"Dear God, Peter, I am *so very, very sorry*," she sobbed, as tears again slid down her face. "When I kissed you, I was only having my fun with you. Father thought it would make you more amenable to his...*plans*. I was never really going to tell anyone," she said as an unfamiliar emotion washed over her—*shame*.

Peter did not respond, her father's fist having delivered a full-on concussion, a tiny trickle of blood still seeping from his nose and a bruised bluish-purple eye swollen shut from the force of the blow. The right side of his face was a spongy mass of bluish-purple also encompassing his nose.

Livinia softly continued, "No man has ever stood up for my honor or defended me, Mr. Cratchit. My father is a monster, and even though I accused you of gross conduct unbecoming a gentle-man, you came to my defense without a thought for your own safety. *Your wife, Charlotte, is the most fortunate woman in the world.*"

And at that moment, looking down at the bleeding, wounded face of their family's guest, for the first time in her life, Livinia Abernathy fell hopelessly in love.

18

VISITORS AND ARM-TWISTING

Ebenezer Scrooge was excited beyond words. A mere week and a half after meeting with Sidney Herbert, he received an envelope from the offices of Parliament at his residence on Belgrave Square. He pulled out a short note that left him at a momentary loss for words upon opening it. Mrs. Dilber saw Scrooge grow pale before he looked up from his library desk with a large smile.

Ebenezer,

I shall be conducting business tomorrow in London at the Royal Home of Convalescent Medicine with Sir Arthur Chadwick until quite late in the afternoon following up on the matter of Captain Bainbridge's conduct at the Battle of the Alma. As we discussed here in my offices, I should like to demonstrate to your discreet band of colleagues that I'm willing to place my good name at the service of your efforts. As I will be concluding my business at approximately 7:30 p.m., I was wondering if I might impose on you for dinner.

I apologize for the short notice; however, it is of the utmost importance that you have the entire folio of testimonies regarding the military conduct of the late Captain Tristan Bainbridge at the Battle of the Alma prepared and ready for me to take away upon my departure. I apologize if this communique seems cryptic, but I do not want to take unnecessary chances. Information of a delicate nature has come to my attention that we must discuss. I shall explain at dinner.

> *Respectfully,*
> *Baron Sidney Herbert,*
> *Minister-without-Portfolio*

PS: I will be accompanied by Miss Florence Nightingale and do sincerely hope you might accommodate us both. She is quite intent on seeing you.

"Mrs. Dilber, we are having esteemed dinner guests tomorrow night. I should greatly appreciate it if you would prepare one of your signature dinners and dessert trays for a party of three. I should think a three-course meal with soup, followed by a roasted rack of fresh lamb and chicken from the butcher, and ending with salads, fine cheese, and liquor will do quite nicely."

"Of course, Mr. Scrooge. Might I inquire as to whom our guests are going to be? Will it be more of your gentlemen acquaintances?" she asked.

Scrooge handed her the note without comment, a mischievous look on his face. He watched her eyes widen as she read.

"Well, Mrs. Dilber, do you think a day and a half is sufficient time to prepare an appropriate dinner for our very own 'Angel of the Crimea?'"

His housekeeper handed the letter back to him with a knowing smile, and without waiting for him to take out his purse, was gone and out the door in minutes, whistling a merry tune. While reaching down, Scrooge scratched an insistent Julius's ruff.

Sir Arthur Chadwick was the administrator of the Royal Home of Convalescent Medicine for Her Majesty's Soldiers and Sailors. He was a former Royal Navy captain and upon his retirement from the Navy had been appointed administrator of the veterans' hospital and convalescent home. In 1855, he had sustained leg injuries from Russian cannon fire aboard his ship-of-the-line, the 118-gun HMS *Ulysses*, while the Royal Navy provided fire support to English and French forces while anchored off Sevastopol. A genial man, he knew he owed his position to former prime minister, George Hamilton-Gordon, 4th Earl of Aberdeen. When he was made administrator, Sir Arthur knew the easiest way to live out the rest of his days in peace was to not "make waves," as they said tongue-in-cheek at the Admiralty. This was doubly the case as Lord Palmerston was now the new prime minister—all Sir Arthur had to do was carefully bide his time until retirement. He was not a mean or vicious man by temperament. His chief fault was that he let the condition of the Royal Home of Convalescent Medicine lapse into a dilapidated state of benevolent neglect with one eye fixed on retiring to his ancestral family home in Yorkshire in a few years. Running the hospital was not tricky work—the doctors and orderlies did their work, the undertakers' vans duly came and went three times a week, and he signed off on the supply requisitions. Therefore, the hospital very much ran itself, if not by beneficent guidance, then an inertia borne of routine. His leg injury prevented him from visiting the sailors and soldiers in the wards with any real frequency, so he took his doctors' word that all was well within the hospital. That was all about to change very quickly.

On a bright autumn morning in early October 1856, a carriage bearing former Minister-at-War Sidney Herbert and a female companion pulled up in front of the Royal Home of Convalescent Medicine. Herbert helped his attractive companion down from the carriage and ushered her into the hospital through a side door to avoid a commotion. Before proceeding to the administrator's offices, they embarked on an informal tour of the wards where the wounded were recuperating. A dark gray veil hid Florence Nightingale's identity. Herbert and Florence did not want the hospital staff alerting Sir Arthur to her presence before Florence had a chance to observe the dismal conditions for herself. The only word Herbert heard during their tour of the wards was a hissed "Scutari," uttered as an epithet more than an observation. From beneath her veil, Florence glided like a phantom through each floor. After some thirty minutes, she had seen enough, and they were on their way to Sir Arthur's offices.

"How does this compare to Scutari?" Herbert whispered to Florence.

"Scutari was worse, but only because of the abysmal temperatures and constant odors. I think the cold of the wards here keeps the smells and vermin somewhat more at bay, but not by much," she answered, her *sotto voce* outrage palpable.

Several minutes later, they were standing in the outer office of Sir Arthur Chadwick before a very flustered Department of War office secretary. Florence Nightingale now had her gauzy veil pulled back from her face.

Sir Arthur sat reading his copy of the *Times of London* when his secretary knocked on his door and entered, closing the door behind him. "I beg your pardon, Sir Arthur, but you have visitors…"

"Visitors?" Sir Arthur asked. "I don't have anyone on my schedule for today, Jenkins. Tell them to make a proper appointment with you for next week, and I will receive them at that time."

"Sir Arthur, I don't think it would be advisable to tell *these* guests you're unable to receive them."

Sir Arthur blustered in a voice meant to be overheard by Sidney Herbert and Florence Nightingale, "Well, unless it's Her Royal Majesty and the Prince Consort, as I told you, Jenkins, they can make a proper appointment and—"

Before he could finish speaking, the door behind Jenkins flew open, and former Minister-at-War Sidney Herbert and Florence Nightingale walked into Sir Arthur's office.

"Hello, Sir Arthur. I'm Baron Sidney Herbert, former minister-at-war, and this is—"

But Sir Arthur was already grabbing his crutch to rise to his feet as he blurted out, "*Florence Nightingale!* You honor us with your presence."

Florence flashed her most engaging smile. "It's my honor to make your acquaintance, Sir Arthur, and I apologize for intruding upon your busy day. I thought I would visit some of the wounded soldiers I met while at Scutari who are now here. I understand you yourself were wounded by Russian cannon fire in the bombardment of Sevastopol. I heard that your flagship, the HMS *Ulysses*, took several direct hits from Russian cannons, and that was when you were injured."

Sidney Herbert knew Florence was laying a trap and did not envy Sir Arthur at all. From the tone in her voice, he could tell Florence was doing everything possible to keep her temper in check.

"Why, yes, Miss Nightingale. Two batteries of long-range Russian guns opened up on us at sunrise."

Given the claimed grievous injuries to his left leg, Florence couldn't help but eye Sir Arthur's alacrity in coming around to the front of his desk to greet her.

"Your leg looks like it has healed quite well for you to be able to move about as well as you do, Sir Arthur."

Minister Herbert winced. As a career politician skilled in the art of the verbal ambush, he knew what was coming.

"Why, yes, I had some of the finest surgeons and doctors in the Royal Navy flotilla tending to me day and night. I was patched up and back in action commanding the HMS *Ulysses* within two weeks," Sir Arthur bragged.

"May I ask you a question, Sir Arthur?" Florence asked sweetly.

"How can I deny anything to our famous 'Angel of the Crimea?'" Sir Arthur replied, eager to ingratiate himself with the famous "Lady with the Lamp." "By all means, Miss Nightingale. I am at your service."

"Then how is it that there are several hundred of Her Royal Majesty's badly wounded sailors and soldiers lying in the wards of this hospital *still* suffering from the same injuries they were being treated for when I was at Scutari Hospital? Not fifteen minutes ago, I saw men pleading with your staff for clean blankets and fresh water. The orderlies were passing them by as if they were common beggars on the street, Sir Arthur." Florence delivered her indictment of the hospital's rank conditions and callous staff with icy fury.

"I saw soldiers with rotting gangrenous stumps of arms and legs lying in filthy beds and hallway cots not twenty minutes ago here in your institution. Other soldiers are suffering from a bone infection called osteomyelitis. At Scutari, our only treatment for that was extensive debridement, saucerization, and wound packing. The affected area is left to heal by secondary intention. As you are not a physician, do you even know what 'secondary intention' is, Sir Arthur? After all, you *are* in charge here."

Florence's eyes blazed as Sir Arthur withered under her verbal assault.

"In plain language, 'secondary intention' healing is dressing the wound with bandages and then hoping God smiles on the poor creature left to lie in his bed. Most of the time, he ends up in a military-issue coffin. It was only through my pleading with Sidney here that the British Sanitary Commission, appointed by Queen Victoria, improved both hospital and general living conditions. I don't envy the job those Sanitary Commission men had trudging through the sewers under Scutari."

Although neither a criminal nor a man of malicious moral character like the disgraced Ainsley Northrup, Sir Arthur knew when he was presented with a damning *fait accompli*. Sitting back behind his desk, he looked up at the impassive Florence Nightingale, asking himself, *Is this woman before me England's beloved "Angel of the Crimea" or an avenging angel straight from the Old Testament?* He quietly said, "The condition of our veterans is of paramount importance to me. Yes, I have relied on reports that were far too rosy from the staff physicians here, and I take full accountability, Miss Nightingale."

Turning the palms of his hands upward on his desk in a gesture of supplication, if not surrender, he asked, "Please tell me your recommendations, and within the bounds of our financial allotment from the Royal Treasury, I will see what can be done."

Sidney Herbert spoke up before Florence could respond. "'See what can be done' is not good enough! Money won't be a problem, Sir Arthur. We are seeking your support for an effort that is simple to request, but difficult in execution. An organization called the 'Honorable Society of Royal Medical Benefactors' will be furnishing the financial resources to begin immediate repairs and improvements to the Royal Home of Convalescent Medicine. *You* have a critical part to play, and I shall not gloss over the issue. We fully expect the same obdurate resistance from the pigheaded British Army doctors in this hospital that Miss Nightingale had to suffer with in Crimea at Scutari. Except *now* there is a difference. The public is outraged, sir, and Miss Nightingale has the direct ear of Her Royal Highness Queen Victoria. Knowing that, you will, without mercy or delay, crush any opposition from the doctors here at your facility to the pending changes in sanitary procedures and building improvements. I frankly do not give a damn if the sensibilities of any doctor here are offended. Those 'doctors' offend Almighty God every time a body leaves here in a mortuary cart due to their neglect."

Herbert placed a document in front of Sir Arthur called "A Directive of Cooperation" for his signature. Sir Arthur picked up the piece of paper with the Ministry of War seal at the topic and began reading the short notice:

To the Attention of Sir Arthur Chadwick,

Administrator, Royal Home of Convalescent Medicine for Her Majesty's Soldiers and Sailors

By Order of the Ministry of War of the United Kingdom of Great Britain and Ireland, henceforth and effective immediately, the practical sanitary procedures known as the "Nightingale Directives" shall be implemented at the Royal Home of Convalescent Medicine for Her Majesty's Soldiers and Sailors. This includes all transfer of all nursing and patient care responsibilities to the initial cadre of "Nightingale Nurses" and their Superintendent of Nurse Staff.

Coincident with the "Nightingale Directives," the administrator and staff of the hospital shall cooperate with building, tradespeople, and contracted parties for all repairs and the physical improvement of the Royal Home of Convalescent Medicine as directed by Minister-without-Portfolio Baron Sidney Herbert.

Any hindrance to the aforementioned improvements and changes to procedure shall be dealt with by this department with the most severe consequences, including a recommendation for courts-martial and dismissal with prejudice from Her Majesty's armed forces and forfeiture of pension for any staff found to be complicit by neglect or willful interference, rank notwithstanding.

By my signature below, I, Sir Arthur Chadwick, fully acknowledge receipt of and concurrence with the contents herein.

Signed, this Third of October in the Year of Our Lord Eighteen Fifty-Six
Fox Maule, Lord Panmure
Secretary of State for War

The repairs to the Royal Home of Convalescent Medicine for Her Majesty's Soldiers and Sailors began toward the end of the next week, to the amazement of patients, staff, and doctors alike. No one knew where the sudden generosity had come from other than a hitherto unknown "Honorable Society of Royal Medical Benefactors." Sidney Herbert's "Directive of Cooperation" from Fox Maule, the Secretary of State for War himself, effectively muted all opposition as word spread among the doctors and hospital that the female visitor who glided through the week before was none other than the "Lady with the Lamp," Florence Nightingale herself. For the first time in many months, smiles and hope, instead of pestilence and disease, began spreading through the wards filled with wounded veterans.

19

SEEKING LIGHT
IN DARKNESS

Later that evening, after leaving the Royal Home of Convalescent Medicine for Her Majesty's Soldiers and Sailors, Sidney Herbert and Florence Nightingale were greeted by a subdued Ebenezer Scrooge at his residence. After dinner had been served, the three retired to Scrooge's library, accompanied by the "felines who would not be denied," Julius and Caesar.

Never one to mince words, Florence looked at Scrooge and asked him point blank, "Have you seen Allyce again since we spoke at Lea Hurst, Ebenezer?"

"Yes, Florence, I've seen her several times when I've visited Charlotte Cratchit, but Allyce has made it clear she does not wish to see *me* or engage me in any conversation whatsoever. It is as if in answering me or breaking the silence when I try to speak to her, Allyce acts like acknowledging my presence will hand me a victory of sorts. As soon as I enter the hospital ward where Charlotte is, she leaves on another task." Scrooge looked very dejected. "I wish I could tell her what is written in my heart, but I see that look on her face when I enter the hospital, and I'm overcome by guilt I cannot forgive myself for."

Sidney Herbert interjected a comment that brightened Scrooge's mood somewhat. "When Florence and I were touring the wards at the Royal Home of Convalescent Medicine, we encountered several members of Captain Bainbridge's unit, the 1st Battalion, Coldstream

Guards. While I was speaking with them, they mentioned a man who toured the hospital recently asking about the actions of Captain Tristan Bainbridge at the Battle of the Alma outside Sevastopol. I can only assume that was you."

Scrooge said, "Yes, Sidney. I was there, and it was after speaking with a number of those soldiers and non-commissioned officers that I became aware of what *true* heroism is. Their stories about the Battle of the Alma and Captain Bainbridge's bravery coincided too closely to have been rehearsed, and besides, what would dissembling gain those poor maimed wretches? Nothing, I say. There would be no point to it. They will live with the consequences of what happened there for the rest of their lives—the wounds, scars, lost limbs, and *lost minds*...all of it. It is especially important to right the wrong that has been done to Tristan Bainbridge's memory regarding that damnable fool, the Duke of Cambridge.

"After I had talked to enough of them, it became apparent that had Tristan Bainbridge not directly led his Coldstream battalion in a charge against the Czarist cannons firing at the Scots Fusilier Guards and Light Division, the Russians would have won the battle. Keep in mind that Tristan's battalion was charging right into the teeth of Russian gunfire. Had Tristan not confronted the impertinent Duke of Cambridge and counterattacked on the Russian flank, we might still be fighting on the outskirts of Sevastopol."

He turned to look at Florence.

"I confess to feeling quite inadequate. Allyce's heart belonged to a true hero while he still lived, and I strongly suspect it belongs to him still. I do not know if anything or anyone can unlock her smile ever again. Charlotte Cratchit is always going on about how many are the days that Allyce's smile is the only thing that gives her hope. But how could the love of a man she holds in open contempt ever hope to be seen as worthy and true?" Scrooge asked in a wistful voice.

Herbert brightened up. "I am not skilled in matters of the heart, Ebenezer, but there may yet be a way we can demonstrate to Allyce that Her Majesty the Queen and England truly appreciate the sacrifice her husband made." He turned to Florence. "Would you kindly tell Ebenezer of your idea?"

"Ebenezer," Florence began. "There *is* a reason that Sidney asked you to compile the verified testimonies of the Coldstream men who lived to tell of Tristan Bainbridge's valor at the Alma River. I have been summoned to Balmoral Castle a week hence by Her Majesty Queen Victoria to speak of my experiences at Scutari Hospital and to formally give her my recommendations for sanitary changes to British military hospitals, whether in the field or here in London."

Florence paused. "I am not a shy woman, Ebenezer."

Herbert could barely suppress a chuckle at her remark, but Florence continued: "It has been made known to me through my father that Her Majesty intends to bestow a special honor on me. It is an honor I do not want or seek but shall nevertheless reluctantly accept for two reasons. First, as a loyal subject of the Crown, I shall not insult our good Queen Victoria by refusing the honor. I will accept her accolades by making it clear that in accepting them, I do so on behalf of every civilian nurse and nun, Catholic or Anglican, who chose to go to Scutari with me. They all traveled with me to that hell on the Bosporus to alleviate suffering, fully knowing what they were volunteering for. Second, I fully intend to ask Queen Victoria to bestow the honorary posthumous peerage of Viscount on Captain Tristan Bainbridge as a nobleman of the British Empire. I would have recommended a knighthood for Tristan. Still, Sidney, who is knowledgeable in such matters, tells me that a posthumous knighthood is quite impossible but that raising someone to a peerage is an act rarely done, but possible, and then only at the sole discretion of the ruling sovereign of England, the queen or king. Several recent governments haven't recommended anyone for hereditary peerages, and the Queen doesn't establish new ones on her authority by mere convention; however, I believe she *would* in the case of Captain Bainbridge, as the evidence in his favor is quite compelling."

"Do you think she will agree to your request?" Scrooge asked, his eyes widening.

"I don't see why not. The Coldstream Guards hold a special place in Her Majesty's heart, and to know that they played a critical part in turning the tide at the Battle of the Alma against the Russians will please her and the Prince Consort to no end. Raising a man like the late Captain Bainbridge to the nobility is perfectly within the purview of Her Majesty in an exceptional case such as this, and I daresay, in this case, most richly deserved. *Tristan demonstrably saved the life of a member of the royal family*, no matter what Prince George says. The evidence is overwhelming in that regard. Besides, Allyce Bainbridge is practically a sister to me, and I would have no problem discreetly communicating to the Crown that if they cannot see a way to honor a brave son of England fallen in battle, then in good conscience, I would have to refuse any honors the Queen wished to bestow upon me. In truth, I would not *dare* refuse, but I am willing to bluff to a certain degree," Florence said with a twinkle in her eye.

Florence turned to Sidney Herbert. "Why don't you tell Ebenezer your idea?"

Leaning forward in his chair, Sidney turned to Scrooge and asked, "Remember when we discussed a fitting memorial to Tristan Bainbridge? Something of lasting value? Well, Ebenezer, I think I've hit upon it."

"Well, it's good *you* have because I've been racking my head doing the same thing without success," Scrooge said.

"Well, Ebenezer, you're responsible for the idea, at least indirectly. You know that we're facilitating the repairs and refurbishment of the Royal Home of Convalescent Medicine. I spoke with the Secretary of State for War, Fox Maule, and obtained a 'Directive of Cooperation' so that all necessary work at the Royal Home of Convalescent Medicine will take place unimpeded by bureaucratic foot-dragging. As so many of Her Majesty's soldiers and sailors suffered grievously in the Crimea, I told the Secretary we should dedicate the refurbished Royal Home of Convalescent Medicine to the memory of Captain Tristan Bainbridge once he is raised to the ranks of the nobility by the Queen and to have a suitable plaque placed near the entrance to the hospital. Florence and I were speaking of it in my office earlier today and came up with a suitable inscription."

Scrooge took the proffered note from Herbert's hand and read it without reaction. Handing it back to Herbert, Scrooge said tonelessly, "I think that would do the job quite nicely."

"Ebenezer," Florence said, "you've been an incredibly gracious host tonight. We appreciate it. I've taken the liberty of explaining Allyce's importance to you with Sidney here, and I must ask you, have your feelings toward her changed? You've seemed rather subdued tonight whenever her name has come up in conversation, and I detect a reluctance to speak about her."

"Florence, you've hit it. My feelings have not changed toward her one iota; if anything, I'm more in love with her than I have ever been in my life. But I confess, a new wrinkle has been introduced into my plan to convince her of my change of heart and win back her affection."

Scrooge glanced toward Herbert before continuing, a none-too-subtle gesture that Herbert picked up on immediately.

Florence reassured Scrooge. "Ebenezer, Sidney here can be trusted with anything you tell us tonight."

"But it revolves around what Jacob Marley told me."

Herbert asked, "Is Jacob one of our 'Honorable Society' whom I haven't met yet, Ebenezer?"

Florence answered matter-of-factly, "No, Sidney. Jacob Marley is Ebenezer's business partner who died thirteen years ago."

Herbert's face was now a mask of confusion.

"I don't understand. Did this Jacob Marley leave behind documents or legal papers that bear upon Ebenezer's situation with Allyce?"

"No, Sidney. It is far more complicated than a legal document," Scrooge said. "I have mentioned in passing that I experienced a spiritual conversion of sorts several years ago and that it came about through the intervention of my late business partner. I have related the entire affair to Florence and, as a competent nurse, she assured me I was not in danger of losing my mind."

Scrooge looked to Florence, seeking support for what he was about to say. She smiled encouragingly.

"Go ahead, Ebenezer. You are among friends."

Scrooge sighed. "Then I shall be direct. Not long ago, I beheld Jacob Marley's shade in Saint Hubert's Church. He told me the only chance I have to win back Allyce's heart, although it is by no means assured, is to enable a spiritual visitation upon her by something called the 'Ghost of Christmas Love.' As Florence is well aware, Jacob's words troubled me, as I have given much thought as to what *great sacrifice* I must make that did not involve my money. I must admit I was at something of a dead end until I met up with Neville Braithwaite for dinner a few nights ago, along with a young American guest he was dining with, a Michel St. Tutelairé. We discussed my problem at length, as the world of spirit is the province of Sir Neville, seeing as he is the vicar of Saint Hubert's.

"Neville came upon a solution to my conundrum that contradicts every sentiment in my heart, but the more I ponder it, it seems like the only logical answer I seek."

Florence interrupted: "Then go on, Ebenezer! Tell us, what is this course of action you must pursue?"

"Well, Neville said I've been looking at this entire situation from the wrong end of the telescope, so to speak. If young Peter Cratchit—"

"Who is Peter Cratchit?" Herbert asked.

"He is the son of my clerk, Bob Cratchit, and he's the husband of a consumption patient Florence's friend and my former fiancée, Allyce, is caring for, Charlotte Cratchit. A quite brilliant young man, Peter is in the United States to determine whether the American end of a prospective business arrangement regarding improvements to the Royal Navy is substantial and worth pursuing. Peter is the guest of Sir Nigel Fairweather-Hawthorne's American business partner, the president and owner of the New York and Pennsylvania Coal and Lumber Company, Mr. Cyrus Abernathy. From Peter's letters home to Charlotte, and as intimated by Jacob's spirit, Peter has been slowly ensnared by the serpent of greed *and* tempted to infidelity by Livinia Abernathy, Cyrus Abernathy's daughter. I can understand the temptation to riches; it almost led me to ruin years ago. Neville told me the only way I may be able to free Peter of these moral snares is by appearing to revert to my miserly former self in leading a competing effort to win the Royal Navy contract. I do not know of any such contract, as I am not familiar with the bidding process for the Royal Navy. Still, if it's large enough to draw the attention of an American industrialist, I'll wager there is not a prospective contract with the Admiralty that our friend in the 'Honorable Society' John Delane hasn't heard of through his contacts."

At that point, Sidney Herbert spoke up.

"There *is* a proposal by the Royal Admiralty Board for a major overhaul of Her Majesty's Navy, Ebenezer. I do not think it is a major secret that some of our greatest capital warships are sixty to seventy years old. The play on words is ironic, but there is a lot of truth to the old dictum that '*time and tide wait for no man.*' The mechanical arts of warfare and sailing ships are giving way to iron warships propelled by great steam engines. What troubles me is that this is a most secret effort, yet one of the most ruthless industrialists in the United States knows enough confidential detail that he is working with an English firm to partner on a proposal."

Looking at Florence with a sense of resignation, Scrooge said, "When I met with Reverend Braithwaite and the young American businessman Michel St. Tutelairé, Michel pointed out what should have been obvious to me from the beginning. This young American gent told me *his* theory as to what the 'sacrifice my gold cannot buy' may be, and it pains me to admit it. This sacrifice and the consequences of my efforts may well result in Allyce's heart once again opening to the possibility of happiness and love, but not with me. I must acknowledge that in setting Allyce's heart free, I may well be setting it free for her to love another man. I must be willing to risk losing her for a second time to give her happiness, however much it pains me to admit. But I will *not* see young Peter Cratchit follow the same path toward greed's damnation that I once walked either," Scrooge declared emphatically. "As I have no family of my own save my nephew Fred, the Cratchits *are* my family. I will not see sorrow and disgrace descend upon them, even if it means I once again lose my good name and reputation."

With the same compassion that compelled her to go to the Crimea, Florence reached out and placed her hand on Scrooge's forearm in a comforting gesture of reassurance.

"We have spoken of my own deep belief in the actions of Divine Providence, Ebenezer," she said. "I have promised not to intercede with Allyce on your behalf at your urging, and now the reasons are clear to me. I believe the hand of God *is* at work here, and I will not interfere. I will follow through on my promises to you; however, now that you have been so forthcoming, it's clear you have a painful and solitary path ahead of you. I have chosen for myself a path to pursue the increased good of my fellow man. I fear you must be willing to risk that same lonely path not only with Allyce, but also your good name in business. It brings to mind the Old Testament verse from

Isaiah chapter 53: '*He is despised and rejected of men; a man of sorrows, and acquainted with grief: and we hid as it were our faces from him; he was despised, and we esteemed him not.*' That is the path you are setting out on, without a guaranteed outcome in your favor."

She looked to Sidney, who spoke up if only to keep up with the conversation.

"Ebenezer, I am a professional man of government and confess I'm not conversant with the world of angels and spirits, but I know Florence's deep faith very well. Only that faith and her determination could have sustained her labors in that Turkish hell called Scutari Hospital. Her words carry an authenticity I cannot deny; they make eminent sense to me. I shall do what I can, but short of feeding you tidbits of information about the Royal Admiralty contract as I learn of them, I fear there is not much else I will be able to do. I do not envy you, my friend."

Scrooge took quick note of the words *my friend*—the famous former Minister-at-War Sidney Herbert did *not* consider him mentally unbalanced.

Herbert continued: "I agree you have a lonely road ahead of you, and as Florence said, you may become an object of mockery and scorn once again. *But you do it for a very noble cause.* Not many men would put their livelihood, riches, and reputations at risk for the love of a woman.

"As for the Admiralty contract, what I do know of it are the barest details. The Admiralty Board issued a formal proposal list to rebuild and refit the Royal Navy's 131-gun *Wellington* class, 121-gun *Royal Albert* class, the 121-gun *Victoria* class, plus the first fleet of ships to be fitted with new high-pressure steam engines and iron armor amidships. I thought it was a highly guarded secret, but in any case, with these newer steam engines, our iron warship navy will constitute the most formidable fleet on the high seas for years to come. One part of this disclosure I find disturbing is that we have eminent men of science working on cannon shells that will explode *inside* an enemy ship after striking it, not merely punch holes in the hull, as cannonballs do."

Scrooge noticed a look of disgust fleetingly cross Florence's face. *Men of science working once again to make carnage and death more efficient.*

Herbert continued: "How Cyrus Abernathy has acquired knowledge of this fact concerns me very much, as the Admiralty Board prides itself on keeping such matters in great secrecy. Abernathy will bear watching."

20

WHAT WERE ONCE VICES

The mood of the meeting of the "Honorable Society of Royal Medical Benefactors" inside Ebenezer Scrooge's stately library on Belgrave Square was somber as John Delane and Sidney Herbert delivered corroborating revelations about the Royal Admiralty Board's Navy contract.

Sidney Herbert spoke up first.

"First off, gentlemen, even though I was the Minister-at-War for Crimea, I didn't realize some of Her Majesty's finest warships are going on sixty years old. Although the details mustn't leave this room, gentlemen, I *can* confirm the Royal Admiralty Board has issued a contract bid tender for the Royal Navy's most extensive warship rebuild and refitting program in decades. The contract value is just north of *four million pounds*, payable by the Royal Treasury through 1885."

John Delane was quick to respond.

"Then that is why my contacts in various shipyards are rife with rumors of a 'certain American' putting forth funds to the tune of half a million British pounds to start, with more to follow, in a bid to win this initiative. That mysterious American *must* be Cyrus Abernathy. He's the only American I can think of who has that kind of money at his immediate disposal. Over and above his financial generosity, he's willing to provide North American lumber at a thirty-percent discount over and above the best offer of any other wood supplier in Europe or the United States for this Navy project. As Abernathy is also president of the New York and Pennsylvania Coal and Lumber Company, he's offering to sell stockpiles of high-grade bituminous coal for our new steam-powered iron warships at a steep discount for the first five years."

As he took his seat, there were grim nods all around as Herbert stood up to speak.

"I know something of this Abernathy fellow. He fancies himself a one-man version of the East India Company, and when he fixes his eye on the jewel of the moment, he will do *anything* in his power to get it, gentlemen. Abernathy is a man without scruple—moral, business, or otherwise. To secure control of our maritime industry, he is willing to put considerable sums of money at risk, all without guaranteed success. I suspect he's paying a considerable sum to someone in Her Majesty's government whom Abernathy thinks can influence the Admiralty Board's final decision. I also have heard of his quick inclination to use unsavory methods to secure a business advantage," he said while glancing at Reverend Braithwaite.

To muttered outrage, Herbert stated, "I fear Abernathy wants to seize control of the entire British shipbuilding industry. Nothing else makes sense. Why would he throw such prodigious sums of money at this effort? My sources tell me he has already saved the John Scott Russell and Company's Millwall Iron Works from the bankruptcy court by quietly buying up fifty-one percent of the company stock. That is where Abernathy, operating under cover of Sir Nigel Fairweather-Hawthorne's Hawthorne and Cavendish Furniture and Carpentry Works, plans to procure new boilers and steam fittings, pipes, copper, and iron smithing for these ships."

"That's absurd, Sidney," Sir Richard Mayne said. "I know Sir Nigel's company well, and they can't build ships. They make furniture, lots of furniture, I'll grant you that much, and they even have a Royal Warrant of Appointment. Still, I cannot accept the leap from making desks and armoires to building and refitting the Royal Navy's 'ships-of-the-line.' It sounds ridiculous on its face."

"With all due respect, Richard, that's where you're wrong," Herbert shot back. "If it were *only* Hawthorne and Cavendish Furniture and Carpentry Works involved here, then I might agree with you, but we also have his *sub rosa* American business partner Cyrus Abernathy to consider. He has ponderous resources at his disposal and a cutthroat willingness to use them. Although Sir Nigel has a rather cunning disposition and outsized ego, he is no match for Cyrus Abernathy. Abernathy is merely using Hawthorne and Cavendish as his stalking horse to put a veneer of English respectability on his plans, and Sir Nigel is too busy looking at his potential profits to see it. Sir Nigel is rather a naive babe in the woods in matters of this import, seeing only *profit*. Abernathy commands one of the largest business empires in America, and he's got a strong presence in a multitude of industries. What Cyrus Abernathy seeks is *control*, gentlemen."

Scrooge laid aside his pipe.

"I think I can provide evidence that proves Sidney correct. Grisham Dockyards in Portsmouth has a loan with my company with the next payment due in two weeks. They just finished the repairs to a Royal Navy 122-gun ship, the HMS *Coventry*, and are not due to begin any repair or refitting on any Royal Navy ship of any substance for the next three months, when they are due to start hull repairs to the HMS *Atlantis*. It is said she struck a reef off Bombay some months ago. Grisham Dockyards' only source of work will be a few merchant clippers, but nothing overly profitable. At most, they'd be able to keep the shipyard in business and the workers employed to make their payrolls until work begins on the refit of the HMS *Atlantis*, but that project itself is due to bring the shipyard only £30,000. The shipyards' outstanding loan balance is for a prodigious sum not due in full for another fourteen years—£280,000, to be paid through 1870. I know because I hold the primary note. A solicitor for the Grisham Dockyards provided me notice today by special courier that Grisham Dockyards will *not* be making its next month's payment in two weeks."

"And how does this affect our discussion, Ebenezer?" Sir Richard asked. "So, they are defaulting on a payment?"

Scrooge smiled.

"I hadn't finished, Sir Richard. The letter said the entire loan balance would be repaid *in full* on the date the current monthly loan payment was due, including all accrued interest and releasing Grisham Dockyards from all outstanding debts. The funds were provided by the First Commerce Bank of New York City through a letter of credit to a commercial account at the Bank of England. Would any of you like to hazard a guess as to who owns the First Commerce Bank of New York City?"

He saw Reverend Braithwaite mouth the name *Abernathy* as the pieces of the puzzle Scrooge pulled together for his audience fell into place.

"One final point, gentlemen. The letter of credit is being deposited into a commercial account for Hawthorne and Cavendish Furniture and Carpentry Works. Why would the relatively modest firm of Hawthorne and Cavendish *Furniture and Carpentry Works* be in the business of paying off an enormous commercial mortgage for a British shipyard?"

Sir Richard Mayne spoke up.

"All right, Ebenezer. I'll concede the point that an American businessman of the nastiest sort has set his sights on Her Majesty's shipbuilding industry and is doing his best to hide his involvement. The question remains, what can *we* do about it?"

"I have given the matter considerable thought, gentlemen, and the solution to our dilemma will be here shortly."

John Delane piped up, evoking good-natured laughter from the group.

"What sort of magic are you going to work tonight, Ebenezer? Are you going to have Florence Nightingale walk in again and solve our problems?"

At that moment, Michel St. Tutelairé appeared around the corner onto Belgrave Square, and walked up to Scrooge's house at a brisk pace. He arrived at the front door and rapped the polished brass knocker three times in succession with his lion's-head-shaped walking stick. When Mrs. Dilber answered the door, St. Tutelairé presented his card and said, "Good evenin', ma'am. My name is Michel St. Tutelairé, and I've been asked to meet with Mr. Ebenezer Scrooge and his associates here tonight."

Mrs. Dilber, who had never heard an accent from the American South before, ushered the tall blond guest into Scrooge's front parlor.

"I'll be telling Mr. Scrooge you're here, sir," she said as she scurried off in the direction of his library.

Knocking at the library door, she heard Scrooge bid her enter. Poking her head through the doorway, she said, "Mr. Scrooge, your guest has arrived and is waiting in the front parlor."

Scrooge exchanged looks with Reverend Braithwaite and stood up.

"Excuse me for a moment. Neville, would you join me?"

Mrs. Dilber remarked in a loud stage whisper, "If you don't mind my saying so, sir, he's got a most unusual way of talking, even for an American."

Scrooge took Mrs. Dilber's elbow and said as he led her off toward the kitchen, "Because he comes from the American South, Mrs. Dilber, and their manner of speech is as different from other parts of America as a Glasgow accent differs from London."

Scrooge and Reverend Braithwaite returned a few moments later with the debonair Michel St. Tutelairé. The "Honorable Society of Royal Medical Benefactors" stood to greet the new arrival.

Reverend Braithwaite spoke.

"This is my good friend Michel St. Tutelairé, the gentleman Ebenezer referred to earlier. He's based in France or thereabouts and is a representative of Sturdy Eagle Fine Wood Products, an American lumber cooperative in Bennington, Vermont. I took the liberty of telling him the purpose of our meeting here earlier today at lunch."

Sir Richard was the first to address the newcomer.

"Your accent is *not* from the northeastern United States, Mr. St. Tutelairé. It rather sounds more like the American southlands."

"I guess I'm guilty as charged, Sir Richard," St. Tutelairé said to the chief of the Metropolitan Police, the irony of his words not lost on the assemblage. "I originally hail from Savannah, Georgia, and the accent follows me as surely as my shadow. At any rate, I may be able to assist with your dilemma in the matter of Cyrus Abernathy. I've crossed swords with him several times back in America, and I know *exactly* what you're up against: a man with a soul blacker than a lump of your Newcastle coal and a heart to match. Some years ago, I dealt his mentor a humiliating defeat before the King, and he has never forgotten it.

"I know there's a rather large contract coming up for repairs to Queen Victoria's fleet, and speaking for my associates, my business colleagues are anxious to establish a foothold in the British shipbuilding industry, not conquer it. Conquest is Cyrus Abernathy's domain. Therefore, Sturdy Eagle Fine Wood Products is willing to put up the sum of £250,000, provided *you* gentlemen are willing to match that as an act of good faith. You need not give me an answer tonight, but I would appreciate hearing back from you within a week."

Reverend Braithwaite looked to St. Tutelairé and said, "I can't speak for all of us until we hold a proper consultation, but I do think we will be inclined to partner with you. I've only got one question, Michel. We've found out that the terms Cyrus Abernathy is offering through Hawthorne and Cavendish are generous to the point of being uneconomical. He's offering a thirty-percent discount over and above the best offer of any other wood supplier in Europe or the United States for this project for Her Majesty's Navy. As Abernathy is also president of the New York and Pennsylvania Coal and Lumber Company, he's willing to sell bituminous coal for our new steam-powered iron warships at a steep discount for the first five years. I don't see how we can possibly match that."

"The region of the United States my company is based in is called New *England*, and I think you'll find we can be just as resourceful. The best way to defeat Cyrus Abernathy is to strike him where he doesn't expect, and I specifically intend to help you gentlemen do just that. As far as his terms of business are concerned, I would leave you with one piece of advice: keep in mind not everything that glitters by the light of the full moon is a jewel," St. Tutelairé said with a hint of mystery.

St. Tutelairé stood up and made a slight bow in the direction of Ebenezer Scrooge. "I should like to thank you for your hospitality, Ebenezer, and it is time I take my leave. May I speak with you in private before I go?" Turning to the rest of the "Honorable Society," St. Tutelairé said, "Gentlemen, it was my honor and privilege to meet you tonight."

He followed Scrooge out of the library. As they reached the front door, St. Tutelairé quietly asked, "If you'll pardon my intrusion in your personal affairs, I'm curious; have there been any further developments with the widow Bainbridge?"

St. Tutelairé's concern touched Scrooge. "I have seen her several times, but neither my politeness nor kindness have any effect. Allyce is still distant toward me. I'm not one to give up easily, but I confess, Michel, her attitude could tempt me to despair."

St. Tutelairé grabbed Scrooge's shoulder in a gesture of support. He had a firm grip for such a slim man.

"Don't lose heart, Ebenezer." Looking around in a conspiratorial manner, he said, "I still think you'll bring about that Ghost of

Christmas Love you mentioned to Neville and me at dinner, one way or another. Your faith will be rewarded."

With a firm handshake, St. Tutelairé slipped off into the night.

Returning to his library, thick with pipe smoke, Scrooge felt his mood buoyed by an optimism he could not place. Perhaps it was this young American businessman with such confidence in his ability to outwit the formidable Cyrus Abernathy. He found his mood was shared by the rest of the "Honorable Society."

Sidney Herbert stood up as if anxious to be the bearer of good news.

"That young friend of Reverend Braithwaite had a most invigorating effect on our little group, Ebenezer. I can't say I've ever heard of Sturdy Eagle Fine Wood Products before, but we're convinced that Mr. St. Tutelairé and his company will deliver on any business commitments made."

He nodded toward Sir Richard.

"Even the one among our number who is paid to be suspicious of people was quite taken with Mr. St. Tutelairé."

Scrooge replied, "I agree. There's something about that young man I like; however, it doesn't relieve us of our remaining dilemma. Abernathy has stolen a march on us regarding the Admiralty Board contracts."

Looking around the room to puzzled looks, he added, "Perhaps I wasn't clear enough. Our intentions are very well and good, but who among us owns a shipyard? I daresay we can't very well purchase one and hope to compete with Cyrus Abernathy at the same time given his wealth."

Sidney Herbert piped up.

"Why not approach Holland and Sons? They have been making fine woodwork for the Crown for many years and hold several Royal Warrants of Appointment to the Crown. I know there's no love lost between John Holland and Sir Nigel Fairweather-Hawthorne.

With their experience, I daresay Holland and Sons would jump at the chance to give Sir Nigel a good comeuppance. They already work with several shipyards, and any one of them would relish the chance to rebuild naval ships."

Scrooge then said, "As we are all men of our word, I propose by a show of hands we each commit to contributing forty thousand pounds each, and that will more than match Michel St. Tutelairé's commitment from Sturdy Eagle."

And as the hands went up around his library, it was resolved that night that the "Honorable Society of Royal Medical Benefactors" was now in the shipbuilding business.

A junior clerk holding a sealed letter knocked on Scrooge's office door the next day.

"Begging your pardon, sir. A gentleman just left this for you," he said as he handed Scrooge the envelope.

Scrooge saw it was addressed to him without any clue as to the sender's identity. He slit the envelope open, pulled out the paper within, and began reading:

Ebenezer,

A matter of singular importance has come to my attention, and I strongly recommend you swear your colleagues to secrecy in this matter for the moment. I have discovered why Cyrus Abernathy can offer the Royal Navy discounted prices for the immense quantities of quality lumber and coal that his competitors cannot match. I have spoken with some of my Sturdy Eagle compatriots, and they tell me Cyrus owns and operates numerous very large logging plantations in North Carolina, South Carolina, and down in Brazil. All this lumber—the oak, pine, and in the case of Brazil, the teak—is produced by thousands of indentured slaves Cyrus Abernathy purchased from African slave traders. These slaves are held in barbaric conditions without a thought to their humanity, and they are subject to brutal treatment at the hand of Abernathy's plantation overseers and bosses. It is routine for them to die in great numbers either from the lash or yellow fever. This wicked stain on the United States will someday require a reckoning, but at present, it remains legal under the law. Abernathy has taken care to hide his widespread ownership of slaves from both Peter Cratchit and Sir Nigel Fairweather-Hawthorne.

I think a judicious word or two to Mr. Delane of the Times *as the Christmas holiday approaches would be enough to arouse the righteous outrage of the British populace. If the Crown enters into contracts with Mr. Abernathy, it could be seen as an official endorsement of slavery. The resulting public outcry against the disgraceful nature of this decision would surely cast great shame upon Her Majesty.*

I respectfully remain, your humble servant,
Michel St. Tutelairé

Scrooge realized Cyrus Abernathy had kept this awful secret held close during his negotiations with his British partners. As good King George III ended the abhorrent practice of slavery and any profit thereof by royal proclamation in 1807, Scrooge decided to sabotage the corrupt deal in a very public manner. Working with Hawthorne and Cavendish competitor Holland and Sons and Michel St. Tutelairé's Sturdy Eagle Fine Wood Products, the "Honorable Society of Royal Medical Benefactors" decided to pool their resources and enter a competing bid against Abernathy/Sir Nigel. As benefactor John Delane was editor-in-chief of the reigning British newspaper of record, the *Times of London*, they decided that right before Christmas would be the ideal time for the *Times* to publish an exposé of Abernathy's corruption and extensive network of slave plantations.

Scrooge pledged half of his fortune to ensure the success of this risky endeavor, almost £650,000.

After thinking it over, Scrooge took Reverend Braithwaite's advice and began displaying a more confrontational temperament and attitude when and where it would leave a lasting public impression.

21 ﻉ

WITH A RUTHLESSNESS
KNOWING NO BOUNDS

Meanwhile, back in New York at Cyrus Abernathy's opulent East 38th Street mansion, Abernathy sat in his study with his daughter, Livinia.

Relishing the moment, Abernathy said, "My dear, we've come to the penultimate act in my little drama with Peter Cratchit."

"I'm afraid I don't understand, Father," replied Livinia. After the way her father had struck Peter several weeks earlier while aiming for Livinia, Abernathy had soon enough forgotten the matter. Peter had forced himself to forget the issue as well, confident that his chance for the fantastic riches Abernathy had promised him would disappear if he were to bring the matter up.

But Abernathy's daughter was an altogether different matter. Although she had begun attending Sunday services with Peter, her motives were now different and motivated by an altogether unexpected sincerity. Despite taking obvious delight in accompanying Peter to Transfiguration Church, she had become the very model of propriety, cultivating a sincere interest in the Christian religion.

"I've confided in you that I aim to raise the New York and Pennsylvania Coal and Lumber Company to great prominence in Europe, starting with England, and thence on to the Continent. At this point, luring young Peter Cratchit away from his employer, Sir

Nigel, is of the utmost importance to my efforts. Now fortune has smiled on my efforts, as I expected it would."

Abernathy picked up an unsealed envelope and handed it to Livinia.

"The captain of the SS *Caledonia* himself delivered that letter earlier today. When you read it, Livinia, you'll know why your cooperation is of utmost importance, *especially* since I'll be departing for London in a fortnight." Livinia had no way of knowing that every word her father was saying was a lie. Abernathy had received the letter earlier that day; however, it was a forgery he had paid a great deal of money for. He couldn't risk having Peter recognize his own script, as the two had spent months together by this point, and Peter wouldn't have been fooled by Abernathy writing the sad message.

Livinia affected a pout as she reached out to grab the envelope.

"Father, I thought you said I was going to accompany you to London for Christmas. If you go with Peter, we'll have only the servants to keep us company over the holiday. The rest of the family is in Chicago, and they won't be inclined to come to New York. That side of the family is Mother's, and they've always..." Livinia hesitated.

"*Detested* me? It's of no consequence, my dear. I find that tiresome lot of farmers and cattlemen to be a petty and jealous lot anyway," Abernathy said. "Livinia, I never said you *weren't* coming to England. On the contrary, it's now critical you accompany Peter to England. Read the letter," he reiterated with a self-satisfied smile.

"But Father, this letter is addressed to Peter from the Royal Consumption Infirmary for Consumption and Ailments of the Chest. I'm not sure reading his correspondence is quite proper. How—?"

"*Read it, Livinia*," Abernathy commanded.

As she unfolded the paper, Livinia's eyes widened in spontaneous shock as she proceeded to scan the short note.

October 28, 1856

To the Attention of Mr. Peter Cratchit
In Care of C. Abernathy
Number 10 East 38th Street
New York City
United States of America

Dear Mr. Cratchit,

It is my sad duty and with great regret that I write to inform you that Charlotte Cratchit expired on the night of October 26. Her attendant nurse, Allyce Bainbridge, told me that Charlotte passed away due to her severe consumption. Nurse Bainbridge was by her side and told me Charlotte passed away most peaceably and that your name was on her lips in her last moments. Arrangements are being made with your parents to take in your children for the moment until a proper home can be found for them on your return. Owing to the consumption that claimed her young life, Charlotte was buried in the churchyard of Saint Hubert's Church with all proper decorum observed.

Nurse Bainbridge told me Charlotte's final wish, may the Lord bless her soul, was for you and your children to find happiness after she was gone and not dwell in sorrow while she now dwells in joy amongst the angels.

On behalf of the Royal Consumption Infirmary for Consumption and Ailments of the Chest, I should like to extend our deepest condolences at your loss.

Respectfully,
Ainsley Michael Northrup, Administrator
Royal Consumption Infirmary for
Consumption and Ailments of the Chest

Already a woman of fair complexion, Livinia turned even whiter as her hand went to her mouth in a gesture of dismay.

"Ohhh no! Father, this is going to *destroy* Peter. He speaks of Charlotte with a devotion approaching Sunday worship."

She was puzzled by her father's smile at her words, his porcine belly shaking as he tried his utmost to contain the bellowing laughter building within.

"I know. Isn't the timing *perfect?*"

"Whatever do you mean?"

Abernathy smiled.

"Livinia, you must promise what you have just read and what I am about to tell you will not leave this room, and if I discover that you have broken your word, you shall spend the next four years at Miss Hayward's School for Delinquent Ladies up in Quebec. I am told Miss Hayward begins her wards' day by scrubbing the toilet floors at 5 a.m. I also guarantee you won't want to be milking cows in her barns when you must walk through an ice storm to reach them from the dormitories."

Abernathy let his threat sink in as a mix of horror and disgust spread across his daughter's face. She thought her father was a truly vile creature to threaten his only child to compel her silence.

"Father, I give you my word. I shall not tell a soul whatever you reveal to me tonight, so help me God."

"That's better; I thought you would see things my way, child. You see, Peter Cratchit hasn't seen that letter yet. Since it arrived on the SS *Caledonia* earlier today, it is my sad duty to deliver it to him, as it says at the top of the note. I wanted *you* to see it first."

"Whatever for, Father?" Livinia was perplexed. "This letter is going to break his heart!"

"Because you need to know ahead of time what a great consolation you'll be to him in his approaching time of grief. Having no one on the voyage to England but sad, disconsolate memories of his beloved Charlotte, you will be his constant companion in his greatest time of emotional trial." Alluding to the earlier incident when he had given Peter a now-healed concussion and fractured nose, Abernathy said, "I'm sure *you* will be on your best behavior in accompanying Peter to England. Of course, once the Royal Admiralty contract is firmly within our grasp and we return to the United States, we can pack his little brats off to an orphanage."

"Come now, Father. I would console Peter anyway, now that his wife has died."

"Of *course* you would, my dear," Abernathy replied in his most patronizing tone. "Perhaps you could give him more Sunday morning *carriage kisses*, eh?" he said with a smirk. "You've comforted a great many men, haven't you, Livinia? A glimpse of ankle here, a bit of décolletage there. It's a good thing you didn't inherit your mother's body, isn't it? You might not be as popular."

"I resent your words, Father." Livinia's eyes flashed dangerously.

"I suppose you do, but spare me your hypocrisy, daughter. I suppose if I had been a better father, my daughter wouldn't be just another notorious New York trollop in expensive clothing." Abernathy sniffed. "But as we say in our poker meetings, one has to play the hand he is dealt."

"'Trollop...?'"

Abernathy eyed his daughter without emotion.

"Let me ask you something, Livinia." Abernathy's hubris had led him into an ethical minefield without realizing it as he tented his fingers on his desk. "If a man asked you to spend an entire night in his company for a dollar, what would you say to him?"

"I would slap his face. What is your point, father?" Livinia asked archly.

"And what if that same man offered you one million dollars in exchange for your virtue, what would your answer be then?" Abernathy said, smirking.

Livinia hesitated as if considering her father's words when in reality, she was pondering whether or not to slap *him* at the insulting accusation against her virtue. Abernathy didn't know it yet, but he had misinterpreted her momentary pause in the worst possible way—one that would contribute to his ultimate undoing.

"What do you take me for, Father?" she asked in a low voice.

"My dear, let's not quibble. We know what you *are*, Livinia. Now, we're just haggling over the price."

In his overweening pride, Cyrus Abernathy had crossed a moral Rubicon Livinia did not realize she possessed until that Sunday when her father struck Peter, who was attempting to defend her. A disconcerting seed of revulsion at her father's insult to her maidenhood and his callous glee upon hearing of the death of Peter's wife took firm root in the soil of her heart. Over the last three months, Livinia Abernathy's painfully chaste love for Peter had slowly grown, despite his oh-so-proper English manners, lack of classical education, and politeness in the face of her various provocations, all of which had so grated on her when he first arrived back in July. Without realizing it, Livinia had come to care quite deeply about the awkward but handsome Englishman and his little family, with the endless stories of his wife, Charlotte, and his children. The days she spent nursing Peter back to health, under the watchful eye of her mother, were now etched in her heart as the happiest days of her life. In her mind, Peter had become Livinia's "knight errant." There were times she ached to cross the bounds of ladylike propriety again and kiss the worry lines from his forehead; however, Livinia was determined, despite her father's mockery, to be a proper Christian lady.

But now the unthinkable had happened, and for once, Cyrus Abernathy had lost control of a crucial part of his intricate plans. Livinia Abernathy, haughty young society heiress and jewel of New York City's high society, had fallen very much in love with Peter Cratchit; but Peter was forbidden fruit, a married man. While the words in the letter her father had just sworn her to silence before reading should have been a source of elation, the only emotion in Livinia Abernathy's infuriated heart was sadness, followed by deep foreboding. Her father was taking wicked delight in tragedy. Livinia had heard of her father's very unethical activities in his business dealings. But this time, there was a small warning voice deep inside her saying Cyrus Abernathy was about to embark on an endeavor that threatened to ensnare her in *real* evil.

"Well?" Her father's voice roused her from her distracted thoughts. "We needn't be unpleasant over things, Livinia. I should think you would be somewhat pleased that you shall have Peter Cratchit all to yourself." One of Abernathy's many personality flaws was that he couldn't hide his hubris.

"Oh, yes…of course, Father," she said, recovering her composure. "It's just that this news is so *sudden*."

"Well, it's not as if we didn't see the writing on the wall for his wife. Consumption devastates the lives of many people, Livinia. I fully expect you to devote yourself to Peter in his hour of need."

"Of course, Father. Don't you want me to be with you when you tell him this news? I feel so…" The normally voluble Livinia was at a loss for words, genuine concern for Peter overriding her fury at her father impugning her virtue to her face.

She's a fine actress, thought Abernathy. He had no way of knowing Livinia wasn't acting. She would console Peter, but *not* in the way her father intended.

Abernathy pulled himself upright, surprisingly spryly considering his enormous four-hundred-pound-plus frame.

"No, Livinia, I will give him the letter myself. I think there will be a suitable chance later today for you to comfort him. I want to leave Peter alone with his thoughts after he reads this."

Livinia knew the letter would bring Peter anything but peace.

Abernathy made his way to Peter's guest suite in the mansion. Although elevators hadn't been invented yet, he stepped into a contraption constructed in his mansion akin to a small room affixed by chains to a sophisticated counterweight system, rather like a very large kitchen dumbwaiter. At the ring of a special bell only Abernathy carried, three hulking servants in the mansion's basement waited until he stepped inside the small "floating room," as it was referred to in the household. Then, with considerable effort, they pulled on the heavy ropes until another butler on the destination floor rang a different bell signaling for them to stop. A heavy iron level-stop was slid into place, preventing any further up or down movement of the chamber.

Abernathy didn't bother to glance at the butler who opened the heavy oaken door when the floating room came to its customary slow stop, the tinkling of chimes announcing its arrival. Abernathy walked down the hallway until his ponderous frame stopped in front of Peter's three-room suite. Peter didn't hear Abernathy's approach because, although Cyrus Abernathy was truly gigantic in every sense of the word, he managed to carry himself with light footfalls. Stifling his malicious grin, he rapped twice in quick succession at the door.

"Yes?" came Peter's voice from within.

"Peter, it's Cyrus. A messenger from the SS *Caledonia* arrived a few minutes ago with a letter for you."

Abernathy suppressed a wicked grin as he heard Peter approaching the door. Peter opened the door.

"Please, Cyrus, do come in."

Abernathy looked around the sitting room/study as he handed Peter the letter he had shown Livinia only a few minutes earlier.

"You always get so excited when a letter arrives from Charlotte. I thought I would bring it up myself. You do tend to push yourself very hard these days."

Maddeningly, Peter bid Abernathy have a seat while, instead of opening the ostensible letter from his wife, he reached for a calculation sheet on his desk.

"Cyrus, I confess I made a slight error in my calculations regarding the board acreage we'll need to fulfill the Admiralty's hull requirements, but as luck would have it, the mistake is in our favor. Our net profit after procurement costs will be eighteen percent, not the fifteen percent I had told you earlier. I used the estimates for standard northern ash, not the southern live oak we had discussed."

"Well, that is good news, but I *am* distressed to find you working on a Saturday afternoon. I know Livinia was disappointed that she had no one to escort her to the opening of the new attraction down at Barnum's American Museum. You know how she goes on when a new cabinet of curiosities opens in the city; she *must* be among the first to attend it. We can review your new calculations first thing Monday morning."

Abernathy handed Peter the envelope closed with the wax seal he had applied only minutes earlier. He tried to dampen whatever look of anticipation he may have had on his face that would betray his knowledge of the envelope's contents.

"I'll leave you to read your correspondence in private, Peter. The family will be gathering in the dining room in forty-five minutes for dinner. Chef Bergammon has prepared a special roast pork dish tonight, and I confess the entire first floor smells like a restaurant."

"No, tarry a moment, Cyrus, and I'll go downstairs with you. I don't think this is a long letter from Charlotte; there can't be more than a sheet or two in here," Peter said as he stood up, grabbed a slender brass letter opener, and slit the envelope open. "I don't want that 'floating room' contraption of yours to make *two* trips."

Peter pulled out the single sheet of paper and began reading. As the meaning of the words started sinking in, he whispered, "Dear God, no...*no*." Not a man ordinarily given to displays of emotion, Peter was helpless to stop the tears of crushing grief as the missive slipped from his fingers onto his desk.

Looking at Peter's ashen face, Abernathy assumed his most solicitous demeanor.

"What is it, my boy? Is everything all right back home?"

Peter's face was a mask of grief. "It's Charlotte, sir," he blurted out, momentarily lapsing into formalism. "The letter isn't from her; it's from the Royal Consumption Infirmary. Charlotte...*my Charlotte is dead*. The consumption took her almost three weeks ago, and I was three thousand miles away when she needed me most."

An inchoate, heart-rending moan of grief escaped his lips as he slammed a fist down on his desk.

"Charlotte is *dead*, and I was off chasing a damned business contract instead of..."

Peter's usual resolute demeanor evaporated as his eyes assumed a glassy appearance. The sudden news of his wife's death overwhelmed him. He felt the room spinning, his legs buckling under him. In stark contrast to the brutal way he had struck Peter in the "carriage kissing" episode with Livinia, Abernathy's bear-like arms shot out and, as Peter keeled over, caught him as he slumped to the floor. Abernathy shouted for the floor butler with all the faux solicitude he could muster.

"Perkins! Get me the ammonia salts *now!*"

Given his immense size and strength, Abernathy lifted the supine Peter and propped him into a rough reclining position on a couch as he waited for the butler. Soon enough, there was a knock at the door.

"Come in, man! This isn't a time for niceties." The floor butler entered, handing Abernathy the small envelope with its vile-smelling contents.

"Go downstairs and tell Jefferson to fetch Dr. Vance immediately! I think our guest Peter has suffered some sort of attack!" he barked.

Perkins stood in the doorway, his mouth agape.

"Perkins! Damn you; tell Jefferson to summon Dr. Vance. Be quick, you idiot."

All in all, Abernathy was quite pleased with his "concerned surrogate father" performance. *And to think those buffoons at the Princeton Dramatics Society wouldn't let me play King Lear.* He sniffed. *More's the pity.*

After waiting several minutes, he waved the open envelope under Peter's nose, letting Peter inhale the noxiously potent vapors. It wasn't long before a disoriented Peter Cratchit sputtered to life, coughing and choking. He looked up at Abernathy in confusion.

"Cyrus? *What...?*" his voice trailed off as he caught sight of the letter on the desk, and his recollection of its contents came flooding back in a rush. Looking up, he asked in a subdued voice, "So it's true, then? *Charlotte is...?*"

"Yes, Peter, I am afraid so. Your Charlotte died almost three weeks ago. There was nothing anyone could have done. Once that wicked malady takes hold of a person, especially if they have a frail constitution, the end is preordained. When you passed out, I thought it in your best interest to read the contents of that sad letter from the SS *Caledonia*. Believe me, my boy, had I been able, I would have moved heaven and earth to save Charlotte's life," Abernathy said. *But there's no way in hell I would have*, he thought.

The pain was etched into Peter's face.

"There was nothing else? No letter from my parents? Nothing from Allyce Bainbridge, her nurse? She was quite devoted to Charlotte."

"From what I understand from the captain of the SS *Caledonia*, an express messenger from the Royal Consumption Infirmary made it to the ship from London just as it was preparing to depart

Portsmouth. Otherwise, it would have been almost another month until you were notified. I assume letters from your family will arrive when the *Caledonia* returns on her next trip to London."

Abernathy twisted the emotional knife with glee.

"Peter, your wife's been cold in the ground for almost a month now. You've got to be a man about this, my boy, and face the situation straight on. Besides, your intentions were good. You originally came here last summer because it would have rebounded to Charlotte's benefit, and she knew that. You just ran out of time."

Unbeknown to Abernathy, his daughter, Livinia, was listening to the conversation from just outside the doorway. For the last few months, her father had been most concerned about Peter's wife, inquiring about her health almost every day, even if just to raise the topic of her suffering and how Peter would alleviate it even more quickly if they could just secure the Admiralty contracts and he received his promised bonus. But now her ghoulish father was referring to poor Peter's wife as if she were a piece of meat rotting in a charnel house. *A piece of meat—the same way he thinks of me,* she thought. *Father, you are truly a vile man. And that's all I've ever been too,* she pondered, *a pretty toy to flit around this mansion for his amusement and to display like a puppet to his friends. A piece of meat.* Suddenly, Livinia could not control her loathing, and she slipped away down a nearby servants' stairway as an unsteady Peter and her father emerged from Peter's rooms.

"You've had a great shock, Peter, and nothing can prepare a man for news like this. I don't think you should be alone right now. Your appetite may be wanting, but I insist that you join us for dinner. I don't care if you only sip a glass of water; at a time like this, you need to be around people who care about you."

Abernathy had gotten his attorney to write the fake letter announcing Charlotte's death not six hours earlier. Cyrus Abernathy was *good,* good at Machiavellian evil. Unknown to Peter, the SS

Caledonia was still at sea, not due to dock in New York City for another three days. Abernathy ensured no further communications from Charlotte or Peter's family that would interfere with his plans would ever arrive at the residence.

At the very moment Peter was reading about her "death," Charlotte Cratchit was fast asleep in her bed at the Royal Consumption Infirmary.

22

THE BEST CHESS PIECES ARE PAWNS

John Delane was as good as his word. Little by little, news of the Royal Admiralty Board's plans for a massive upgrade to the quality and the firepower of the Royal Navy were leaked in his *Times of London* to the general public in a piecemeal fashion. The vast majority of readers—if they ventured any opinion at all—thought it more than past time to reinvigorate Her Majesty's Royal Navy. Any reader who followed the stories with genuine interest knew the pertinent details anyway. Still, Delane had convinced the "Honorable Society of Royal Medical Benefactors" that the issues at stake with Abernathy required approaching the overall situation with the finesse of a chess grandmaster, with all the deliberation this entailed.

With the cooperation of Minister-without-Portfolio Sidney Herbert, Delane also began to feed stories in a similar manner to American newspapers as well via dispatches. Although they couldn't help but come to the attention of Cyrus Abernathy (which they were intended to do anyway), the stories in the *Times of London* began to prominently feature Ebenezer Scrooge as leading the exclusive British bid as only a mere nuisance to the Hawthorne and Cavendish/Abernathy effort to win the massive naval contract. Given his penchant for seeing the business world through his Machiavellian chess lens, Abernathy always saw himself as the black king; however, his opponent, in this case personified by Scrooge, was invariably cast as

"The Defeated." Here and there, the pieces in the newspaper were "salted" with references to Ebenezer Scrooge's reawakened cruelty and cunning. These slowly trickled their way down to Scrooge's personal relationships, with the inevitable negative consequences.

Bob Cratchit timorously rapped on the door frame at Ebenezer Scrooge's office entrance.

"Begging your pardon, sir, but may I have a word?"

Scrooge looked up.

"Of course, Bob. Please sit down. You look troubled."

Bob couldn't lift his baggy eyes to meet those of his employer; he hadn't gotten much sleep of late, dividing his time between work, visiting Charlotte, and home life.

"Well, begging your pardon, sir, for the past couple of weeks, since those stories have been appearing in the *Times*, many people have been remarking on your ill temperament. If *I've* done anything to give offense, I want you to know that I—"

Scrooge held up a hand, cutting off his clerk.

"No, Bob, I know what you're thinking, and you've not done anything wrong. However, there are sensitive things afoot that require me to swear you to secrecy, even from your own family. Are we in agreement?"

"Of course, sir."

"I'm taking quite the chance, taking you into my confidence, Bob," Scrooge said. "Do you trust me?"

"Of course, sir. After all you've done for our family and meself, how could I not trust you?"

"Then if you see a brooding man of dark countenance stalking the streets of London who resembles the wicked man you once knew me to be, all I can tell you is do not put your faith in *appearances*, Bob. I'm taking on quite the challenge in wresting the Royal Navy contracts away from that wicked Cyrus Abernathy and his stalking horse, Peter's employer, Sir Nigel."

"But, again, begging your pardon, Mr. Scrooge, if your efforts to win the Royal Admiralty contracts are successful, it will damage Peter's career beyond measure. Charlotte already suffers from both the consumption and the thought that Peter is already ill-influenced by that man Abernathy and his daughter. Why would you cause either of them such pain? *Why would you do that?*"

Scrooge replied, "Bob, let me answer your question with one of my own. Does the surgeon stop operating because the patient is screaming?"

A confused Bob Cratchit, said, "No, sir."

"Then trust me, Bob. On my solemn word as a Christian gentleman, *not everything is as it seems.* I am never going back to the man whose memory I detest, although there will be times it may seem that way. You must have faith that no matter what rumors or gossip you may come across, even if it's from some of my associates at the London Royal Exchange, it is all rubbish."

23❧

WHEN A BRAWLER
MEETS FEAR

Cyrus Abernathy arrived to great acclaim in London in the late afternoon of December 8 aboard the SS *Caledonia*, with Peter and Livinia to follow on another ship arriving a week later. He knew from newspaper accounts that his partnership with Sir Nigel Fairweather-Hawthorne was considered the odds-on favorite to win the announced Admiralty Board bidding competition for the massive Royal Navy contract. Articles seeded by Delane in his *Times* hinted that the Admiralty Board had already chosen the Abernathy/Fairweather-Hawthorne consortium, but the official announcement wouldn't be made public until December 19. While Peter and Livinia were still at sea for another week, Sir Nigel greeted Abernathy as the SS *Caledonia* docked and escorted Abernathy to check in to the prestigious Saint Regis Hotel in London's tony Mayfair district. Hotel staff bustled around the huge hotel putting up gaily decorated Christmas decorations as they anticipated the upcoming holiday.

"Would you like to have dinner this evening, Cyrus?" Sir Nigel asked. "I haven't seen you since June, and we have much to discuss. The Saint Regis has already begun serving a succulent goose prepared Christmas-style, stuffed with either oysters or walnut dressing."

"I'm afraid we'll have to postpone dinner until tomorrow, Nigel," Abernathy said. "Parts of the crossing were a bit stormier than my stomach cares to tolerate these days, and I think I would rather get a good night's rest."

"Of course; how inconsiderate of me. I do beg your pardon," Sir Nigel replied. "I have meetings with my cousin at the Admiralty Board tomorrow morning, and then I return to my office around one o'clock. We can meet then. Why don't we open my new bottle of 1839 Lagavulin scotch over a game of chess, and then off to an early dinner? Perhaps Grenville will be able to join us with any new news about the Admiralty Board's deliberations. Besides, we can toast our pending good fortune as an early Christmas gift to both of us!"

"Excellent, Nigel," Abernathy said as he turned to go up to his suite, thankful it was on the hotel's second floor. With his massive frame, climbing flights of stairs was not Cyrus Abernathy's forte. "I will see you then. I will have all the latest supplier estimates if your cousin requires any updates. They haven't changed much, but I'm sure we can sharpen our quills a bit if we have to make any adjustments."

After the hotel valets unpacked Abernathy's mountainous luggage, he gave them a generous tip and closed and locked his door. The coming weeks should be the crowning moment of his opening business gambit to cripple the British shipbuilding industry, just as the height of the Christmas season approached. However, on his first night in London, Cyrus Abernathy, notwithstanding the consumption of a pint of premium whiskey procured for him by an ingratiating concierge, couldn't sleep.

Despite trying to distract Peter Cratchit with Livinia, Peter's ultimate infidelity on the transatlantic voyage with his daughter was no sure thing. Abernathy remained convinced that having the brilliant Peter as part of the Abernathy family was instrumental to his competitive position in every future endeavor. Abernathy realized he had made a critical mistake in losing his temper with Livinia back in October and striking Peter in his blind rage instead. Although Peter was in no position to contradict him, Abernathy did his best to reassure Peter that the events of that Sunday morning were a rare and most regrettable aberration brought on by years of frustration at being a father of a vehemently headstrong daughter.

The truth was that earlier in his life, the mountainous Abernathy had been a most fearsome street brawler. He was also one of the only people to ever defeat the Five Points Bowery Bhoys' infamous street gang leader, William "Bill the Butcher" Poole, in a fight.

Abernathy had learned that some of the stevedores unloading his ships were being extorted for money by Poole's gang. The captain of the SS *Caledonia* had shown up bloodied at Abernathy's door two years earlier with a note from the notorious Poole, telling Abernathy that Poole expected a one-hundred-dollar "protective payment" for every shipload of cargo destined for the New York and Pennsylvania Railroad Company. After the incident, Abernathy took matters into his own hands.

Resolving to send a very public message to Bill the Butcher and any others of his ilk with similar ideas for extorting money from him, one winter evening, Abernathy took twenty of his largest, toughest railroad employees down to Poole's bar in the Bowery. Walking into the establishment attired in one of his most expensive, delicate silk suits to look the part of a large, effete dandy, the hulking Abernathy demanded in a loud voice that "the little sissy-boy coward Poole" show himself. Poole, who didn't fear anyone due to his own well-founded reputation for brutality—which included beating men to death and gouging their eyes out—strutted out from behind the bar. Not recognizing Abernathy, instead mistaking him for a braggart, uptown dandy, Poole wasted no time in conversation and took the first swing. Abernathy stopped Bill the Butcher Poole's punch in mid-swing, his fearsome grip crushing the bones in Poole's fist. Poole's other hand came whistling around with a razor-sharp fighting knife aimed at Abernathy's jugular just as Abernathy delivered an uppercut punch to Poole's solar plexus. Abernathy's punch not only lifted him off his feet and knocked the wind out of Bill the Butcher, it broke four ribs and caused Poole internal injuries that required almost a whole month from which to recover.

Nobody had ever meted out punishment like this to Bill the Butcher. Seeing their boss being thrashed by this cocky, uptown giant of a stranger, the Bowery Bhoys sprang to his defense, but Abernathy's thugs were ready for them. Poole's men were armed with lead pipes, but Abernathy's burly toughs all had two-foot lengths of iron railroad chain hidden inside their black leather overcoats. The ensuing fight lasted only five minutes, but Poole, his gang, and his beloved bar were *wrecked*.

Standing over, looking down at the bleeding, gasping Poole, Abernathy said, "Nice to finally make your acquaintance, *Mr. Poole*." As Poole lay struggling to pull in a breath on the floor, Abernathy crouched down, lifted him by his collar, and hissed, "If you remember nothing else from this day, let this be your lesson, *Billy Boy*. I am Cyrus Abernathy, and I don't take kindly to gutter scum stealing money from my ships or my company. Try your little games with me again, and you have my word; there won't be enough of you left to stuff inside a pickle jar."

Back in his London hotel suite, as the December sun slid below the horizon and the streets of London grew dark, Abernathy eyed a second pint of whiskey, thinking it would calm his nerves. He began pacing the floor of his spacious suite at the Saint Regis Hotel. Second-guessing his natural assumption Livinia would seduce Peter by the time they arrived in London was a rare strategic error in judgment for the crafty Abernathy. Therein lay his great love of chess, a most gentle warfare that permitted him to hone his cunning—and now he feared he had lost his "queen," so to speak. Abernathy's greatest fear was that if Peter saw his ailing wife, Charlotte, still alive, the normally reserved Peter would be furious at Abernathy's treachery and ruin Abernathy's plans before the contracts could be inked.

Every hour that passed turned that *possibility* into a *likelihood*. After that Sunday evening in October, he had no doubt that Peter would destroy everything Abernathy had carefully worked to build over the past few years with a vengeance. Peter's devotion to Charlotte would nullify Abernathy's plans for a union between Peter and Livinia. Not a man to leave anything to chance, Abernathy resolved to take care of this particular loose end as a grieving Peter on the high seas fast approached England, thinking his beloved wife dead and buried.

He knew only one way to allay his growing apprehension. Abernathy resolved to pay the ailing Charlotte a stealthy visit in the Royal Consumption Infirmary that very night and smother her in her bed. When she was discovered lifeless the following morning, the Royal Consumption Infirmary's staff would naturally assume she died of her consumption during the night.

Abernathy immediately felt relief wash over him as he pulled the cord for the concierge service. As he was the hotel's most important guest by far, at least on this night, the concierge raced to the suite and knocked.

"Come in," Abernathy called out.

On entering, the concierge gave a curt nod and asked, "How may I be of service, Mr. Abernathy?"

"Tell me, do you happen to know when the hospitals around here close to visitors? I know it's far too late already this evening, but it would be good to know for future reference," Abernathy said with a greasy smile. "I have a distant English relation who had his leg amputated from a war injury and I would like to surprise him while I'm in London."

"Well, sir, most of those sorts of places close to public visits right at seven o'clock, so's the night staff has a chance to get up to speed, in a manner of speaking. Will you need anything else?"

Abernathy dug two gold sovereigns out of his vest pocket and slid them across the suite's writing desk to the concierge, who accepted them with wide eyes. He assured the discretion of the concierge with promises of more on delivery of further discreet "favors."

"Well, from time to time, I may require special, umm, *conveniences* that require maximum discretion," Abernathy said, winking broadly. The concierge naturally assumed a *none-of-my-business* deferential attitude.

"Will you be needing anything *tonight*, sir?"

"Well, yes, I will require the services of a large hansom cab for an hour or two around nine thirty. As you can see," Abernathy said, looking down at his ponderous girth with a self-deprecating gesture, "an ordinary cab will not do. I need a cab chosen with your degree of discretion and trustworthiness, and I will pay the driver very well for his understanding of my requirement for privacy. I also need to enter and exit your establishment in a most discreet fashion." Abernathy raised his hands in false modesty. "Can you arrange these things for me?"

The concierge smiled and said, "There is a service door at the bottom of the stairs opposite your room that opens onto the alley to the right of the main hotel building. That door can be opened from the outside by your room key, Mr. Abernathy. I will ensure there is a cab according to your requirements waiting there at nine-thirty."

"Wonderful," Abernathy said with a smile. "That will be all for the moment."

Two hours later, Abernathy set out alone from the opulent Saint Regis Hotel in Mayfair at nine-thirty to pay Charlotte a very private visit. He told no one in his entourage of his plans and, after leaving the hotel by the special side door, climbed into a rather large, empty hansom cab waiting in the alley. Abernathy told the driver the address of the Royal Consumption Infirmary, and the larger version of the cab that seated four people facing each other pulled away at a brisk trot.

No sooner had Abernathy glanced down at his pocket watch than he jerked his head up, sensing a familiar but unwelcome presence in the large cab with him. An American voice with a velvety southern twang from behind a copy of the *Times of London* removed all doubt.

"You know, Cyrus, despite your, uhh, *proclivities*, I should think a man of your learning would be somewhat acquainted with the Good Book. Are you familiar with the Old Testament? I have always found the implications in the Book of Deuteronomy's thirtieth chapter quite *instructive*."

Cyrus Abernathy looked up with a visible start to see Michel St. Tutelairé sitting across from him in the cab! Abernathy blinked in astonishment; he was *sure* the carriage was empty when he climbed inside. The lithe St. Tutelairé was dressed in an elegant bespoke black wool dinner suit with a long frock coat, bow tie, expensive gold pocket watch on a fob loop, and he gripped a long gold lion's-head-topped ebony walking stick.

St. Tutelairé gave a disdainful smile on seeing the look of recognition mixed with consternation wash over Abernathy's face.

"It's been a long time, hasn't it, Cyrus?" Except in St. Tutelairé's southern accent, Abernathy's name came out as *SAHHH-RIS*.

"Isn't it a bit late to be visiting patients at the Royal Consumption Infirmary? But then, we both know, the great Cyrus Abernathy doesn't let minor trifles like 'playing by the rules' get in his way, does he?" St. Tutelairé said in a mocking tone. Frozen by a fear beyond his ability to comprehend, Abernathy sat in mesmerized silence as St. Tutelairé continued.

"In fact, Cyrus, the reason for your little clandestine visit to the hospital tonight is to ensure Charlotte Cratchit does not live to see another sunrise, isn't it? I can only imagine what an inconvenience to your grand plans it will be when Charlotte recovers from her consumption, and she *will* recover," the disquietingly serene St. Tutelairé declared with an ominous note of disapproval.

What the hell was St. Tutelairé doing here? How had he entered the carriage unnoticed, and how had his old nemesis discovered his plans? Abernathy was too stunned by this revelation of his murderous plans to respond, much less interrupt St. Tutelairé's patronizing reproach, so the American southerner continued.

"May I give you a bit of unsolicited advice, Cyrus? If I can paraphrase that chapter of Deuteronomy, *y'all have a choice to make*. Now, I recommend you return to the Saint Regis Hotel and choose a nice late dinner with some of your business compatriots. I'm sure the kitchen will reopen for the great Cyrus Abernathy." Again, a tone of condescension entered Michel St. Tutelairé's voice quite distinctly. "Might I recommend their foie-gras-stuffed petite goose with oyster and French white truffle sauce? It would be eminently satisfactory to a man with your gustatory discernment. A gourmand like you could pair that with a bottle of Saint Regis 1851 Chateau Rieussec Sauternes. The 1851's notes of apricot, butterscotch, ginger, and citrus stand up very well to the foie gras' rich texture.

"I can assure you dinner would be far preferable to smothering poor Charlotte Cratchit in her bed tonight. We both know you've killed a fair number of people who have gotten in your way, Cyrus, but Charlotte Cratchit shall not die this night, not by your hand nor by another's," the American said with steely menace. Abernathy was still trying to process how St. Tutelairé could know of his wicked purpose in going to the Royal Consumption Infirmary, especially after his careful efforts to ensure secrecy.

As the large cab slowed to stop, St. Tutelairé tipped his hat and casually said, "Well, here we are, Cyrus. Y'all have a good night now," patronizingly patting Abernathy's knee as if he were a small child. The cab stopped, and the mysterious American alit; however, when Abernathy looked out the cab window, there was no sign of St. Tutelairé. The street was deserted, and the cab was right back in the alley next to the Saint Regis Hotel, right in front of the service door Abernathy had exited moments earlier. A dread fear he hadn't known in years kept him motionless in the carriage for some time.

24

PERDURING EVIL MAKES ITS GAMBIT

Shaken, but undeterred due to the perduring blackness of his heart, Abernathy ignored the cognitive dissonance of his experience with the mysterious American, returned to his hotel suite, and promptly summoned the concierge. Not wishing to cause a scene he knew would only spread among the gossipy hotel staff like wildfire, Abernathy knew the situation called for a much more *delicate* approach.

"I left as we discussed at nine thirty, and there was a cab waiting outside the service stairway side door as I requested; however, it was already occupied."

The concierge flushed red in mortal embarrassment.

"Sir, I assure you on my word as an employee of the Saint Regis, I made the arrangements myself according to your specifications—a large, vacant hansom carriage for your exclusive use and a very discreet driver." Drawing himself to his full height, he said in a slightly aggrieved tone, "The Saint Regis prides itself on a high level of exactitude in catering to our guests. You are no different, Mr. Abernathy—I assure you."

Knowing there was something not quite right with Michel St. Tutelairé's peculiar talent for having shown up at precisely the wrong time, Abernathy didn't press the issue and instead let the matter drop.

"Can you arrange for another carriage in twenty minutes? *An empty carriage this time?*" Abernathy asked.

"Of course, sir. I shall meet you downstairs shortly before eleven o'clock, and I will ensure, in your presence, that the carriage is indeed empty. Will that be satisfactory?"

Letting the concierge draw his own conclusion, Abernathy let out a coarse laugh and said with a lecherous wink, "Of course! Mustn't keep the lady waiting, eh?"

Twenty minutes later, another hansom cab pulled up outside the side door to the Saint Regis and, after the concierge checked the inside of the carriage and confirmed to Abernathy it truly *was* unoccupied, Abernathy set off for Charlotte's hospital again. He handed the driver a crown when the cab arrived and said, "Wait here. I shan't be long."

After Abernathy's insistent knocking, the sullen attendant who answered the front entrance door refused to let Abernathy in until he poured five sovereigns into his meaty hand and showed them to the attendant, whose eyes lit up. The attendant opened the door and snatched up the proffered gold coins. The imposing Abernathy then pressed five more sovereigns into the attendant's hand and gutturally whispered, "And that's for forgetting I was ever here. Now, just point the way to the Third Floor Consumptives Ward." The attendant nodded, pointing at the dimly lit stairway, and silently withdrew to a desk hidden in the Stygian shadows near the front door.

Abernathy made his way up the stairs to the now-silent, darkened ward where Peter Cratchit said his wife was convalescing and, carefully counting the beds, made his way to where Charlotte Cratchit lay sleeping. He glanced around and satisfied himself that no one, *especially* Michel St. Tutelairé, was in the room other than the fitfully sleeping patients, some snoring, some moaning in their sleep. Abernathy grabbed the down feather pillow from the chair next to Charlotte's bed with both hands. Smiling with evil satisfaction, he intended to make quick work of his wicked task.

As he adroitly brought the pillow down over Charlotte's face with a deadly grace borne of experience, Abernathy found one of his meaty forearms suddenly clenched in the viselike grip of a Royal Consumption Infirmary orderly who'd quietly materialized out of the darkness. Not wanting to risk the hue and cry that would be the catalyst of an embarrassing public scene in the dimly lit ward, his heart pounding, Abernathy allowed the orderly to take the pillow from his grasp without protest and acquiesced to being led out into the hallway.

25 ❧

THE UNHOLY CANNOT
REMAIN HIDDEN FOREVER

Preparing to vent his faux outrage at this rough treatment by a mere hospital orderly, Abernathy gazed into the orderly's face, illuminated in the hallway gas light, only to have the blood drain from his own. It was *Michel St. Tutelairé*—now dressed in the white uniform of a Royal Consumption Infirmary attendant. Once again in his velvety Georgia accent, St. Tutelairé sighed with more than a hint of exasperation and asked Abernathy as if reproaching a recalcitrant child, "Cyrus, Cyrus…what am I to do with you? The foie-gras-stuffed petite goose back at your hotel would have been a far wiser choice than attempted murder, yet evil still rules your heart. I told you before, *I have my orders*; no harm shall come to Charlotte Cratchit. And don't think of offering me the ten sovereigns I've already returned to your purse. Gold will not avail you this night."

All the while, the slim St. Tutelairé inexorably manhandled Cyrus Abernathy's ponderous frame down several flights of stairs and toward the Infirmary front door with no more effort than if he were guiding an invalid to the Infirmary solarium for a bit of fresh air. As the incongruous pair reached the street outside the hospital, the original large hansom cab Abernathy engaged when he first encountered the preternaturally unnerving St. Tutelairé was again waiting at the curb.

Abernathy paled further as St. Tutelairé began speaking in fluent Latin. From the recesses of his mind, Abernathy understood every terrifying word: "Heed my words carefully, Cyrus Abernathy, for I have been sent as a warning. Your wickedness is tempting the terrible wrath of God. When you signed your contract with His ancient adversary on that accursed October night in 1822, your pride blinded you to the condition that the evil document promising power and riches did not grant you power over innocent life. Death will not visit Charlotte Cratchit this night."

Abernathy's massive frame scrambled into the cab with the terror of a man who'd now come face to face twice in one night with what *couldn't* be real: an irresistible power beyond his comprehension that knew his deepest, darkest secrets. Despite their brief and hostile encounters in the United States, Abernathy now knew that whatever Michel St. Tutelairé claimed to be, he was no "American lumber businessman."

How on earth does he know about the contract I signed back in 1822?

A long-forgotten "business associate" had assured the young Princeton graduate on that evening that by promising certain things to "the Lord of This World," Abernathy would reap untold power and riches as a result, so in his heedless greed, he gladly pricked his thumb and affixed his fat fingerprint to the ancient parchment document. Besides, who read the fine print, especially if it was in a dead language?

As the carriage door slammed shut with an audible *chunk*, its lock clicking into place, Abernathy took a moment to dare a glance back at the hospital through the cab's rear window. St. Tutelairé was once again clothed in his black suit and long frock coat, except for the impossibly magnificent, luminous wings Abernathy saw slowly unfold from St. Tutelairé's back. And they were *not* the delicate, translucent wings out of a child's fairy tale; they were the mighty, densely feathered wings of an enormous eagle. Abernathy, in his terror, retained the presence of mind to realize that St. Tutelairé was no mere mortal—his adversary this night was a mighty and very angry *angel*.

Abernathy's panicked gaze locked eyes with those of the now-ethereal Michel St. Tutelairé, whose eyes glowed with baleful bluish-white fire. St. Tutelairé brandished his now brightly glowing walking stick at the retreating cab like a war sword. Bringing the night's encounter with St. Tutelairé full circle, Abernathy heard a paraphrase of Deuteronomy in St. Tutelairé's voice, this time in perfect English:

"I, Mī Kā'EL, command thee in the name of the Eternal One to depart this place, thou unclean son of Cain. Because thou hast cast thy lot with the angel of the pit, I have arrayed Myself against thee."

Upon hearing these damning words resonate with awe-inspiring power and an authority brooking no challenge, the mortally terrified Cyrus Abernathy profusely soiled himself.

Arriving back at the Saint Regis Hotel fifteen minutes later, Abernathy unlocked the hotel's alleyway door and came as close to running to his suite as his gargantuan size would permit, trailing a disgusting, putrid mess. Once inside, he placed his ruined clothing inside a laundry bag outside his door and rang for the night concierge, who showed up at his door in a matter of moments. Wrinkling his nose at the foul smell emanating from the laundry sack, the concierge knocked on the door to the suite.

He didn't have time to ask what Abernathy required before he heard a timorous, quivering voice from behind the suite door that did not sound at all like the commanding, tyrannical presence the hotel staff was all too familiar with.

"*Look down*," the concierge heard. He did so, and two gold sovereigns slid out from under the door. "They are to assure your discretion in this matter, my good man. I became quite ill while I was out tonight, and I want those clothes burned; do you understand me?"

Knowing nothing of Abernathy's harrowing evening, the concierge took him at his word.

"I assure you this bag will be immediately tossed into the hotel furnace. Is there anything else, Mr. Abernathy?"

"Y-y-yes," Abernathy stammered. "You will want the night cleaning man to wash the stairway coming up to this floor from the side entrance door. And not a word of this to anyone, or I will have your job before the sun rises. Am I clear?"

"Very clear, sir. I hope your stomach is more at ease in the morning."

26

HONESTY'S PAINFUL PRICE

Livinia Abernathy awoke early and looked out her first-class state-room berth on the deck of the steamship SS *Arctic* while the ship was still a good day's time away from docking in Portsmouth. The December North Atlantic Ocean was turbulent that morning, but not any more so than the first part of the crossing. She looked down the length of the ship and knew she'd see the solitary figure at the railing gazing with dead eyes fixed on the eastern horizon in the direction of the British Isles. Throughout the trip, Livinia observed him at different times during the day, and her heart broke seeing Peter buffeted by the icy winds and salt spray, his hands often frozen to the ship's iron railing. Livinia felt powerless to ease his grief.

She still remembered that awful week when Peter would only fitfully open his swollen eyes, looking about the room without seeing anything. Dr. Vance had placed small wooden splints inside and outside Peter's nose. Livinia and her mother dutifully tended to Peter as his face healed, regularly applying cold compresses and ice to reduce the swelling on the right side of his face. Under her mother's ever-watchful eye, Livinia took charge of the regular rotation of people who nursed Peter's injuries. Livinia longed to gently cover Peter's injured face with soft kisses of loving contrition as if they might hasten his healing, but she could not. *She would not.* At the time, before receiving Charlotte's death notice from the Royal Consumption Infirmary, Peter was a faithful, devoted husband, and in the days and weeks since the awful incident with her father, she grew to appreciate what *that* kind of love might be like.

Yes, Livinia was in love with Peter, but she knew, because of his devotion to his late wife, that Peter's heart could remain locked away inside a shell of solitude and grief. In the twelve days since they had departed New York City, there had been many occasions when Livinia had to procure pitchers of warm salt water to slowly pour over Peter's hands and free them from the railing, with Peter oblivious to it all. Livinia could only conclude the pain in his heart was greater than any physical pain he might endure—including the blow from her father.

Livinia dressed quickly and put on her coat, scarf, and padded leather gloves as the Second Mate knocked on her door.

"Miss Abernathy, Mr. Cratchit has been out there over half an hour, and the captain is becoming concerned again."

Livinia opened the door and said, "Very well," then asked, "Do you have the water ready?"

The Second Mate responded by lifting a brass pitcher for her to see. They proceeded out to the deck and over to Peter. The Second Mate slowly poured the warm seawater over Peter's near-frostbitten hands as Livinia gently pried them loose from the railing.

"Come, Peter," she gently urged. "We must go inside now. You'll be of no use to your children if you're sick."

Peter didn't resist as Livinia and the Second Mate guided him through the open hatchway and out of the winter gale. The next day would bring them within sight of England and thence up the Thames to dock in London.

It would be a decidedly mixed blessing.

27 ⊰

TIMING IS EVERYTHING

As if Cyrus Abernathy's utter humiliation at the hands of Michel St.
Tutelairé were not enough, a week later to the day, on December
15, two days before Peter and Livinia Abernathy were to arrive in
London aboard the SS *Arctic*, John Delane's *Times of London* newspaper ran the headline "ABERNATHY-FAIRWEATHER NAVY BID
INSULTS CROWN WITH SLAVE LABOR." Thus, the opening
shot of Ebenezer Scrooge's salvo against the machinations of Sir Nigel
Fairweather-Hawthorne and Cyrus Abernathy was fired. In a bold
front-page story, it revealed the scandal that, according to "impeccable sources," the Cyrus Abernathy and Sir Nigel Fairweather-
Hawthorne consortium intended to use slave labor from American
and Brazilian plantations to supply Great Britain with wood products for the Royal Navy fleet rebuilding program. The British public was appropriately outraged, and the instantaneous outpouring of
public indignation explained why the joint Abernathy/Fairweather-
Hawthorne bid was returned from the Admiralty Offices with the
word "*REJECTED*" boldly scrawled across the first page of the bid in
bright red calligraphic pen, signed by Secretary of State for War, Fox
Maule, himself. Ebenezer Scrooge and the rest of the "Honorable
Society of Royal Medical Benefactors" noted with grim satisfaction
that Britain's highest military authority had rejected the Abernathy/
Fairweather-Hawthorne bid.

Despite the still-appealing but higher-priced bid from the consortium Ebenezer Scrooge had put together with Michel St. Tutelairé's

Sturdy Eagle Wood Products and London's premier woodworking firm, Holland and Sons Fine Furnishers and Outfitters, the Admiralty Board delayed awarding the final seven-year £4.5 million contract pending the results of a parliamentary inquiry into what the British press now called the "Abernathy Slavery Scandal." The following day's *Times* reported that a two-year £1.5 million "interim contract" was awarded to Scrooge's alternative joint American/English lumber cooperative. As the contract was not for the initial £4.5 million value, Ebenezer Scrooge lost two-thirds of his investment—a sizable portion of his contribution.

His reputation in Europe tarnished for the foreseeable future, an enraged, humiliated Cyrus Abernathy stormed into Sir Nigel's offices, his wrath on full display, the incident with Michel St. Tutelairé having receded like a bad dream. All gaiety associated with the approaching Christmas was immediately silenced as Abernathy stomped into the offices like an angry bull. Sir Nigel rather enjoyed the carols sung by his happy office staff; however, they ceased immediately on Abernathy's appearance. "O Come All Ye Faithful" fast gave way to a pensive silence.

Abernathy roared at his British partner, "Why in the Devil's own name did you reveal to the Admiralty Board we were sourcing the lumber from plantations that use slaves?"

Cowering behind his desk, Sir Nigel croaked, "I've not said a word to anyone, Cyrus. I didn't even know until that blasted headline came out that we were using wood connected with slavery to begin with. You never said a word. I assumed the lumber was at such a low cost because you were willing to accept the losses to establish us and then make the costs up in the future."

Abernathy stood there, pondering the truth of Sir Nigel's statement. Then, a thought struck him like a thunderbolt.

"*Cratchit!* It must have been your little weasel, Peter Cratchit! That worm traveled with me everywhere except Brazil. Are you sure he never said anything to you, Nigel?"

A terrified Nigel only sputtered, "If he had, Cyrus, I'd have told you right away our bid would be untenable because of the slavery angle. It is common knowledge that most people here abhor slavery. It's been almost fifty years since King George III abolished it."

Unable to refute Sir Nigel's logic, Abernathy's wrath only intensified.

"First, that little church-monkey clerk of yours turns my daughter into some virtue-chasing angel, and now he's single-handedly destroyed everything I've worked for here in England. *This shall not stand*, Nigel, unless you wish to share the blame with him. I'm becoming quite weary of these little islands called Her Majesty's kingdom. It's not bad enough I have to be reminded of the *Crown* and how the mighty British Empire ran from the Americans in 1783 with its tail between its legs like a whipped cur, leaving behind thousands of loyal British subjects like my own family, but now the Abernathy name will be dragged through the mud *all over again!*" Abernathy's voice quivered in proportion to his growing rage and, in a swift motion that belied his size, he grabbed a terrified Sir Nigel by his coat lapels and slammed him up and into a wall, with Nigel's feet dangling a full foot off the floor.

"Unless you wish to share the 'credit' for proposing to rebuild the Royal Navy using slave labor and officially committing perjury to your Ministry of War with the contract offer, you're going to help me nail that little toad Peter Cratchit to the wall. Remember, you signed the proposal to the Secretary of State for War, too."

Abernathy stared into Sir Nigel's terrified eyes.

"Do we understand each other, Nigel?" as Abernathy let go of Sir Nigel's lapels.

Abernathy didn't even wait for a reply as he quickly calculated that he had spent roughly $800 having Peter accompany him around the East Coast of the United States. This did not account for the food and lodging at the Abernathy residence, which had suddenly become worth a small fortune.

"How much did you give Peter as an advance for his travels?"

"Fifty gold sovereigns," Nigel replied.

"Well, even if he managed to save it all, and I know he hasn't, there's no way Peter Cratchit can repay the equivalent of seven hundred pounds in American dollars due to me on demand, is there? What happens here in England if a man cannot satisfy his debts?" Abernathy demanded.

"Why, the creditor party obtains formal 'Articles of Indebtedness' from a magistrate, and the Metropolitan Police carry the debtor off straight away to King's Bench," Sir Nigel said.

"King's Bench? What's a 'King's Bench'?" Abernathy demanded.

"It's a *where*, Cyrus," Sir Nigel answered. "King's Bench is the most punitive debtors' prison in London. Sometimes a man will disappear into that filthy place for the rest of his life if he can't satisfy his debts. If you leave my name and that of Hawthorne and Cavendish Furniture and Carpentry Works out of any proceedings, I can help you get your revenge."

A relieved smile crept across Sir Nigel's face, where mere seconds earlier a mortal terror had taken root that he'd soon witness one of Sir Richard Mayne's Scotland Yard detective squads burst into the premises with his name on an arrest warrant.

"Then we'll have to make sure he'll never be able to satisfy those debts, won't we? I think it is fitting Peter Cratchit is presented with Articles of Indebtedness when the SS *Arctic* docks here tomorrow. He'll be unable to pay, and it'll be off to King's Bench with him, courtesy of the Metropolitan Police.

"I won't deny Livinia her special Christmas holiday in London, but then it'll be straight back to America for me on the first available ship," Abernathy rued. He had been checkmated in his larger plan to avenge his father, but he would still savor this smaller victory in the debtors' court.

The SS *Arctic* made its way up the Thames River on a cold December 16, 1856. As Peter and Livinia prepared to depart the ship with the other passengers, Livinia's spirits were lifted as she noticed knots of carolers scattered here and there about the wharf, with earnest, but slightly off-key versions of "God Rest Ye Merry Gentlemen" competed with "O Little Towne of Bethlehem: for donations of a farthing or tuppence. They also spotted a small knot of London Metropolitan Police officers milling about the bottom of the gangway. Then, Livinia noticed one man towering above them all. "Peter, look; it's Father!" she exclaimed.

As porters began removing the first-class passengers' baggage from the SS *Arctic*, Peter and Livinia saw a scowling Cyrus Abernathy with a clutch of officers from the Metropolitan Police pointing at them. As the two reached the bottom of the gangway, a police officer clutching papers in his hand asked, "Are you Peter Cratchit?"

No sooner did Peter manage to croak out a surprised "Yes" than he was grabbed on either side by a police officer.

Before he could utter a word of protest, Peter was handcuffed and hustled into the back of a Metropolitan Police van with the words "*King's Bench*" painted on the side in gilded letters, pulled by a pair of sturdy quarter horses.

Livinia raced up to her father.

"Father, what is the meaning of this? Why has Peter been arrested?"

"Your devious little knight-in-shining-armor has been embez-zling from both me *and* his boss, Sir Nigel," Abernathy retorted. "We're going to make sure he never sees the outside of the King's Bench Debtors' Prison until he needs a cane to walk."

As a smug Abernathy turned to see the van with Peter trundle off into the distance, Livinia tore loose from her father's grasp while he was momentarily distracted.

"Livinia!" he bellowed, but as he looked around the sea of people milling about the wharf, Abernathy realized that not only was Peter Cratchit gone, but so was his daughter.

Ebenezer Scrooge, Peter's father, Bob Cratchit, and Michel St. Tutelairé watched the distressing drama play out from a discreet dis-tance. They had gone down to the pier to properly welcome Peter home for Christmas and were taken aback by the turn of events. They saw the beautiful young woman with Peter tear loose from Cyrus Abernathy's grasp and deftly disappear into the milling wharf side tumult.

"I'll go after the young woman; she must be Abernathy's daugh-ter, Livinia," said St. Tutelairé with a knowing look. "Judging by her father's face, he didn't expect that kind of defiance from her. Knowing Cyrus's temper, if he catches up with her, I fear in his rage he may forget Livinia is his daughter and a lady, despite her faults. Y'all best go to King's Bench Prison and see to Peter Cratchit."

"I've promised to visit Charlotte this afternoon, good sir," said Bob Cratchit. "She was expecting me to have Peter with me. This is going to come as a great shock to her."

Scrooge grabbed Bob Cratchit's shoulder.

"Bob, remember our chat about the surgeon continuing to operate even if the patient is in pain. After we speak with Charlotte, I'll be off to

King's Bench myself to see about Peter straight away and then meet you at your home later for dinner."

But not before collecting Sidney Herbert and Metropolitan Police Chief Mayne, Scrooge thought. *I'm going to need their help with this mess.*

The two men turned to speak with Michel St. Tutelairé, but he had already vanished in pursuit of Livinia Abernathy.

Livinia had just been helped into a roomy coach, desperate to get away from her father and just as determined to help Peter Cratchit. Before answering the driver's query as to where she was going, she heard a honeyed American southern accent behind her as a man climbed into the cab.

"Hello, ma'am. Cabs seem to be in short supply this mornin', so I don't suppose y'all mind if we share a ride?" asked the suave Michel St. Tutelairé.

Livinia recognized the American southern accent at once and, as she assumed the stranger to be one of her father's hirelings in pursuit, she reached to unlock the door on the opposite side of the carriage to make a quick getaway, but to her vexation (and St. Tutelairé's bemusement), the door handle would not budge.

Livinia turned to him, eyes blazing.

"I don't care who you are, sir. You will *not* be taking me to my father."

St. Tutelairé gave a gentle chuckle.

"You're right, Miss Abernathy. I'm not taking you anywhere *near* your father, given his foul mood at your defiance. I assure you, however, I am the last person on earth your father wants to see right now," he said, taking her hand and lightly brushing his lips over the back.

Livinia's mind reeled as she gathered her wits.

If he's not one of father's men, how did he know my name? she wondered.

"Michel St. Tutelairé at your service, Miss Abernathy. I am working, well, for your father's…*competitor*, shall we say? I am also a good friend of the Cratchit family, and it's now my responsibility to see you safely away from your father's grasp. I have personal experience with, shall we say, his more malevolent tendencies, and trust me when I tell you he is *not* well-disposed toward you or Peter Cratchit right now. He has had his way with Peter for the moment, but that will be rectified in short order."

Leaning out the side window, he called to the driver, "My good fellow, kindly make haste for the Belgravia Park Grand Hotel!"

"My father will spare no expense in hunting for me, Mr. St. Tutelairé," Livinia quavered. "Hiding me in an expensive hotel won't help you."

St. Tutelairé turned to Livinia, smiling in reassurance.

"And that is why you're going to the Belgravia Park Grand Hotel. I have been acquainted with the family who owns the hotel for quite a few years now and it's quite touching how devoted they are. I have arranged for you to have accommodations waiting for you there under the name of a long-deceased member of the French royal family, Princess Marie Louise Le Marche. According to the hotel's register, Princess Marie checked in seven weeks ago. A 'friend' of mine who bears a striking resemblance to you has been seen coming and going from the Belgravia Park Grand Hotel many times before your ship docked today. There is no possible way your father will know to look for you there, not even if an errant member of the hotel staff should want to betray your whereabouts to your father. You will be quite safe; just remember to speak your fluent French whenever you are in the presence of others and use your accomplishments as a *dramatist* in pretending to be a poor speaker of the English language."

Still on guard, though bewildered that St. Tutelairé knew of her fluency in French, Livinia asked, "How do I know I can trust you, Mr. St. Tutelairé?"

"Miss Livinia, many years ago, I suffered the indignity and pain of seeing my boss betrayed by a man with the same blackness of heart that unfortunately consumes your father, and I was *ordered* not to intervene. Don't you think if I were going to inflict the same anguish upon you, I would have spared myself the charade of pretending to rescue you? I could have brought you right back to your father at the docks instead of going to all this trouble."

Livinia bit her lip in thought as the carriage proceeded to the Belgravia Park Grand Hotel.

Back at the offices of Hawthorne and Cavendish Furniture and Carpentry Works of London, an enraged Cyrus Abernathy paced the floor of Sir Nigel's office, fixated on where Livinia had gone.

"Livinia has never been to London, Nigel; that little tramp could be *anywhere* in your city. Now, what do I do?"

Sir Nigel tried to assuage Abernathy's anger by using logic.

"Look, Cyrus, your family has no relations or friends in London, correct? You also said she was not one to carry any considerable sum of money on her person either."

"So what, Nigel? What's your point?" Abernathy growled.

"Well, she knew the name of Peter's company...*this* company, to be exact. I should think even if she only has a few crowns to rub together to get by on, sooner or later, she's going to have to turn up here and apologize to you," Sir Nigel observed.

Abernathy rubbed his beard stubble as he contemplated Nigel's words.

"So, you're proposing that I don't go out searching for Livinia, that London itself will bring that repentant child to your offices sooner or later?"

"Yes!" Sir Nigel exclaimed. "In the meantime, this Monday or Tuesday will be the formal booking of Mr. Cratchit at King's Bench Magistrate Court. While we wait for Livinia to show up, you can tally up the real cost of my disloyal senior clerk first-class's stay with you in New York City and squiring him around the United States for five months. If you play your cards right, Peter Cratchit will have amassed such a huge debt that the only daylight he'll ever see again will be through the high bars of his prison cell window."

At the mention of Peter's pending booking at King's Bench Magistrate Court, Abernathy snapped his fingers.

"Nigel, I've got it! The answer to finding Livinia was staring us in the face all along. We don't have to wait for her to show up *here*. That tart of a daughter saw the name on the wagon's side that took Peter off to debtors' prison. If she doesn't show up by Thursday, I'll wager she shows up for those proceedings to try to comfort him. All I need do is have a few hired men in the courtroom to make sure she can't leave until I can grab her, and then we'll be aboard the SS *Caledonia*'s next departure for New York right after Christmas!"

I certainly hope so, thought a worried Sir Nigel. The more time he spent in the presence of the irate Cyrus Abernathy, the more he dreaded it.

28

CONNECTING THE DOTS

Later that afternoon, Ebenezer Scrooge and Bob Cratchit pulled up in front of the Royal Consumption Infirmary, where they proceeded to Charlotte's bedside. She looked up, expecting to see her beloved Peter, but saw only her father-in-law and Ebenezer Scrooge. Her eyes blazed in disappointment.

"Where's Peter?" Charlotte demanded.

"Well, there was a bit of a problem on his arrival, my dear," said Bob.

"What do you mean, a problem?" she demanded.

Scrooge did not want Bob Cratchit to be the bearer of bad news, so he took the opportunity to speak up.

"When the SS *Arctic* docked in London this morning, Sir Nigel and Cyrus Abernathy had him arrested and taken off to King's Bench."

As Charlotte's eyes filled with tears, she looked up at Bob Cratchit.

"Is this true? Has Peter been taken to King's Bench?"

"I'm afraid so, my dear. We haven't got the full gist of it, but he's being accused of running up debts in America that he can't repay."

Rounding on Ebenezer Scrooge, Charlotte burst out.

"This is all your fault, Ebenezer Scrooge!" She broke into a violent hacking spell that soon passed enough for her to continue her tirade, bringing a concerned Allyce Bainbridge within earshot.

"The hospital was abuzz yesterday that you and *your* business partners had beaten Peter's company to the Royal Navy contract by accusing Mr. Abernathy of using slaves to mill his wood in America.

I say damn you and your hell-bound greed, Ebenezer Scrooge. I shall hate you forever."

It was at that precise moment that Charlotte caught Allyce Bainbridge's eye.

"Allyce! Have this vile excuse of a man removed *now*. I don't ever want to hear the name Ebenezer Scrooge again, except as a curse on someone's lips."

An equally distraught Bob Cratchit tried in vain to console Charlotte.

"My dear, we don't know all the facts yet. Why don't we—"

"Father," Charlotte began, "the only fact I know is that my Peter is now a prisoner at King's Bench because of your boss's greed," she declared, tears now streaming down her crestfallen face.

Allyce came up to Bob and Ebenezer.

"You have distressed Charlotte enough, and she is already in a very frail state. I will have to ask you to leave, especially you, *Mr. Scrooge.*" There was no mistaking the resolve in Allyce's voice or the open contempt in the look she shot Scrooge.

As the two men headed for the door, Allyce sat beside a sobbing, disconsolate Charlotte.

"I'm sure things will clear up for Peter, Charlotte. Everything I know of him speaks to his honesty and loyalty. While I might question his prudential judgment in certain areas"—with neither woman having to mention the name *Livinia Abernathy*— "he is a good man."

"But if Uncle Ebenezer knew Peter's fortunes were tied to this arrangement with Mr. Abernathy, who seems to be a man of the most disagreeable sort, why would he set out to wreck the arrangement and destroy Peter in the process?"

Allyce pondered the question before answering.

"Remember the *Times* said the Royal Navy contract was worth millions of pounds? The Ebenezer Scrooge I had the good sense to walk away from has returned with a vengeance. When he was younger, he was a grasping, greedy man, and for all his efforts to pretend otherwise, he remains just that. Ebenezer Scrooge has again proven he doesn't have a kind bone in his body, and nothing on earth will convince me otherwise."

When his secretary informed him that Ebenezer Scrooge was waiting in his outer office, Minister-without-Portfolio Sidney Herbert bounded from his office, a happy smile on his face.

"You've done it, old boy," Herbert said, clapping Scrooge on the shoulder. "The papers are full of stories that the nasty giant Abernathy has received his comeuppance. It's quite the Christmas gift for us all, eh?"

Then, he saw Scrooge's face.

"Ebenezer, what's wrong?"

"*Everything*, Sidney," Scrooge said. "Somehow, Cyrus Abernathy conspired with Sir Nigel to have Peter thrown in King's Bench the moment the SS *Arctic* docked late this morning. I was there with my clerk, Bob Cratchit, the lad's father, and Michel St. Tutelairé. I thought perhaps I might prevail upon you to accompany me to King's Bench to explain that there's been a terrible miscarriage of justice. Now Peter's wife is blaming us, or more specifically *me*, for Peter's plight."

Sidney Herbert paused to ponder the turn of events.

"Then, if that is the case, I think we'd better go round and collect Sir Richard Mayne. He may be able to use his influence as chief of the Metropolitan Police Department to intercede on Peter's behalf."

A half-hour later, Ebenezer Scrooge and Sidney Herbert were sitting in front of a sympathetic chief of the Metropolitan Police Department. Finally, Sir Richard stood up and faced the two gentlemen.

"My friends, although I see the hand of that snake Cyrus Abernathy in this vile affair, once my men have collected a prisoner for King's Bench with formal Articles of Indebtedness, not even someone of my position may intercede on his behalf before his booking and hearing. As today is Tuesday, they won't happen until at least Monday morning and afternoon, five days hence. And that will depend on the numbers of prisoners on the docket to be arraigned."

Scrooge's face fell.

"Then I have failed Peter...*and Charlotte*," he said in a barely audible whisper.

Sidney Herbert looked to Sir Richard.

"So, Peter Cratchit has been thrown into that hellhole, and there is nothing to be done about it?"

"I didn't say *that*, Sidney," Sir Richard replied. "I have some influence with the warden at King's Bench and will see to it that Peter is held in one of the cells reserved for indebted nobility. The food is quite passable, and his quarters—even though a prison—will be quite satisfactory until we can get this matter sorted out."

Scrooge then spoke up.

"Why can't I just make good the funds from my own money that young Peter is accused of having stolen, and then the debt will be settled?"

Sir Richard smiled at Scrooge's eager magnanimity and innocent ignorance of court procedure.

"Ebenezer, it's not that simple. For you to walk into court with the necessary funds to settle Peter's debts would be the same as a guilty plea by young Peter, and *that* scarlet letter would follow him for the rest of his life. It would only serve to prevent Peter from ever obtaining another position with any decent firm in England."

Scrooge sighed.

"So, there is no point in going to King's Bench today, is there?"

"Well, not either of *you*," replied Sir Richard. "I, on the other hand, will be leaving for the prison within the next half-hour to speak with the warden and to have a word with Peter. Remember, gentlemen," he said with a grin meant to reassure Scrooge, "the 'Honorable Society of Royal Medical Benefactors' is not to be taken lightly."

The next morning, Scrooge arrived at his offices to find another sealed missive from Michel St. Tutelairé waiting for him.

My Dear Ebenezer,

I know you and Mr. Cratchit are most concerned about the whereabouts of Peter's traveling companion, Miss Livinia Abernathy. You need not worry; she is under my protection in a place where her father will not find her despite the considerable resources at his disposal. There are duplicitous aspects to her father I fear she must learn for herself, but do not be troubled. As I have said, she is under my protection. I shall see you promptly Tuesday afternoon at Peter's indictment hearing and sentencing at King's Bench. I suspect his accusers suffer from hubris and have overplayed their hand, but we shall see what Providence decides.
Ever your servant,

Michel

Saturday, December 20, dawned crisp and cold in London. Livinia Abernathy awoke to find a small envelope slid under her door while she was still sleeping.

20/12/1856

Miss Livinia,

Should you seek more information about Charlotte Cratchit (and I can't recommend strongly enough that you do), the Royal Consumption Infirmary on Oxley Street is normally closed to visitors on Saturdays. I happen to know that Mrs. Cratchit's nurse, Allyce Bainbridge, will be there today should you wish to inquire about Charlotte. I have arranged for you to be admitted to the premises for a short while.

I urge you to take my advice and go. Allyce Bainbridge has had a very hard life, and she's emerged relatively unscathed in heart and soul. I think it would greatly rebound to your benefit to meet her. She may be able to reveal more about Charlotte Cratchit (and your father) than you realize.

Your humble servant,
Michel

Livinia dressed and ate a light breakfast. The butterflies in her stomach wouldn't permit more than toast, jam, and tea before departing for the Royal Consumption Infirmary. Her heart beat wildly within her chest for reasons she couldn't quite place, but soon settled down. On reflection, she realized that her de facto protector, Michel St. Tutelairé, was an extraordinary individual. He had been as good as his word. Although there were plenty of stories and splashy advertisements about a "wealthy runaway daughter" in the London papers by her American father, offering a prodigious reward for information leading to her safe return, there hadn't been a single inquiry at the

Belgravia Park Grand Hotel about her or the elusive Princess Marie Le Marche.

The carriage she had arranged to take her to the Royal Consumption Infirmary arrived at ten, and by ten thirty, Livinia Abernathy was walking into the building. Speaking in broken, French-accented English, she asked, "Where might I locate ze Superintendent of Nurse Staff for Royal Consumption Infirmary, yes?"

Livinia batted her eyelashes in her most alluring manner possible at the flustered young male orderly manning the front desk that Saturday.

"Yes, Miss. That would be Superintendent Bainbridge. I believe she is making the rounds of the Third Floor Consumptives Ward." He gestured toward the stairway.

"Just go up those stairs and then to the right." He grinned.

"*Merci, Monsieur.* You are most kind."

Pretending to be European royalty comes easily, she thought as she walked up the stairs. Her heart pounded in her breast like a hammer. Perhaps it was because she was about to come face to face with the last person to have seen or spoken with Charlotte Cratchit before the poor woman died of consumption.

Reaching the third floor, Livinia turned to the right and, dropping her *faux* French accent, she asked the first nurse she encountered, "Where may I find Superintendent Bainbridge?"

Allyce looked at the wealthy young American woman standing before her. Holding out her sanitized hand in greeting, she said, "I'm Superintendent Allyce Bainbridge. How may I be of assistance, my dear?"

Swallowing hard, Livinia forged ahead.

"I'm told you were Charlotte Cratchit's nurse before she…well, *before* she died of consumption. Is that correct?"

Allyce thought that perhaps the young American woman standing before her was playing some sort of game, but the searching, pleading look on Livinia's face told Allyce she believed her words to be the truth.

Still incredulous, Allyce asked, "I beg your pardon, Miss?"

Livinia stammered out, "I…I just wanted to know what sort of woman Mrs. Cratchit was. I had heard so many delightful things about her from her husband, Peter, while he was visiting my family in America that I felt compelled to seek you out, Mrs. Bainbridge. I was given to understand you knew her quite well. I should also want to thank you for the care you provided Mrs. Cratchit before she died. It will be of great comfort to her husband."

Livinia saw the bewilderment on Allyce's face and said, "I think this will explain things better than I can."

She searched her purse, fumbling about for something, and soon pulled out a letter written on a single sheet of creased paper and handed it to Allyce.

As she reached for the letter, Allyce suddenly felt a wave of nausea and a pit in her stomach. This young lady was very much in earnest. That meant something was *very* wrong with Peter Cratchit, especially given the recent headlines in the *Times* about Cyrus Abernathy and the scandal over procuring lumber for the Crown with slaves. She looked down and began reading, her hand coming up to cover her mouth as she mouthed a silent "Oh no…" Allyce was looking at an accurate reasonable facsimile of the hospital's stationery, but the letter's words caught her heart in her throat. The letter was dated October 28, more than two months after Ainsley Northrup's removal as the hospital administrator, yet it bore his forged signature. But that was *nothing* compared to the contents, as the letter claimed that Charlotte Cratchit had died almost two months earlier! Who would be so cruel as to write Peter Cratchit a letter trying to deceive him into thinking his beloved Charlotte was dead? As she reread the note, a specific detail caught Allyce's attention:

To the Attention of Mr. Peter Cratchit

In Care of C. Abernathy

With sudden clarity borne of her well-honed intuition, that had to be *Cyrus* Abernathy, Allyce realized. Suddenly, many of the details Peter had written about in his letters to Charlotte began to make sickening, consistent sense. It also explained the dearth of recent letters from Peter to Charlotte.

"Miss, would you please follow me?" There was only one way to solve this riddle, and Allyce resolved to cut this Gordian Knot.

Walking down several rows, she stopped in front of a bed where Livinia saw a pale, wan-looking woman drinking tea. She turned to the mysterious American visitor.

"Miss, this is Charlotte Cratchit. Charlotte, this is…" Allyce turned to a suddenly pallid Livinia. *The poor girl looks like she's seen a ghost,* Allyce thought.

Turning to Livinia, Allyce said, "Where are my manners? We haven't even been introduced. *You* know who *I* am; may I have the pleasure of knowing with whom I am speaking?"

Livinia smiled nervously, swallowing several times before she caught Charlotte Cratchit's eye, her face red with humiliation. She gathered her courage and declared, "I am Livinia Abernathy."

Allyce thought for a moment she was going to have to catch Livinia, as the poor girl looked as though she were going to faint from shock and humiliation, but the daughter of Cyrus Abernathy was made of sterner stuff. Managing to smile as she regained her composure, Livinia looked at Charlotte and said, "We have much to discuss, and reading the sign downstairs, I know we have only a few moments together."

She turned to Allyce. "Nurse Bainbridge, I am forever in your debt."

Livinia sat down next to an astonished Charlotte and said, "My father, Cyrus, gave Peter this letter two months ago saying you died of consumption on October 26 and that your children had been taken in by Peter's parents." She looked down into her lap in embarrassment. "Peter wrote letter after letter to his parents, Nurse Bainbridge, and even Mr. Scrooge, imploring them for any news about what had happened, but my father made sure every letter Peter wrote 'disappeared.' Peter was in such a state of shock at the news of your 'death' that he was quite inconsolable. My wicked father prevailed on Peter to stay in New York and finish the contract work they had undertaken and justified it by saying nothing further could be done in the matter of your death. My father told Peter the best he could do now to honor your memory was to provide your family the *best* possible life, which meant *money*. Everything boils down to money with my father, Mrs. Cratchit.

"I feel so ashamed for believing my father's lies and going along with his schemes. You must think me a horribly immoral woman, but I want to assure you, your husband Peter was nothing but a loyal husband to you and a perfect gentleman in my presence for the entire time he was in the United States."

Livinia looked down at her hands in her lap, twisting her fingers together.

"Mrs. Cratchit, I see now my father is a most evil man, a vile beast, and your Peter could not be more opposite to him in *every* way possible. You should be very proud. I cannot believe my father faked your death in a vain effort to push us into a romance. It was *never* going to work, especially after your husband saved my life."

Charlotte's eyes went very wide at Livinia's last statement.

"My husband *saved your life*, Miss Abernathy?"

"Please call me Livinia. I am ashamed to admit it now; however, I must give you a full account of things. I had a bit of innocent fun at Peter's expense one Sunday after church in early October, but my father became enraged and struck me on the face in front of Peter at dinner for my impertinence. I think my father was starting to doubt my utility as a pawn in his business game with Peter and his employer. Perhaps due to my father's influence, I have obeyed the Fourth Commandment more in violation of it than observing it, as I have never truly honored my father or my mother. When I tried to lie my way out of my problem, Father grew ever angrier and resorted to violence. He is a gigantic man, almost seven feet tall and weighing four hundred pounds. Peter saw what I didn't; my father was making quite a huge fist to strike me again, and Peter jumped up to intervene. Father's punch, meant for me, caught Peter full in the face, broke his nose, and cracked his orbital eye socket, according to our family physician, Dr. Vance. He said that were it not for Peter's gallant gesture, my father would have most certainly killed me had his fist connected with *my* face instead of Peter's. Your husband is made of stern stuff, Charlotte."

Charlotte blinked her eyes in astonishment. The Abernathy woman she suspected for months of trying to lure her husband into adultery was sitting by her bedside, regaling her with a story of how Peter had saved her life and telling her how lucky she was to have Peter to begin with!

Charlotte grabbed Livinia's gloved hand, ignoring hospital rules.

"Thank you, Livinia," she said in a husky whisper as tears rolled down their faces. "Your father must be tearing London apart looking for you. Whatever will you do?"

"I am under the protection of a group of London merchants and government officials known only to me as the 'Honorable Society of Royal Medical Benefactors.' They have assured me of their protection until I can leave the country next week, the day after Christmas."

Allyce's ears perked up at hearing of the "Honorable Society" mentioned in this context. How were *they* connected to this? From her conversations with Dr. Entwistle, this Honorable Society of Royal Medical Benefactors seemed to have its finger in many a pie that did not involve medicine.

Livinia continued: "These men are concerned that my father and his English business partner, Sir Nigel, are conspiring to invent new charges to keep Peter in King's Bench Debtors' Prison for many years. Are you familiar with an American gentleman named Michel St. Tutelairé? I take it he is one of the men in this remarkable 'Honorable Society.' He has assured me that my father's wicked schemes will come to naught, and I must believe Peter's welfare is included in that statement. I don't know *why* or *how* he intends to thwart my father, for Father is not only vexatiously headstrong, but has unlimited financial means at his disposal. He didn't come out and exactly say it, but Mr. St. Tutelairé is certain my father has good reason to fear him, and I've never seen my father fear *anyone*. Mr. St. Tutelairé doesn't present an intimidating presence, but there is something formidable about his personality, like a warrior girded for battle. When he speaks, it is clear he will brook no challenge."

Livinia stood up and said, "I have taken up far too much of your time, Mrs. Cratchit. Again, I hope you accept my most sincere apology for the anguish I have caused you. I am not as blameless as Peter; he was blind to my father's ultimate machinations. If my presence will make any difference, I intend to be at the indictment and sentencing of Peter at the King's Bench Magistrate Court Tuesday next if my testimony may do your husband any good."

Charlotte looked up at Livinia and, through eyes rimmed with tears, said in a husky whisper, "Will you assure Peter I am still among the living and give him my love, Miss Livinia?"

"Of course, Mrs. Cratchit," Livinia said. "It's the very least I can do. May I visit you afterward?"

Charlotte nodded at Allyce Bainbridge, who was hovering at a discreet distance.

"That will depend on Allyce."

Allyce smiled in response and gestured that it was time for Livinia to leave. After Allyce had escorted Livinia out of the room, she said to her,

"I heard what Charlotte asked you. I suggest you return the following morning, as it shall be Christmas Eve, and I expect this place to be rather quiet." As they stopped by the small basin in the hallway filled with lightly lavender-scented water with a tincture of bleach, she gestured for Livinia to remove her gloves and wash her hands.

"Give me your gloves; I will have them properly cleaned and returned to you on your next visit. Now please wash your hands, as we can't risk spreading consumption, especially so close to Christmas."

29 🎋

THE PRICE OF REDEMPTION

Tuesday, December 23, 1856, dawned bleak and cold. Livinia took a light lunch and tried to concentrate on a worn copy of Jane Austen's *Pride and Prejudice* as she watched the hours pass on the clock on the wall. At last, as she heard the majestic clock at the north end of the Palace of Westminster, the clock tower the locals affectionately called "Big Ben," sound the hour of 2 p.m., there was a light rap at her door. Her heart leaped at the pattern, two short raps, a momentary pause, then another light rap. It was the signal Michel St. Tutelairé used for Livinia to recognize it was he at the door.

She heard his dulcet accent through the room door.

"Are you ready, Miss Livinia? Peter Cratchit will appear in the docket within the hour, and they tell me there is always limited space in the public gallery at the King's Bench Magistrate Court."

Livinia breathed a sigh of relief as she grabbed her purse, her coat in hand, and rushed to open the door. St. Tutelairé stood there with the slightest smile on his face when he saw her look of concern.

"Be of good cheer, Miss Livinia. We must hope that Providence will have its way and maleficence is thwarted, my dear," he said, pronouncing it in his accent more like *mah deah*. "Come, our carriage awaits," he added, helping Livinia put on her coat and taking her arm.

"Are you *quite sure* we will be safe from my father, Michel? I know how he is always plotting, and I have no doubt he will have the building and courtroom watched."

As they walked down to the waiting carriage, St. Tutelairé couldn't help a small chuckle.

"Miss Livinia, I can assure you that *anything* your father may be planning will come to naught. You have my word of honor; you are quite safe. However, I have no doubt your father will be there, as he is one of the principals, along with Peter's boss, Sir Nigel, pressing the embezzlement charges contained in the Articles of Indebtedness against poor Peter," St. Tutelairé said as he helped Livinia into the carriage.

A thought occurred to Livinia as the carriage set off for King's Bench Debtors' Prison. *Peter hasn't been before the magistrate yet. How can Michel know the specific charges against him are embezzlement?*

St. Tutelairé glanced at Livinia from the opposite seat in the carriage, and she caught the hint of a reassuring smile.

Cyrus Abernathy and Sir Nigel sat in the Accuser's Section of the King's Bench Magistrate courtroom, scanning the visitors' viewing gallery for any sign of Livinia. The five husky, well-dressed body-guards Abernathy had hired and placed among the viewing gallery crowd scanned the faces of all women coming into the courtroom. They compared cheap paper copies of a daguerreotype handed out earlier by Cyrus against the face of every woman entering. They had orders to detain Livinia under the pretense that she was a "runaway daughter," if any court officers questioned them. Livinia was already seated among the crowd of court spectators, but for some reason, none of her father's hirelings recognized her, nor did her father see her at first, despite their coordinated search. The plan was that when Abernathy *did* see her, he would remove his stovepipe hat as a signal and, using his fingers, gesture to his bodyguards in the visitors' viewing gallery just where his wayward daughter was sitting. London's Metropolitan Police chief, Sir Richard Mayne, had taken the afternoon off to sit among the section reserved for government officials and special "Friends of the Court," as was his right. He had rescheduled his afternoon appointments to witness the proceedings on behalf of the men of the "Honorable Society" to fill them in later that evening at dinner. His gaze met Michel St. Tutelairé's.

The defendants shuffled into the dock, a disheveled Peter among them. Livinia gasped in worry when she saw Peter's appearance, not only unkempt but also dazed and haggard. She felt Michel St. Tutelairé's hand squeeze hers in reassurance. She spied her smirking father and Sir Nigel sitting together, Sir Nigel smiling at Abernathy's comments, both men in quite the jocular mood. Together, they had conspired to trump up further charges totaling almost £1,200, amounting to a life sentence debt judgment against Peter.

The afternoon's proceedings droned on in a dull manner, with each hapless defendant preceding Peter having his charges read aloud and sentence duly passed. As the debtor just before Peter stood to take the stand and have his Articles of Indebtedness read before the court, Abernathy gave a start of recognition at a young woman sitting in the visitors' viewing gallery.

Livinia!

He had just removed his stovepipe hat in triumph, signaling to his men that his daughter was sitting among them when he felt a shock course through him. As he took his hat off and his hired thugs began scanning the women among them, the gentleman sitting next to Livinia raised his head, his face emerging into view from beneath the brim of his hat. *It was Michel St. Tutelairé.* Abernathy's blood ran cold as he realized that not only was his preternatural arch-nemesis among the spectators, but the mystery of Livinia's whereabouts for the last week came into sharp focus; she was being protected by that *thing*, St. Tutelairé.

The two caught each other's gaze. Sudden terror rooted Abernathy to his seat while a slight smile danced about St. Tutelairé's face as he nodded at Abernathy.

Abernathy heard St. Tutelairé's voice in his head. *I admire your tenacity, Cyrus, but it won't avail you in this place either.*

Livinia gave a panicked start as she recognized her father, but then she saw his smug triumph give way to a very uncharacteristic look: *fear.* Abernathy couldn't break his gaze away from St. Tutelairé as an unseen force locked his gaze on that of Livinia's protector. Just as Peter Cratchit's name was read out and the Articles of Indebtedness were spelled out in full, Cyrus Abernathy saw Michel St. Tutelairé blink his eyes in the slow manner of a sleepy cat. When they opened, they flared with the same baleful bluish-white fire Abernathy last saw when he fled the Royal Consumption Infirmary in terror after St. Tutelairé thwarted his attempted murder of Charlotte Cratchit. No one else present in the courtroom saw this except for Cyrus Abernathy.

Abernathy was mute with fear, his panic palpable at seeing his nemesis again. His hands gripped the railing in the Accuser's Section with a hold approaching *rigor mortis.* Livinia didn't acknowledge her father other than a quick look of recognition. Sir Nigel had no idea of his business partner's silent panic attack until the Articles of Indebtedness were read out against Peter Cratchit. He turned to the mute Abernathy, urging him to respond to the judge.

"Cyrus?" he asked. "Cyrus, you *must* speak up! They're reading the Articles against Peter, and you insisted on being the principal signatory."

But Abernathy remained speechless in terror next to Sir Nigel. Nigel scanned the visitors' gallery and recognized Abernathy's missing daughter, Livinia, but Abernathy gave no sign of seeing her anymore. Sir Nigel also couldn't see Michel St. Tutelairé. Nigel had no idea what so terrified Abernathy into silence but was compelled to stand and address the court himself instead.

"Your Honor, I am Sir Nigel Fairweather-Hawthorne of the firm of—" But Sir Nigel was cut off mid-sentence by the magistrate.

"You are out of order, sir," said an annoyed magistrate. "Is Mr. Cyrus Abernathy, the signatory of these Articles of Indebtedness, present in this courtroom to speak to the allegations or not?"

Addressing the court, Sir Nigel gestured toward the silent Abernathy.

"This is Mr. Abernathy, Your Honor. He is suffering from a medical infirmity arising out of his voyage from America and has authorized me to testify on his behalf as to the veracity of the charges."

Becoming annoyed and anxious to be home for dinner, the magistrate asked Sir Nigel, "Very well. Under penalty of perjury, do you so swear that the charges of indebtedness in the amount of one thousand, two hundred british pounds sterling owed by the defendant, Mr. Peter Cratchit, to Mr. Abernathy and yourself upon demand are true and accurate?"

Sir Nigel again looked down and noticed heavy beads of sweat trickling down the stricken Abernathy's brow. *What in the bloody blazes is wrong with you, Cyrus? You have a violent mouth for* everything, *and now, when it counts the most, you're a stupid statue?* Sir Nigel fumed, willing him to speak but receiving not so much as an acknowledgment from the perspiring Abernathy.

"Yes, Your Honor. Each charge before you in the Articles is complete and accurate," Sir Nigel said.

The magistrate turned to Peter and asked him, "Do you have anything to say in your defense as to these charges, Mr. Cratchit?"

Peter opened his mouth to object but couldn't find his voice. His world had caved in around him, and the depression of his circumstances overwhelmed him to the point of muteness. Livinia

Abernathy was almost in tears, praying Peter would defend himself before the court.

Finally, unable to contain her concern, despite knowing it would mark her as a target for her father's wrath, Livinia rose to her feet.

"Peter!" she shouted at the top of her lungs.

"Charlotte is alive! I saw her last night at the Royal Consumption Infirmary. *Charlotte is alive!"* Livinia screamed, her voice rising in pitch as deputy bailiffs hurried toward her for disturbing the court proceedings. The Chief Magistrate vigorously banged his gavel as he tried to restore some semblance of order before pointing it up at Livinia in the Visitor's Gallery.

"Have that woman removed at once! I will not have these august proceedings turned into a circus."

Peter Cratchit craned his head upward; as Livinia's voice burned through his haze of despair and misery. *Charlotte? My Charlotte… alive?* he thought. *But Cyrus…that letter from the Royal Infirmary.*

Livinia turned to Michel St. Tutelairé, who was still engaged in a staring match with her father across the courtroom. From the look on her father's face, Livinia had never seen him so mortally terrified. She had no idea Michel St. Tutelairé was causing a phrase to reverberate in her father's mind: *Because thou hast cast thy lot with the angel of the pit, I have arrayed Myself against thee.*

St. Tutelairé turned and gently grabbed Livinia's arm.

"Mah deah," he drawled. "I fully appreciate your intentions, but you've drawn a trifle of unwarranted attention to yourself. I suggest we make an expeditious departure," as he urged her to the Visitor's Gallery exit.

After asking a mute Cyrus Abernathy one final time if he wished to say anything on his behalf, the court magistrate pronounced judgment against Peter Cratchit and had him remanded to the King's Bench Debtors' Prison to serve his sentence until the overwhelming debts were repaid. The Chief Magistrate banged his gavel to signal an end to the day's proceedings as the bailiff announced, "This court shall reconvene tomorrow at 11 a.m. to hear the final cases on the docket." He turned to the official Friends of the Court bench rows, where Sir Richard and several of his senior officers from Scotland Yard sat and momentarily caught Sir Richard's eye. Sir Richard betrayed no sign of recognition other than again giving the slightest nod before standing to depart with his men.

Livinia and Michel St. Tutelairé walked unseen past Abernathy's hired bodyguards and court officers still frantically searching for her, at which point he escorted her back to her hotel. Once inside her suite, she turned to St. Tutelairé.

"I'm sorry, Michel, but after seeing Charlotte still alive at the hospital, I couldn't contain myself. I don't know what compelled me to cry out to Peter, but I knew I couldn't let my father's games go on any longer.

"I don't know what happened to my father, but I know his talent for cunning. Right when he should have sprung his trap on me, all color drained from his face. I have never seen *anything* frighten Father, but I can tell he was most terrified of *something*, Mr. St. Tutelairé."

"As I told you, Miss Livinia, I have a strong antagonism with your father going back many years, and he undoubtedly did *not* expect to see me with you in court. There were also at least five men near us looking for you, not including the court bailiffs, but it would seem they failed in their task as well," St. Tutelairé said. "With the money at his disposal, your father really should hire better help. As for your outburst regarding Charlotte, who knows? Had you not made your concerns so vocally known, perhaps I should have been compelled to do so myself."

Livinia pondered his words and, as she was quite intelligent in her own way, she intuited something otherworldly had transpired between her father and St. Tutelairé in the courtroom, and it had made her father very, *very* afraid. *Who are you, Michel St. Tutelairé?* she thought as he hurried off. *What* are you?

After the commotion inside the King's Bench courtroom, Sir Richard and his detectives waited in the Great Hall outside. After a few minutes, Cyrus Abernathy and Sir Nigel emerged from the courtroom. As Abernathy drew abreast of where Sir Richard was standing to the side, Sir Richard moved to intercept him, blocking his way.

"Mr. Abernathy?" Sir Richard asked in a low voice. "I am Sir Richard Mayne of the London Metropolitan Police Department."

The blustery response rising in Abernathy's throat died before it reached his lips when he heard the words "London Metropolitan Police Department."

Sir Nigel broke in. "What is the meaning of this?" he demanded. "We've done nothing wrong! We were the *plaintiffs* in the case of that embezzling little scoundrel, Peter Cratchit."

The chief of the London police was dry and perfunctory in his reply.

"You'd best come along too, Sir Nigel. We need to speak about a matter of some delicacy, best discussed in private." Sir Richard's words came out more as a command than a request as he gestured toward an open door adjacent to the courtroom. "This way, gentlemen."

The small group of men proceeded into the conference room where, once inside, one of Sir Richard's detectives ostentatiously locked the massive oak door and pocketed the keys. Sir Richard gestured for the two businessmen to have a seat at the table before sitting opposite them with a genial affectation.

"Mr. Abernathy," he began. "I'd like to start off by inquiring if you are familiar with the Royal Infirmary for Consumption and Ailments of the Chest here in London. Before you answer, I should remind you, sir that you are in the presence of the London Metropolitan Police Department."

"I don't have the slightest idea what you're talking about," retorted Abernathy. Sir Nigel gave Abernathy a baffled sideways glance. This was definitely more than he bargained for.

In contrast to the belligerent manner he'd used to face down Joseph Billingsly, Sir Richard assumed a calmly detached demeanor with Abernathy.

"If you insist young Mr. Cratchit is guilty of embezzlement, then it's only fair that I remind you that lying to the Metropolitan Police is also a prosecutable offense as well, Mr. Abernathy, regardless of your wealth or social station."

Having recovered somewhat from his unnerving experience in court, Cyrus Abernathy's confrontational bluster returned with a vengeance.

"*Do you know who I am*, Sir Richard?" Abernathy sneered, a tone of menace in his resonant voice. "Do I need to remind you that threatening a distinguished visitor to your country with perjury can have unpleasant repercussions? I am rather good friends with Mr. Dallas, the American Minister to the Court of St. James."

Ignoring Abernathy's implicit threats, Sir Richard smiled and responded, "Mr. Abernathy, I'm very well aware of *who* you are. Might I remind you of *where* you are? Your ability to intimidate so much as a church mouse ended the moment you crossed the threshold of this building." He smiled indulgently before continuing.

"Your reputation as an aggressive negotiator precedes you, Mr. Abernathy. Let's get down to business, shall we?"

He pulled a letter from his breast pocket, slid it across the table to Abernathy, and motioned to a nearby pen and inkwell.

"This document is a 'Recording Letter of Debt Renunciation' in the matter regarding Peter Cratchit. I suggest you sign it, and we can all be off to enjoy our respective evenings."

Abernathy scanned the paper, his eyes going wide with surprise that quickly turned into glowering anger. He attempted to rise, but a pair of enormous Scotland Yard detectives grabbed his shoulders and roughly shoved him back down into his seat. Sir Richard had come prepared.

"I will not sign that document," Abernathy angrily declared. "Peter Cratchit embezzled from *us*, and *I* have not committed perjury. You'll live to regret this, Sir Richard."

Sir Nigel shifted nervously in his seat. Devious business plots *were* his stock in trade, but defiantly facing off against the chief of Scotland Yard was not something he'd bargained for. To make matters worse, Abernathy was now threatening Sir Richard Mayne himself. Was he mad?!

Sir Richard serenely looked Abernathy in the eye and said, "I'll ask you again, are familiar with the Royal Infirmary for Consumption and Ailments of the Chest?"

"And I'll give you the same answer *again*," Abernathy sneered, his voice dripping with contempt. "I don't know of any consumptives here, much less any consumption hospitals in London."

Sir Richard calmly turned to the police secretary, diligently taking down the official notes of the meeting at a side desk, and said, "I want the record clear on this matter. Mr. Abernathy now faces *two* counts of perjury, in addition to one count of trespassing against a royal medical establishment and the charge of attempted murder at the aforementioned royal medical establishment."

This time it was Sir Nigel who burst out, "I don't know anything about *attempted murder!*" He cast a panicked look at the defiant Abernathy and, using his feet, tried to push his chair away from his erstwhile business partner.

Sir Richard took out a sheaf of parchment papers and placed them in front of the blustering Abernathy.

"These are sworn affidavits of staff and several patients at the Royal Infirmary for Consumption testifying that on the night of December 8, you were seen entering the premises by the main entrance and then hastily departing in a carriage ten minutes or so later. The description in each affidavit matches you perfectly. You're a man who would stand out in any crowd, Mr. Abernathy."

"I know all about forging documents, Sir Richard," Abernathy spat out. "I'm sure Scotland Yard has done it when it has suited your purposes. Show me an actual witness whom I can confront to his face. You can't, *because there isn't one.*"

Sir Richard sighed in what Abernathy mistook for an admission of surrender. At that moment, there came the sharp rapping of a walking stick's brass head on the outside of the locked oak door several times, that only grew more insistent as the seconds passed.

"Aren't you going to answer that door?" Abernathy finally blurted out.

Sir Richard didn't blink as he called out, "Please, do come in."

A look of momentary confusion flitted across Abernathy's face as no one moved to unlock the sturdy door, but the heavy brass lever handle started to turn of its own accord nonetheless, and the door began to swing open. The color drained from Abernathy's face as a dapper Michel St. Tutelairé stepped wordlessly into the room as if the door had never been locked in the first place. St. Tutelairé glanced at Sir Richard and stood silently gazing at Cyrus Abernathy and Sir Nigel.

Sir Richard, having played his trump card, turned back to Abernathy.

"You told me I had no witnesses to your attempted murder of a patient at the Royal Consumption Hospital." Nodding toward St. Tutelairé, he said, "I beg to differ with you, sir, but I have here a most impeccable witness prepared to testify in criminal court that you tried to smother Charlotte Cratchit in her bed on the night of December 8."

There was no longer any hint of a supernatural gleam in St. Tutelairé's eyes, but it was not lost on Abernathy that the angel had just effortlessly entered the room through a massive oaken door, *locked from the inside.*

Sir Richard turned back to a now visibly cowed Abernathy and said, "I believe you are well acquainted with Mr. St. Tutelairé. He is prepared to testify in court that he personally witnessed you trying to smother a consumption patient, Mrs. Charlotte Cratchit, on the night in question. I am assured by the highest authority that Mr. St. Tutelairé will make an unimpeachable prosecution witness."

Sir Richard spread his hands magnanimously.

"But, if you are prepared to see reason, Mr. Abernathy, we are willing to drop the charges against you in return for your immediate signature on the Recording Letter of Debt Renunciation and your immediate departure from the United Kingdom, never to return. As they say in chess, Mr. Abernathy, *checkmate,*" as a confident Sir Richard placed a pen in front of Abernathy.

His heart pounding in his barrel-like chest, Cyrus Abernathy knew when he was beaten. No one in the room had acted the least bit surprised when Michel St. Tutelairé impossibly entered the locked chamber door without a key. He quickly scribbled his name on the letter renouncing the debt charges against Peter and rose to his feet.

"Am I free to go?"

Sir Richard smiled. "Of course, and do enjoy your dinner." He glanced at Michel St. Tutelairé and couldn't hold back one final sarcastic riposte.

"I know you're staying at the Saint Regis Hotel, Mr. Abernathy. Might I suggest the foie-gras-stuffed petite goose with oyster and French white truffle sauce? A gourmand like you could pair that with a bottle of Saint Regis 1851 Chateau Rieussec Sauternes. The 1851 Chateau Rieussec stands up very well to the foie gras' rich texture."

Abernathy blanched and understood too well the origin of Sir Richard's dinner recommendation. He could not exit the room quickly enough, followed by an ashen Sir Nigel. Neither man said a word.

$$\sim$$

The members of the "Honorable Society of Royal Medical Benefactors," who met that evening for dinner at Ebenezer Scrooge's elegant residence at 38 Belgrave Square were in a festive mood, especially with Mrs. Dilber's best efforts at serving a holiday season dinner on short notice and a variety of Christmas seasonal drinks, like mulled wine and hot buttered rum. In attendance were Ebenezer Scrooge, Sidney Herbert, John Delane of the *Times*, Sir Richard Mayne, Reverend Neville Braithwaite, and the enigmatic Michel St. Tutelairé. The repairs at both the Royal Consumption Infirmary and the Royal Home of Convalescent Medicine had been completed ahead of schedule and in time for Christmas, so there was an air of palpable Christmas cheer among the gathered men—with the exception of Ebenezer Scrooge. Both Sir Richard Mayne and Michel St. Tutelairé related the foregone results of the proceedings against Peter that afternoon at the King's Bench Court and the meeting afterward with Cyrus Abernathy and Sir Nigel Hawthorne. Peter Cratchit had been found guilty on each count of the Articles of Indebtedness and condemned to serve his sentence at King's Bench Debtors' Prison, but this injustice was temporary in the extreme.

As Scrooge passed around detailed ledger sheets to everyone, he announced that as a result of the Royal Commission of Inquiry into the so-called "Abernathy Affair," as the public dubbed it, the assembled businessmen who had consented to help finance the competing bid had lost a collective £1.1 million. Scrooge revealed that his own business fortunes had taken a financial loss approaching well over half a million pounds.

"Gentlemen, I feel I must apologize to each of you. Had I not persuaded you to join me in this misbegotten adventure, you would not be sharing the disgrace of this moment with me," he said as he hung his head. "This entire affair began as a result of encountering a love from my past who I am afraid will now remain forever distant and has now cost each of you a considerable sum on my account."

Sidney Herbert puffed his pipe, stood up, and gripped Scrooge's shoulder.

"Ebenezer, there is no nobler cause than love. As for my 'losses,' they more than balanced out because we rehabilitated not just one but *two* immense hospitals here in London. We relieved *suffering*, man, suffering on a huge scale. That in and of itself is worth more than any numbers in a bank account."

Looking around at his nodding compatriots, he continued: "Not only have we alleviated suffering, but I'm certain adoption of the 'Nightingale Procedures for Medical Sanitation' will set a new world standard for sanitary care of the sick everywhere."

"Here, here!" resounded among the small gathering.

Then, it was Sir Richard Mayne's turn to speak. "Don't forget; had we not fought that scoundrel Abernathy with such vigor," he said with a smile toward Michel St. Tutelairé and John Delane, "Her Majesty Queen Victoria would have suffered a grievous blow to her dignity and reputation. *That* could not be permitted. Not to mention that we put an end to Ainsley Northrup looting the Royal Consumption Infirmary to line his own pockets."

Michel St. Tutelairé raised his brandy snifter and stood in turn. "Gentlemen, this is no place for modesty. I would like to propose a toast in keeping with the season. Here's to *Mistah* Ebenezer Scrooge," the American said in his easy drawl as Scrooge tried in vain to demur. "It was his love for a woman and his determination to atone for a wrong he had done to her years ago that set these noble efforts in motion."

$\sim$

After dinner, Michel St. Tutelairé and Livinia Abernathy set out again for the Royal Consumption Infirmary. Allyce Bainbridge had consented to await the arrival of the two before departing for the night, as she knew Charlotte Cratchit was awaiting word of the day's court proceedings. Soon the three stood by Charlotte's bedside as Allyce roused the sleeping woman.

"Charlotte! Charlotte!" she whispered in the darkened ward. As Charlotte roused from her fitful slumber, she looked up to see Allyce standing there, along with Livinia Abernathy and a tall, well-dressed American who introduced himself as Michel St. Tutelairé.

"Do you have any word of Peter?" she asked. By the group's solemnity, she could tell that the day's news wasn't good.

"I'm sorry, Charlotte. It didn't go well for Peter," Livinia said apologetically, as yet unaware of Sir Richard's subsequent meeting with Cyrus Abernathy and Sir Nigel. "Peter either wouldn't or couldn't speak in his defense. Although my father Cyrus tried to speak, something prevented him from doing so. Even so, Peter's boss, that dreadful Sir Nigel, made a compelling case for the charges of debt. The chief magistrate had no choice but to pass down the maximum sentence. I broke with all decorum and cried out that you were still alive, hoping that Peter might hear me, but we were ordered removed from the courtroom. At least he knows you're still among the living and that Father's letter was a fraud." The dimness of the ward prevented those assembled from seeing Michel St. Tutelairé's eyes narrow at the mention of Cyrus Abernathy.

Charlotte choked up at the knowledge that she might never see her husband again. "If only that damnable Ebenezer Scrooge hadn't interfered with the Royal Navy contract, my Peter would be home with our dear little children decorating the Christmas tree," she wept, overcome with sadness. "I shall die in this wretched place; Peter will die in King's Bench, and it is all Ebenezer Scrooge's fault." Moved by compassion and pity, Michel St. Tutelairé stepped forward and knelt by her bedside. Disregarding all infirmary protocol, he embraced the disconsolate Charlotte, whispering to her in reassurance.

"Charlotte, please let me assure you that the injustice done to Peter will be corrected just as soon as it can be arranged," he whispered.

Moved more, at the moment, by frustration and annoyance at the mention of her former betrothed than concern for Charlotte, Allyce Bainbridge stepped up. Allyce leaned over St. Tutelairé, grabbed his shoulder, and hissed, "I'm sorry, sir, but we have very strict rules here about physical contact with the consumption patients. I'm afraid I must ask you to stand up and step back."

She received the shock of her life when Michel St. Tutelairé glanced up with a smile that dazzled even in the ward's dim light. A bright twinkle of blue light flared in his eyes as a strong energetic warmth Allyce couldn't fathom ran up her arm where she had grabbed St. Tutelairé.

"You needn't fear for my safety, Superintendent Bainbridge," he gently said in his soft southern accent. "I assure you; I am quite safe, and so is Mrs. Cratchit." No one present saw his hands gently clasped about Charlotte momentarily shine a deep golden glow against the fabric of the Infirmary gown's back, as the dread consumption in her lungs disappeared at the archangel's touch. Too shocked to speak, Charlotte drew in a sudden, deep breath in surprise, unencumbered by the congestion that had plagued her for months.

Livinia pulled Allyce aside and quietly said, "I wouldn't worry about Michel contracting consumption. I'll grant you he is a most peculiar personage, but I doubt there is any disease that can fell him. *Trust him, Allyce.* The Ebenezer Scrooge whom Miss Charlotte blamed for Peter's plight is the reason Michel is here tonight in the first place."

After a few more minutes passed, Allyce gave Charlotte a light sedative to induce sleep.

Half an hour later, Livinia and St. Tutelairé approached the Belgravia Park Grand Hotel. As he escorted Livinia to the threshold of her suite past the fragrant wreaths and mistletoe adorning the hallway walls, she turned to St. Tutelairé and said, "Everything is such a mess, Michel. Peter is locked away in that awful prison, and I fear Charlotte will succumb to her consumption if she loses the will to fi—" St. Tutelairé pressed a finger to her lips. The unexpected gesture spoke of love, not romantic love but *agape*, pure supernatural love borne of spirit.

"Hush, Miss Livinia," he said with a smile. "You must have faith. You have been of more consolation to Charlotte Cratchit than you can know. Even now, her consumption fades away, and Peter has mere hours before he is released." Before she could say anything in response, his lips grazed the back of her hand in his trademark genteel gesture, and he was gone.

Just before 11 a.m. the following day, a hired coach pulled up to King's Bench Magistrate Court, and a timorous Cyrus Abernathy entered the building. He approached the bailiff.

"I must speak with the presiding chief magistrate," Abernathy demanded, but without his customary bluster.

"I'm sorry, guv'nor, but 'is Honor is in 'is chambers preparing the remaining cases from yesterday and can't be disturbed," the bailiff said.

Abernathy raised his voice again, "I *must* speak with the presiding magistrate. I have pressing information in a case that was before the court and demand to see him. I shall not be long."

But the bailiff was used to such bluster, and again, he rebuffed Abernathy.

Losing his temper, Abernathy knocked aside the shocked bailiff with a meaty paw and burst into the magistrate's chamber.

"I must speak with you about a case that was prosecuted before you yesterday afternoon," Abernathy sputtered.

"This is a most serious breach of the court's procedural dignity, sir. I will not be treated like an ordinary shoe salesman in a cobbler's shop," retorted a surprised but annoyed chief magistrate, putting down his cup of eggnog.

"It concerns the matter of Peter Cratchit's debts to the Hawthorne and Cavendish Furniture and Carpentry Works of London, as well as the American New York and Pennsylvania Coal and Lumber Company."

"And who might you be, sir?" asked the chief magistrate, still taken aback by the breach of protocol.

"I am Cyrus Abernathy, president of the American New York and Pennsylvania Coal and Lumber Company and principal signatory of the Articles of Indebtedness against Mr. Peter Cratchit presented in your courtroom yesterday afternoon."

"And?"

Abernathy took out a sealed and notarized letter from his inner coat pocket and handed the Recording Letter of Debt Renunciation to the chief magistrate, who took a letter opener and broke the seal. Withdrawing the letter, he began reading:

24th December 1856

To the Chief Magistrate, King's Bench Debtors' Court,

I, Cyrus Abernathy, do now and in perpetuity, forswear any monetary claim against Peter Cratchit. I absolve and release him, his family, and heirs in perpetuity from any financial bounds alleged against his person in the matter of the attached "Articles of Indebtedness." As the principal signatory of those Articles, I renounce them of my free will and with the full consent of my business associate in this same matter, Sir Nigel Fairweather-Hawthorne of the Hawthorne and Cavendish Furniture and Carpentry Works of London.

Signed and notarized this Twenty-fourth Day of December 1856
Cyrus Abernathy
President, New York and Pennsylvania Coal and Lumber Company

The chief magistrate looked up from reading the letter and saw the stunned bailiff appear in the doorway, moving toward the towering Abernathy in an attempt to avenge his wounded pride. He dismissed him back to his desk with a sharp jerk of his head meant to indicate *I've no time for this madness right now. I shall handle this.*

Waving the letter renouncing the charges against Peter, he turned back to Abernathy and said, "Is your decision final, sir? Once I affix my name and court seal to this document and hand it to the bailiff to enter under lock into the court records, you will have no further recourse against Peter Cratchit in any court within Her Majesty Queen Victoria's realm. Your request for a change in the magisterial judgment is quite unusual. I will grant it only because this is Christmas Eve, and I am charitably inclined to overlook your most uncommon breach of protocol. *Am I clear, Mr. Abernathy?*"

Abernathy gave an abject nod as the chief magistrate counter-signed the Recording Letter of Debt Renunciation. The chief magistrate motioned for the bailiff to come forward for the document. The bailiff dripped hot sealing wax upon the letter, noted the registry number in his index book, and then placed the debt renunciation letter inside a locked safe.

As Cyrus Abernathy turned to go, he asked one final question.

"When will Peter Cratchit be released from this place?"

"Today, Mr. Abernathy, if I am permitted to get on with the business of this court. *Good day*, sir," the chief magistrate said, more as an imperative than a politeness. What Abernathy could not know was that Sir Richard Mayne had already apprised the chief magistrate that very morning over breakfast of the gross miscarriage of justice in the matter of Peter Cratchit and, should Cyrus Abernathy show up to renounce his claim of debt, justice would be best served by accepting it and closing the case forthwith.

30 &

THE GHOST OF CHRISTMAS LOVE

Despite his doubts, on Christmas Eve 1856, a week after the announcement was made on the front pages of the *Times of London* about the "Abernathy Lumber Slavery Scandal," the efforts of Ebenezer Scrooge bore fruit.

Upon arriving home from work after a late shift at the Infirmary, Allyce was greeted by her niece, Penny, when she entered her East End London flat.

"Are Geoffrey and Amanda already asleep?" Allyce asked.

"Yes, Aunt Allyce. They were ever so excited that Father Christmas was going to visit them this night. It was so cute; they kept imploring me to reassure them that they were good enough to receive a bit of fruit or candy in their stockings from Father Christmas," Penny said as she helped her aunt remove her winter coat.

"Oh, they've been good enough to deserve more than a piece of fruit or candy," Allyce smiled.

Allyce reached into the bag, pulled out a package, and handed it to Penny.

"Merry Christmas, my dear. Do humor me and open it now?"

Penny blushed as she took the package from Harrods, the prestigious London department store. Opening it, she pulled out a knitted cashmere scarf and a pair of robust winter mittens. Penny broke into a wide grin and hugged Allyce tightly.

"Oh, Auntie Allyce, this is far too generous, but since I love them, I shan't say no. Thank you ever so much!"

A weary Allyce smiled at her niece and then looked at the modest Christmas tree in the parlor. "That's just to wish you a very Merry Christmas and to thank you for all your help."

Allyce bit her lip.

"I *do* wish I was here to finish decorating the tree with the children tonight. I know how much they look forward to it. Chauncey from the Infirmary was kind enough to use his lunch hour to do a bit of Christmas shopping for me today." She held up the bag from Harrods department store.

Penny took a small musical ornament of St. Michael the Archangel, his little gilded sword held high, and handed it to Allyce.

"They wouldn't go to sleep unless I promised that you'd put their father's special remembrance ornament on the tree."

Allyce took the delicate swiveling St. Michael music box ornament and moved to hang it in a prominent place on the Christmas tree where her children would be sure to see it on Christmas morning, proof that their Aunt Penny had kept her word while they slept. Stepping back to admire the diminutive but gaily decorated tree, Allyce swayed on her feet from working twelve-hour days for the past four days, prompting Penny to react in alarm.

"Aunt Allyce, we must get you to bed. You'll do no one any good on Christmas Day if we can't rouse you from exhaustion. I've got everything ready to go for dinner tomorrow; all you need to do is take care of yourself. Geoffrey and Amanda need a mummy who can smile at them tomorrow," Penny insisted.

Complying with her niece's urgings, Allyce first went and gently kissed her children's serene little foreheads—fast asleep in their beds—even as the rowdiness of the rough-and-tumble East End Whitechapel streets permeated up to her flat from below. "I love you, my dears," she whispered and was surprised when Geoffrey muttered in his sleep, "I love you, Mummy." After leaving the children's bedroom, she bid her niece good night as well.

Allyce made her way to her own bedchamber, almost too tired to change into her nightgown. She sat on her small bed debating whether or not she had the strength to stand up and get a sleeping gown from her large armoire—a gift from her late husband—when she noticed a soft golden-hued light seeping from around the edges of the armoire doors, like summer's dawn in some far-off Elysian Fields. She had just about convinced herself that her sleepy eyes were playing a trick when, to her utter astonishment, Allyce saw the apparition of a small golden-haired child begin to appear right in front of the armoire. The radiant little boy grew in form and substance until he looked as real as her son, Geoffrey, his long blond hair as gloriously brilliant as sunrise over the Channel. He walked right up to Allyce, sitting on the side of her bed, reached out with one of his diminutive hands, and took her own in his.

"Who, who are you?" Allyce squeaked. The sight of this child came as quite the shock, even though he radiated an ineffable peace and consolation.

The shining child looked right at her, smiled, and said, "I am brought here to you this Christmas Eve night through the sacrifices and loving devotion of one who is known to you. You may call me the 'Ghost of Christmas Love,' Lady Bainbridge."

Still wary, but falling under the irresistible spell of this beautiful child, Allyce managed to say, "Gentle Spirit, I am only an ordinary widow, and my husband died far off in the Crimean War. Why do you address me so, and who is so devoted to me that it causes you to disturb me this night?"

"My Lady, the one who labored so ardently on your behalf to bring me to you this night is your former betrothed of years ago, Ebenezer Scrooge."

At the mention of Scrooge's name, Allyce's face darkened, and she overlooked the fact that this creature had addressed her as "Lady Bainbridge." Gathering her courage, Allyce decided that if this vision were truly only a hallucination, she was far too tired to have her emotions trifled with, especially this night of all nights.

"Good Spirit, I know Ebenezer Scrooge. Although he may have cultivated an aura of gentility and good humor, he has not changed his ways," she said bitterly. "I know for a *fact* that he remains a hard-hearted grasping miser without a soul. In just this last week, he has caused the good and gentle husband of one of my patients at the Royal Consumption Infirmary to be sentenced to King's Bench Debtors' Prison in a spiteful contest over his own god, the gold sovereign. Ebenezer does not care that this poor man may never again see the light of day and, for all I care, Ebenezer Scrooge can rot in Hell."

Despite Allyce's vehemence, the Ghost said, "I know what you *think*, Lady Bainbridge, but you do not *know* the truth." When Allyce gave the impression that she was dismissing the spirit as a symptom of overwork and fatigue by moving as if to lie down in her bed, the ethereal child commanded, "Lady Bainbridge, you will arise and take my hand."

Allyce was not intimidated by the otherworldly personage, but neither did she dare disobey the authority in its voice, so she did as she was told. When the glowing hand only the size of her son's clasped hers, she felt a strong wave of warmth pass through her, invigorating her weary mind and body.

"Appearances can be very deceptive, Lady Bainbridge. Let me ask you: Do you know who formed and nurtured the efforts of the 'Honorable Society of Royal Medical Benefactors?' It was Ebenezer Scrooge these many months. Despite the occasional appearance of malice caused by circumstance, he has been working tirelessly night and day to improve the Royal Consumption Infirmary for the common lot of all patients there, but the plight of Charlotte Cratchit especially moved his heart.

"Although she remains ignorant of it, even now Charlotte Cratchit's lungs have been purged of consumption and she will shortly be on her way home, due in no small measure to the efforts of another such as myself. He was also brought forth by Ebenezer Scrooge, though without his knowledge. There are many who carry the touch of the Divine Physician."

Allyce immediately thought of the enigmatic Michel St. Tutelairé and the feeling that surged up her arm when she grabbed him at the Royal Consumption Infirmary.

"Ebenezer fell in love with you again when he visited Charlotte in the Royal Consumption Infirmary those long months ago, but the plight of the suffering souls in the old Infirmary moved his heart far beyond a reawakened love for you to a higher love, *caritas*, a proper charity for his fellow man. For many years, he has not been the memory you cling to of a grasping, greedy miser, though his heart aches with an unrequited love…*for you*."

Allyce found the courage to challenge the smiling Ghost of Christmas Love again. Despite her feelings of renewed vigor, they did not penetrate her heart.

"Spirit, I have two questions for you. Why do you insist on calling me 'Lady' Bainbridge, and if, *if* Ebenezer has repented and worked these wondrous changes you speak of, then why hasn't he told me any of this? There is no way he could have worked these changes, even with the men of the 'Honorable Society.' I am certain neither Ebenezer nor any of his compatriots know a single detail of the 'Nightingale Procedures' my friend Florence perfected in that reeking excuse of a hospital at Scutari."

Though she felt rather triumphant, her satisfaction soon turned to exasperation when the Ghost of Christmas Love declined to answer her question as to why he addressed her as Lady Bainbridge and instead waved his other hand. A shimmering tableau began resolving on the opposite wall of her bedchamber. To her great surprise, Allyce recognized the Nightingale family estate, Lea Hurst, in Derbyshire as it slowly came into focus. The scene changed once more, and she saw Florence Nightingale sitting deep in conversation in Lea Hurst's elegant atrium during high tea with her family. Allyce recognized Florence's parents and Florence's elder sister, Parthenope. Then, the man deep in conversation with a smiling Florence turned his head slightly…and it was Ebenezer Scrooge!

The enchanting spirit child again spoke. "Remember to discern between what you *perceive* as true and what *is* true. You now behold wherein Ebenezer gained the knowledge you claim him ignorant of. Search your heart, Lady Bainbridge. Would the Florence Nightingale you know have lent her assistance to such a man if she thought his motives purely mercenary, to be merely part of a tawdry effort to gain your affections? Would she have invited him as a fêted guest of her family at Lea Hurst if that were the case? Remember, Florence Nightingale had to daily cope with the most manipulative and wicked elements of your English Army while she was in the Crimea, and she certainly has the intuition and experience to determine when someone is contriving to toy with her. I assure you: Ebenezer could not do so if he wanted to. You know Florence does not suffer fools lightly."

"Well, then if this is the case, why hasn't Ebenezer spoken to me of any of his 'benevolent' efforts, especially when he played such a large part in Peter Cratchit ending up in King's Bench Debtors' Prison?"

Fixing Allyce with a steady gaze, the glowing Ghost of Christmas Love gently but firmly remonstrated with Allyce, asking her, "And wherein is it written his obligation to give an account of his deeds to you, Lady Bainbridge? Is it not in Holy Writ, *'But when thou doest alms, let not thy left hand know what thy right hand doeth: That thine alms may be in secret: and thy Father which seeth in secret himself shall reward thee openly.'?"*

The issue of why the Ghost continued to address her with the title *Lady* nagged at Allyce for reasons she could not give voice to, so she tugged on the hand of the small spirit child and asked again, "Spirit, I want to know why you continue to address me as *Lady* Bainbridge? I am a commoner, a widow, and a poor one at that. I am not of noble birth, nor was my late husband Tristan a member of the peerage. I would rather you speak to me by my given Christian name, Allyce."

The Ghost of Christmas Love cocked his head as if listening to an invisible personage speak, nodded his head in understanding, and he returned his gentle smile to Allyce.

"Where I come from, we are bound under Authority and must therefore obey in matters of command. If you *command* me to call you 'Allyce,' Lady Bainbridge, I am compelled by that same Authority to address you as such."

Allyce felt a momentary melancholy as if she were forcing this sweet creature to do something it would rather not do. She sighed in resignation, still thinking the entire episode to be a bizarre dream, then spoke in a somewhat regretful tone.

"Good Spirit, if it humors you to call me Lady Bainbridge, then by all means, you have my consent." She wasn't sure, but it appeared for an instant the glowing child sighed with relief.

The scene at Lea Hurst and the Nightingale family faded away, to be replaced with a scene where Scrooge appeared in modest dress, as if he were no longer a wealthy banker trying to impress his friends at the London Exchange. He was sitting in the library of a well-appointed yet not opulent house. Two cats were curled up fast asleep near his feet as Scrooge puffed his pipe and stared into the roaring fireplace on a frigid winter's night.

The Ghost of Christmas Love spoke again. "In endeavoring to defeat the American industrialist, Cyrus Abernathy, and his English partner, Sir Nigel Fairweather-Hawthorne, Ebenezer lost a considerable part of his fortune. Yet, I bid thee, Lady Bainbridge, gaze upon his countenance. Does he appear to be embittered at the loss of so much money, or does he instead carry himself with an aura of peace? No, it seems he cares more for the welfare of the two orphaned cats he has taken in than his own comforts."

"Then you speak of a different man, Spirit. The Ebenezer I know would sooner toss those moggies out into the street rather than indulge animals living in his house."

It was then that Allyce found herself an invisible presence along with the spirit on that drizzling, cold autumn night in Eaton Square Gardens Park when Scrooge first encountered the tiny, abandoned kittens. As she and the Ghost of Christmas Love looked on, she saw Scrooge smile to himself, pause, turn around to crouch, and slowly speak to a group of rose bushes.

Is he mad? Allyce thought. "Spirit, is it within your power to permit me to hear what he is saying? I cannot imagine Ebenezer Scrooge speaking to a group of rose bushes unless he had lost his mind."

The Ghost of Christmas Love smiled in benevolence and nodded. She saw the slightest hint of movement near the base of the spreading rose bush and heard Scrooge speaking in a surprisingly gentle tone of concern.

"Come now, my little friends, I don't doubt your bravery, but it's getting much too dark for a couple of intrepid explorers like you to be out and about by yourselves on a wet night like this. I'm sure we can convince Mrs. Dilber to part with a nice little piece of leftover chicken or a wee bit of beef, eh? I'll even see that it's washed down with a nice saucer full of cool water."

Despite her skepticism, Allyce saw Scrooge's hand dart out and emerge with two tiny, malnourished kittens who had been abandoned in Eaton Square Gardens Park to fend for themselves. He smiled in triumph, carefully slipped them inside the pockets of his greatcoat and hurried off. Allyce was given to understand by the spirit these kittens Scrooge had rescued were now the grown adult cats she saw curled up and purring by the fire in his library. The Scrooge she knew appeared to have lost much of financial value, yet it couldn't be denied he looked to be at peace with himself, preferring the company of two small cats to a roomful of his pompous business associates at the Royal London Exchange.

"Spirit, if this is truly a new side to Ebenezer, then you also know of the darkness of heart that held him in its grasp. Tell me why I should place my trust in a reformed miser with only Lady Poverty and two little cats for companionship. I have my own two children, Amanda and Geoffrey, to look after."

The Ghost replied, "Lady Bainbridge, if a man falls to the bottom of a rocky well in pursuit of a noble cause, he has no place to climb but *up.*"

Allyce was then shown another scene, in which her children—now appearing several years older—alighted from a carriage outside Saint Hubert's Church with their mother and Ebenezer Scrooge.

Disconcerted by the implications of this particular vision, Allyce remained silent. The Ghost of Christmas Love spoke again.

"Lady Bainbridge, if you can let go of the past and trust in Love, the Love born in a Judean stable long ago, you'll never again need fear for your children's spiritual or material welfare."

Allyce found herself in an obstinate, resentful mood. She demurred and refused to acknowledge the simple merit of the Ghost's statement. Her intransigence caused the Ghost of Christmas Love to assume a different demeanor, becoming impatient with her stubbornness. He swept his hand across her field of vision and sternly admonished her with the voice of a grown, mature man.

"Lady Bainbridge, thou prideful daughter of Eve, you who hold forth a gentle heart to all except the True Love I have shown thee, that man of sincere heart whom thou would spurn and despise…*behold!*"

31 🦂

IMPLICATIONS AND REPERCUSSIONS

Before realizing what had happened, Allyce found herself as an invisible presence, along with the Ghost of Christmas Love, standing outside King's Bench Debtors' Prison, where Peter Cratchit was confined. Ebenezer Scrooge was in animated conversation with another well-dressed, handsome man of quite noble bearing. She had no way of knowing Scrooge was speaking with Baron Sidney Herbert, Florence Nightingale's close friend. The main gate suddenly opened, and a well-dressed gentleman she didn't recognize led several shabby but incredulous debtor inmates to a waiting row of merchants and factory owners, their debts not only mysteriously satisfied in full, but each man given a chance at a fresh beginning. Allyce realized one of these men was a bewildered Peter Cratchit. Her suspicion was confirmed when he strode up to Ebenezer Scrooge and embraced him in a tight hug. Allyce marveled that Scrooge didn't recoil from being embraced by an unkempt, dirty ex-convict. Peter Cratchit, Ebenezer Scrooge, and Sidney Herbert then climbed into an awaiting coach, which soon departed. She then beheld Peter knocking at the door of his home to be ecstatically greeted by an obviously cured Charlotte and their children.

Allyce and the Ghost of Christmas Love were next transported to a juvenile union workhouse entrance. A group of young orphan children had emerged blinking into the bright light of day to families who had arranged to adopt them. Another gentleman on horseback, whom Allyce assumed was yet another member of the mysterious "Honorable Society of Royal Medical Benefactors," was watching the scene, and Allyce gave a start. She turned to the Ghost of Christmas Love.

"That's Reverend Braithwaite!" Allyce exclaimed. "He was assistant vicar at Saint Mary's Church on the High Road. It was my childhood church in Ilford."

As the confused but happy children were led away toward waiting carriages by their new adoptive families, Reverend Braithwaite smiled. He tipped his top hat to the warden of the juvenile workhouse, tugged on the horse's reins, and wheeled his whinnying mount around to trot at a brisk pace back into Central London to Saint Hubert's Church.

Allyce and the Ghost of Christmas Love then found themselves standing in the Royal Consumption Infirmary, in the time before Ainsley Northrup was unceremoniously dismissed. Allyce and the Ghost of Christmas Love stood near Charlotte Cratchit's bed as invisible onlookers.

They listened as Charlotte poured out her fears about the Abernathy family's malignant influence on her husband to a sympathetic Scrooge. As they watched, an elderly man's bed across from Charlotte's collapsed without warning, and Scrooge rushed to help even before the orderlies could react and reach the patient. At that moment, Allyce realized that Scrooge had been visiting Charlotte on Sundays to avoid her, as Sunday was the only day of the week Allyce would not be there.

"Merely *seeing* you, Lady Bainbridge, had become far too painful for Ebenezer Scrooge to bear. Yes, there were times it was unavoidable, but for the most part he paid his visits of support and consolation to Charlotte when you were not there."

"Pray, Spirit, *why?*" Allyce asked with some indignation. "Did he fear seeing me that much? Was it his guilt for breaking my heart that kept him from facing me? That would betray cowardice, not love."

Before the Ghost of Christmas Love could answer, the scene changed to an elegant board room at the Royal London Exchange, where Ebenezer Scrooge was hammering the top of a sturdy oak table with his fist, passionately addressing a group of well-dressed men.

"As God is my witness, gentlemen, our efforts here to amass money and profit in the name of being 'good businessmen' will all come to naught if we cannot assist the most vulnerable among us here in Her Majesty's realm. Our affluence carries a heavy responsibility, and we will one day answer before the Almighty for it. *We* must be the eyes and ears for Her Majesty Queen Victoria and the voices of our suffering countrymen who have no voice to cry out to her.

"Do you even realize at this very moment how many of our fellow citizens lie slowly dying of consumption in that fetid hellhole excuse of a hospital called the 'Royal Consumption Infirmary'? Yet within these comfortable surroundings, our greatest concern is measuring sovereigns, crowns, and shillings in our bank accounts! I have spoken at length with Miss Florence Nightingale. She has assured me the conditions of our hospitals here in London are little better than that cesspool of a British hospital at Scutari near Constantinople. And, gentlemen, it is the truth when I tell you Scutari Barracks British Army Hospital near Crimea *was built over a cesspool.* When Nurse Nightingale arrived, a dead horse was floating in the fresh water drinking pond."

In his anger, Scrooge poured a cup of murky water from a pewter pitcher into a crystal goblet and placed it in the middle of the conference table.

"There, gentlemen, is a glass of water from a putrid water tank just outside the Royal Consumption Infirmary. Go on, stouthearted men of England, drink heartily! According to our chief medical officer at Scutari, *'British men are made of stern stuff!'*"

The assembled businessmen looked at the beautifully adorned goblet with undisguised disgust, yet not a single hand reached for the cup.

"If we do not show the same common decency to our fellow man here in our United Kingdom, we do not deserve to call ourselves subjects of Her Royal Majesty, Queen Victoria."

The scene shimmered once again, and Allyce found herself in her childhood town of Ilford. The only way she recognized it was that the Ghost of Christmas Love had brought her to the graveyard side of her home parish church, with its unique steeple and adjacent parsonage. She saw the now tilted and worn tombstone where her parents, Robert and Lillian, lay in eternal rest.

The realization dawned on Allyce that Ilford was no longer the idyllic small town she remembered frolicking about as a child, playing with her young friends. She took some measure of comfort that she could still see the great dome of Saint Paul's in the distance, but so much else in the town had changed. Ilford now seemed to have been swallowed up by the spread of London City, itself.

"This is my childhood home, Spirit, yet it is strange to me," Allyce wondered aloud. Tall wooden poles like sailing ship masts stood spaced out along the side of the streets, with what looked like heavy ropes slung into every building. Rails ran down the middle of old Cranbrook Road, where a long, sleek railway carriage without a steam engine to propel it whizzed along at an alarming speed. Stranger still was the variety of every sort of horseless carriage and conveyance that jounced along the cobblestone streets of her youth. Some were small vehicles capable of holding only two or three people, but others were larger affairs owned by merchants and businesses of every sort, and all made the most noisome racket as they sped along Ilford's streets and byways. There was not a horse to be seen.

It was then that Allyce took note of the people of Ilford, but it wasn't their odd manner of dress that caught her attention. All of them hurried along about their business with an air of palpable tension and fear, every so often craning their heads to gaze skyward.

"Tell me, Spirit, why are the townsfolk so frightened? I confess so much of Ilford is now so strange to me that I shouldn't recognize it except for Saint Mary's Church, but I cannot see why they hurry along so fearfully."

The Ghost of Christmas Love remained silent, a sad look on his normally serene face. Suddenly, Allyce heard the wail of a great horn in the distance, its frightful pitch rising and falling like a warning voice calling out danger's approach. At the sound of the great horn, every person in sight ran into nearby buildings or fled down nearby stairways on the sidewalk beneath signs labeled "METRO—EMERGENCY SHELTER." Soon, except for the sound of the ominous horn, Ilford looked like a ghost town. The Ghost of Christmas Love pointed up over the church steeple in the direction of the fields beyond.

"Behold England's sad future, Lady Bainbridge."

At first, Allyce saw nothing, but soon heard the frightful droning of great machines. She shrank in fear as she glimpsed six giant metal birds coughing smoke from their iron beaks, climbing noisily into the azure skies beyond Saint Mary's toward the English Channel. As Allyce looked upon this incredible sight, thunderous noises like the explosion of hundreds of cannon shells rocked Ilford and nearby London, where enormous gouts of orange flames blossomed like flowers from the depths of Hell, and great clouds of rising black smoke soon obscured St. Paul's great dome on the horizon. Allyce saw the building right in front of her spontaneously erupt in fire and dust, and she—although an insubstantial presence along with the Ghost of Christmas Love—still felt the very ground under her tremble in concussion. Allyce cried out in terror, instinctively attempting to grasp the spirit for protection.

"Has the Devil himself come to Ilford? Pray, Spirit, say this is not the Apocalypse of Holy Writ!"

The Spirit of Christmas Love remained silent, wearing a mournful expression, but Allyce's view changed to the grassy fields on the other side of Saint Mary's Church, where she saw nine more of the intimidating iron birds lined up along the bumpy field's edge. Men raced busily about each vehicle, disconnecting ropes and cables from the great mechanical birds' noses and quickly hauling away wheeled carts laden with boxes as each prepared to follow the first six into the sky, three at a time. Men climbed up onto the wings and into the very bodies of these bird-machines of war, while around the meadow filled with the pandemonium of war, great cannons pointed at the sky and barked fire at unseen dangers.

Allyce and the Ghost of Christmas Love were standing next to one of the great iron birds when she received a tremendous shock that almost caused her to swoon. A man dressed in strange green pants and a shirt with a bright yellow vest, odd hat, oversized spectacles, and heavy bags hanging over his stomach and back ran up to the flying machine. He climbed into the metal bird of war and pulled a mask with a hose resembling an elephant's trunk over his face, but not before he momentarily locked widened eyes with Allyce from the RAF Spitfire cockpit. Then, flames and smoke erupted along the iron bird's nose as the pilot engaged the engine starter and magneto switches, which caused the great fan blades at the very front of this strange iron bird to spin in halting fashion.

As the ground crew scurried away, Allyce gasped. *This man's face was that of her late husband, Tristan!* Reeling from this emotional shock, she cried out to the Ghost of Christmas Love, "It cannot be Tristan; he is dead but these past three years!"

The Ghost solemnly said, "Lady Bainbridge, you now behold that many years hence, a great war will come to your fair land, begun by a wicked ruler of greater Germany, thirty and six years after mankind learns to build these flying machines. Mankind will master the sky as the hawk and falcon now do. The heroes you see will fight valiantly for His Royal Highness the King, and they will be known as the 'Royal Air Force.'

"This man whose appearance caused you such consternation climbing into the flying machine is your great-grandson, Tristan Bainbridge III, the 4th Viscount of Umbria. Your late husband's blood will flow brave and strong in his veins as his machine takes flight to battle Great Britain's enemies. As I speak these words, fate has decreed he will toil for his daily bread as a Manchester chimney sweep; however, if the River of Time alters its course but slightly, as you have seen, your great-grandson Tristan will ride these steeds of the air into battle, inflicting great damage to the wicked men from Germany raining destruction down upon your fair land."

Having just settled into the cockpit of his Supermarine Spitfire, RAF Squadron Leader Tristan Bainbridge III frantically ran through his pre-flight checklist. The air raid horns warned of the approaching German Luftwaffe bombers as they inexorably droned across the English Channel to rain their deadly loads on England. Bainbridge, or "Triss," as he was known to his fellow pilots in the 65th Fighter Squadron, had a huge passion for flight and a deep hatred of the German planes trying to bomb Britain into submission. When World War II came to the British Isles, the Germans soon resorted to massive, unrestricted bombing of English cities, the infamous *Blitz,*

hoping to force Britain to sue for peace. It was only due to the fierce courage of outnumbered pilots like Triss, who took to the skies in a lopsided duel against the Germans, that Great Britain wasn't battered into submission.

As his flight of Spitfires prepared to rumble in formation across the makeshift airstrip of Royal Air Force Station Fairlop near Ilford, Triss yanked his headgear on before checking his navigation maps. He glanced down to tell his ground crew chief, Harry Glenister, to disconnect the engine battery charging carts when he was stunned to see an attractive middle-aged woman in an antique dress who bore a startling resemblance to his grandmother in her younger years, with a small blond child, standing off the port wingtip of his Spitfire. *What on earth were civilians doing here?* He craned his neck to the starboard side of his rumbling fighter and warned Ground Crew Chief Glenister that civilians were standing off the port wingtip. He again glanced to port...and they were gone! They were in great danger if they were in the vicinity of his plane.

Crew Chief Glenister carefully checked around the Spitfire, and there was no one except the ground crew preparing to trundle away the battery cart in preparation for the plane's takeoff. He glanced up to see Triss craning his head, looking around the plane. *Poor fellow's going daft*, Glenister thought. *That's what comes from flying nine alert missions against the Luftwaffe in two days.* Triss was one of the squadron's very best pilots, twice an ace, but he would be of no use to the 65th if combat flight fatigue caused hallucinations, and England needed all her pilots during the Nazi onslaught.

Glenister cupped his hands and yelled up to Triss.

"We checked 'round your Spitfire, and there are no civvies! Repeat, *no civvies!* You're cleared to take off. Get the hell out of here before Jerry hits London again!"

32 ⊰

SURRENDER TO LOVE

Whether unable or unwilling to believe the alarming visions of the future war the Spirit of Christmas Love revealed to her, Allyce's heart remained obstinate.

"We have one final place to visit until you return home to your children and niece, Lady Bainbridge."

Allyce and the Ghost of Christmas Love returned to her own time and were now in front of the Royal Home of Convalescent Medicine for Her Majesty's Soldiers and Sailors. Allyce immediately felt a twinge of pain and regret at seeing the hospital where Tristan would have recovered from his injuries had he not died in the Crimea. The notoriously run-down hospital was now brightly clean—not merely newly painted but also furnished with all-new beds, operating rooms, and shining new medical equipment.

Allyce looked to see the Ghost of Christmas Love standing near the entrance to the refurbished hospital.

"I bid thee, draw close, Lady Bainbridge," the Ghost said, a new note of respect evident in his voice. "You must read this plaque affixed here by Royal Decree only a few weeks ago."

Allyce found herself in front of the gleaming new bronze dedication plaque at the Infirmary entrance. As she read the words engraved on the large gleaming brass plaque firmly affixed to the wall and their implication set in, Allyce's eyes uncontrollably brimmed with hot tears of understanding. As they overflowed and slid down her cheeks, her heart blazed spontaneously into rekindled love, even as her shoulders shook with involuntary sobs. She realized everything shown to her by the Ghost of Christmas Love's tableau had demonstrated that though Scrooge may have fallen in love with her again on seeing her at the Royal Consumption Infirmary, he was indeed a changed man in many ways. His was again the heart of the man she had fallen so deeply in love with in her youth. Scrooge was now a man who had genuinely set out to alleviate suffering at great personal cost to himself, much as her friend Florence Nightingale had, only for far different reasons.

At that moment, Allyce Bainbridge realized love truly manifested in many ways. The Ebenezer Scrooge who broke her heart and whose memory she had nursed a deep grievance against had indeed died years ago, to be morally reborn like the mythical phoenix from the ashes. Ebenezer Scrooge carried the day *and* won Allyce's heart, although he was unaware of it, as she gazed upon the plaque honoring her husband:

> The New Royal Home of Convalescent Medicine
> for Her Majesty's Soldiers and Sailors is dedicated
> to the Memory of Captain Tristan Bainbridge,
> 1st Viscount of UMBRIA: Hero of Crimea,
> Loving Husband, Dedicated Father, and Loyal
> Subject of Her Majesty Queen Victoria
>
> *Dedicated this day XV NOVEMBER MDCCCLVI*
> *ANNO DOMINI by her Royal Highness Victoria,*
> *Queen of the United Kingdom of Great Britain and*
> *Ireland, and Prince Albert Saxe-Gotha-Altenburg*

In a somewhat more conciliatory tone, the Ghost of Christmas Love asked, using her given name for the first and only time, "Allyce, do you now understand why I was constrained to call you *Lady* Bainbridge? As Queen Victoria has deigned to confer a rank of nobility upon your late husband, Tristan, for saving her nephew's life in the Crimea, hereafter you will always be *Lady Bainbridge*. Though still a child, your son, Geoffrey, is now Geoffrey, the 2nd Viscount of Umbria."

Allyce found herself back in her bedchamber, standing before the Ghost of Christmas Love.

As his smiling image slowly faded away, he spoke one final time.

"Your Ladyship, you have beheld what has happened, what is now, and the strands of what may yet be. What I *cannot* do is usurp your free will. Know that everything you have been permitted to see this night has been procured by the actions of a man who realizes that his love for you may never be reciprocated yet undertook them regardless of personal consequence. I bid thee farewell, Lady Bainbridge."

And with a smile radiating ineffable joy, the glowing Ghost of Christmas Love faded away as if he had never been in the bedchamber at all.

Christmas Day 1856 dawned cold and snowy. Livinia Abernathy and Michel St. Tutelairé stood by the gangway of the SS *Andromeda* as it prepared to depart Portsmouth for the United States. Livinia wiped hot tears from her eyes as she reluctantly prepared to board the ship.

Michel St. Tutelairé pressed a small pouch of gold coins into her hand.

"Here is two hundred dollars for when you arrive in Philadelphia; it should suffice to keep you in good stead until your mother arrives from New York. Telegraph her courtesy of Reverend Houghton at Transfiguration Church. He will be discreet in bringing the message to her, and she will meet you in Philadelphia two days after. Although regrettable, she has realized the need to get away from your father, as he will vent his wrath in every direction after his humiliation here. As some of your father's...*discomfiture*...was directly my doing, I am obligated to see you safely out of his grasp."

He continued: "I have arranged for an additional sum of money to be made available to you and your mother that will enable you to begin your new life far from New York in a comfortable yet modest manner with your mother's family in Illinois. Everything has been made ready."

"But I...I have not even purchased passage home yet," Livinia hesitated, glancing at the SS *Andromeda*. Looking up into St. Tutelairé's smiling face, she uttered, her lower lip quivering. "I am going to miss you, Michel. How can I ever repay you for—?"

He softly put a finger to her lips.

"Repayment is neither sought nor asked for, Miss Livinia. The best way to repay me is to return to the United States and become the lady of dignity and grace you were destined to be from the moment you were born. We shall let Providence see to the rest."

As hot, salty tears freely trailed down her cheeks, Livinia pulled a small, unsealed envelope from her coat and handed it to St. Tutelairé.

"You will see that Peter and Charlotte Cratchit receive this? I trust it will explain my feelings properly."

St. Tutelairé pulled out the note inside and read.

Christmas Day 1856

Dear Peter and Charlotte,

I write this note in humble and abject apology. My father used my haughty pride and entitlement to inflict great anguish upon you both. For that, I am truly sorry and sincerely beg your forgiveness. I have come to realize the love you share between yourselves renders you far richer than I can ever hope to be.

If I ever cross your memories or you should think of me, I hope it is pleasant for you. Please remember that there is an Abernathy in America who will always regard your family with the greatest esteem and the highest affection.

> *May God bless you and your family, now and always,*
> *Livinia Abernathy*

Livinia looked into St. Tutelairé's piercing eyes as he tucked the note back into the envelope and inside his coat.

"It is a gracious and noble thing you do, Miss Livinia," he said reassuringly. "I will see that Peter and Charlotte receive this as soon as possible."

"Michel?"

"Yes, Miss Livinia?" he replied.

The tears continued falling as she spoke.

"You know, I truly love him, but I leave England knowing my love must remain forever unrequited. I started out playing a tawdry game with Peter at my father's instigation, thinking it would be to my profit and amusement, but I didn't know my heart would find a champion in Peter. *I will not easily forget him,*" she said as another quiet sob escaped her petite frame. St. Tutelairé embraced her in a comforting hug.

"I shall not forget *you* either, Michel. I truly thank God you came into my life when you did. You saved my life every bit as much as Peter did, and I shall miss you."

St. Tutelairé smiled into Livinia's searching eyes with his own gently penetrating gaze.

"He knows of your repentance and gratitude, Livinia. I can assure you of that." St. Tutelairé reached into a waistcoat pocket and handed her a small silver medal of Saint Michael the Archangel on a silver chain.

"Remember: should you need me, call on me, and I shall be there for you. You have been marked as one of the Master's favorites."

As Livinia looked down for a moment to examine the image on the medallion, the meaning in his words suddenly hit her. When she looked up to thank St. Tutelairé, he was gone.

The next morning, Ebenezer Scrooge found himself once again sitting in Saint Hubert's Church with only flickering beeswax candle flames for company. Soft sounds emanated from the nave of the church. Scrooge thought, *Neville is already puttering about his vicar's duties, preparing for Christmas Octave services later today.*

Examining his thoughts, Ebenezer Scrooge realized he had done everything humanly possible to fulfill Jacob Marley's cryptic advice about Allyce, yet Christmas Day had come and gone without any change.

"Jacob!" he cried out in frustration to the empty church, "I tried *mightily* to follow your mysterious words, and to what avail? With the exception of our 'Honorable Society' persuading the Crown that Tristan Bainbridge was truly worthy of a peerage for his bravery and the rehabilitation of the two hospitals, my only recompense was for an innocent man to be locked away in King's Bench Prison. I would gladly have changed places with poor Peter until we obtained his freedom," an anguished Ebenezer Scrooge groaned.

He leaned forward and clutched his head between his hands in mental anguish before lifting his head to stare at the cross over the altar in prayer. "You alone know I truly love Allyce Bainbridge with all my imperfect soul. I am no war hero like her noble Tristan, but I swear I would lay down my life for Allyce and her children with a glad heart. But instead, everything I touched in my quest for redemption in her eyes turned to ashes in my mouth. *Where did I go wrong?*"

Back in the nave of the cavernous church, Michel St. Tutelairé and Allyce Bainbridge listened as Scrooge poured his heart out. After some moments, Allyce turned to St. Tutelairé with a questioning look. He smiled and silently urged her forward, gesturing toward the stricken Scrooge.

"There kneels a man in need of medicine only you carry, that within your heart, Lady Bainbridge," he whispered. "Go to him."

"Thank you, Michel," she whispered. Momentarily overcome by uncharacteristic shyness, Allyce glanced down at the parasol in her hands. St. Tutelairé was nowhere to be seen when she looked up, but Allyce wasn't surprised. Since her encounter with the Ghost of Christmas Love, Allyce strongly suspected Michel St. Tutelairé was no mere mortal, but a vehicle of divine agency. She began walking down the center aisle toward Scrooge.

Unaware of Allyce's approaching presence, Scrooge implored with humble agony in his breaking voice, "I am a man lost. What must I do to be worthy of Allyce's forgiveness, much less win her heart? Lord, you alone can read my wretched soul. Have my sins so condemned me that I must walk this life alone?"

Absorbed in the agony of his tortured thoughts, Scrooge was oblivious to the soft rustling of a Victorian dress brushing against the waxed oaken church pews. A gloved feminine hand delicately came to rest on his shoulder and startled him out of his sad reverie. He turned around to look up with astonishment into Allyce's loving gaze, a tender smile on her face that he last beheld what seemed like a lifetime ago. He stood up in shock, not daring to believe his eyes. Scrooge opened his mouth to speak, but Allyce gently brought a finger to his lips, hushing him, and as the two embraced, Scrooge's tearful face came to rest on her shoulder.

Filled with love and a newfound respect, Allyce Bainbridge's tender voice broke through his sadness like soothing balm poured over a burn wound, gently breaking the stillness of the old church.

"No, dearest Ebenezer. I do not think you will walk through this life...*alone*."

Looking down from the choir loft of Saint Hubert's Church, the smiling apparitions of Jacob Marley, the small golden-haired Ghost of Christmas Love, and the Archangel Michael in the guise of a serene Michel St. Tutelairé slowly faded from sight.

Epilogue

Christmas Day 1868 was uncharacteristically cold and snowy in London. December had been of average temperature, hovering in the mid-forties, but Christmas week was ushered in with an arctic blast that sent temperatures plummeting. The freezing temperatures brought the first white Christmas in memory, when a good eight inches fell on Christmas Eve and started up again the next day as heavy snow fell from midday onward. Scrooge was now a spry seventy-four-year-old man of leisure, having sold his firm several years earlier. The intervening twelve years since his rekindled romance with Lady Allyce Bainbridge had been the happiest years of their lives. Allyce, now fifty-eight, still worked three days a week at the Royal Home of Convalescent Medicine for Her Majesty's Soldiers and Sailors. Dr. Creighton, the hospital administrator, now getting on in years, was increasingly dependent on Allyce for her expertise in medical and administrative matters.

Given his age, Ebenezer spent his time mostly as a doting grandfather to Viscount Geoffrey, Lady Amanda, and their respective toddlers. As it was already 4:30 p.m., having spent Christmas day with Scrooge and Allyce, the families had bundled themselves tightly against the snow and set off into the deepening night for their homes, laden with gifts from Father Christmas. Ebenezer and Allyce settled down for an evening in the drawing room to quietly enjoy each other's company and watch the snow falling through the large picture window next to the Christmas tree.

A poignant expectancy hung in the air when suddenly, the miniature sword on the memorial St. Michael ornament of Tristan Bainbridge hanging from the tree began to glow with warm golden light, and the tiny angel decoration began to spin on its swiveled hanger. The tiny music box hidden within its base began playing the tinkling notes of "Angels We Have Heard on High." Husband and wife both looked on, entranced, as neither of them had gotten up to wind the music box ornament, nor was there enough light for St. Michael's tiny sword to cast its ethereal gleam. What they privately called their 'tiny Christmas miracle' happened each Christmas night since Ebenezer and Allyce were wed in 1857.

"Tristan," Allyce whispered, a wistful tone in her voice as she stroked the fur of a sleeping Julius on her lap. Scrooge bore Allyce no jealousy, for he knew her late husband's battlefield sacrifice was critical in rekindling their love. Fascinated, they sat watching the ornament put on its gently twirling performance for almost half an hour when there was an unexpected knock at the door. Caesar raised his head off the ottoman he was sleeping on and both cats instinctively looked to the front parlor.

"Who could it be, Ebenezer?" asked Allyce. "It's almost six o'clock."

Scrooge gave a happy shrug as unexpected visitors were not uncommon on Christmas.

"I don't know, my love, but I shall see to the door straightaway. It's a wonder anyone is about in this storm."

He proceeded into the entryway of their spacious home when the knocking at the door began again more insistently. A babble of cheerful voices sounded from outside the door.

"Open up, Uncle," Peter and Bob Cratchit called out in unison. "We don't want to become icicles!"

"It's the Cratchits come for a Christmas visit!" Allyce exclaimed. She hurried to the front door as Scrooge opened it to reveal Peter and Bob Cratchit standing with their wives, Charlotte and Emily.

"Do come in out of the cold," Scrooge exclaimed as a gust of icy wind blew a burst of snowflakes through the threshold. Their wives exchanged sideways grins as if they were bursting to tell a secret.

"I do so hope you'll pardon the inconvenience, sir," Bob said, "but we've also brought along guests who were quite insistent that they be permitted to accompany us to see you; a military couple, Colonel and Mrs. Nathan Wainwright."

"Well then, come in, all of you," exclaimed Scrooge. "Where are these guests of whom you speak?"

As they entered the Scrooges' home, Charlotte and Emily stepped to either side to reveal a woman in an elegant coat standing next to a tall, ruggedly handsome military officer in a United States Army overcoat and dress uniform. A mischievous twinkle gleamed in the women's eyes.

Peter said, "Uncle, Colonel Wainwright is the newly appointed Military Attaché of the United States to the British Ministry of War and Court of Saint James. He and his wife arrived in London a week ago and were most eager to see you."

Scrooge was puzzled, as he didn't immediately recognize the Cratchits' guests or why an American military diplomat would visit himself and Allyce on Christmas. However, Allyce's eyes grew wide with recognition as she rushed forward with a cry to tightly embrace Colonel Wainwright's wife.

"Livinia!"

THE END

Acknowledgments

The author wishes to acknowledge the following people for their help in making this work come to life.

The legendary Charles Dickens for providing me with a rich tapestry of characters to draw from. Bestselling author, the late Malachi Martin. Richard Gould, for providing me with a flow of constructive criticism. Thanks to Eric H., who encouraged me to reinvent myself after becoming disabled.

I want to give a special mention to Alan Parsons and the late Eric Woolfson, whose music not only inspired my writing but also became a reassuring companion during more late nights than I remember.

About the Author

Robert (Rob) Marro Jr. is a native of Brooklyn, New York. Prior to his twenty-five-plus-year Wall Street career combatting international financial crime and money laundering, Rob started with a brief stint at the White House: the Executive Office of the President. This was followed by over twelve years as a covert operations officer in the CIA Clandestine Service, focusing on classified programs in pursuit of US national security policy and Presidential Decision Directives. He has also served as a standing member of the US Department of Defense Special Operations Command's (SOCOM) J-36 Counter-Threat Working Group at MacDill Air Force Base in Tampa, Florida. Rob is a graduate of the Catholic University of America in Washington, DC, with a BA in Soviet/Russian Studies and is also active in the film industry. Along with major Hollywood studio projects currently in development, he was an executive producer and featured in the 2016 Netflix film *Hostage to the Devil* about the acclaimed author and controversial Vatican exorcist, the late Father Malachi Martin. *Ebenezer Scrooge and the Ghost of Christmas Love* is his debut novel. Although medical issues preclude certain activities, Rob still enjoys photography, writing, and World War II history.